"She's right," Morales said to me. "If we want in on this, we're going to have to fight for it."

Gardner tipped her chin to acknowledge his support. "Just be sure you keep the MEA out of it at the hospital. Since Prospero is technically still a BPD detective, use her badge to show credentials. I don't want someone calling Duffy and him tattling to Eldritch."

I clenched my teeth. Since I shared a last name with one of the most famous coven leaders in Babylon, I wasn't exactly incognito in the Cauldron. Once I flashed my badge, someone would notice the name and remember it if Duffy came sniffing around for answers. "I just want to go on record that I still think this is a bad idea."

"Noted," Gardner said. "Now, get out of here and find me something I can use against Eldritch."

BY JAYE WELLS

Prospero's War

Dirty Magic

Cursed Moon

Deadly Spells

Prospero's War Short Fiction

Fire Water

Sabina Kane

Red-Headed Stepchild

The Mage in Black

Green-Eyed Demon

Silver-Tongued Devil

Blue-Blooded Vamp

Sabina Kane Short Fiction

Violet Tendencies

Rusted Veins

Fool's Gold

DEADLY SPELLS

PROSPERO'S WAR: BOOK 3

JAYE WELLS

www.orbitbooks.net

Orbit
Hachette Book Group
1290 Avenue of the Americas, New York, NY 10104
HachetteBookGroup.com

First Edition: February 2015

Orbit is an imprint of Hachette Book Group, Inc. The Orbit name and logo are trademarks of Little, Brown Book Group Limited.

The Hachette Speakers Bureau provides a wide range of authors for speaking events. To find out more, go to www.hachettespeakersbureau.com or call (866) 376-6591.

Library of Congress Cataloging-in-Publication Data:

Wells, Jaye.
 Deadly spells / Jaye Wells.—First edition.
   pages ; cm.—(Prospero's war ; Book 3)
    ISBN 978-0-316-22842-8 (softcover)—ISBN 978-0-316-22841-1 (ebook)
 I. Title.
 PS3623.E46898D43 2015
 813'.6—dc23
                                                2014036591

10 9 8 7 6 5 4 3 2 1

RRD-C

Printed in the United States of America

*This one is for Kevin Hearne, the almighty
Taco Pope and only male member of the Laser Vaginas.*

"No man is rich enough to buy back his past."
—*Oscar Wilde*

"What's past is prologue."
—*William Shakespeare*

Chapter One

There was a body in the church.

Even if Duffy's phone call hadn't alerted us to that fact, the line of news vans along the street would have tipped me off. Murders always made the media swarm like flesh flies on a corpse.

Outside the yellow police tape, reporters wielded microphones and cameras like weapons, and they shot questions like bullets at anyone wearing a badge. Special Agent Drew Morales and I were bundled up in coats and street clothes instead of cop uniforms, so they let us pass without too much trouble. If they'd known my partner and I were members of the Magic Enforcement Agency task force, they wouldn't have been so dismissive.

In addition to the journalists' vehicles, two CSI vans were parked at the curb. I cursed silently. Any scene that required that many forensics wizards had to be a clusterfuck of epic proportions.

The call had come from Detective Patrick Duffy an hour earlier. Given the tense track record between Babylon PD and our MEA task force, they'd only have called us in to consult if the murder had ties to the dirty magic trade. The most likely scenario in this case was that the victim was a known player in one of the three major covens. Still, why the church? Dirty magic covens rarely set foot in houses of Christian worship— not even to commit crimes.

Adrenaline and dread made the hairs on the back of my neck prickle. Adrenaline because I loved my job, and working coven cases was my specialty. Dread because coven-related murders were always messy and never easy to solve.

"Any guesses?" Morales said.

"The vic?" I shook my head. "We'll find out soon enough."

He shot me his trademark smirk. "You're no fun."

"It's Sunday night and I'm working a murder. Sorry for not being the life of the party."

He put an arm around my shoulder. "Beats the paperwork you were working on before Duffy called."

I expelled my breath on a laugh. "No shit."

I grabbed the handle to the door and noticed streaks of white corrective fluid across my knuckles. Before Duffy's call, I'd been pecking away at case reports and cursing the MEA's refusal to automate the extensive forms we had to fill out after we'd wrapped a case.

Through the gaping wound that used to be the church's ceiling, a helicopter's spotlight created a strobe-like pattern in the sanctuary's shadowed corners. I ducked under a large wooden beam blocking our path. The structural damage had allowed a late-season snowstorm to have its way with the interior. Splintered wood and glass shards stuck out of the snow like skeletal hands. Broken windowpanes gaped like missing teeth in a battered face.

If you squinted hard, you could imagine this run-down temple in its heyday. Barrel-vaulted ceilings, gleaming woodwork, high stone arches, and stained glass that would have glowed like jewels in the late-afternoon sun. But now there was no sun—only the helicopter's lights. And instead of a temple, it looked like a tomb.

The old church was just one of many sad relics of Babylon's steel empire. Some might see the empty shell of a church as a symbol that God had turned His back on the city. The truth was, even if God existed, He wasn't the reason the economy had collapsed. Ask any of the old-timers—the ones who were too worn down to bother with lying—and they'd tell you the real culprit in Babylon's slow death: magic.

Several of the other abandoned buildings on the street had been torn down years earlier, leaving behind lots choked with weeds and trash. Yet for some reason, this old church had been allowed to remain. Maybe some people believed God would come back to Babylon, after all.

As I walked up what used to be the aisle, a familiar uniformed officer turned to call out, "Hey, Prospero, you don't call, you don't write…"

"I came to collect that twenty you owe me, Santini." He'd been one of the few patrolmen who hadn't treated me like a pariah back when I was still a beat cop.

He motioned toward his crotch. "I got your money right here."

"You'd have to pay me a lot more than twenty bucks, Jimmy."

Raucous laughter echoed through the old sanctuary. Murder scenes are usually tense, for obvious reasons, and any chance to add a little levity to the grim task of cataloging some poor bastard's final moments was leaped on with forced enthusiasm.

Farther up the aisle, I spotted Duffy standing next to the

altar. Even on a good day he wore a perma-frown, but this night, among the snow and the wreckage, and the blood, his expression was downright grim. He was speaking to Valerie Frederickson, one of my friends from the CSI squad. Val was a fellow Adept and one of my few allies at the BPD.

Behind the pair, a sheet covered the body, which was splayed out on the stone altar like a sacrifice to old pagan gods. In the snow in front of the altar, someone had painted a symbol using a liquid that was too darkly red to be anything but blood.

"Prospero," Val called. "Hey, Morales."

I waved and picked up my speed to get the shit circus under way. Circumventing the bloody symbol, I joined them by the altar. "Who we got?"

"That's what I was hoping you could tell us." His tone hinted that asking us for help was costing him a lot of pride.

Detective Pat Duffy used to be on the homicide beat for a precinct in an upscale Mundane area of Babylon. But last year, after his work on a case involving the murder of Babylon's former mayor, he'd been made head of homicide for the Cauldron precinct, which handled crimes in Babylon's magical slums.

Before his promotion, Duffy had rejected Gardner's invitation to join the MEA task force—twice. None of us could figure out why he'd been so opposed to the move, especially since as an Adept, he shouldn't have problems working under and beside other Lefties. But apparently he did. Now every time any of us had to work with him, it was twice as difficult and five times as frustrating as it should be. But since he was Captain Robert Eldritch's new favorite, we were forced to deal with the guy.

"Who called it in?" I asked.

Standing beside me with his arms crossed, Morales loomed like a large shadow. Even though he outranked me, I was the one who knew the covens best, so he was letting me take the lead.

"Homeless freakhead across the street called it in," Duffy said, using the term for a potion addict. "Unis found him in an abandoned gas station across from the church. He gave an initial statement, but it didn't make much sense. He was spouting nonsense and half-frozen, so I called an ambulance to take him to Babylon General. Once he's lucid, I'll head over to get an official statement."

"All right." I blew out a breath. "Let's see who's behind curtain number one."

Val flicked back the covering.

The limbs had been severed from the trunk and arranged around the body. "Where's the head?" Morales asked.

Val nodded toward a covered statue next to the altar. Wearing a grim expression, she slowly pulled the sheet away. On top of a marble pedestal, a kneeling angel cradled a severed head.

"Shit!" The outburst escaped my lips like a bullet from a gun muzzle. The sound echoed off the crumbling walls and the banks of snow. I felt rather than saw everyone in the ruins freeze. Tension rose like a plasma dome over the crime scene.

The empty eye sockets and the blackened potion burn in the center of the forehead were important clues, but they hadn't unsettled me. Instead, it was the bull ring hanging from the nose and the close-cropped gray hair that made my stomach flood with acid.

"One of your old friends?" Duffy was asking if I knew the victim from my days as the scion of a dirty magic coven.

I swallowed hard and dragged my gaze from the face of the man I'd known since I was born. "H-his name is Charles Parsons. On the streets they called him Charm."

"Figured he was Votary from the tattoo on his wrist." Duffy's tone was filled with contempt, and he flicked a glance at my left arm.

Without thinking, my right hand moved to cover the matching Ouroboros on my own wrist, which permanently marked me as a *made* member of the Votary Coven. I'd left the coven ten years earlier and started a new life, but not everyone was willing to let that old life stay in the past. "He was Abe's left hand—his enforcer."

A parade of black memories goose-stepped through my head.

The last time I'd talked to Charm was on the worst day of my life. As both the next of kin and the leader of the Sanguinarian Coven, Uncle Abe had been the one to tell me that my mother had died, but Charm had stood nearby with his arms crossed. That's how I'd always remember him: standing with his head bowed like a bull ready to charge. Lots of people had been afraid of Charm, but I'd always found comfort in his steady presence.

After my uncle had told me the news, I'd cried myself out and screamed until I was hoarse. Abe hadn't known how to comfort me, but Charm had offered me a cigarette and patted me on the arm. "It's not your fault, Katie," he'd lied. Abe had told me my mom overdosed on a potion I'd cooked, and Charm had listened patiently as I broke down with guilt. Charm hadn't been a man of many words, but he always listened. That's why he'd been such an asset to Abe—he heard everything.

"Kate?" Morales prompted.

I shook myself and tried to ignore the grief smudging my vision. There'd be time for mourning later. Now I had a job to do. "After my uncle got pinched and thrown into Crowley, Charm took over as the day-to-day leader of the crews still loyal to the coven."

I scanned the crime scene again to avoid looking at Charm's sightless eyes. Now that I knew who the victim was, it put a whole new light on the visible evidence. As I did, I scrolled through a mental Rolodex of possible enemies.

"What are you seeing, Prospero?" Morales asked.

"The blood in the snow," I said. "It's an ankh, I think."

His knees popped as he knelt closer to the symbol. "Sangs?"

I nodded. The Sanguinarian Coven specialized in blood magic, and a lot of their Arcane symbolic language revolved around Egyptian hieroglyphs. But the ankh was especially damning because the new leader of the Sangs, Harry Bane, had one tattooed on his forehead.

Morales rubbed his lower lip and looked up at me. "Think it's retaliation for Ramses?" Ramses had been Harry Bane's father, who had been murdered the previous November.

"The old leader of the Sangs?" Duffy asked. "What about him?"

"I was just wondering if this is some sort of grudge hit," Morales said, not looking in my direction. "After Ramses died, chatter on the street speculated that the Votaries were responsible."

Duffy crossed his arms. "His death was ruled a suicide."

Morales and I exchanged a quick look. Ramses had been murdered while in protective custody. The cops charged with his care claimed he'd hanged himself rather than face standing trial for his crimes, which included distribution of an Arcane substance and murder. But Morales and I both knew that was bullshit. We also knew the rumors were sort of true. Uncle Abe had put out the hit on Ramses from prison, but no one could prove it.

"Well?" Duffy prompted.

"Street thugs don't tend to put too much stock in police

reports, Detective," I said. "All it takes for this to happen is one Sang corner boy looking to prove himself."

"Still, that was months ago," Morales said in a thoughtful tone. "Why get revenge now?"

"I have a feeling once we have that answer we'll have our guy," I said.

"Murder weapon been found yet?" Morales asked.

Val shook her head. "Doubt we will. The body was obviously moved here after they dismembered him. ME should be able to tell us whether they cut him up before or after they hit him with whatever potion caused that forehead burn."

I shuddered at the possibility Charm might have been alive during the ordeal. Morales touched my arm and shot me a concerned look that seemed to ask if I needed to leave. I shook my head and cleared my throat. "Are there any other wounds? Gunshots?"

Val shook her head. "Nothing visible, but we'll know more once Franklin gets him back to the morgue." Thomas Franklin was the medical examiner, who should be arriving any minute to collect the body—or the pieces of it, anyway.

"Question is—why move the body here?" Duffy rubbed his lower lip and narrowed his eyes.

I looked at the ankh on the ground. "I know Harry Bane isn't exactly a candidate for Mensa, but does it bother anyone else that there's so many obvious clues that he's behind this?"

"Explain," Duffy said.

"This church is just inside Sang territory. If someone wanted us to think this was their handiwork, this is the perfect place to leave the body. It's on their turf but not so far that some other coven member getting caught here couldn't make a quick escape."

"Hold on," Duffy said. "You said you thought this was a revenge hit by the Sangs?"

I shook my head. "I said it appears that way. It's possible someone just wanted us to think that."

Morales blew out a long breath. "Jesus. We need to keep these details out of the news. If the Votaries believe this is a Sang hit, they'll come out with guns blazing to avenge Charm."

Duffy opened his mouth, but a voice called out for Val. We turned to see a tall black man entering the sanctuary. "There's Franklin now." She gathered her evidence kit. "I'll go fill him in so he can get started."

"Let us know what he finds," I said.

"Sure thing." She turned to go.

"Excuse me?" Duffy said, sounding exasperated.

"What?" She froze and shot him a confused look.

"Why would you call the MEA with details about my case?"

Val glanced from Duffy's boorish expression to my annoyed one and back again. "I'll let you two figure that out. Bye." She marched away, lugging her evidence case.

I raised a brow at Duffy. Next to me, Morales crossed his arms and looked down at the older man.

"Don't flash those fed intimidation glares at me," he said. "Homicides are the BPD's."

"Something you seemed to have forgotten when you called us in to explain your crime scene to you," Morales said.

Duffy's eyes narrowed. "I appreciate the help, but this was never an invite to team up. I assure you Captain Eldritch will agree."

I barely managed not to call bullshit or roll my eyes. Duffy was clearly still pissed at us for stealing his thunder on the Babylon Bomber case five months earlier. He'd been called in after Mayor Owens had been killed, but Morales and I were the ones who solved the case and got all the credit in the media.

"Why don't you call Eldritch and ask if he agrees with your plan to lock federal agents out of a case involving players in our ongoing investigations?" I suggested.

"You damned well know he's at that Mayor Volos's inauguration party."

My lips curled up at the mention. I'd been invited to that party, too, but luckily I had a great excuse for begging off: I hated the new mayor. He knew it, too, but had sent that damned invite anyway to screw with me.

"Gardner's there, too, right?" Duffy said, triumph clear in his tone. "Guess you'll have to take it up with her in the morning."

By then Duffy would have already warned his boss, Eldritch. Unfortunately for us, Captain Eldritch had his eye on a promotion to chief under the new mayor, and would fight tooth and nail to get a big coven bust on his résumé.

"All right," I said. "Fine. We'll let the brass decide. But don't call us next time you need someone to save your ass."

With that Morales and I turned our backs on the sputtering detective. As we marched back down the aisle, Val and Franklin stopped talking to shoot us apologetic glances. That's when I realized every uni and CSI wiz in the place was watching us leave, which meant everyone had heard the exchange.

Except Charm, I thought. The man who used to keep his ear to the ground for the Votary Coven would never hear anything again. With one last look toward the altar, I thought, *Rest in peace, big guy.*

Chapter Two

Half an hour later Morales and I walked into task force headquarters carrying bags of burgers.

The front door of the building still bore the sign for Rooster's Gym, which was the name of the old-time boxing club that used to inhabit the second-floor space. Inside, a set of narrow steps dumped us into the massive room that served as our office. Old wooden planks covered the floor, and large steel windows added to the ambience. In the center of the floor, the old boxing ring still stood, only instead of hosting fights it now served as the place where our team duked out strategies on cases.

To the right of the entrance, a couple of temporary walls had been erected to seal off the lab the team wizard used to break down potions and create Arcane tactical weapons. To the left, a row of old metal desks bore ancient desktop computers—a couple even had typewriters. Only the best for the MEA.

The scent of old sweat and ozone filled the air. The sweat was a relic from the old days, but the ozone was a sign that someone was cooking potions.

"We're back," I called. "And we brought dinner."

"In here," a muffled voice responded.

Morales walked toward his desk, which butted up against the boxing ring. I set down the food and detoured toward the lab. But before I reached it, a loud popping noise exploded from the area. A plume of purple smoke curled toward the ceiling and was accompanied by the sound of coughing.

I ran the rest of the way. Behind me, the sound of Morales's boots striking the wooden floor planks echoed as he followed.

I skidded into the doorway in time to see my little brother, Danny, turn. Large goggles covered the top half of his face, but the bottom half was all smiles. "Hey, Kate!"

"What happened?" I demanded.

Kichiri Ren, our team wizard, turned to look at me. The members of the team called him Mez, which was short for Mesmer. He wore a white lab coat over his vintage vest and slacks. He pushed a pair of goggles up off his face and onto his dreadlocks, which were studded with various charms and amulets. He was the only Asian man I'd ever seen with dreads, but somehow he pulled them off. He coughed and waved his hands to dissipate the purple smoke. "Everything's under control."

I shot him a skeptical look. "That's the second explosion today."

"Third," Danny corrected.

I raised a brow at Mez, who cringed. "There was a slight mishap while you guys were gone."

"Cool, right?" Danny grinned. He pushed his own goggles back. Sweat and potion residue formed an outline where the protective eyewear had been. The effect made him look younger than his sixteen years, especially when paired with the excitement making his eyes shine like a little kid's on Christmas morning.

"Everyone okay?" Morales said at my shoulder.

Mez shrugged. "I'm teaching him how to actively charge a Spagyric tincture. He just charged it a little too much." He clasped Danny on the shoulder as if he was proud of him. "I'm telling you, Kate, the kid's got some mojo."

Danny's smile was so proud, I felt the corner of my own mouth turn up in response. "'Course he does," I said. "He's a Prospero."

For the last five months, Mez had been teaching my little brother the ins and outs of cooking clean magic. After months of Danny needling me about wanting to learn magic, I'd only relented when Mez agreed to be the one to teach him. Even though I was also an Adept, my specialty was dirty magic, but I didn't want Danny anywhere near that kind of knowledge. I was hoping that learning the clean side of the Arcane arts would distract the kid from wanting to learn the old family business.

"Just be sure not to blow up the building, okay, Danny?"

He rolled his eyes. "Whatever."

"How'd it go with Duffy?" Mez busied himself putting on thick rubber gloves and cleaning up the mess while we spoke.

I leaned against the doorway and looked at Morales. He blew out a breath and answered. "The good news is someone killed a major player in the Votary Coven."

Mez paused from cleaning to look up. "How is that the good news?"

"Because the bad news is Duffy is fighting to keep the case all to himself," I said.

"Why'd he ask you to come, then?" Danny demanded.

I shot my little brother a warning look. He'd been hanging around enough that he clearly considered himself a member of the team, which he absolutely was not. I pulled a dollar out of my pocket. "Why don't you go buy a soda in the locker room?"

A flare of rebellion flashed on his face, but I hardened my look enough to let him know any arguments would have consequences he wouldn't like. "Fine," he muttered. As he passed, he snatched the bill from my hand but refused to look at me.

I glanced back at Mez, who deadpanned, "Why'd he ask you to come, then?"

"I heard that!" a pouty voice called from the other side of the gym.

I rolled my eyes and shook my head. Some days I wondered which one of us was more likely to survive Danny's teenage years. Every day it looked more and more like I'd be the big loser, which was curious seeing how I was the one legally permitted to carry weaponry. "He said it was professional courtesy," I said, ignoring the moody teen, "but really he needed me to identify his vic for him."

Mez made a disgusted sound. "I'll never understand why Eldritch made Duffy head of the Cauldron murder squad. The guy doesn't know dick about coven politics."

"Exactly," Morales said. "Which is also why he refused to listen when we warned him that the covens might use Charm's death as an excuse to start a war."

"Who's Charm?"

I crossed my arms in an effort to corral the emotions swirling in my chest. "He's been running what's left of the Votary Coven since Abe went to Crowley."

Mez tilted his head. "You knew him?" I nodded, trying to appear dismissive, but Mez saw through it. "I'm sorry, Prospero."

I shrugged. "It was a shock but not exactly a surprise. Dirty living usually leads to a dirty death, you know?" Even though I believed the words I'd spoken, it didn't lessen the emotions I was struggling with. The truth was, Charm's death had brought up a lot of memories I usually kept under lock and key. Seeing him dead had taken me right back to the night I'd found out my mom had died. Grief was like that sometimes, snagging individual strands of your life and tangling them until you can't remember what's immediate and what's past.

Luckily, both men seemed to accept my comment about Charm's death being inevitable and moved on.

"You call Gardner?" Mez asked.

"She's on her way in now," Morales said. "She sounded relieved to have an excuse to leave the ball."

"You mind keeping the kid busy for a little longer?" I asked Mez. "I need to call Baba to see if she can come get him." Baba was an elderly witch who used to be our neighbor. But about a month ago, she'd moved in with us after she'd missed a couple of rent payments and almost been evicted. It had taken some convincing, but I'd eventually talked her into living with us rent-free in exchange for all the help she gave me with Danny.

"I don't mind dropping him off once we're done cleaning up," Mez said.

I checked my watch. It was already close to nine, which meant Baba was already in bed reading one of her romance novels. "If you don't mind, that would be a huge help."

"It's no problem," he said. "It's on my way anyway."

Right then Danny returned with his soda. "What'd I miss?"

Morales ruffled his hair. "Boring cop stuff."

Danny looked up at my partner and grinned. "Please, nothing you guys do is boring."

I snorted to cover my brief spurt of jealousy. If I'd tried that buddy-buddy stuff with Danny, he would have yelled at me for embarrassing him and then refused to speak to me for days. But Morales and Mez could do no wrong in the kid's eyes because, unlike me, they were cool. Asses.

"We brought burgers if you're hungry," I said.

"Where from?" Danny asked, his tone suspicious.

"Burger Shack."

The kid's eyes rolled so hard he probably saw the back of his brain. "Mickey's is better."

Morales shot me a smirk. "Told you."

"It's also on the other side of town," I said pointedly. "No one's gonna force you to eat it." I turned on my heel and left all three males staring after me. I could practically hear the three of them share silent looks that said "Chicks, man," as I walked away.

I grabbed a burger from the bag and took it back to my desk. A stack of file folders sat next to the typewriter I'd abandoned when Duffy's call had come in a few hours earlier. At the time, I'd been eager to leave the reports behind in favor of actual police work.

When I'd joined the Magic Enforcement Agency, I thought life would be a nonstop ass-kicking party. While our most recent bust of a cosmetics ring that sold illegal vanity potions to rich ladies had been successful, it hadn't exactly gotten my heart racing. The last time we'd really gotten our hands dirty had been last October's Babylon Bomber case. The perp then had been a real nut job who thought he was the god Dionysus. He'd tried to kill Morales and me before blowing up a dirty magic bomb over the city. I didn't exactly enjoy people trying to kill me, but I did savor the adrenaline rush of the grittier cases. That's why I'd been excited when Duffy called. That feeling had only intensified once I'd found out it was Charm who had been killed and realized what was at stake.

Morales strolled up to my desk. He shoved a few of my fries into his mouth. "You okay?"

I looked up at him. "Yeah."

But even as I spoke the words, my mother's face appeared in my mind. She was smiling and pulling on her coat. Telling me she had to run an errand, but she'd be back before Danny woke up from his nap. Before she walked out the door, her eyes had been bright. "Thing's are looking up for us, Katie. I just know it."

If Morales saw the lie in my eyes, he decided not to comment. That's one of the things I liked about Morales. He'd let me talk when I was ready, and if I was never ready he'd accept that, too. He grabbed a handful of fries. "How you wanna play this with Gardner?"

I opened my mouth to respond, but the sound of a door opening interrupted, followed by the *click-clack* of shoes on the steps. A cold breeze whooshed through the gym a moment before Special Agent Miranda Gardner appeared at the top of the steps.

Instead of rising to greet her, I froze in my chair with my mouth hanging open. Gardner was usually one for sensible business suits and low-heeled shoes, but that night she wore a long gown in a modest navy hue, which was jazzed up by a sheer overlay dotted with beads and crystals. I wasn't sure if it was the formfitting silhouette of the dress or the fact she was wearing makeup that surprised me more.

A low whistle carried over from the direction of the lab. "Lookin' good, sir!"

Gardner's smoky eyes narrowed as she turned an ice-queen look at Mez. The wizard put his hands up and backed away. Without a word, she kicked off her ridiculously high heels and padded angrily across the worn wooden floors toward Morales and me.

As she approached, her glare dared us to comment on her appearance. My partner cleared his throat and stood straighter. "Evening, sir," he muttered.

She tipped her chin quickly. "My office."

I rose from my seat and exchanged a wide-eyed look with my partner. He shook his head. "Here we go," he said under his breath.

I walked into the office first. Gardner was standing in profile behind her desk. As I watched, she spread open the high slit on her skirt and unbuckled her thigh holster. "Thank Christ. That thing's been chafing me all night." She looked up and saw me in the doorway with Morales looming at my back. "Well, come in."

We spilled through the door and took the two chairs facing the metal desk. A sign on the desk reminded us that our boss would tolerate no bullshit before five p.m. It was well after five, but I was pretty sure she didn't want any bullshit right then, either.

She finally dropped into her seat. "All right, so," she said, looking back and forth between us, "after you filled me in on the phone, I've been thinking about how to approach this." She pulled her sparkly earrings from her ears and tossed them on the desk next to her Glock. "Duffy didn't report what was happening to Eldritch, so we have some time."

"How do you know Duffy didn't call him?" I asked.

"I was at his table," she said with all the joy of a woman who'd spent her night with people she couldn't stand. "He didn't get any calls."

"That's good," Morales said. "We have some time, then."

Gardner pressed her lips together. "I'm not sure this is a hill we want to die on, guys."

I frowned. "How do you figure?"

"When I left the party, Eldritch was smoking a cigar and drinking Scotch with the mayor. It's looking more and more like Chief Adams will be promoted to commissioner, which means Eldritch is campaigning hard-core for the position."

I sighed. "Never mind that Duffy is the last person who should be leading a case involving the covens."

Gardner nodded. "Agreed."

"So what are we going to do?" I asked.

She sighed and leaned back in her chair. "The mayor wouldn't be too happy for his first week in office to be remembered as the start of a coven war. I could play that angle with Eldritch." She tapped her fingers on her desktop as she thought it over. "Didn't Duffy say he has a witness?"

Morales nodded. "He was sent to Babylon General."

Gardner sucked on her teeth. "Well, start there. If we can gather enough evidence pointing to a coven hit, Eldritch will have to give us the case."

I went still. "Sir, you want us to interview Duffy's witness?"

She raised a brow. "Is that a problem?"

"It's not exactly kosher to horn in on Duffy's witness before he's had a chance to talk to him."

"I thought you wanted this case?" she demanded.

"I do—it's just, if Eldritch finds out, any chance of cooperation will go down the drain."

She leaned forward. "Do you think Eldritch would hesitate to interview one of our witnesses if he thought it would benefit him? I know this is tricky for you since you technically still report to Eldritch, but if we delay we'll risk any chance of gaining traction on stopping the coven war."

I sighed. "Easy for you to say. If he finds out I went behind Duffy's back, he'll fire me."

"I'll handle Eldritch." She laughed bitterly. "You just get me some evidence to strengthen our case when I talk to the captain tomorrow."

"She's right," Morales said to me. "If we want in on this, we're going to have to fight for it."

Gardner tipped her chin to acknowledge his support. "Just be sure you keep the MEA out of it at the hospital. Since Prospero is technically still a BPD detective, use her badge to show credentials. I don't want someone calling Duffy and him tattling to Eldritch."

I clenched my teeth. Since I shared a last name with one of the most famous coven leaders in Babylon, I wasn't exactly incognito in the Cauldron. Once I flashed my badge, someone would notice the name and remember it if Duffy came sniffing around for answers. "I just want to go on record that I still think this is a bad idea."

"Noted," Gardner said. "Now, get out of here and find me something I can use against Eldritch."

Chapter Three

At the hospital we went straight to the information desk on the main floor. We had next to no information about the witness, so we decided Morales would work his charm on the nurse to get a room number.

The woman behind the desk was in her late forties with graying hair, wrinkles around her mouth that hinted at a lifelong love affair with nicotine, and a voice like steel wool. "Help you?"

Morales leaned an elbow on the counter. "Hi there, Donna," he said, reading her name tag. "One of our witnesses was brought in a little bit ago, but we don't have his room number."

"Need to see a badge."

Morales shot me an expectant look. I pulled back the edge of my leather jacket to flash the badge clipped to my waistband. Donna held out her hand. With a sigh, I removed it and handed it over.

"Where's yours?" she said to Morales.

"Forgot it in the car," he said with a rueful grin. "I could go get it, but it'll take a few minutes since we had to park in the remote lot."

Donna pressed her lips together. "What's the patient's name?"

My partner flashed some teeth. "Our buddy asked us to come talk to the witness but he didn't give us a name."

She crossed her arms and gave him a schoolmarm don't-bullshit-me frown. "Why don't you call your buddy and find out the name?"

"It's a sensitive case, Donna." Morales leaned farther over the counter to whisper. "Murder. Our detective friend is busy informing the deceased's family, and we're on somewhat of a time crunch. You understand."

Donna's right eyebrow arched up like a pissed-off cat. "Oh, I understand."

Realizing that Morales's plan to charm the woman was crashing and burning, I pushed in next to him. "Detective Prospero."

Her expression changed. "Kate Prospero?"

"Yeah," I said slowly.

"I saw you on the news a few months back. You're a real hero."

Beside me, Morales grumbled, "I was on the news, too."

I nudged him with my elbow. "I was just doing my job, ma'am. Which is what we're trying to do right now, too. It would be a huge help if you could see if there was a homeless man brought in about two hours ago. He would have arrived by ambulance."

"Oh!" Her eyes widened. "You mean Hot Pocket."

I shot Morales a look, but he shrugged, as if he couldn't make sense of it, either. "Hot Pocket?" I asked.

"His real name's Dale Schmidt, but 'round here we call him Hot Pocket."

"Why is that?"

"You don't want to know." She smiled like the Mona Lisa. "Anyways, he was brought in about the time you said. According to my friend in the ER, he was mumbling something about a dead body."

"That's probably him, then," Morales said. "Do you have a room number?"

She typed something into her computer for a moment. While she looked it up, I turned to Morales. "Hopefully he's had enough time to sober up so he can shed some light on what happened."

Donna snorted. I shot her a questioning glance, but she kept her eyes on the screen. "What?" I asked.

She looked up then. "Oh, sorry. It's just Hot Pocket's a professional potion freak. He's never totally sober. But I'm sure he'll be as helpful as he's able." She looked back down at the screen, but an amused smirk hovered on her crepe-paper lips.

"According to this, he's already been moved from the ER into a room. You can go on up." She rattled off a room number and directions on how to reach the correct wing of the hospital. "Good luck, Officers. You'll need it."

With that cryptic send-off, we started our journey to meet the mysterious Hot Pocket.

When we reached the floor Donna had indicated, we found a uniformed cop standing outside the witness's room. Morales stopped me just off the elevator and pulled me down a side hall for a strategy session.

"Looks like Hot Pocket's got a bodyguard," he said. "You know him?"

I glanced around the corner for another look. "Nope," I said. "He must be a rookie. They wouldn't waste a seasoned guy on an assignment like this."

Morales nodded. "That's good."

"How should we play this?"

"Just follow my lead."

I nodded but didn't say anything. No sense reminding him that his plan to take the lead hadn't gotten us very far with Donna. "Yes, sir." I performed a mocking salute.

Morales grinned. "I kind of like it when you call me sir, Cupcake."

I frogged him in the ribs. "Don't get used to it, Macho."

He rubbed his sore side. "All right, let's hit it. Remember to act natural."

I followed him back around the corner and toward the door. The closer we got to the uni, the more I was convinced my rookie theory was right. His posture was too straight and his uniform too perfectly pressed and creased for him to have been on the job long. It reminded me of my early days on the force. Back when I still felt like a superhero in my uniform—ready to dispense justice and make the bad guys pay. I found myself sort of envying the kid in front of the door for still being able to function in the black-and-white world where there was an obvious line between right and wrong.

As we approached, the kid stood straighter. "Evening," Morales said in a friendly tone. "Detective Duffy got caught at the crime scene and asked us to pitch in and interview the witness."

The kid's eyes narrowed. "Duffy didn't call me."

Morales sighed. "Listen—" He squinted at the kid's shiny name tag. "—Officer Harper, is it?" The kid nodded. "If you want to call Detective Duffy, be my guest, but I'm guessing he won't be too happy to be bothered. You ever work a murder scene?"

Harper shook his head. Morales made a clucking sound with

his tongue. "Gruesome stuff. Plus the media's breathing down Duffy's neck. When we left he was in a pretty shitty mood." Morales shrugged. "But, hey, you want to call him and ask him why he sent us to do his job, that's your business."

The green officer blinked a couple of times. "Maybe it's best not to bother him."

"A wise decision." Morales nodded, as if it had been Harper's idea to begin with. "Is Mr. Schmidt awake?"

"Yes, sir. A nurse is in with him now."

Morales clapped the guy on the shoulder. "Appreciate your help. We'll be in with him for a little bit if you need to go hit the head or grab some coffee."

Harper's shoulders went back another inch. "I'm not supposed to leave my post, sir."

"Good answer." Morales clapped the guy on the shoulder. "I was testing you."

I had to bite my lip to keep from laughing.

"Thanks for your help." Morales took my arm and pushed me through the door, where we ran headlong into a fabric room divider.

"Knock, knock," I called.

"Come on in," a male voice answered.

I pushed the curtain back. A male nurse was leaning over the patient and attaching some sort of device to his right side. "Oh, sorry," I said quickly and started to back away.

"It's cool," said the man in the bed. "Buck here was just finishing up."

"The new bag's in place," the nurse said. "We've added an antibiotic potion to your saline drip to deal with the infection, but we'll need to keep the area clean."

The man called Hot Pocket's lower face was covered with a scraggly beard. His shaggy hair was the color of muddy water shot through with gray. The color of the orange juice he sipped through a straw contrasted nicely against his apple-green skin. His odd complexion color was the result of a longtime dirty magic habit. If I had to guess, he probably favored some sort of abundance potion—the kind that's supposed to bring fame and fortune to the user, but more often exacerbates envy and leaves the user desperate for more attention.

Morales cleared his throat. "Mr. Schmidt? We're with the BPD," he half lied. "We were hoping you could answer some questions about what you saw at the church earlier tonight."

Schmidt set down his juice and wiped his mouth with the back of his green hand. "Mr. Schmidt was my daddy. You can call me Hot Pocket."

In his voice was the clear invitation to ask him the story behind the nickname. But I wasn't about to go there. If the hospital staff knew him well enough to give him a special moniker, it meant the reason was probably extremely disturbing.

"You're all set," said Buck, gathering his supplies. Once he was done, he passed by carrying a bag filled with something I really hoped was not shit. I stepped back out of his way.

"Make sure they bring me my dinner soon," Schmidt called after the nurse. He received a quick wave before Buck closed the door behind him. "So," I said slowly. "What can you tell us about what happened at the church?"

"Already told the guy at the scene. Doody?"

"Duffy," I corrected, biting my lip.

"Right, Duffy." He put his hands behind his head, which made his hospital johnny stretch across his torso. It made the suspicious lump on his right side more noticeable. "I was freaking pretty hard earlier, but I know what I saw."

"May I?" I indicated a chair next to the bed. When he nodded, I sat down and opened my notebook. "If you wouldn't mind going over it one more time? What were you doing in the gas station when the murder happened?"

"Turning tricks." This was said with a straight face and a matter-of-fact tone.

I paused with my pencil hovering above the pad. "By turning tricks you mean—"

"Selling my body for potion money."

I bit my lip to hide my shocked smile. Morales cleared his throat.

"Err, Mr. Schm—Pocket," Morales said, "you are aware we're cops and you just admitted to breaking, like, three laws."

Hot Pocket sat up a little straighter. "Are you going to arrest me?" he asked in a hopeful tone.

"Not at this time," I said quickly.

"Oh." His face fell. "That sucks."

"Wait," Morales said, "you want us to arrest you?"

"Prison's a lot more comfortable than the streets." He shrugged. "Three hots and a cot, right? Plus my special skills are in high demand in the can."

Before I could quickly change the subject, Hot Pocket pulled his hospital gown to the side to expose the colostomy bag attached to a hole in his abdomen. "There's some real sick fucks'll pay good money for two minutes with my stoma."

Bile rushed into the back of my throat. Morales took a step back, as if the distance would protect him from the mental image. The room was silent for a good thirty seconds as we each struggled to figure out how to respond to the disturbing revelation.

"Wait," Morales said, recovering first, "*that's* why they call you Hot Pocket?"

The green man smiled proudly. "Partly. They call me Pocket on the streets, but the nurses added Hot on account of all the STDs."

My hand found its way to my mouth. I wasn't sure whether the move was meant to cover my horror or keep in the vomit that threatened to make an appearance all over the sterile hospital floor.

Oblivious to the distress he was creating in two veteran cops who'd seen their share of fucked-up shit, he continued, "I'm kind of a celebrity around here."

I tapped my pencil on the pad in a rapid staccato. "Maybe we could get back to what you saw at the church?" I asked hopefully.

A quick knock sounded at the door before it opened to reveal an orderly bearing a covered tray. "Dinnertime!"

The patient clapped his hands. "Hey, Bob! You bring me a juicy steak?"

The orderly laughed. "Chicken and rice today."

"Aww, man," Hot Pocket said.

"Behave yourself and I'll get you some of them graham crackers you like."

"Sweet!"

The orderly nodded at us with a smile. Clearly Hot Pocket hadn't been lying about being a regular around the hospital. We waited until the guy left and the patient started eating before we continued.

"So about the church?" I prompted.

"Well," Hot Pocket said over a mouthful of chicken, "about five thirty a loud noise woke me up." He swallowed loudly. "I went to one of the windows and saw a white van had pulled up to the side of the church."

"You get the license plate number?" Morales asked hopefully.

Hot Pocket shook his head. "Anyways, a dude and a big cat got out and dragged a huge bag to the building."

"Wait—a cat?" I asked. No wonder Duffy had sent the guy to the hospital if that's the story he'd told at the scene.

Hot Pocket grimaced and shook his head. "Huge." He extended his green arms to the side. "Black, too. Bad luck."

Morales cleared his throat and shot me a look. I ignored him. "What did the cat do?"

"At first I thought I was just trippin' balls, right? But I rubbed my eyes and sure enough when I looked again, it was still there. It seemed like the cat was in charge 'cause the other dude was following it."

"Can you describe the man?" I asked.

"He was wearing all black. Like a cat burglar? Ha! Get it—cat burglar?" He glanced at me to see if I was amused. I forced a weak laugh. "Anyway, I didn't see the man's face or nothin' on account of he was too busy dragging a big bag behind him."

"How confident are you with the time?" Morales asked.

"Pretty sure. I checked my watch."

"You wear a watch?" Most junkies don't accessorize because those items could be sold for cash or traded for a fix. Plus, they tended to invite beatings from other freaks looking for things to pawn.

He fished around under his pillow and produced a brass pocket watch. "Belonged to my daddy. Still runs like a top, too." He held it up so it caught the light as it spun. I leaned forward as if to admire it. "It's tricky having stuff like this on the street so I keep it where the sun don't shine."

I froze with my hand in midair. "Uh?"

"Luckily, once the doc rerouted my plumbing my pooper became convenient for storage."

I lowered my hand with as much grace as I could muster and wiped it on my jeans. I hadn't touched the watch, but just hearing the story made me feel like I needed a scalding-hot shower. "How long were they in the church?" My tone sounded strangled to my own ears. I chanced a glance at Morales, who was looking at me with exaggerated patience.

"About twenty minutes. I waited another ten after they left to go see what they was doing. That's when I saw the body." He shivered. "Ooh boy, I never run so fast in my life."

"Is there anything else you can tell us about when they left— the man and the cat?" I asked.

"Mm," he said over a mouthful of juice. "I almost forgot to tell ya. When they walked back out, the cat was a man."

I tilted my head. "Two men walked out? You're sure."

"Yep. The same guy who walked in and another fella who was wrapped up in a blanket that covered his head." He nod-ded enthusiastically. "And when I went to look there wasn't no cat in there."

I frowned toward Morales, who looked like he was about three seconds away from walking out of the room and never looking back. "We appreciate your help, Hot Pocket." I moved to hand him a card. "If you think of anything else, please call me."

He took the card and nodded. "Hold up—Prospero? You one of Old Abe's relations?"

I nodded. "His niece."

"And you're a cop?" Hot Pocket shook his head. "Ain't that a trip? And here I thought I was the black sheep of my family."

"Thanks for your time," Morales said, shooting me a grin. With that, we left the room.

Officer Harper nodded at us as we exited. "Get what you need?"

I paused. Morales didn't stop to talk. Instead he headed toward the nurses' station to speak to Buck the nurse. "Hon-estly?" I said to Harper. "I have no idea if that was helpful."

He looked at a loss for how to respond, so I waved good-bye and went to join Morales.

"He's excited y'all are here," the nurse was saying.

I frowned at him. "Why's that?"

Buck waved a hand. "Oh, Hot Pocket loves attention."

"Tell me something," Morales said. "He told us about his nickname. Is it true that he—"

"Oh sure. He's a minor celebrity around here."

"But what he does, it's . . . dangerous, right?" Morales asked.

The orderly's smile faded. "Of course it's dangerous, but so's being a potion freak. And being homeless, for that matter. You wouldn't believe the degrading shit people do to score dirty magic." He shook his head. For the first time, I noticed the permanent bruises under his eyes and the jaded tilt to his mouth. "Naturally, we try to convince him to stop risking his life like that, but in the end it's his decision. Best we can do is treat him when he comes in, give him a couple of hot meals, and make him comfortable until he ends up ODing, gets stabbed by a trick, or dies from health complications."

"That's a pretty fatalistic view," Morales said.

"He's a potion junkie, Detective," Buck said with a sad smile. "Fatalistic is the only option. Now, if you'll excuse me, I need to go give Mrs. Strauss a sponge bath." He walked away whistling, as if he didn't have a care in the world.

Morales turned toward me with his brows raised and blew out a breath. "What do you think?"

I shrugged. "Even if Hot Pocket didn't hallucinate the whole thing, we still don't have enough to go on to convince Eldritch to give us the case."

"Agreed," Morales said. "Can you imagine how he'd react if we told him a catman killed Charm?"

I huffed out a laugh. "Hey, it's the Cauldron—weirder things actually have happened."

Morales pushed himself away from the desk and started walked toward the elevators. "I think it's time to call it a night. I'll call Gardner and fill her in. Maybe after sleeping on this we'll be able to come up with a new angle."

I nodded, but prayed sleeping on it wouldn't require any dreams about Hot Pocket's special gifts.

Chapter Four

I dreamed about the church. The pristine snow glinted sharp as knives in the helicopter's lights. Only this time, instead of Charm, the body on the altar belonged to my mother. The highlight of the nightmare was the moment when her eyes popped open in her disembodied head. Two blue lips parted and hissed at me, "Murderer."

Needless to say, when I woke the next morning I felt about as refreshed as a zombie rising from the grave. Only instead of brains, I needed coffee.

Danny was already at the kitchen table. I yawned and nodded a greeting. He didn't look up from his phone, but every few seconds he managed to bring a spoonful of cereal to his mouth without spilling milk.

I stuck a filter in the coffeemaker and scooped in grounds. "Anything interesting planned at school today?"

Heavy silence greeted my question. I turned to see what had happened to the game soundtrack. Danny was staring at me with a betrayed expression.

"What?"

"You're supposed to speak to my class today."

I closed my eyes and cursed silently.

"You forgot," he accused.

I opened my eyes and scrambled to cover my slip. "Not at all. I just momentarily blanked."

"Whatever, Kate."

"Danny, cut me a break, okay? I was up late and haven't had any caffeine. I would have remembered eventually." I turned to pour some coffee into my mug. "Morales, Mez, and I will be there."

"You promise?" The kid shot me a threatening look that reminded me a lot of the one I used on criminals all the time.

"Yes, sir." I saluted. "Should I bring lots of embarrassing naked baby pictures of you, too?"

He rolled his eyes. "That's child abuse."

I grinned at him. "Will Luna be there?"

His expression went dead serious. "Kate."

"What?" I asked, all innocence.

"I swear to God if you do anything—"

I laughed. "Give me some credit, kid. I'm not going to embarrass you in front of your *girlfriend*."

His cheeks went bright red. "She's not my girlfriend," he mumbled. After that, he tuned me out and turned his attention back to the game. Electronic beeps and bops and zings filled the kitchen once again. While I waited for the coffee to finish brewing, I turned on the small TV on the counter.

A morning news show was on. I turned up the volume to compete with the racket coming from Danny's game and

34

fill my coffee cup. The perky blonde on the screen flashed a thousand-watt, potion-whitened smile at the camera. "Babylon's power brokers turned out in droves last night to help new mayor John Volos celebrate his inauguration."

I groaned over the rim of my coffee cup as an image of Volos popped up on screen. On a normal day, he looked handsome, if imposing, but in the tux he'd donned for the ball he was downright devastating. I took a sip of scalding coffee to distract myself from those traitorous thoughts.

"Mayor Volos, what will be your first act as mayor?" the reporter standing next to Volos asked.

He looked into the camera, as if he were speaking directly to me through the screen. "I intend to follow through on my campaign promises. My number one priority as mayor will be to reduce violent crime in Babylon. To that end, I'll be creating a committee on how to best stem dirty potion traffic in the Cauldron."

"A committee," I snorted. "How about raising cops' salaries so they don't have to worry about paying their rent while fighting your war on dirty magic?"

"Huh?" Danny said, looking up from his game.

I shook my head and punched the Off button. Instead of listening to a man I didn't like, and sure as hell didn't trust, I needed to get to work.

However, before I could escape to grab a shower, Baba shuffled into the kitchen. My septuagenarian roommate used a purple cane decorated with yellow crescent moons as a walking aid. She wore black leggings, white tennis shoes, and an oversized T-shirt with three howling wolves and a full moon emblazoned across her chest. Her gray hair was pulled back into a long ponytail.

"Help me, will ya?" she groused instead of saying hello.

Danny rushed forward to take the bag from her free hand and pulled out a chair for her at the table.

"Morning," I said. "Coffee?"

She waved a hand. "Tea. You know coffee gives me the runs."

I scrunched up my nose and put on the kettle. "What's in the bag?" I warmed up my own coffee and leaned against the counter.

She frowned, as if she'd forgotten she'd brought a bag in with her. "Oh!" Her face cleared. "Some stuff for my new job."

"Since when do you have a job?"

"What? I do things," she said. When I just stared at her, she finally relented. "Okay, it's a volunteer thing, but it's still work."

"That's great, Baba."

Lately, I'd noticed her age catching up with her. Baba used to spend most of her time at the Babylon Senior Center, flirting with the silver foxes, playing bingo, and participating in a smutty book club. But lately she'd been sticking closer to home. By that I mean, butting into our business more than usual. Her having something new to do might mean I'd get a little less grief from the meddling witch about my own lack of a personal life.

She opened the zip-top bag and handed an item from inside to Danny.

"Cool," Danny said in a halting tone. I leaned over to see what was in his hand. It was a glittery unicorn sticker.

"Kids love stickers!" Baba exclaimed.

"Baba?" I said carefully. "Where exactly are you volunteering?"

She shifted in her chair to look at me. "The Babylon Community Center. You remember—it's the place Mayor Volos opened last fall?"

I choked on my coffee.

Baba tilted her head and threw a dish towel at me to mop the coffee stains off my shirt. "Careful," she said.

36

"Thanks." I cleared my throat. "How—why?"

She sat up straighter. "The mayor himself called me."

My eyes narrowed. "John Volos called you?" And she hadn't mentioned it to me before now? Something smelled rotten in that kitchen, and it wasn't just the trash Danny had forgotten to take out.

"There's some new pilot program that pairs seniors up with at-risk youth." She beamed. "John said he thought of me immediately."

"Hmm." Better to make noncommittal noises than to speak my mind on the subject of Volos. "And you didn't mention this why?"

Her gaze skittered toward the kettle. "That's ready." A split second later the pot's high-pitched whistle cut through the air. I turned to take it off the stove but didn't let the task distract me. "You were saying?"

"I thought I'd told you." She shrugged. "Guess my memory ain't what it used to be."

"Uh-huh." I wanted to call her on her lie. Baba might be old, but her memory was just fine.

I poured hot water over the special tea bag she'd made from herbs she'd grown in her old garden. The new neighbors had ripped out the garden almost immediately after moving in, but we had plans to plant a new one in my backyard once spring officially sprang.

A horn beeped from the street. I glanced out the window. My best friend waved back from inside her car. "Pen's here," I said to Danny. Since she was the counselor for the school Danny attended, she normally drove him in the mornings.

He jumped out of his seat and gathered his backpack. "Don't forget to come today," he called as he ran out the door.

I pressed my lips together and dunked the tea bag with

increasing force. "I would have remembered," I muttered to myself.

"Huh?" Baba asked. When I shook my head, she waved an arthritic hand, dismissing the topic. "Anyway, I was hoping you could take me."

"Where?" I looked up from stirring the bag three times counterclockwise.

"The community center," she enunciated. "Are you feeling okay? Maybe you need some of my special tea."

"Uh, no thanks."

Even though I'd relaxed the total ban on magic in my house, I was terrified of Baba's concoctions. She liked to give them names that reflected their uses, like *Lose Dat Ass Tea* or, even more disturbing, *Sexy Juice*. Call me crazy, but I preferred not to ingest sex teas brewed by senior citizens.

Plus I didn't trust Mundane magic, as a rule. Most of it was just intention and flashy rituals instead of the actual transformative magic that Adepts were trained to use. If all that wasn't enough to convince me, she also often used herbs that caused decidedly nonmagical side effects, such as painful cramping or explosive diarrhea.

"Do you think you could give me a ride?" she asked. "It's on your way into the office."

"What—today?" I set her cup of tea next to her hand.

"Thanks." She nodded. "Yeah, this morning."

"Why not take your car?"

She shifted uneasily in her chair and looked away. "I'm running low on gas."

Something in her posture and tone set off an alert in my gut. Baba had only lived with us for about a month, but in that short time I'd become painfully aware of how dire her financial situation had become. When her husband died, she'd been left with Social Security and modest savings as her only income. But with rents on the rise as our neighborhood got more gentrified and the cost of food and medication going up, she simply hadn't been able to keep up.

Having her move in had been a mutually beneficial situation. She didn't have to pay me rent because she did so much to help me with Danny. But I was starting to worry about what would happen when her health deteriorated to the point where herbal remedies and kitchen witchery couldn't cut it anymore.

"How will you get home, though?" I asked. "I'm probably going to be out of reach most of the day."

She waved a hand. "I'll either get one of the other volunteers to drop me or I'll grab the bus."

She could have taken the bus there this morning, too, but I didn't point that out. For some reason she thought she needed me to take her. It would only add a couple of minutes to my commute, and, frankly, I found it hard to deny Baba most favors. Besides, this way I could check out the facilities and make sure she'd be safe there. "Okay," I said, "I'll grab a shower and then we can head out."

Chapter Five

An hour later I pulled my run-down Jeep, Sybil, up to the curb outside the Babylon Community Center. The two-story brick building stood on what used to be an empty lot. Just behind the building, concrete sealed the old entrance to Babylon's abandoned subway tunnels. The Arteries, as they'd been called, used to be ruled by the Sanguinarian Coven. The space used to be a maze filled with potion freaks looking to get high off magic, but now they were empty tombs haunted by the ghosts of blood-magic fiends.

The new community center blocked any view of the old entrance to the Arteries. The building's design was clean and modern—a sculpture of steel and glass. The sign in front read: DEDICATED TO THE CHILDREN OF THE CAULDRON. Beneath that line was a list of benefactors, the first of which was John Volos.

If the tunnels had once been a symbol of Babylon's downfall, the community center—and by association its founder, John Volos—were being touted as a beacon of the city's bright future.

Inside, the lobby held a visitors' check-in desk and a seating area. Kids' toys were piled into plastic bins, and colorful artwork decorated the walls. Farther into the facility there were basketball courts and classrooms, where arts-and-craft classes were offered.

"I need to check in," Baba said.

I helped her toward the desk, where a friendly woman handed her a clipboard with paperwork attached. As soon as Baba bent her head to fill out the forms, I started to tell her I would leave her to it, but a gust of wind from the front door grabbed my attention. I turned to see who had just entered and froze.

In the doorway, wearing a black trench coat like any respectable villain, was Mayor John Volos.

He was speaking to an Asian woman who looked vaguely familiar, but I was too busy trying to figure out how to slip away without him seeing me.

"Hey, it's John," Baba said. I closed my eyes and cursed. "Yoo-hoo—Mr. Mayor!"

I opened my lids. "Thanks, Baba."

"What?" she muttered.

Volos looked up midsentence. The instant his gaze landed on me, his words dried up. I raised my chin. I'd be damned if I was going to cower like a rodent trying to avoid a predator's attention.

His head tilted, as if he, too, couldn't believe we were running into each other in this of all places. The woman next to him perked up and said something to the cameraman who'd followed her and Volos into the building. That's when I realized where I'd seen the woman before: on the evening news.

Volos started toward me with determined strides. The journalist and cameraman followed hot on his heels.

"Kate, what an unexpected and pleasant surprise." Since he was a fellow Adept, Volos held out his left hand to shake mine. The heat of his palm engulfed mine, and his grip was tighter than necessary. I couldn't help but wonder if it was his way of warning me to behave in front of the journalist.

"You're up bright and early after the inauguration ball, Cinderella."

"You know how it is—no rest for the wicked." His smile was tight. "Sorry you couldn't make it. You were missed."

"My ball gown was at the cleaners."

The corner of his mouth twitched. "What brings you to the community center?"

"Just giving your newest volunteer a ride." I nodded toward Baba. "It was nice of you to ask her."

The smile that spread across his lips was hesitant, as if I'd thrown him off guard by paying him a compliment. "We're lucky she agreed." He raised his voice so Baba could hear him. "I know she's got a busy social schedule chasing the eligible bachelors at the senior center."

"Damn straight, kiddo," she said, chuckling.

"Detective Prospero." The reporter edged her way into my personal space. "We haven't officially met. I'm Grace Cho, Channel Seven Action News." Her black hair was long, and the perfect waves could only have been achieved with the aid of a vanity potion. Her makeup was camera-ready, but with natural light flooding into the lobby instead of studio lights, the cosmetics looked caked on and garish. However, there was no denying she was naturally beautiful, and the determined expression on her face told me she was used to being underestimated because of her looks.

I shook her right hand with mine, as was the custom when one of the greeters was Mundane. "Seen you on TV."

"Grace here is doing a piece on my first week as mayor," Volos said.

I nodded because it was polite, not because I cared.

"You must be so proud of Mayor Volos," she said with a practiced smile. She turned to the cameraman and gave him a signal that had him lifting the lens. A red light lit up, indicating we were being recorded.

I flashed a look at Volos. "Um."

"It must be exciting to have your old friend become the first Adept mayor of our city," Cho prompted.

I gritted my teeth and tried to remind myself to behave. "Sure," I said. "Exciting."

"Unfortunately Kate and I haven't seen each other in a while," Volos said, stepping in front of the camera. "The campaign took up so much of my time, and Detective Prospero has been keeping our streets safe."

The reporter looked from John to me with a speculative gleam to her eyes. "I just had a great idea! Detective, if you have a moment, I'd love to have you answer some questions about growing up with the mayor."

"I'm sure Detective Prospero is busy," John said. "Right, Kate?"

The unease in his tone amused me, but as it happened I'd rather get a pelvic exam from Freddy Krueger than reminisce on camera about my past with Volos. "Actually, he's right. Crimes to solve and all that."

"That's right." Cho stepped around Volos. "Is the MEA task force investigating the murder of Charles Parsons?"

Volos's gaze slammed into me like a punch. But I couldn't react to his surprise at the news because I had to fend off the reporter. "I'm not at liberty to disc—"

Cho motioned to the cameraman to keep rolling. "Do you have any leads?"

I held up a hand. "No comment." I glanced at Volos. Something in my expression must have warned him I was about two seconds from losing my patience.

"Ms. Cho, have I introduced you to Baba?" He steered the journalist toward my neighbor, who patted her hair. "She's helping us out with a new pilot program at the center that pairs at-risk kids with senior citizen mentors."

Cho looked like she wasn't ready to give up trying to get me on the air, but the steel in Volos's voice encouraged her to let the matter drop—for now. She fished a business card from her purse. "Call me and we can set up a time for an interview." She shoved the card in my hand just as Volos took my arm and pulled me toward the door.

I glanced over my shoulder in time to see Cho turn and start asking Baba questions. I smiled at the excitement on the witch's face. Grace Cho might have thought she was about to get a simple fluff piece out of the old woman, but I'd put money on Baba talking her ear off until Cho had to beg for mercy.

Volos pushed the door open and ushered me out into the cold. He didn't let go until we were out of sight of the door. "Sorry about that."

I pulled away and shrugged. "Not as sorry as I am."

"Charm's dead?" His politician's smile had disappeared and his tone was deadly serious.

I nodded and rubbed the chill from my arms.

"You okay?" He stepped closer. "I know you guys got along."

"That was a long time ago."

"Had you seen him since—"

"No," I cut in. I definitely didn't want to talk about my mother's death with him.

44

His expression hinted that he knew better than to believe I was unaffected, but he let the matter drop. "Who did it?" he asked.

I sighed. "Don't know yet."

"Come on, Kate, I know you have a theory."

"Why don't you ask Eldritch? His top murder detective is refusing to let us assist."

"Because I'm asking you," he said. "Friend to friend."

I wanted to remind him we weren't friends, but resisted because we had been—more than, actually—a long time ago. Whatever issues we had personally now, the fact remained that John and I had shared history that I couldn't seem to escape completely. He had every reason to want to know about Charm's murder—both as a former member of the Votary Coven and as the mayor of the city that would feel the aftershocks of the crime. "We're still working out angles, but someone definitely wanted Charm's death to make the news."

Volos frowned. "I just can't believe he's dead. Figured that guy would outlast all of us."

"See, that's the difference between us. I can't believe he lasted this long."

He tilted his head. "How you figure?"

"Abe's been in Crowley for five years. I can't believe some ambitious corner boy didn't try to take Charm out to gain rep before now."

"Is that what you think happened—one of the Votary crew took him out?"

I shook my head. "I honestly don't know." I glanced at my watch. "Speaking of, I really need to get going."

He smiled, but the expression didn't reach his eyes. "Wait, how's Danny?"

I held up my hands. "Let's not do this, okay? I'm late and you've got a world to dominate."

He crossed his arms. "Running away?"

"No, John." I sighed, not bothering to disguise how tired he always made me. "I'm just leaving." I started to walk around him.

"You've always been great at that."

I ignored that. "Have a nice day, Mr. Mayor."

The corner of his mouth lifted. "Watch your ass out there, Detective."

With a quick, awkward wave I walked away. All the way back to the car, I could feel him watching my ass for me. Jerk.

When I got in the car, my phone buzzed with a text from Morales asking where I was. I typed *on my way* and hit Send. After the surprise run-in with Volos, I was looking forward to spending my day dealing with potion freaks and murderers.

Chapter Six

Twenty minutes later I pulled into the parking lot outside the gym. Morales's SUV was already there, as were the cars for the rest of the team. I gathered my gear and headed across the lot.

My foot had barely touched the top riser of the staircase when Gardner called out, "You're late."

She stood next to Morales's desk with her arms crossed. The gown she'd worn the night before had been replaced with a brown pantsuit and a cream-colored shirt. Next to her, my partner leaned back in his desk chair with his battered cowboy boots propped on the desktop. He shot me an I-told-you-so smirk. Guess that explained why he'd been texting.

"Sorry, sir," I said. "Had to make a detour on my way in." No way in hell was I about to mention that a conversation with Volos had kept me. That was a sure invitation to get teased.

Most of the team knew enough about my history with the city's new mayor to have plenty of ammunition to throw at me every time he was mentioned.

I took off my coat and stashed it at my desk. "What have I missed?"

"Well," Gardner began with a sigh, "I called Eldritch to discuss the case."

"And?"

"He's not budging. According to him there's not enough evidence to treat this as anything but a murder. Unless something new comes to light that indicates a larger coven conspiracy involving dirty potions, we don't have any jurisdiction."

I sighed. "So we have to wait until the coven war starts?"

Gardner crossed her arms. "Not at all. I said we don't have cause to take over the murder investigation. We can still start beating the bushes to see if anything shakes loose on the coven side of things."

I frowned. "Sir, it's going to take a miracle to keep that from Eldritch and Duffy."

"Duffy will be busy with the witness and waiting on the forensics to come back. Until he's got something concrete he won't be able to move on a warrant to search Harry Bane's residence."

"Right," Morales said. "But we can just stop by for a visit—see if he's acting strange."

"Harry always acts strange," I said, "but it's probably not a bad idea."

"I'm thrilled you approve," Gardner said in an arid tone. Clearly she wasn't loving me pushing back on going behind Eldritch's back on this, but she wasn't the one who'd be out of a job if he found out what we were doing. Still, my gut was also telling me that we'd be called on to help with the case eventually, anyway. Better to risk pissing off Eldritch than to fall behind and have to play catch-up once the shit hit the fan.

Right then Shadi Pruitt joined us at Morales's desk. She wore jeans, a flannel shirt, and tennis shoes. Her black hair was pulled back into a low ponytail. She tipped her chin at me in greeting before addressing Gardner. "You want me to head out, sir?"

Gardner nodded. "Shadi's going to set up surveillance near the crime scene. See if there's any suspicious activity—coven members coming by, the like."

Shadi preferred to work cases alone, which meant she got a lot of the surveillance duty. That worked out great for me because that was my least favorite part of the job.

Morales glanced at his watch. "It's a little early in the day for Harry to be awake. Maybe we should swing by and see if Aphrodite Johnson has heard any rumors about who killed Charm."

At his mention of the time, something clicked in my head. "Oh shit," I said. "What time is it?"

"Just after ten. Why?"

"We have to speak to Danny's class today."

Morales muttered a curse.

"Reschedule it," Gardner said.

"We've already had to reschedule it twice," I reminded her. "The club usually meets after school, but they rearranged the schedule to accommodate our request that it be earlier in the day. If we cancel now they won't invite us back, which wouldn't reflect very well on the MEA." I didn't mention that Danny would stop speaking to me if I disappointed him. Again.

"I don't know," she hedged.

"It'll only take an hour, tops," I rushed to say. "We can go see Aphrodite, do the school thing, and then swing by Harry's after lunch."

"All right." She sighed.

"Thanks, sir."

She nodded curtly. "Mez is at the BPD labs to see if he can sweet-talk any hints out of your friend Val about the physical evidence. He can fill you in on what he's found when you meet up at the school. We all set?"

Nods all around.

"Keep your heads down so we don't raise any alarm with the BPD. You find anything, you call me immediately."

As we moved toward the stairs to head out, I exchanged a look with Morales. "Eldritch will know what we're up to before nightfall," I muttered so as not to be heard by the boss.

He shook his head. "Have a little faith, Cupcake." He nudged me with his shoulder. "If things go our way, we'll have the perps arrested by then anyway. Then no one will give two shits about us overstepping."

As we emerged into the frigid morning, I shot him a look. I wished I could share his faith, but when cases involved the covens, things usually got messier before they got easier.

Chapter Seven

Morales parked at the curb outside the office building that served as headquarters for the Mystical Coven of the Sacred Orgasm, aka the O's. The building itself was nothing special—five floors of brick and a rotating door with a discreet brass plaque announcing the establishment as THE TEMPLE OF COSMIC LOVE.

Inside, though, the place was little more than a fancy brothel where orgasms were considered mystical rites and sex potions could be purchased for exorbitant tithes to the coven's Hierophant, Aphrodite Johnson.

The O's were a special case among the Cauldron's three main dirty magic covens because they'd gotten themselves registered as a religious order with the government. That meant they didn't pay taxes, and they got away with a lot of bullshit by claiming their crimes were religious expression.

Morales walked around the car and met me on the sidewalk. "I still can't get used to the idea that Aphrodite's one of our snitches now."

After Mayor Owens was killed, Aphrodite had been arrested for the murder. But it turned out Dionysus, aka the Babylon Bomber, had framed the Hierophant. However, once Dionysus was dead and Aphrodite had been cleared of the murder, s/he'd made a deal with the powers that be to act as an informant in exchange for us ignoring the fact s/he'd interfered with our investigation.

"No shit," I said. "Let's hope s/he's got something useful to tell us." The combination pronoun I'd used for the Hierophant was a necessity because of Aphrodite's being a sacred hermaphrodite. S/he was literally half male and half female. Sometimes the masculine right side was in charge and sometimes the feminine left side took over, but until you knew which gender you were dealing with it was safest to use the combo. Among other things, Aphrodite was notoriously easy to offend, and since the hermaphrodite's favorite pastime was revenge, it paid to be careful.

When we walked into the lobby, the Hierophant's bodyguard nodded, as if he'd been expecting us. "S/he's not here."

I leaned on the tall counter separating the desk from the lobby. "Do me a solid, Gregor, and tell her it's us. I'd hate to have to create a scene."

The man's eyes narrowed. Gregor was about as wide as I was tall. He was bald with a pronounced forehead and crooked nose that made his head look like a meaty fist. His expression told me he wasn't impressed by my threat. "The Hierophant is not here," he repeated with exaggerated patience. "S/he loaded all the girls on a bus this morning and headed out of town."

My stomach dipped with disappointment. In addition to

wanting to question the Hierophant about Charm's murder, I'd also been hoping to speak to her privately. Several months earlier s/he'd hinted s/he knew something about how my mother died. Back then, s/he'd refused to tell me what s/he knew, but I was hoping to convince Aphrodite to reconsider that position. Charm's death had dredged up lots of old ghosts, and knowing someone had information I didn't about her death was like an itch in the back of my throat. But Aphrodite wasn't there, so I pushed down my frustration and focused on getting answers. "Why did she skip town?"

"I reckon the reason you're here has something to do with the decision."

"Charm's death? Why?"

Gregor sighed like a martyr. "Suppose s/he didn't want to get caught in the crossfire."

I couldn't help but think that if the Hierophant believed it was too dangerous to stick around, my hunch had been right. The covens were going to explode into violence if we didn't find Charm's killer ASAP.

"Where did they go?" Morales asked.

"Went to visit Aphrodite's cousin Fontina Douglas."

I blinked. "Who is that?"

"Hierophant of a coven down in Atlanta."

I sighed. "Any chance you could give us Aphrodite's cell number?"

"Aphrodite don't believe in cell phones. Says the waves block kundalini energy or some shit."

"We could call Fontina," I said.

Gregor looked me in the eye and lied. "Don't have the number."

I pursed my lips and shot him a don't-bullshit-a-bullshitter glare. Most likely, Aphrodite had left instructions to keep her real location a secret. Probably she wasn't even in Atlanta, but holed up in some safe house.

"Did Aphrodite know who was behind Charm's death?" Morales asked.

Gregor smiled at us with a hint of pity. "I'm just the help."

Time to try another tactic. "Why didn't you go with her to Atlanta?" From what I'd seen Gregor was never far from his boss's side.

"I volunteered to stay back and make sure the temple's safe if the covens go to war."

"Gregor, I know your loyalty is to Aphrodite," I said. "But it seems we all want the same thing."

"Oh yeah? What's that?"

"To prevent a coven war," I said slowly. "If you tell us what you know, we might be able to do that."

He laughed. The sound was rusty and grating, as if his throat wasn't used to making the sound. "You got bigger problems than you think. The least of which is believing we're on the same team." He chuckled again and shook his head. "You know the way out."

◆ ◆ ◆

We got back in the SUV and Morales started the engine, but he didn't pull away from the curb. "That was a waste of fucking time."

I rubbed my hand over my face. "Not entirely."

"How you figure?"

"It's meaningful that Aphrodite skipped town and took all her girls," I said. "We might be able to use that later to convince Eldritch of the threat."

"What was the deal with his reaction to you mentioning a

coven war?" Morales said, tapping his fingers on the steering wheel.

I shook my head and sighed. "Maybe he was fucking with us."

"Or he doesn't believe we could stop a war."

"Possibly. I mean, arresting Charm's murderer won't make the Votaries suddenly feel justice has been served."

Morales ran a hand through his hair, leaving the dark-brown locks spiky. "Maybe we're looking at this all wrong. What if there's something else going on?"

"Like what?"

He dropped the car into Drive and pulled away from the curb. "Fuck if I know."

I put on my seat belt. "We got some time to kill before the school thing. Should we swing by Harry's now?"

Morales shook his head. "There's not enough time to go all the way to the junkyard and then get back across town. Get in touch with Mez and see if he can meet us a few minutes early to go over what he got at the lab."

I nodded and pulled out my phone to text the wizard. "Let's hope his morning's been more productive than ours."

Chapter Eight

B y the time we made it through the Bessemer Bridge traffic and all the way to Danny's school, we were only about fifteen minutes early.

We decided to wait for Mez in the lot so we could talk about his findings before heading in. Right after Morales parked the car, my cell phone rang. I glanced at the number and frowned because the caller ID said it was Grace Cho calling. "Prospero."

"Detective, Grace Cho—Channel Seven Action News," she said, as if the channel was part of her proper name. "We met this morning."

"Yes, hi," I said without much enthusiasm.

"I have a proposition for you. Since I'm already doing a story on the city's first Adept mayor, I thought it would be a great follow-up piece to do a story on you, too."

"I can't imagine why you'd think that was a good idea."

Morales shot me an amused glance even though he didn't know who I was speaking to. Cho, however, ignored my sarcasm. "As an old friend of the mayor's and a high-profile Adept in your own right, you'd make a perfect subject for a story."

"I'm gonna stop you right there," I said. "I'm way too busy chasing criminals to sit down for an interview."

"That's the beauty of this, Detective. You don't have to sit down with me at all. I'll just shadow you for a couple of days."

"So not gonna happen." I laughed. "Even if I wanted to do it, there's no way the MEA would approve it."

"I guarantee I could convince them."

I shook my head at the woman's balls. "I said I'm not interested. Good-bye." With that, I disconnected. As I did, I realized how much I missed the old phones where you could really hang up on someone instead of tapping a screen to end an unwanted call.

"Who was that?" Morales asked.

"Reporter wants to interview me." I shook my head. "Long story." I was saved from having to elaborate as Mez's potion-powered sports car hovered into the lot. He steered the vehicle into a spot near ours; a loud hiss sounded as it lowered to the ground.

We got out and met him at his back bumper. "You made good time," I said. He'd been at the BPD lab building, which was a good ten minutes farther from the school than the temple we'd come from.

"That's the beauty of being able to use the PPV lane." Mez grinned and patted the side panel of his pride and joy. The special lanes on the freeway for potion-powered vehicles had been controversial but necessary, since unlike regular vehicles they had a special mode that allowed them to hover over the road.

"I'm telling you guys," Mez continued. "You gotta get rid of that dinosaur gas guzzler you two ride around in." He looked at me. "And that disgrace of a Jeep."

"Hey!" I protested. "Sybil's family." Buying my own wheels had been of one of my first acts of independence after I'd left the coven. Sure, she broke down a lot, but her dents and scratches gave her character.

"How about you, Morales? Chicks dig sports cars."

Morales crossed his arms. "I prefer to keep my tires on the road as God intended."

Mez shrugged. "Suit yourself, Luddite."

"How'd it go with Val?" I asked.

Mischief lit up the wizard's eyes. The midday sun sparked off the charms in his dreads. That day, he'd used a potion to change his hair's color from its natural dark brown to a mix of auburn and black that coordinated with the embroidery on his vintage silk vest. "She still won't go on a date with me."

I shot him a cut-the-shit look. After the way our morning had gone, I wasn't in the mood for banter.

"Oh! You meant the case," he said. "According to the ME, there weren't any additional wounds besides the sites where the limbs had been severed. The cause of death is being ruled Arcane."

"The potion burn on the forehead?" Morales asked.

Mez nodded. "They've run occult tests on the body, and Val claims she's never seen a potion like this one in the Cauldron before."

I perked up. "Really? What was in it?"

"She needs to run some additional labs, but her initial ones revealed some sort of paralytic toxin."

"Meaning?" Morales asked.

"Meaning the potion paralyzed the vic to the point of his lungs and other body systems shutting down."

"Did Franklin determine when the dismemberment happened?" I asked even though I wasn't sure I was ready for the answer.

Mez looked at me with a sympathetic expression. "They did it after he was dead."

I expelled a relieved breath. "That's good." The possibility that he'd been alive during the torture had been eating at me ever since we'd left the crime scene. During my nightmares the night before, there had been a really vivid episode where Charm screamed for me to help him as Uncle Abe sawed at his arm. Maybe this new information would prevent that horror show from being a repeat performance.

Morales patted me on the shoulder. I shot him a quick but unconvincing smile.

"Val's going to run those other tests to try to track down the source of the toxin," Mez continued. "Maybe that'll help us narrow down the type of magic used, at least."

"That's great," I said. "We really need something to break soon. Otherwise it's going to get harder to justify sneaking around."

Morales shot me a look I couldn't decipher. But before I could question him, the sound of a bell ringing signaled it was time to head into the school.

"All right." I blew out a breath. "Time to go mortify the kid."

◆ ◆ ◆

Facing down criminals with potion guns was downright relaxing compared with standing in front of a classroom of bored teenagers. Especially when one of those teens was your own little brother, who didn't look bored at all. Instead, with his crossed arms and warning scowl, he looked downright hostile.

"And that is how we file the paperwork for a search warrant," I concluded. "Any other questions?"

At the back of the classroom, Mr. Hart, the teacher who sponsored Don't Use Dirty Elixirs, or DUDE, gave me a thumbs-up. That day he wore his uniform of tweed blazer, indie band concert T-shirt, worn jeans, and Converse sneakers. He was cute in a hipster sort of way.

When we'd arrived, Mr. Hart had greeted each of us warmly, but I was the only one he'd hugged. At the time, I'd caught Morale's posture stiffening, like a pack animal sniffing a competitor, but I'd written it off. Still, ever since that moment Morales had been suspiciously sullen.

Beside me, Morales pointedly cleared his throat, and I realized I'd been smiling at the teacher. I shook myself and schooled my features. "Any other questions?"

"How big is your gun?" A girl from the front row batted her doe eyes at Morales. Several feminine giggles greeted this question.

My partner came around the desk, and an audible gasp of appreciation filtered through the room. In the girl's defense, Morales did sort of look like an alpha hero from one of Baba's romance novels. His dark hair and scruff gave him a dark and mysterious presence. Add to that biceps bulging against his shirtsleeves and a world-class ass cupped in worn jeans and you had yourself the stuff of carnal daydreams. No doubt about it, Drew Morales was totally swoon-worthy.

When he wasn't being an ass, my practical side amended silently.

His weapon lay on the desk with the beakers, defensive wands, and brass cuffs we'd brought as props. He lifted the gun and cleared the chamber as a safety precaution before holding it up for the class. "Glock 22 .40-caliber." He cleared it again before returning it to the holster. Silence followed as everyone waited for him to elaborate, but he was clearly not in a chatty mood.

"What about you, Mr. Ren?" called Mr. Hart.

Mez stepped forward, and another round of dreamy sighs came from the girls. He wasn't brawny like Morales, but he had his own sort of man-of-mystery appeal. That day he wore a duster-length black coat with a black silk vest with alchemical symbols embroidered in red and black thread. His high cheekbones, shrewd brown eyes, and broad forehead were enhanced by the mane of dreadlocks. He stood just under six feet tall in his socks, but he typically wore black lace-up wing tip boots that edged him just over the mark.

"As a civilian employee of the MEA, I'm not cleared to carry Mundane firearms." A ghost of a smile flirted with his lips as he spoke, proving he was very well aware of the effect he was having on his audience. "But I still have plenty of Arcane weapons at my disposal." He snapped and a shower of purple sparks danced from his fingertips.

I tried not to roll my eyes. Mez was an impressive wizard, but the little display he'd just done was nothing more than a cheap illusion. However, the kids, most of whom were cocooned in Mundane life, ate it up and clapped like he'd just made a building disappear.

After Mez's showboating, I stepped forward to answer. "Each MEA agent and BPD officer is allowed to choose from a list of approved weapons. I use the same gun as Morales." I pulled a different weapon from my left-hand holster, cleared it, and then held it up. The girls didn't even look at me as I spoke, but now that I was talking about firearms I had a lot of the boys' attention. "But I mostly use this salt flare gun." I tapped the barrel. "It holds two rock salt shells. The salt isn't lethal, but it's a great deterrent and it works to disperse magic in potion freaks."

"You ever been shot?" The boy who asked looked to be about

seventeen or eighteen—a senior. He had the features of a Kennedy and the entitled posture of a young man used to privilege.

"Yes," I admitted.

"What's it like?"

"It hurts."

"Have you ever killed anyone?" I didn't like the way his eyes got a little too bright at the prospect.

"No," I lied.

The kid sneered, as if he assumed this answer meant I must not be a real cop. He turned to Morales. "What about you, Slick?"

"Special Agent Morales," my partner corrected. Clearly he'd gotten a rotten-apple vibe from the kid, too.

Richie Rich nodded. "Well? Have you?"

Morales looked the guy in the eye. "No, I have not."

A disappointed groan filtered through the room. These kids thought they were grown-up enough to handle the truth, but we knew better. Most of them came from wealthy families and had never had their safety threatened. They wouldn't last five minutes in the Cauldron after sundown. The kids I grew up with—the same kind Danny would have known if we'd stayed in the Cauldron—would have eaten these kids for dinner if they'd turned down the wrong street in their mothers' BMWs.

"Detective Prospero," Mr. Hart called out, "what's it like being an Adept arresting other Adepts?"

The room went quiet. I suppose I shouldn't have been surprised Mr. Hart brought up the topic, but I was. "Um," I began, "it's really no different from arresting anyone else. I'm a woman but I don't have a problem arresting another woman. Why would I feel differently about arresting someone just because we both happened to be born left-handed?"

"But didn't you grow up in a coven?" This from the same guy who had been interested in whether we'd killed anyone.

"So?" I shot him a look that should have warned him it was in his best interest to change topics fast.

"So"—he dragged the word out, totally ignoring my fair warning—"I heard you and your brother used to live in the Cauldron." He turned in his seat to look at Danny. "Your whole family was in the dirty potion business, right?"

I shot a quick glance toward Danny, who slid down in his seat as if he wished to dissolve into the floor.

"What's your name, son?" I asked the guy.

He smirked and leaned an elbow back over his seat. "Pierce Rebis."

The air dropped lower in my lungs. "Any relation to Anton?"

A viper's smile. "That's my daddy. You know him?"

"I haven't had the pleasure." Anton Rebis had been the candidate who ran against John Volos for mayor. The family had a long history in Babylon and came from old steel money. Rebis had run on a platform of traditional Mundane values, and had gone hard against Volos's being the first Adept to run for mayor in the city. In the end, the conservative candidate had been undone by his own hubris when it came to light that his traditional lifestyle included spending money on underage hookers.

Pierce looked primed to follow in his father's footsteps. He was the kind of guy whose voice caused the weaker members of the herd to retreat into themselves. Considering all that, it didn't surprise me that he was the one who asked about my notorious past in such a blunt manner. However, the looks some of the kids were now shooting Danny worried me.

Meadowlake accepted very few Adept students. Besides Danny and his friend Luna, who was also looking uncomfortable, there were only two other Adept students in the upper school—a freshman and a senior, neither of whom was in the club.

"It's true that I grew up in a coven," I said. "But the day I was sworn in as an officer of the law, I vowed to protect and serve all the people of Babylon. I take that responsibility quite seriously."

Morales stepped up. "Detective Prospero's background has been a huge asset to our team. Without her expertise and experience with the covens, we wouldn't have been able to have the success rate we've had."

Next to Danny, Luna raised her hand. A riot of black curls surrounded a delicate pixie's face. Her eyes were wide and intelligent, and when she blinked they appeared downright owlish. "You caught the Babylon Bomber, right?"

I shot the girl a grateful smile for helping to defend my honor. "Special Agent Morales and I stopped him together," I corrected. "In fact, the entire task force as well as the BPD pitched in. It was a team effort."

Luna raised her hand again. "Is it ever okay to use dirty magic?" Her voice was timid and her hands trembled, as if having all the attention on her was physically painful. Pierce groaned and rolled his eyes. She kept her large eyes trained on me, as if it felt safer than looking his way.

"That's actually a great question." Mez stepped in to give me some breathing room. "The truth is that there is no such thing as good or bad magic. Whether you're using clean methods or unregulated dirty cooking, there are risks involved. Either way, you're ingesting products that alter your body's chemistry in some way."

"But people who cook dirty magic are criminals," Pierce shot back.

I motioned to Mez that I'd field that one. "Not everyone can afford the expensive ingredients and licensing required by the government to cook clean. Not everyone cooks dirty to turn a profit. Some people do it out of desperation."

Pierce snorted. "Liberal bullshit."

"But as agents of the government," I said louder to drown out his pessimism, "it's our job to make sure those unsafe and unregulated products aren't sold on the streets."

"Mr. Ren, you're an Adept, too, right?" Luna asked.

The wizard nodded. "Yes, although I was trained in clean methods of cooking at Thoth University." The mention of the most prestigious university of the Arcane arts in the world didn't even make them blink. After a moment passed without applause, Mez cleared his throat. "After I graduated, I got a job working for Sortilege Inc., developing new products for the home consumer—vanity potions mainly. But then I got recruited away by the MEA to support their agents with crime scene investigation, potion analysis, and defensive magic potions—all using clean magic."

I frowned because I had the feeling he'd skipped a few steps in there. But considering how the kids' eyes were glazing over now that the guns were put away, I didn't blame him.

"Clean potions hurt people, too," Luna said in a soft voice.

Mr. Hart rose from where he leaned against a table. "I think we're out of time for today!" he said in an overly cheerful tone. Mez snapped his mouth shut on the answer he was about to deliver. Once at the front of the room, the teacher turned to face the class. "Let's give the officers a hand for taking time to speak with us."

A smattering of halfhearted clapping rose from the mostly ambivalent crowd. My gaze sought Danny again, and found him staring at the floor like he wanted to bore through it with his gaze alone.

My chest felt heavy. I'd intended to impress the kid and maybe help raise his stock among his classmates by speaking to the class, but I was worried I'd only managed to make things worse.

The kids started to collect their things to head to their next class. Danny moved more slowly than everyone else. I prayed he would wait until we got home to lay into me.

"Thank you all so much for coming," Hart said. Mez nodded, but Morales busied himself with packing away the items we'd brought to show the kids.

"It was our pleasure," I said.

Hart put a hand on my arm. The warmth of his palm radiated through my shirt. "I was hoping I could chat with you a minute?" he asked. "In private."

From the corner of my eyes, I saw both Danny's head pop up and Morales's gaze zero in on that hand on my arm. I kept my gaze aimed at Hart's pleasant face and tried to ignore the looks being shot our way. "C'mon, Morales," Mez said. "Help me carry this stuff to the car. And you have class, right?" he asked Danny.

Danny nodded and trudged out of the room. Since he saw himself as Mez's apprentice, he wouldn't dare question the wizard. Meanwhile, Morales hefted a large box from the table and shouldered past the teacher. I cringed inwardly at his rudeness. He'd been in a mood ever since we arrived, but I chalked it up to him being restless about the detour. Probably he just wanted to get back on the case.

Once they were gone, I turned to Mr. Hart. "What did Danny do?" The kid was usually pretty good, but for the last six months he'd had these outbursts of rebellion, which arrived as unexpected and fiery as solar flares.

"Huh? Oh! No. Danny's been great. Perfect."

I tilted my head. "Didn't anyone ever tell you it's illegal to lie to a cop?" I softened the tease with a grin.

A golden eyebrow rose in response. He leaned in closer and lowered his voice. "Does this mean you're going to cuff me?"

Probably, he felt he was being shocking, but I spent my days busting the scum of the earth. A little flirtatious innuendo was hardly going to make me blush. Still, I found his effort adorable.

I opened my mouth to play along, but a loud gagging sound erupted behind me. Turning my head, I saw Danny in the doorway miming sticking his finger down his throat. When he saw me glaring at him, he stopped and scowled at me. "Forgot my algebra book." He grabbed it from the desk and turned to go, casting disturbed glances between his teacher and me. Just before he walked out the door he whispered, "Gross."

With my cheeks hot, I turned back toward Mr. Hart. He looked as uncomfortable as I felt.

"I'm so sorr—"

"Do you want to grab a drink with me?" Hart blurted.

My mouth snapped shut. We'd flirted a little here and there, but I never thought he'd actually ask me out. Now that he had, my mind swirled with questions. What would Danny say? Was it unethical for a teacher and a student's guardian to meet socially? Did I even want to go out with him? He was cute, sure, but totally Mundane in all senses of the word.

I was quiet so long, his shoulders drooped. What the hell, Kate, I thought, grabbing a drink together isn't a big deal. "How about tomorrow night? Spinelli's—say six o'clock?"

The color on his cheeks was high as he expelled a relieved breath. "It's a date, Detective."

I grinned at him. "All things considered I think you can call me Kate."

His responding smile had a twist of impishness to it. "It's a deal, Detective Kate. And you can call me Brad."

"Prospero." Morales loomed in the doorway like a dark cloud. He didn't spare a glance for the teacher. "We got an appointment at the junkyard."

I cleared my throat. "Yep." I turned to Brad. "Just call me if anything changes, okay?"

This time it wasn't a charming grin he flashed, but a wolfish smile. "See you soon, Detective Kate."

Chapter Nine

On the way to find Harry Bane, Morales was pretty quiet. Both hands flexed on the steering wheel, and his eyes focused on the road with too much intensity.

"Any word from Shadi?" I asked.

He jumped, as if he'd forgotten I was there. "No. Gardner called while we were taking stuff to the car," he said in a distracted tone. "Not much new to report."

I frowned at him. "All right. What gives?"

He glanced at me but looked away quickly. "What?"

"You're acting weird."

His spine straightened. "No, I'm not."

"Whatever." I turned away from him, knowing he'd tell me when he was good and ready—not a moment before. There's this odd sort of intimacy that grows with someone when you spend the bulk of your waking hours together. That's how

I knew he was pissed about something, but damned if I was going to drag it out of him.

"Is that why we went to do that stupid talk today?" He turned to look at me.

"What?"

He paused a beat before laying it on the table. "You're hot for teacher."

My head whipped around so fast I gave myself vertigo. "Excuse me?"

He shot me a quick glance before looking at the road again. "Are you really going out with that guy?"

My cheeks heated immediately. While I had no real reason to be guilty, that's exactly how I felt.

"Well?" he prompted.

"I think so."

Morales nodded slowly and his expression didn't change, but a muscle in his jaw contracted. "Bad idea, Cupcake."

My eyes narrowed. "I don't recall asking your opinion on the matter."

"Right," he said stiffly. He took a turn a little too fast, and the weight of the SUV shifted to bump me against the door.

"Watch it," I snapped. "I don't know why you're so bent out of shape. What I do in my free time is none of your business."

He shot me a raised brow. "What about Danny, Kate?"

Now I knew he was pissed. He only called me by my real name when he was upset. "What about Danny, *Drew*?" And I only used his when I was pissed off.

He must have finally heard the warning in my tone because he softened his posture. "It's going to be awkward for him at school once it ends badly."

I lowered my brows. "Where do you get off?"

"It's my duty as your friend to let you know when you're being an idiot."

My mouth fell open. "If anyone's being an idiot it's you, you smug asshole."

"Fine, whatever." His voice was hard as concrete. "I still don't trust the guy."

"Why? Because he's nice?"

He snorted. "You're letting your hormones blind you. The man's got a past. I'd bet my badge on it."

"First of all, fuck you for the hormone comment." Months ago, under the influence of a truth potion, I'd been forced to admit it had been a while since I'd had sex. Throwing it in my face now was a low blow. "Second," I said pointedly, "we all have pasts, don't we, Drew?"

The glare he shot at me should have set my eyebrows on fire. I met the look without flinching. Finally, he took a deep breath and released it slowly, as if releasing the pressure valve on his temper. "I'm just saying be careful."

"I don't know whether to feel insulted that you think I wouldn't be careful or pissed that you think I'm not capable of knowing that without you tell me. I'm a grown-ass woman, and what I do with my hormones is my own fucking business."

He grumbled something under his breath. But I was saved from having to respond when he turned onto the street leading to the junkyard. About halfway up the road, a set of tall gates barred entrance to the Babylon Refuse and Recycling Center. A fancy name for a dump more likely to feature dead bodies than a recycling machine.

The Sanguinarian Coven used to be headquartered in the Arteries, the old abandoned subway tunnels that ran under the Cauldron like an ant colony. But after the city sealed all the entrances to the tunnels, the Sangs had to scramble to find new turf. Luckily for Harry, before his father died, Ramses Bane had diversified his empire into the sanitation business, of which this junkyard was the putrid crown jewel. Now Harry ran the coven from a throne of trash, which was fitting since he was about as friendly as a junkyard dog.

We pulled up to the gates in front of the dump around a quarter till two—late enough for the brat prince to be awake. Morales punched the red button on the intercom. The box buzzed and crackled for a moment before a confrontational voice shot out from the speaker. "Fuck you want?"

"It's Morales and Prospero."

"So?"

I shot a glance at Morales. Harry's henchmen knew who we were, so either they were fucking with us or the asshole in charge of the intercom that day wasn't one of the normal guys. I didn't recognize the voice, but that didn't mean much since covens tended to have high goon turnover.

"Tell Harry we're here for a friendly chat but we'd be happy to have an unfriendly one downtown instead."

"He's not accepting visitors."

I leaned over Morales, who pushed the button for me. "Put Harry on."

"He's indisposed." Before the guy could take his finger off the button a loud scream came through the speaker.

Morales raised a brow. "Sounds like someone got here before us."

"Let's go." I threw open my door and ran to the gate. Morales met me there. I expected to have to climb it to gain entrance, but the mechanism that locked it was broken, as if someone had pried it open with a crowbar. I removed my gun from my holster. "Look alive."

72

We entered the dump with our guns drawn and our eyes scanning the piles of trash for ambush. The air here was heavy and hot despite the near-freezing temperature. The stench of rotting food and decomposing rodents was like a punch in the nose. We moved past that part of the junkyard as fast as possible. I knew from previous visits that the trailer Harry used as a makeshift office was just on the other side of a mountain of auto body parts. Up ahead the towering hill of old carburetors and engines rose like a rusty modern art sculpture. The good news was it hid our approach. The bad news was we had no idea what waited for us on the other side.

We paused in front of the pile and formed a plan. "You go right, I'll go left," Morales said. "I'll approach from the front and you work your way to the back of the trailer. Hopefully we'll meet in the middle without either of us gaining a bullet hole."

"Should we call in some backup?" I asked.

Right then another loud scream reached us. Morales shook his head. "No time."

I nodded in agreement and took off toward the right. On the edge of the steel mountain I peeked around toward the trailer. In the dirt near the steps leading to the front door, a rottweiler lay too still in a pool of blood.

I frowned. Last time we'd been to the junkyard, there had been two dogs. Part of me hoped the missing pooch had escaped its friend's fate, but the other part was worried about stumbling into a frightened animal.

The good news was there weren't any bad guys with weapons outside the trailer. However, raised voices were coming from inside. Unfortunately, the trailer only had one small window and it was on the door, so peeking in to get a head count was out of the question.

Just then Morales came around the other side of the pile and began making his way toward the door. He waved his gun at me to indicate it was safe to make my move. I ran to the side of the building. In the shade, the air was cold as a slap. I made my way to the corner and peeked around the back. Another door and set of stairs provided a rear exit. I began to edge toward the steps. As I moved, I kept my ears cocked for sounds of what was happening inside.

A man yelled, and it carried through the thin walls. A deeper but no less menacing voice joined it. Then a high-pitched whimper cut through the air and made my neck tighten. The wall at my back vibrated from movement inside. I raised my gun and pointed it at the door in case Morales's arrival through the front door prompted an exodus out the back.

I was five feet from the back steps. A loud bang exploded through the trailer as Morales crashed through the front door. "MEA, put your guns down!"

The trailer rocked and the sounds of struggles vibrated through its walls. The back door burst open. A male in a black hoodie rushed out.

"Freeze!" I yelled, projecting my voice.

He looked up in shock. The lower half of his face was covered in a bandanna. His foot slipped and he skidded down the steps.

I jumped forward. "I said, freeze."

The man complied, his shoulders up near his ears but his head facing down.

"Hands on your head!"

He placed his palms behind his neck. The move pulled the cuffs of the hoodie back. Along his arms, several alchemical symbols had been tattooed in stark black ink.

I tensed to pull away the items concealing his identity, but a low growl sounded from my right.

The hairs on the back of my neck went stiff as needles. From the corner of my eye, I saw a shadow move. A split second later, a massive jaw slammed down around my ankle. "Oh shit!"

The dog shook its head, knocking me off balance. I slammed to the hard-packed dirt. My salt flare flew from my hand to land under the trailer.

The guy in the hoodie blinked in shock for a moment. Then he took off like a bullet through the junkyard.

"Freeze!"

The only response was a growl from the dog. It shook its massive head again, like my ankle was a particularly juicy treat. Pain bolted up my leg. "Morales!"

"Busy here!" came the muted response inside the trailer. A loud thump echoed inside the metal box, making the walls shake.

I worked my fingers into the beast's slobbery mouth. My fingertips slicked against sharp canines and fleshy gums. Luckily my jeans and leather boots prevented the massive teeth from sinking into my flesh. But with each second, the jaws ratcheted down farther, like a vise. If I didn't move quickly, the pressure might snap ligaments or, worse, bone. Shooting the damned dog was out of the question, but I wasn't about to just let it maim me.

Ribbons of drool dripped from my fingers. I wiped my left hand on my jeans, ignoring the moisture seeping through the denim. Then I did what I would have done to any human who refused to release me—I punched the beast in the eye.

The dog whimpered and released its grip long enough for me to scoot quickly out of the way. Unfortunately, the punch had only surprised it. Each step felt like my ankle was wrapped in lightning, but with speed born of adrenaline, I pulled myself up the steps and burst through the back. I slammed it closed a split second before the dog's blocky head bashed into the metal door like a wrecking ball.

I slumped against the panel. "Shit." My ankle throbbed and my heart felt like it wanted out of my chest.

The silence behind me had gravity to it. I turned slowly.

The first thing I spotted to my right was a heap on the floor. Harry Bane's body was too still and covered in blood. His walking stick lay broken across his body. At the top of the splintered staff, the crystal skull was slicked with red.

The second person I saw was Morales. He stood motionless and tall with his hands up. "Told ya I was busy," he said apologetically.

The third person in the room was about six feet, maybe two twenty. His skin was deep black. Not the brown of an African American man, but a deep onyx color that could only be achieved via magic. Some sort of scarification marred the side of his face—perhaps the result of an accident or a branding iron or the keloid scars of a tattoo that hadn't healed right. His front teeth had a gap the size of the Lincoln Tunnel, and his eyes were silvery with cold intent.

The weapon he pointed at Morales wasn't a Mundane pistol, like a Glock or a Sig. Instead it was a modified pellet gun—a Merlin Px4. That meant the barrel held potion pellets instead of bullets. I wished that made me feel better, but it didn't. There was no telling what kind of dirty magic that asshole was aiming at my partner.

I reached for my salt flare, but at the same moment I touched the empty holster, I also realized the flare was still under the trailer. Without blinking, I grabbed my Glock from my other holster and pointed it at the assailant. "Drop your weapon!"

He didn't flinch. It was clear he was the ringleader of the two assailants. The one who'd scampered away was obviously a lackey. Unlike the guy who'd run, the man I was looking at wouldn't have hesitated to put a bullet through my skull while the dog attacked.

"Drop the gun, *vadia*, or your partner will need a saline enema." His voice held the spice of an accent I couldn't place, but sounded Latin American.

The saline enema he mentioned was a reference to the fact that powerful potions required a massive cleansing with salt water to wash away the dirty magic.

Bam! The rottweiler pounded the door. In between each hit, it growled.

I glanced at Morales. His shoulders were up by his ears, but his expression had gone poker-blank. His right hand twitched. To the uninitiated eye the move could have looked like a nervous tic—after all, he had a gun pointed at his head.

"Now." The man pointing the gun at my partner was no jittery street thug caught in a bad situation. His hands didn't shake. His voice didn't rise. And when he looked at me to underline his command, I had no doubt that he would shoot Morales if I didn't comply.

"All right," I said slowly. I made a show of holding the Glock by its stock and slowly lowering it to the ground.

"Kick it over here." I did, kicking it with just enough force to take it to the middle of the room—halfway between us. Kicking it all the way over gave him two guns, but that way left me a chance to dive for it when the firefight broke out.

My heartbeat pulsed in my ears like a hammer rapping against a hollow steel drum. It echoed through my body with sickening inevitability—a rhythm of foreboding. In the corner, the pile of bloody rags moaned. The hellhound was still banging on the door. My eye twitched from the assault to my nerves.

"The BPD is already on its way," I said. "We called for backup the minute we exited our car."

"Didn't anyone ever tell you it's a sin to lie, Detective Prospero?"

I smothered the dread that rose from him using my name so casually. "I'm afraid you have me at a loss, Mister—?"

A low, evil laugh came from his blackened lips. "Tell Special Agent Morales that he needs to stop thinking about playing the hero."

I flicked my gaze toward Morales. A muscle jumped in his jaw.

Bang! The dog hit the door again, but instead of the repeated impacts getting farther apart as the dog tired, they were speeding up.

I feinted right. Mr. Black's gun swiveled so fast I didn't even see it move. Time slowed. My hand grasped the doorknob, twisting as I fell to the moldy carpet. A rush of cold air. Then a hulking and very pissed-off rottweiler barreled through the door.

Morales leaped behind the desk to take cover. I rolled toward my gun.

Mr. Black cursed. He got off a shot as the dog plowed into him. The rottie yelped, but the sound was swallowed by a fierce snarl.

I came up into a crouch and took stock. The dog blocked my view of Mr. Black's face. The pair rolled across the floor in a tangle of growls and grunts, fists and sharp teeth. There was blood. Lots of it.

The dog whimpered and slid off the man. The entire right side of the dog's body was paralyzed. Its left twitched and a confused growl emerged from the left side of its drooling mouth. Whatever was in that potion was draining the fight from the dog. The man's left arm was bloodied, and he switched the potion gun to his right hand.

I pointed the gun at him. "Freeze, asshole!"

He paused in his effort to sit up and watched me with his two ghostly pale eyes. A shudder shivered through my body, as if someone had walked across my grave.

But before I could issue another command, the man's mouth moved, like he had a marble rolling over his tongue. I frowned. "Stop what you're doing." I took a menacing step forward.

His jaw clamped down. Reddish-orange smoke leaked from between his black lips. My heart tap-danced inside my chest. But before I could figure out what he'd just done, his body disappeared.

Poof.

Gone.

The dog whimpered from its spot on the floor. I stepped closer to check on it, and realized its body was totally paralyzed. On its forehead a poison-green slick of gel indicated the spot where the potion ball made its impact. The fur there had already burned away, leaving charred skin.

Across the room, Morales was kneeling over Harry's bloody body. "He's still breathing."

"Thank Christ," I breathed. "I'll call it in." I pulled out my phone and punched the numbers.

"Sir, we've got trouble. Walked in on two men trying to kill Harry Bane."

"Is he alive?" Her tone was preternaturally calm.

"I think so." I glanced down at Bane. He wasn't making sounds anymore, but every few seconds the fingers on his left hand twitched. "Perps got away, though. We need Mez."

A muttered curse. "We'll be there ASAP."

Blood and drool slid down the walls like wet paint. I glanced toward the dog, whose sides heaved with the effort of pulling air into its lungs. "Oh, and call animal control. We got a dog here who's had a pretty shitty day."

I hung up the phone. "Cavalry is on the way, Macho. You okay?"

He leaned back on his ass. "Peachy." I patted him on the shoulder and knelt down next to him to get a better look at Harry, who didn't look peachy at all. Only patches of his pale white skin showed through the abrasions and rapidly spreading bruises. His long white hair was streaked dark red with drying blood. Both eyes were swollen shut. The black ankh tattooed on his forehead was supposed to be a symbol of life, but the blood smeared across it hinted Harry Bane wasn't far from death.

"Harry?"

No response.

I shook his shoulder. "Hieronymus?"

Nothing.

I clasped my left hand into a fist with my middle knuckle jutting out above the others. Three hard rubs of the knuckle up and down his sternum didn't produce a reaction, either. Sucking in a breath, I raised two fingers to his jugular. A weak beat tapped against my fingers. I blew out the breath and fell onto my butt next to my partner.

"He's alive," I said quietly. "Barely."

"Good. Because I'm gonna kick his ass when he wakes up."

I nodded in agreement. Harry's death would have been no great loss for the Cauldron. However, given the fact we had no fucking clue what was going on, he was the only one who could shed light on the shit show we'd stumbled in on. I glanced over at Morales. His eyes were open and he stared at Harry's still body.

I nodded. "Did you see what happened?"

Morales dipped his chin. "You mean the abracadabra Mr. Black pulled? Yeah. I kind of hoped I'd hallucinated it, though."

I forced a smile and shook my head. "Just before he disappeared he bit down on something in his mouth. Best guess is he had some sort of potion capsule in there that allowed him to pull the disappearing act."

"You ever seen something like that?"

I paused as my ears picked up the whine of sirens in the distance. "Nope." Through the noise, the Grand Wizard of the Sanguinarians lay still as a corpse covered in the blood that was so sacred to his coven. I nudged his foot with mine. "You've got some 'splainin' to do when you wake up, Harry."

◆ ◆ ◆

An hour later the ambulance carrying Harry Bane pulled away from the junkyard with sirens blaring. A cop followed in a cruiser. A uniformed officer would be stationed outside Harry's door until further notice. Two reasons: One, they'd be there if Mr. Black decided to return to finish the job. Two, if Harry woke up before we could get there, they'd make sure he stayed put.

Morales and I were rock-paper-scissoring to see who had to go explain to our boss why we hadn't called for backup.

"Damn it," Morales said. "Best two out of three."

"Morales? Prospero? Get your asses in here."

"Ha!" Mez laughed. "Looks like you're both in trouble." I shot him the bird before following my grumpy partner toward the trailer. As we approached, we stepped out of the way of the animal control guys, who were carrying the poor rottweiler away from the trailer. A long trail of saliva from the doped doggy's mouth dragged on the ground behind them. As they passed, I patted the old boy on the head. "Make sure he gets a steak or something tonight."

The guy in the front snorted. "Right, lady."

I paused. "Wait, what's going to happen to him?"

"We dosed him with saline, but he's pretty far gone." The dog's breathing had a wheeze to it that hinted it wouldn't be long until the lungs shut down permanently.

I frowned. "Isn't there anything else you can do?"

The lead guy adjusted the dog's hefty weight with a put-upon sigh. "We're just doin' our job." I shot him a glare until he squirmed. "We'll make him as comfortable as we can."

I sighed and shook my head as they carried the too-still dog away. "Poor mutt."

Morales watched me for a moment before responding. "That mutt attacked you. If it weren't for your boots you'd be on the way to the hospital for rabies shots."

"He was just protecting himself."

"You're a trip, Prospero," he called after me. "I've heard that same excuse from dozens of criminals."

"Yeah, well, a lot of criminals are animals, too." With that, I limped my way toward the trailer. Morales followed me, but he wisely kept his mouth shut.

Inside, we had to tiptoe over puddles of blood to reach Gardner. "What's up?"

She crossed her arms, scanned the room with narrowed eyes, and then speared Morales and me with a no-bullshit look. "Tell me."

"Right," I said, "we showed up to talk to Harry like you asked us to do. When we got here, it was clear he was in immediate danger."

"No call for backup?" she asked.

I shot a pointed look at my partner. After all, he'd been the one to make the call to skip it.

"There was no time," Morales said. "Once we heard Harry scream we understood the threat was too immediate to hold off. Besides, I was under the impression we were trying to keep our involvement on the down-low."

Gardner crossed her arms and sighed. "Tell me about the assailants."

"One got out the back door and took off," I said.

"And how did that happen?"

"The dog, sir," I said, pointing at my ankle. "It attacked as I tried to apprehend the perp."

"How did you get away from the dog?"

Beside me, I felt Morales look at me, too, as if he'd been wondering the same thing. I looked Gardner in the eye. "I punched him, sir."

Morales's hand came up to cover a sudden cough. Gardner looked intently up at the ceiling for a moment before continuing. "Go on. What about the man in here?"

"He had skin as black as the barrel of your gun," Morales said. "His two front teeth were gold with a big gap between them."

Something in her gaze changed and her posture became more alert. Before she could speak, Mez joined our party. "The med wizes think Harry was dosed with a potion, too," I said. "His injuries were severe, but when they checked his pupils they were dilated and the irises were pale blue."

"Shit," Morales said. "Let's hope they can do something to override the magic. We need him conscious."

Gardner sighed again. "How did the other perp manage to escape?"

I looked her in the eye. "I believe he had a potion capsule hidden in his mouth."

"Wait," Gardner asked, "he just disappeared?"

"Gone." I snapped my fingers.

"You're serious?" she asked.

"Unfortunately yes."

"I've heard of such potions existing, but never seen one in action," Mez said.

I shook my head. "Me either."

"Hmm. I'll do some digging and see if I can find anything on how they're made. May not lead to the perp, but it wouldn't be a bad weapon to add to our arsenal."

The sound of a new car arriving outside carried into the trailer. A moment later a door slammed and a man's raised voice echoed. That was all the warning we got before the thin metal door flew open and Captain Eldritch barreled inside. He looked around long enough to take in the blood and the three of us staring at him. His angry gaze zeroed in on Gardner. "Did we or did we not have a conversation this morning?"

She frowned. "We did."

"Then do you want to explain to me why you went behind my back?"

"Prospero and Morales were here to question Harry Bane on an unrelated matter when they discovered he was in danger."

Eldritch's face morphed from annoyance to confusion. "I don't give two shits about Harry Fucking Bane. He's not my problem anymore." His gaze zeroed in on my face. "No thanks to you."

My stomach dipped. "What?"

"Explain yourself," Gardner said.

He crossed his arms. "About an hour ago, I got a call from the chief. Seems the mayor had a little chat this morning with Prospero here about the murder of Charles Parsons."

Morales and Gardner both shot me accusing glances. "That's

not exactly true," I said. "I ran into Volos when I was dropping Baba somewhere. He asked me about Charm's murder and I told him the BPD was handling it. That's all." Okay, I'd skipped a couple of steps, but the gist was true.

Judging by the sneer twitching under Eldritch's mustache, he wasn't buying my story. "Regardless, Mayor Volos convinced the chief it was in our best interest to hand over the case to the MEA."

Gardner made a derisive snort. "Thanks for letting us know in such a professional manner, Eldritch."

He paused. "Wait—you really didn't know?"

After Gardner shook her head, Eldritch started to chuckle. She pursed her lips. "Since this is our case, I guess that means you can go now."

He held up a hand. "Not so fast. We need to have a discussion about a field trip to Babylon General last night." Eldritch crossed his arms and shot Morales a look that dared him to lie. "You know anything about that?"

Morales smirked at Eldritch. "Sir, things were kind of confusing last night. What with your lead detective calling us in for a consult because he doesn't know enough about his own beat to identify a major player in the dirty magic trade and then telling us to keep our hands off his case." He shrugged. "You can't blame us for being confused."

"Prospero?" Eldritch said. This was where things were going to get really tricky. Technically, I was still an employee of the BPD. They'd loaned me to the MEA, which paid for my overtime, but the city of Babylon paid my salary. That meant the man staring me down was still my boss. However, Gardner was also my boss, so admitting to interviewing Duffy's witness would throw her under the bus. Basically, I was screwed no matter who I pissed off.

"Sir, I—"

"Prospero and Morales went to the hospital on my orders," Gardner cut in. "We were going to write up their findings and share them with Duffy as soon as possible."

The relief I felt over the first part of her statement was ruined by the lie in the second half. With these two I often felt like a marionette whose arms were being yanked in opposite directions by two puppeteers.

Eldritch looked unconvinced. "For the record, if I ever catch one of your people interfering with one of our investigations, I'll charge you with obstruction." He rounded on me. "And you, *Detective*, will find yourself out of a job."

"Sir," Morales said, "Duffy himself didn't believe the witness was reliable. Our conversation with him supported that position."

Eldritch cocked his chin. "Well, we'll just have to take your word for it, since Mr. Schmidt is dead."

Frost crept along the back of my neck and down my arms. "What? He was fine when we left him."

"Damnedest thing." He shook his head. "The officer guarding the room said that after two unnamed cops"—he shot us a weighted look—"stopped by claiming Duffy asked them to interview the witness, no one went in or out except hospital staff."

"He was pretty sickly," Morales said. "What was the cause of death?"

Eldritch looked at all of us with a deadpan expression. "Knife through the eye socket."

"What?" Gardner's expression went pale. "You're sure? What kind of knife?"

Eldritch frowned. "Forensics said it was some sort of South American model."

"Shit," Gardner said. "A façon?"

The captain nodded. "What do you know?"

"It's classic *A Morte*." Her tone was heavy and her complexion was milky green, as if it couldn't decide whether she was scared or nauseated.

"The Brazilian cartel?" Morales asked.

"*A Morte*'s wizard assassins use what they call *O olho de Deus*—the Eye of God. It's sort of a cartel calling card." Gardner turned toward Morales and me. "When you said Harry's attacker had black skin I started to suspect, but this cinches it. There's a hit man they call Pantera."

"Panther," Morales translated, looking at me. "What was it Hot Pocket said about the cat?"

"Wait." Eldritch held up a hand. "Who's Hot Pocket?"

"Duffy's witness," Morales said. When Eldritch opened his mouth to ask the inevitable question, it was Morales's turn to hold up a hand. "You really don't want to know, sir."

The same feeling I'd felt when the dogcatchers walked out with the half-dead rottweiler rose in my throat. Pity? Yes, that was it. Hot Pocket hadn't been a paragon of humanity, but, like the dogs, he'd been caught in the crossfire of someone else's war. The irony was that his murder should have made his dreams of fame a reality—it at least warranted a couple of inches in the newspaper ("Homeless Man Murdered in Coven-Related Violence"). But with a new mayor in office and a coven war brewing, I doubted it would even get a couple of lines of coverage.

I cleared my throat and rejoined the conversation. "Hot Pocket said a large black cat was at the church last night."

Morales shot an inquiring look at Gardner. "Ring any bells?"

Gardner's already pale face went ashen. "What the fuck is he doing in Babylon?"

"Who?" Eldritch demanded in an exasperated tone.

Gardner grabbed her purse and grabbed her cell. "I need to make a couple of calls." She started for the door.

Eldritch stepped in her path. "Now, hold on just a damned minute—"

She pushed him out of the way. "Meet me back at the gym," she said to Morales and me.

"What about Harry?" Morales called.

"We need extra detail on him—including someone in his room." With that, she ran out the door. "Call Shadi and tell her to head over there."

"What the fuck was that about?" Eldritch threw up his hands.

Morales's expression was uncharacteristically grave. "Gardner's had several run-ins with *A Morte* in the past. If she's right and the man who beat Harry is one of their hit men, we're looking at problems way worse than a coven war."

Eldritch's confrontational expression fell. "I'll get those extra bodies on Bane, but we're already getting more calls about coven violence than usual. Besides, the BPD isn't at the MEA's beck and call."

"Yes, sir," I said.

"And, Prospero?" he said. I raised my brows. "Remember where you came from. I could put you back there in a heartbeat."

My skin suddenly felt too heavy.

"Excuse me, Captain," Morales said, "Detective Prospero was following orders from her superiors. Just like you're following your orders by surrendering the case. You don't like what she's being asked to do—take it up with Gardner." With that, Morales pushed me ahead of him. "Let's go."

My mouth hung open all the way through the trailer, past

Eldritch's rage-red face, and out the door. It wasn't until the door closed behind us that I recovered my wits. "Holy shit," I whispered. "I'm gonna pay for that later."

"Nah. He's just blustering to save his ego." He put an arm around my shoulder. "Hot Pocket died under the watch of a BPD officer. An officer who let us past him without verifying we should even be there. If Eldritch raises a stink, he'd have to expose his own cop's incompetence first."

Even though he'd just ensured I was safe from repercussions, the increasingly nasty tone of this investigation left a bad taste in my mouth. Political maneuvering was the thing I hated most about my job, and it was becoming more and more necessary to keep my ass out of a sling.

"What now?" I asked.

"Now we head to the gym and hope that whatever Gardner's finding out from her sources isn't bad news."

Chapter Ten

On the way back to the gym, Morales called Shadi and sent her to the hospital to watch Harry. He promised one of us would be there in a few hours to relieve her. Until Harry was conscious and we got his statement, the task force members would take shifts watching him twenty-four seven.

Mez had been confused after Gardner stormed past him at the junkyard without a word, but we'd filled him in. Now he was in his car following us back to the office.

After he hung up, Morales settled back into his seat with a sigh. "What a fucking day, huh?"

I nodded. "Doesn't sound like it's going to get better, either."

"What's the real story with Volos?" he asked, his tone tight.

"I was telling the truth. Baba is volunteering at the community center. I went to drop her off this morning and there he was. We didn't talk long because he had some reporter with him. But she's the one who told him about Charm—not me. He asked me a couple of questions, but I told him it wasn't our case." I hadn't mentioned that the man who'd just gotten us the case also had put me in Grace Cho's crosshairs. Part of me wanted to call him and thank him for strong-arming Eldritch, but the other half wanted to punch him for interfering in my life—again.

"Why do you think he called the chief, then?"

I shook my head and sighed. "I gave up trying to understand Volos's motivations for anything a long time ago."

"Still." Morales looked at me with a raised brow. "In this case, his maneuverings appear to be in our favor."

I snorted. "Sure, if you consider having to track down a dangerous cartel assassin a favor."

He nodded absently, his eyes on the road. "You ever hear the story on Gardner's past with *A Morte*?" He asked the question casually, leaving himself wiggle room to say it was her story to tell in case I hadn't heard.

"About her team getting ambushed?" I nodded. She'd also intimated that one of the undercover officers lost in the massacre had been her lover.

"It was all the talk in the MEA for weeks after it happened." He shook his head in disgust. "People were placing bets on whether she'd even have a job to come back to after her leave of absence."

"From what she said it didn't sound like it was her fault."

"Didn't matter." He shrugged. "Someone higher up needed to assign blame to someone's name. Since it was her team and her undercover guy who got made by the cartel, she was the obvious choice."

"But she's running this task force now."

"It was touch and go for a while," he said. "For a couple of years she got assigned to some real shit details. But then some-one decided there needed to be a task force in Babylon. None of the usual suspects would go near the job." He glanced at me. I just nodded, because I believed it. Babylon had a reputation for being a city without a future. I could see it being a real dead-end assignment for any ambitious MEA agents looking to rise in the ranks. "So they had no choice but to give it to Gardner, but they made no bones about the post being provisional. If we don't close cases, they'll close us down."

I crossed my arms and looked out the window at the passing landscape. A man limped down the sidewalk with a trash bag over one shoulder clasped in a palsied hand. His skin was green, like Hot Pocket's had been. I tore my gaze from the depressing scene and rubbed my eyes. I wished I could say Hot Pocket's death was a rare occurrence in the Cauldron, but, sadly, power-less addicts like him were discarded like trash daily. "I got the impression Gardner saw this assignment as her way of making good."

He nodded. "But now that *A Morte*'s in the mix things are going to get tricky. It's bound to dredge up a lot of shit for her."

We were driving through Votary territory. Buildings were covered in graffiti of alchemical symbols—mostly griffins and winged serpents hatching from eggs. But here and there I also spotted a circle with an arrow jutting from it. The paint looked fresh, with trails dripping from it like blood. I pointed the image out to Morales. "That's not good."

"It looks like the male symbol."

I nodded. "Also Mars, which is ruled by masculine energy."

"Mars was the god of war, right?" He spoke it as a question, but his tone told me it was rhetorical. "Christ, I hope Gardner's intel on *A Morte* helps us find this guy fast."

A block or so later, we passed a corner store where three thugs in black hoodies slouched against the stoop waiting for their next customer. Seeing them reminded me of the guy who'd gotten away. Yet another confusing angle to the case. Why would a Votary wizard be hanging out with an *A Morte* shaman?

I cleared my throat, keeping my eyes on the sidewalk, as if Pantera himself might suddenly appear. "What happens if we don't find him?"

He was silent so long that I looked over. Finally, he said, "Best we don't even entertain that as an option."

Chapter Eleven

Gardner stood in front of a large whiteboard inside the boxing ring. In her hands she held a thick file folder. The whole team was there, except Shadi, who was already at the hospital keeping an eye on Harry.

"The Brazilian cartel calls themselves *A Morte*," Gardner was saying. "It means 'the death' in Portuguese. No one knows the leader of the entire operation, but the players the MEA does know about are mostly powerful shamans who capitalize on the black-market demand for regulated rain-forest ingredients in dirty magic potions."

The government had cracked down on imports of herbs and plants from the rain forests back in the 1990s. They claimed the regulations were meant to control the quality of ingredients used in sanctioned clean magic labs as well as to prevent dirty magic practitioners from getting their hands on them, but the hefty tariffs on those items also helped fill Uncle Sam's coffers.

"After magic pushed out cocaine and heroin as America's favorite addiction, *A Morte* began supplying to dirty covens along the East Coast of the US," Gardner continued. "In addition to selling hard-to-get ingredients for a premium, they also dabble in human trafficking to supply workers for the sex magic covens."

She removed a picture from her file folder and tacked it to the board. "This is Hector Souza."

The picture was grainy, but there was no mistaking the man's pitch-black skin. "That's him," I said, "the guy from the junkyard."

"That's what I was afraid of," Gardner said. "Like I said, they call him Pantera. He's an Amazonian shaman who specializes in shape-shifting potions."

I glanced at Morales. "A big black cat." His expression tightened as the meaning of my comment hit home.

"Explain," Mez said.

"Duffy's witness from Charm's murder said he watched a big black cat walk into the church, but a man walked out."

Gardner nodded and crossed her arms. The move made the tiger-eye cabochon ring on the middle finger of her left hand wink in the light. She'd once told me she bought it after her team was killed and never took it off. Tiger eye was the stone of truth and logic and she wore it on her Saturn finger, which governed responsibility and security. "When he's in his human form, his skin stays pitch black—a side effect of using the potions for so long."

"Have you had any experience with this guy, sir?" Mez asked carefully.

"If you're asking if he was involved in murdering my old

team, the answer is no. But he does work for the same asshole who issued the kill order on them."

The mood in the room shifted. Up until that point, we'd all been tiptoeing around the tragedy in her past. But having her bring it up seemed to ramp up the tension. As if she'd summoned a ghost into the room.

She cleared her throat. "From what I understand, he's sort of a specialist for the cartel. They bring him in to help establish new territories. Once he gets a foothold, the cartel brings in someone else to run the operation."

"Does *A Morte* supply to any of the Cauldron's covens?" Morales asked me.

"As far as I know, Uncle Abe only used Canadian suppliers," I said, "which means all the other coven leaders would have, too."

"Do you know why he preferred the Canadians?" Gardner asked.

I shook my head.

"Maybe with Abe in prison someone decided to switch up the supply chain," Mez offered.

I shrugged. "It's possible but not probable. Charm was loyal to Abe so he wouldn't do something like that without permission."

"But the Votary crews fractured after Abe went to prison, right?" Morales said. "Maybe someone decided a new supplier would give them a leg up on the competition."

"Maybe," I said. "But I also don't get why this panther guy would go after Harry Bane."

"Right," Morales said. "He tried so hard to make it appear as if Harry killed Charm."

"If Souza's goal is to start a coven war," Mez said, "Harry's death would look like a retaliatory hit by the Votaries for Charm's death."

"The guy who got away when the dog attacked me was definitely Votary," I said. "He had alchemical tattoos all over his arms. But he didn't have an Ouroboros that would indicate he was a *made* member. I'm wondering if he was the same guy Hot Pocket saw with the Panther at the church."

"So you're thinking an ambitious Votary wiz went in league with *A Morte* to kill Charm and then helped try to knock Harry out of the game, too?" Mez asked.

"It's just a theory," I said. "But I don't get what *A Morte* would gain by manipulating a coven war."

"It's possible Harry Bane and Charm refused to work with the Brazilians," Morales said. "So Souza decided to remove them from the picture altogether."

We all fell silent for a moment as the implications settled in. Finally, Morales blew out a long breath. "Okay, so what's our next move?"

"Start with the Votaries. See if you can find out who was playing wingman to the Pantera today."

"We should drop in to see the Wonder Twins," I said, referring to my favorite snitches. "Maybe they've heard something."

"Good plan," Gardner said. Her tone seemed slightly less tense now that we were working on a plan. "Keep in touch with Shadi, too. I want you two there when Harry Bane wakes up."

Once Morales and I nodded, she turned to Mez. "Stay with the potion angle. Now that Eldritch has handed the case over, you should be able to get all the lab reports and samples from Val. Maybe something in the potion can tie Hector Souza to Charm's death."

Mez rose and nodded. "The BPD labs are notoriously slow, but once I have the sample back here I should be able to break it down fairly quickly. Then I could get to work on trying to figure out how this guy zapped out of here."

"All right," Gardner said. "I don't need to remind any of you how serious this situation is. We already have two murders and one attempted murder tied to this case. We need to find Pantera before he creates any more chaos."

She didn't mention the pressure the MEA would now put on her because of the *A Morte* connection, but she didn't need to. We all knew the stakes.

We all rose to get busy, but Gardner called out, "Prospero— a word in my office?"

My stomach dropped. Morales shot me a curious look, but I shook my head since I had no idea why I was getting called to the office. All I knew was those invitations rarely involved good news. With my mind scrambling to figure out how I'd screwed up this time, I climbed down from the boxing ring and followed her to the cramped room.

The door had barely clicked shut behind me when she rounded on me. "You got anything you want to tell me?"

I tilted my head and eyed her. Without any hints to go on, I jumped on the first thing I could think of that might have pissed her off. "I'm sorry I didn't tell you about running into Volos, but I swear I didn't ask him to call Eldritch—"

"Not that." She waved a hand. "I assume Volos has his own reasons for interceding on our behalf. Until those motivations are revealed, I'm just going to focus on solving the case without losing any more lives."

I frowned but nodded. "Good. So what did you call me in here for?"

She crossed her arms. "You get any calls from the media lately?"

Taken off guard, I spoke slowly. "Yeah, actually. This reporter was with Volos this morning and I guess she decided I'd make a good story. She called right before we spoke at Danny's school to propose an interview."

Gardner sighed and leaned back in her chair. "I can't believe she called you directly. She called this morning right after you left to see Aphrodite. I told her it was out of the question."

"That's what I said, too. I can't believe she called me after you said no. She seemed confident she could talk you into agreeing."

"Reporters are a particularly aggressive form of parasite."

A smile tugged at the corners of my mouth. "For the record, even if you had agreed I would have refused."

Gardner pursed her lips, narrowed her eyes, and steepled her fingers. "You're telling me that you'd defy a direct order?"

I nodded. "When it comes to inviting a camera into my private life, yes, sir."

She nodded. "I'll be sure to make a note." She looked back at her laptop. "Guess it's a good thing our policies forbid such a thing."

"That's it?" I asked.

She looked up. "Is there something else?"

I blew out a breath. "I guess not."

"Good. I really need your head in the game right now." She sighed and rubbed her mouth with her left hand. The shadows behind her eyes were no wonder given her personal history with *A Morte.*

I stepped forward. "Sir, I promise we'll get this asshole." I didn't mention the past because I knew she wouldn't want to discuss it. Nevertheless, she seemed to accept the unspoken support I was offering.

"Don't just promise, Prospero. Make it happen."

I stood straighter. "Absolutely."

"Go on, then."

When I came out of the office, Morales was pacing near the desks. "What was that about?"

I shook my head. "I'll tell you later. You ready to go see Little Man and Mary?"

He sighed and threw his newspaper on the desk. "I need to hit the ATM first."

Chapter Twelve

Normally, our favorite snitches received us in a run-down park near one of the abandoned steel factories. But since this March had been colder than snowman's taint, they'd moved their operation indoors to an apothecary.

Morales glanced at the sign over the door and raised a brow. "Black Cat Commissary?"

"Think it's an omen?" I said in a dramatic tone. Truth was, the name was a coincidence. I'd been to this place months earlier to meet with our informants about the Dionysus case. He was shooting me a questioning look, so I playfully nudged his shoulder. "I'm joking. Not everything is portentous—even in a magical slum."

When we walked in, a bell rang over the glass door. The guy who ran the apothecary was measuring out some sort of blue powder onto a scale. He looked up and frowned, as if he knew we wouldn't be buying anything. "They're in the back."

I nodded my thanks and continued farther into the store. Behind the counter, a long mirror was lined with shelves bearing containers of powder, herbs, and oddities, like chicken feet and dried animal eyeballs. The rest of the store was filled with shelves bearing sundries and homeopathic remedies. I'd never checked the storeroom, though I was pretty sure our friend behind the counter had a sideline of selling illegal potion ingredients. But we weren't there to harass black-market potion peddlers. We'd come for information.

Next to the set of stairs leading to the second-floor apartments, a raised platform held an old-timey shoeshine stand. A tank of a woman spilled over the edges of the chair. She wore a man-sized white T-shirt with yellow pit stains and polyester plaid pants that looked straight out of a Goodwill bin. Her lanky brown hair was pushed behind her ears like an inconvenience. The tiny being strapped face-out in a baby carrier on her chest was asleep.

"Hey, Mary," I said.

"Hi, Lady," Mary said, her voice thick. She looked at Morales and waved. "Mister Man."

Over the last few months, Mary had become more accustomed to Morales, so he'd been deemed trustworthy enough to deserve his own nickname. "What's happening, Mary?" Morales said, grinning at her.

"Baby sleeping," she whispered. With a large hand, she gently patted Little Man's belly.

"Any chance he's waking up soon?" I whispered back. "We're kind of in a hurry."

"You inconsiderate assholes are always in a hurry." Little Man's eyes stayed closed. "Why's today any different?"

"You know why we're here?" I asked.

A tiny lid opened. "Charm?"

I nodded.

"I'm pretty tired today, Prospero." His rosebud mouth opened into a broad yawn. "I'm gonna need some help waking up."

I shot a look at Morales, who rolled his eyes and removed his wallet. He took out a twenty and waved it under Little Man's nose. "How's that?"

The homunculus's eyes popped open. His tiny hand snatched the money out of Morales's palm and had it hidden in his diaper before either of us could blink. He smacked his rosebud lips and stretched like a kitten. "I'm suddenly feeling ready to take on the day."

"Glad to hear it," Morales said. "Now, about Charm…"

Little Man sat up a little straighter in the carrier, leaving an elbow against Mary's flat chest. "That's some bad juju there."

"What's the word?"

Little Man nodded. "Votaries think it was Bane." He sighed. "But I don't know." He clucked his tongue against the roof of his mouth. "Something don't feel right about that."

"True enough," I said. "Some asshole beat the shit out of Harry this afternoon. Would have killed him if we hadn't interrupted."

"Revenge?" LM asked, raising a single hairless brow.

I shook my head. "We don't think so."

The other brow rose to match the first. "Interesting." The homunculus crossed his arms.

"Has there been any chatter about one of Charm's lieutenants wanting to climb the ranks?" Morales asked.

Little Man shrugged. "There's always chatter about motherfuckers wanting a bigger piece of the pie. I wouldn't rule it out."

"You got a name?"

LM rubbed his chin with his tiny hand. "Nothing specific. But I did hear something. The Votaries are holding a memorial for Charm tomorrow."

My brows rose. "Really? Where?"

"The Red Horse. You know it?"

I nodded and explained for Morales. "It's a bar favored by a Votary crew led by a real pain in the ass named Puck."

"If it were me, I'd stop by and see if anyone's acting like the new cock of the walk." LM waggled the skin where his eyebrows would have been if he'd had any hair.

"Wouldn't be a bad idea," Morales said.

I snorted. "Hell yes, it would be a bad idea. I used to belong to that coven, remember? Walking in there with a badge on my hip is like begging for a beating."

Unfazed, Morales pursed his lips. "Or they'll be so shocked by your balls they'll let something slip."

I sighed. "We'll talk about it later." I turned back to LM, who'd been watching the exchange with his chin in his tiny hand and a rapt expression on his face. "What about Aphrodite?" I asked him. "Any chance s/he's wrapped up in this mess?"

LM laughed. "Please, the he-bitch don't leave bodies behind. You know that."

Morales and I exchanged a glance. It was true enough from what we knew of the Hierophant of the O Coven.

"Either way, this city's in for some shit."

"That's what we're afraid of," I said.

"You better shake a leg, then, Prospero. Because some people in the Cauldron been waiting for an excuse to unleash for years."

"You heard anything about a new player coming in from the outside?" I asked carefully.

Little Man frowned. "Like who?"

I shrugged. "Just covering our bases." I didn't want to mention *A Morte* to LM. If he didn't know about the threat, I didn't want to be the one responsible for him spreading the news.

"I ain't heard anything about a new wiz. Hell, we got enough assholes who are already in play."

"All right." I sighed. "I trust you'll call us if you hear anything we can use, right?"

Little Man nodded. "Of course, but I doubt I'll be hearing much."

"Why not?" Morales asked.

"Ain't you been listening, Macho? War's coming. Only an idiot would be on the streets. Mary and I are gonna hide out in our apartment till the smoke clears."

"Regardless," Morales said, "call us if you hear anything." He pulled another twenty out of his pocket.

Little Man's eyes widened. So did mine. My partner wasn't usually so generous with the payoffs.

"Shit, Macho, for that I'd do a hell of a lot more than call you." The homunculus pursed his lips and made a kissy noise.

"Keep it in your diaper, Pinkie Dick."

Little Man threw back his bald head and laughed. "Oh man, it's good to see you guys. Watch your asses out there, okay? We worry."

More like they worried about the prospect of losing the extra income, but it was still nice of him to pretend he cared. "See ya around, Little Man. Bye, Mary."

"Bye-bye, Lady and Mister Man."

We turned to go, but before we took three steps Morales's phone buzzed.

"It's Shadi." He answered and listened for a couple of moments. "See you in an hour," he said finally.

"What's up?" I asked.

"I'm gonna go relieve her at the hospital. She's gotta go get her kid."

I froze midstep. "Shadi's got a kid?"

Morales shot me a confused look. "Of course."

"But I thought she was—you know."

He laughed. "What? Lesbians have kids, too, Cupcake."

"*Single*," I corrected. He raised a pointed brow as if to remind me I was single and raising a kid.

"You know what I mean." My cheeks heated. "She's never mentioned a kid."

He shrugged and pushed the door open to let me step onto the sidewalk. "Shadi doesn't talk about her personal life much."

"How old is the kid?"

"Four. Shadi and her former partner split when Kesha was a baby."

"Wow," I said. "I still can't believe it. She never takes time off."

"Her mom lives with them and helps out, but she had something else going on this afternoon so Shadi can't hang out at the hospital."

"Okay," I said slowly. I was still trying to absorb the idea that Shadi and I had a lot more in common than I had thought. I looked at my watch and realized it was already after six. "I need to call Pen and tell her I can't meet up with her tonight."

He clicked the button to unlock the SUV. "Shadi said Harry's still totally out. Why don't you head home and I'll call if he wakes up?"

I paused with my hand on my door. "Are you sure?"

He shrugged. "There's no point in both of us sitting around the hospital. I'll drop you at your car."

That decided, we hopped in the car. On the way, I called Pen and told her to bring extra beer. I had a lot to discuss with my best friend after the fucked-up day I'd had.

Chapter Thirteen

Two hours after Morales dropped me at my car, I was sitting at my kitchen table with Pen. Since it was too cold to sit on my back patio like we usually did, we claimed the kitchen table. Luckily, Danny had a ton of homework so he'd locked himself in his basement bedroom to work, which meant we could talk without censoring ourselves for his sixteen-year-old ears.

Pen's dark-brown hair was pulled back into a bun. Before coming over, she'd changed into comfy yoga pants and a pink sweatshirt that made her brown skin glow. Pen was petite in stature, but she had a personality that belonged in a much larger body. Even her laugh was robust—the kind that came from deep in the belly and was released with abandon. I'd missed that laugh over the last couple of months, and the chance to catch up and joke over a couple of beers was just what the doctor ordered after my shitty day.

Pen

Pen took a sip from her beer and leaned back in the chair. "Tough day?" I asked. Pen was the counselor at Danny's school. I'd tried to stop by and say hi after we'd finished our talk with DUDE, but she'd been meeting with a student.

She laughed and nodded to the ice pack on my ankle. "It was nowhere near as exciting as yours." I'd already filled her in on the altercation at Harry's junkyard after she'd taken one look at my swollen ankle and demanded details.

I shrugged. "I'm pretty sure dealing with spoiled teenagers every day feels a lot like getting mauled by rabid dogs."

"No shit," she said. "Although to be fair, it's usually the parents who are foaming at the mouth when little Muffy and Preston get suspended for 69ing in the girls' locker room."

I snorted. "Is that what happened today?"

She shook her head. "Nah, that was last week. Today—" She sighed. "Today, a girl came into my office claiming she'd been raped."

The air in the kitchen changed, as if any sudden movements would make the air spark. "Oh?" I said carefully.

Pen's focus remained on the table, but she lifted the beer for another long swallow, as if trying to wash away a bad taste.

"Do you want to talk about it?" I prompted.

She shrugged, stealing a glance at me. "She wouldn't tell me who it was."

I frowned. "Do you think she was telling the truth?"

"About being raped?"

I nodded.

She pressed her lips together. "Yeah."

I didn't ask how she knew. Instead, I said, "If she won't give up a name, why did she come to you?"

"She's worried she might be pregnant." The word lay there

on the table between us like a loaded gun. "Wanted to know her options."

"Jesus, Pen. What did you tell her?"

"That's the rub. She said if it turns out she is, she wants to abort."

I slapped my beer on the table. "Christ, Pen. How old is she?"

"Fifteen."

"So she'll need parental permission." According to state law, all minors had to have a parent's consent for the administration of an abortive potion at a government-approved clinic.

"She asked if there's a way around the permission."

I scrubbed a hand over my face. "Stop right there. If you tell me anything else, I'll have to report it."

"Jesus, Kate, I'm not going to help her get a back-alley potion. Give me some credit."

I held up my hands. "No judgment, okay? I know the laws haven't kept up with the times. But since I'm on the federal task force I can't afford to have even the appearance of being an accessory to helping a minor break the law."

"Right. And I can't afford to have my license revoked. Besides, I'm not going to be responsible for sending that child into the Cauldron to get a dirty potion from a charlatan wizard."

I leaned back and crossed my arms, thinking over the options. "How long ago did the rape happen?"

Pen cleared her throat, as if it were tight. "Couple of weeks."

"She has a couple of weeks until she knows for sure, then."

"In the meantime, my concern is the guy who did it." Pen rubbed her arms, as if cold. "She said she was working on a project with him after school and he made a pass at her. She refused and he seemed to back down. He even offered to get her a soda to make up for it."

"A real Prince Charming, huh?" I said.

My friend made a disgusted face. "Anyway, next thing she knew she woke up and he was standing over her doing up his pants."

Chilly dread slid under my skin. "He slipped something in the drink."

Pen nodded.

"There's a potion making the rounds at colleges and high schools," I said. "It's a clean potion originally used as a sleeping pill for severe insomnia. The kids call it DTF. There are even fan pages for the potion on social media sites."

"What does *DTF* stand for?" Her tone was flat, as if she didn't really want to know.

"Down to fuck."

Pen paled. I couldn't blame her. Just saying those words made nausea bloom in the back of my throat. I'd seen humans do all sorts of horrible things to each other, but this felt way too close to home. Not just because it had happened at Danny's school, but also because of Pen's own past with sexual abuse. Dealing with this case was clearly already taking a toll on her, and I hated knowing it would only get worse.

"Why didn't she report him?" I asked.

Pen picked at the label of her beer. "She was scared. Her attacker told her no one would take her word over his. He even said the school might take away her scholarship."

"Scholarship?" My eyes widened. I paused, wondering if I should even say what I was thinking. Meadowlake didn't offer many scholarships. In fact, only one was offered to each incoming class in the upper school. That meant it was one of four kids—one of whom was Danny's special girl. "Pen, it's not—" I leaned forward and whispered, "Please tell me it's not Luna."

Pen hesitated and her gaze lowered. "You know I can't tell you." I'd been friends with this woman for a decade, and her body language was screaming guilt.

"Fuck—it *is* her." My stomach recoiled. Just that afternoon I'd spoken to the girl and had no idea she'd been suffering under the weight of such a horrible secret. "Jesus."

Her head jerked up but her shoulders slumped in surrender. "You can't tell Danny."

"Of course not," I said, lowering my voice.

"Her mom works two jobs and her dad is gone. This school is her big chance to improve their lot."

"And then some privileged asshole uses that against her." I smacked the bottle on the table, wishing it were the attacker's head instead.

Pen leaned forward on her elbows. "What are our options here? Legally."

I chewed on my bottom lip. "If she'd gone and gotten a rape kit done this would be a lot easier. Since she didn't, it's going to be his word against hers. And since she won't give you a name..." I trailed off, letting Pen come to the conclusion without saying it out loud.

"I'll keep working on her, but she made me swear not to tell anyone. She seemed really scared that he'd find out she talked." I just nodded because there wasn't anything to say to make the situation less shitty. "But you know what really worried me?"

I shook my head.

"She seemed way more worried about being pregnant than the fact she'd been violated. It was almost as if she blamed herself."

"That's common with rape victims."

"I know," Pen snapped.

111

"Hey." I tilted my head down to catch her gaze and reached across to touch her hand. "I know you do. And I'll help in any way I can. You know that."

Pen swallowed hard and nodded. "Thanks, Kate. I'm just worried there's not much we can do, you know? I told Principal Anderson we might have a sexual predator among the student body but he brushed me off."

I patted her hand before withdrawing to grab my beer. I didn't want to tell her it was hopeless. During my time as a cop, I hadn't worked on too many rape cases, but it was well known that they were incredibly difficult to prove. But charges couldn't even be filed without Luna naming names. Still, given the stigma rape victims faced, I couldn't blame the girl for not stepping forward.

But more than the shitty odds of proving the case, I was worried about Pen herself. The previous fall she'd had a horrible car accident that resulted in some broken bones and, worse, a broken sobriety. In an effort to relieve the pain of her injuries, she'd fallen off the wagon and taken pain potions. While she seemed to have kicked the urges quickly, the stumble had affected her emotionally. I knew she was still attending Arcane Anonymous meetings, but she'd also been more withdrawn in general.

While I pondered all that, Pen finished off her beer and went to get another, grabbing one for me, too, without asking. When she came back her expression had cleared, as if talking it out had alleviated some of her worries. That or she simply had decided it was time to change the subject. "Enough of that. What's up with you besides being attacked by dogs?"

For the first time in a long time, I actually had something else to talk about besides work. "Well...something very interesting happened at the school today with Mr. Hart."

Her eyes widened. "Spill it, sister." According to Pen, all the single women at Meadowlake had crushes on the guy.

I sucked on my teeth for a moment to draw out the suspense. "He asked me out."

"Shut up!" She leaned forward. "Tell me everything."

After I told her about the awkward conversation that ended in setting the date, she frowned. "Where was Morales when all this happened?"

"He walked in at the end and overheard." I forced a casual shrug. "He read me the riot act about it later."

She snorted. "I just bet he did."

"What's that supposed to mean?" I couldn't quite meet her eyes.

"Please, Kate, that boy's sweet on you and you know it, too."

"He is not." I adjusted uneasily in my seat.

"Mmm-hmm. Didn't you tell me he left the ball in your court?"

I sighed. "Sort of."

Pen shook her head. "Why haven't you followed up on that?"

I took a swallow of beer before answering. "It's too complicated."

Her eyes narrowed. "Because you work together or because you think he'd be too difficult to control?"

This was the problem with having a counselor as a best friend. She never let me wriggle out of difficult discussions. "Both," I admitted grudgingly.

"Plus it probably dings your ego that he called you on your bullshit last time."

"Hey!"

"Girl, please. The more emotionally unavailable that boy is the more you want his D."

"I do not."

"Uh-huh." She smiled knowingly. "Okay, so how does Mr. Hart fit into this?"

"I don't know if he does." I shrugged. "He just asked and I said yes."

"Do you like him?"

"He's nice," I said. She looked unimpressed by my passion. "Smart and cute," I added quickly. "Normal in a good way."

There went that eyebrow again. "I see."

"What's that supposed to mean?"

"Relax." Pen raised her hands. "Drew's hotter than Georgia asphalt in August. He's exciting and dangerous. But most of all, he challenges you."

I couldn't really argue with any of that. "So?"

"So." She dragged out the word. "Maybe you're going out with Mr. Hart precisely because he's the polar opposite of Morales."

"Maybe it's just that I want to have a nice date with a normal guy."

"Hmm."

I was saved from having to continue that painful conversation when Baba waddled in with her cane. She had on an acid trip tie-dyed housecoat, and her long gray hair was pulled up into a bun on her head. She yawned and nodded at us. "Commercial break." She went straight to the fridge and removed a large glass pitcher filled with a liquid the color of urine from a dehydrated hobo.

Pen frowned at the drink the old woman poured into a glass. "What's that you're drinking?"

Baba took a good long swallow and let out a satisfied *ahh* before answering. "It's kombucha."

"What the hell is that?"

"It's fermented tea. It balances the flora in your gut," she said. "Of course I added a little bit of an herbal kick to it."

I didn't want to touch the topic of gut flora, so I raised a brow and asked about the other part. "What kind of herbal kick?"

A small burn escaped her lips. "Just some willow bark and goldenseal for my arthritis."

I shook my head. "You really need to go see a doctor about that, Baba."

She laughed. "With what money?" She shook her head and took another sip. "Besides, they'd just give me a prescription for Maslin's Tincture. This works just as well and is way cheaper."

I shot her a skeptical look.

"You wanna try it?" Baba asked us.

I shook my head immediately.

"I'll try it." Pen took the cup from Baba and sniffed. Her nose instantly wrinkled, but she took a sip anyway. Judging from the expression on her face, she regretted volunteering the instant it hit her tongue.

"Well? What do you think?" Baba asked, a knowing smile on her face.

"It tastes like carbonated vinegar."

"Great, right?" Baba said.

Pen thrust the cup back at the woman.

"Suit yourself," Baba said. "Just means more for me."

Pen took three chugs of her beer to rinse the kombucha from her tongue. Baba pulled out a chair and settled into it. "What are you two talking about anyway? Normally you're cackling like lunatics in here, but it's been suspiciously quiet."

I shrugged and busied myself reading my beer label. "Just work stuff."

Baba made a dismissive sound at the mention of our jobs. In her opinion, modern women spent too much time being stressed out because of their ambitions. Her husband had been a handyman and she'd supplemented his modest income by selling homemade remedies to neighborhood ladies using their pin money or allowances. "You both need hobbies."

I snorted. "Who has time for that?"

"Where a person spends their time is the truest indicator of their priorities."

I gritted my teeth instead of responding. It was easy to judge other people when you spent your day watching TV and brewing suspicious teas. I didn't have the luxury of deciding not to work because someone else was paying the bills.

A foot kicked mine under the table. I looked up to see Pen shooting me a look. Apparently she'd been able to read my mind with her scary therapist skills. I scooted lower in my seat as regret washed through me at my uncharitable thoughts.

"So how's your new gig at the community center going?" I asked.

"Great!" Baba said, sitting up straighter. "They paired me up with some really sweet kids."

"You'll be able to make a real difference there." Pen sighed.

"Uh-oh." Baba leaned forward. "What's wrong?"

Pen leaned forward and set her arms on the table. "I don't know. It's just that playing counselor to a bunch of privileged kids is wearing thin."

"That's not all you do," I said. "There are kids there with real problems that you're helping." I shot her a meaningful look.

She pressed her lips together but nodded. "I know. It's nothing." She waved a hand. "I should feel lucky." She took another drink, as if trying to force down a bitter pill.

"Anyway," Baba said, "the center is great. Oh, I forgot to tell you, Kate."

I raised my brows. "What happened?" I braced myself to hear about some delinquent who'd given her shit.

"That news lady—the one who was there with Volos?"

My brows slammed down. "Grace Cho."

Baba nodded. "That's the one! She came back this afternoon."

"What did she want?" I asked.

"That's the weird part," Baba said. "She had all these questions about you."

I slapped my hand on the table. "That bitch."

"Why would a TV reporter be asking questions about you?" Pen asked.

Before I could answer, Baba spoke for me. "Grace Cho wants to do a special interview with Kate!" She sounded excited, as if she thought this would be my big break. For what, I had no idea. "She said she was interviewing people who knew Kate as pre-research." Baba looked at me with an accusing glance. "You didn't tell me you agreed to do an interview."

"That's because I didn't."

Baba frowned. "She sounded pretty confident the story was on."

"What kinds of questions did she ask?"

"Just about how we knew each other and stuff."

It was the "and stuff" that worried me. Baba had never met a stranger, and her default setting was at too much information. "What did you tell her?"

Baba shot me a worried look. "I didn't tell her any of your secrets or anything."

"What secrets?" I shot back.

She raised a gray brow. "Mmm-hmm. Anyway, I told her I wasn't going to answer any questions without clearing it with you first."

I sighed. "That's good, Baba. Thanks."

Baba nodded. "She seemed particularly interested about your time in the covens, and your relationship with John."

I pointed at Baba. "That's exactly the stuff I don't want aired in public. Jesus, can you imagine?"

"Either way, you're going to have to play this carefully," Pen said. "If you pissed her off she's likely to do an exposé or something out of spite."

"If she contacts you again, let me know," I said to Baba.

Baba drained the rest of her urine tea and let out a sigh. "Yes, ma'am." She grunted and pushed herself up from the table. "Okay, my tea's kicking in. If I don't come out in half an hour, send in a search party." With that, the old witch cackled and waddled away.

Chapter Fourteen

On the way to the hospital the next morning to meet Morales, I turned on the police scanner for company. Even though it was early, there was a lot of chatter. Apparently, a few Sanguinarians had been jumped by a group of Votaries the night before. The perps had run off before the cops arrived, but one of the Sang boys had died on the way to the hospital. The other two survived, but had to undergo treatment for broken limbs and hexing.

I cursed out loud as I turned my Jeep into the hospital parking lot. Chances were good the attack happened in retaliation for Charm's death. I didn't believe for a second that the Votaries hadn't heard that Harry Bane, who was the leader of the Sangs, had been beaten within an inch of his life the day before. Most likely some Votary wiz had taken credit for beating Harry, which had inspired others to declare open season on the Sangs.

Morales met me by the elevators at Babylon General. He'd called me at the butt crack of dawn to tell me Harry was awake and with the doctor. I'd thrown on my clothes and hightailed it over to help him do the interview.

"You been here all night?" I asked.

He shook his head. "Gardner took the overnight shift. I got here to relieve her just before Harry woke up."

I raised my brows in surprise. "Gardner took a shift?" As the special agent in charge of the team, she never took those kind of crap details.

He nodded. "She relieved me at midnight. Just showed up and told me to go home. Said she hadn't been able to sleep. Guess this *A Morte* stuff is weighing on her."

I didn't have a response to that, so I changed the subject. "You hear about the three Sang guys who got jumped last night?"

He shook his head.

"They claim the attackers belonged to a Votary crew. One of the Sangs died."

He sighed and shook his head. "Harry better be in a talking mood."

The halls were quiet as we walked toward Harry's room. The door was open and inside, a doctor bent over the bed. We loitered by the entrance while he did his thing. I took the opportunity to watch Harry before he put his guard up.

His normally thin face was swollen into an odd shape from all the contusions. Streaks of blood still clumped in his white hair, and the edges of the black ankh on his forehead were blurred from all the bruising. The doctor moved to the right, allowing me a better view of Harry's mouth. His lips were split and when he opened them to gasp, black gaps showed where teeth had been knocked out.

"You're a very lucky man, Mr. Bane," the doctor was saying.

That comment elicited a groggy laugh from the wizard. "Don't feel...lucky," he wheezed.

The doc patted him on the shoulder. "I'll be back in a couple of hours to check on you. In the meantime, let the nurses know if you need more pain potion."

With that, the doctor turned to exit. He paused when he saw Morales and me loitering in the doorway. "Take it easy on him. He's still in bad shape."

While Morales promised the good doctor we'd follow his orders, I met Harry's slitted gaze. The swelling prevented him from showing much emotion, but a hissed curse escaped his lips. Guess he wasn't any happier to see us than we were to be there.

Once the door shut behind the doctor, I grabbed a chair and straddled it. Resting my chin on my hand against the back of the chair, I shot the patient a sympathetic look. "You look like shit, Harry."

"I almost died yesterday. What's your excuse, bitch?" He dragged his watery gaze from me to stare at the ceiling, as if dismissing us.

I raised my brows. "Hey, Morales?"

"Yeah?" He stood at the end of the bed with his arms crossed.

"Jog my memory here. Whose ass did we save yesterday?"

"Some shitbag wizard."

I snapped my fingers. "Oh yeah. I remember now. Couple of bad guys beat a pitiful son of a bitch with his own walking stick." I looked at Harry. "Any of this ringing a bell?"

Harry shot me a venomous look. "Can't say it does."

"Well," I said with faux concern, "it's no wonder, seeing how they were giving you a total beat-down before we saved your sorry ass."

He snorted. "If you call getting attacked by my dog rescuing me."

I tilted my head. "Ah, so you do remember some things."

"Cut the shit, Prospero." He smacked his destroyed mouth. "What do you want?"

I leaned back and crossed my arms. "Gee, I don't know. Maybe you could start with telling us why a cartel hit man would want to frame you for Charm's murder and then turn around and kill you?"

"Life's a big mystery." He tried to shrug, but the effect was ruined by a pained wince.

I laughed. "Good to see they didn't beat your sense of humor out of you."

"You know what I think?" Morales said. "He doesn't know shit."

"Hmm," I said, pressing my lips together. "I don't know. I mean Harry's the head of his own coven. Surely he knows everything that happens in the Cauldron."

While Morales and I pretended Harry wasn't in the room, the wizard watched us with an increasingly bullish expression.

"Didn't you hear?" Morales said with a smirk. "Word on the street is Harry's been losing influence."

"Bullshit," Harry said. "I got plenty of influence. Otherwise why would that asshole try to set me up?"

I raised a brow. "You tell us."

He squeezed his eyes shut for a second before opening them again. "Doesn't matter now anyway."

"Hate to break it to you, Harry, but it matters a whole hell of a lot." I leaned forward to force him to look at me. "Even if we could just chalk up your beating to a personal beef with another wizard, we can't overlook the fact your assailants attacked a federal agent and a BPD detective."

"You won't find him."

"Find who, exactly?" Morales asked.

"I don't know his name, okay? I don't know anything."

I paused and really looked at Harry. "You're scared."

He didn't respond. Simply tipped his chin and looked at the broken finger on his left hand.

I'd known Hieronymus Bane since we were kids. He'd had his ass kicked plenty of times because of his ego and chronic verbal diarrhea. But the thing about Harry was, he was too stupid to stay down when he was beat. I'd watched him dust himself off and raise his chin to threaten larger kids who clearly outfisted him. Being the son of the powerful wizard of the blood coven had instilled in Harry an electrifying sense of entitlement that prevented him from ever feeling totally outgunned.

But right then, I saw true fear in his eyes. It was the haunted look of a man who knew he'd finally gotten himself into a situation he couldn't bluster his way out of.

"Let us help you." My tone was sincere. Because if Harry was scared, that meant we probably had good reason to be, too.

He snorted. "Right."

Morales and I exchanged a look. Time to try a different tactic. "The guy with the black skin," my partner said. "You ever seen him before yesterday?"

Harry touched the tip of his tongue to one of the empty sockets in his mouth. "Nuh-uh."

"What about his helper?" I asked. "We know he's Votary. You got a name for us?"

Harry's pause was imperceptible. Almost. "Nope."

Most likely Harry planned on dealing with that guy without interference from law enforcement. All the more reason to head to Charm's wake after we were done with Harry. If his goons got to the Votary guy before we did, we'd lose the chance to get intel from him.

Morales napped his notebook closed. "We're wasting our time. Let's go, Prospero."

Harry's head jerked up. "What are you going to do?"

I paused in my exit and turned back toward him. "We got a long day ahead of us. We've gotta review every computer and file folder we found in your trailer."

His chin came up. "You won't find shit about the black guy in there."

I leaned forward. "No, but they'll give us enough dirt on you to put your ass in prison."

"I didn't do anything wrong!"

"You're obstructing our investigation," Morales said with a raised brow.

Harry deflated against his pillow. "I don't know anything, okay? I was in my trailer watching porn when those assholes busted in and started whaling on me."

"Bye, Harry," I said. "I'd tell you to stay in town, but given your injuries I'm pretty sure you're going nowhere fast."

"Wait—you're just going to leave me here? What if he comes back to finish the job?"

"You got so much influence I suggest you get a couple of your guys here to watch your ass," Morales said.

With that, we marched out the door and let it shut behind us.

In the hall, Morales blew out a breath. "That was a waste of time."

"No shit." I shook my head.

"You ready to go pay your respects to the deceased?"

I sighed. "Not really, but that's never stopped me before."

Chapter Fifteen

Half an hour later we were driving through the heart of Votary turf. "Pull in here." I pointed him to a lot across the street from the Red Horse.

The peeling white paint on the cinder-block building was covered in spray-painted alchemical symbols that marked the place as the territory of the Votary Coven. The front door was painted black, and a red neon sign above it displayed the anarchy symbol. A frigid wind scattered trash across the sidewalk while a bum huddled on the corner of the building like the world's worst bouncer.

"You take me to the nicest places, Prospero," Morales said.

"If you're nice, I'll take you out for a burger after."

"You ever been to a Votary wake?" His leather jacket creaked as he turned to look at me.

I cringed.

"Shit, sorry," he muttered. "I forgot about your mom."

I shrugged off the apology and ignored the cold echo of grief that thrummed through my midsection. "There was no wake for her. Just a funeral." Memory of Danny's tiny, warm hand in my cold palm as we walked up the aisle in the funeral parlor toward her open casket. The sick feeling of dread at seeing the garish makeup on her too-still face. The cloying scent of carnations and lilies. The black cloud of guilt hanging behind my painfully dry eyes.

Morales cleared his throat. I shook off the past and tried to focus on the present. "More than likely this wake is just an excuse to drink a lot and jockey for position in the coven."

"Are you expecting to find any old friends in there?"

"Even when I belonged to the coven these people were, at best, *frenemies*." I sighed. "Keep your gun close."

We got out of the car and jogged across the street. My salt flare was a comforting weight against my side. I knew if shit went down we'd be sorely outnumbered, but I was hoping we'd get through this without weapons being drawn.

The door opened and Morales stood aside to let me go in first. Music scraped the air like the yowls of a pissed-off cat. I suddenly wished I'd thought to bring some earplugs in addition to my guns. The scent of smoke and beer saturated the thick air. The only lights in the place were spotlights aimed at the stage, where four men thrashed around like they were having seizures.

A very large man stepped into my path. "This is a private party."

I squinted up at him. Didn't recognize him, but I knew the type. Probably worked as muscle for the coven when he wasn't harassing people in the bar. Tattoos covered every inch of exposed skin—including his bare scalp. "We're friends of the deceased."

He squinted at me. "Name?"

I looked him in the eye. "Kate Prospero."

He looked up at me with new interest. "You related to Abe?"

"Yes." I wasn't giving him any more than that. Didn't matter; it was enough.

"Cover is twenty."

This was the first time I'd ever heard of a cover charge for admission to a wake, but I wasn't about to argue with the man. I tossed a look back at Morales. He pressed his lips together and forked over the money. The bouncer checked Morales's ID without incident, and we carried on into the bar. "You're an expensive date."

"Add it to my tab."

We worked our way through the crowd toward the bar. I didn't bother to lower my head in case anyone recognized me. The bouncer didn't know who I was, but I could already feel the gazes of several members of the audience. It was only a matter of time until a confrontation happened.

As far as wakes went, it wasn't exactly conventional—the bar setting notwithstanding. The only signs it was a memorial at all were the bottle of rye whiskey and framed picture of Charm on the stained green felt of the pool table. The image was of the bull of a man with his head thrown back as he laughed at something. I recognized the image because it had sat on the mantel at Uncle Abe's house for years. Abe always loved that picture because it pissed off Charm, who rarely even smiled, and hated having what he considered a weak moment captured for posterity.

At the bar, I ordered two beers even though it was only ten thirty in the morning. In a pinch, beer bottles made excellent weapons. Plus, even though everyone already knew we didn't belong, that wasn't an excuse to rub it in by looking like a couple of teetotalers.

Morales turned away with his elbows resting behind him on the bar. "You've got an admirer at three o'clock," he said under his breath.

I lifted the bottle to my lips, pretending to drink, and looked out of the corner of my eye. Sure enough, a blonde was watching me from other end of the bar. Most likely she was some Votary tough's bitch, but there was knowledge in her eyes that told me she was more than just an overly made-up face. I set down the beer and turned my back toward her, confident Morales would warn me if the polecat attacked from behind. "Don't recognize her."

"She recognizes you," he said. "And judging from the look on her face, she's not a fan."

I was going to reply that she should get in line, but at that moment the band finally finished their song. The crowd's vigorous cheering had a forced edge to it, as if everyone was afraid to be caught not clapping.

A broken guitar hung from the lead singer's left hand as he approached the mike. The sides of his head were shaved, but he'd left the middle long in a lazy Mohawk. He wore a ratty wife beater, baggy jeans, and scuffed Doc Martens with skulls painted on the sides. "We'll be back in fifteen. Stick around—or not, we don't give a fuck."

I nodded toward the Johnny Rotten wannabe. "That's Puck," I whispered to Morales. "This place is his crew's turf. I'd bet money he's the heir apparent now that Charm's gone."

Puck tossed the remains of the guitar down and jumped off stage. He strutted through he crowd as if he expected their adoration, and, of course, he got it. I tracked his progress through the mirror over the bar, and Morales's stillness indicated he was doing the same.

The blonde from earlier approached Puck. After an enthusiastic kiss where he grabbed her ass through her short skirt,
she whispered something to him. I knew the instant she told
him we were there because his gaze zeroed in on us like a laser.
Ripping my gaze from the mirror, I lifted the beer bottle and
took a long swallow. Duty be damned. I wasn't going into this
confrontation without some liquid fortification. I wasn't worried about Morales lecturing me considering his own beer was
already half-empty.

"Kate Prospero." I flicked a glance toward the mirror to see
Puck standing with his hands on his hips behind me. Morales
continued to lean against the bar in a casual pose, but I could
feel the heightened tension coming off him.

I turned slowly, taking my time so Puck would know I
wasn't one of his flunkies who'd jump just because he deigned
to speak to me. I took another sip of my beer before I answered.
"Hello, Puck."

His eyes narrowed. "I go by Pain now." Despite his slacker
getup, there were very real muscles on display. His eyes were
light blue, which contrasted against his dark hair, but it wasn't
the color that was unsettling. It was the glow of lunacy behind
them. The ruthlessness.

I cocked a brow. "Pain, huh?"

He ignored the mocking edge to my tone. "And I hear
you're a detective now. You got a lot of fucking nerve showing
your face here—today of all days." These words were said in a
calm tone that hinted at some sociopathic tendencies in young
Puck—err, Pain.

"I wanted to hear your set."

The corner of his mouth lifted. "What'd you think?"

"It was certainly...loud."

His eyes narrowed. "Who's your pig friend?" Behind Puck, the entire bar had gone silent. I wondered if this was why we hadn't been harassed when we'd arrived. Everyone had been waiting to see what their new leader would do.

My partner pulled away from the bar. "Morales."

"Well, Detective Morales"—neither of us corrected his mistake. Saying either of us worked with the MEA in that crowd would be like begging for a bullet—"did your partner here tell you who I am?"

"You mean besides being a mediocre musician?"

Those crazy eyes glowed with anger. "You want to start something, dick?" His followers closed ranks behind him, and there was no doubt they'd follow through on any threat he issued.

I held up my hands. "Relax. He doesn't know who you are."

Morales's eyes shifted toward me, as if he couldn't tell whether I was bluffing or not. I turned to him and dropped the bomb. "Old Puck here—excuse me, *Pain*, is not only a highly respected wizard of the Votary Coven, he's also the cousin of our esteemed mayor, John Volos." Saying that name had an immediate electrifying effect on the crowd, as if I'd thrown chum in the water.

"Get out," Morales said. He turned toward Puck. "That true?"

Puck crossed his arms and spit on the floor. "The wizard part is true, but I disowned that treacherous motherfucker."

I frowned at him. "Oh, Puck. Say it ain't so. You used to worship him." I turned toward Morales. "He used to follow us around and beg John to let him carry his wand and stuff. It was heartwarming, really."

"Shut the fuck up with your lies, bitch." Puck slashed a hand through the air. The move exposed his wrists, which, as expected, were covered in alchemical symbol tattoos. I couldn't get a good enough look at them to verify they were the same ones I'd seen at the junkyard, though. "That disloyal asshole shows his face around here and I'll remove it with a bullet."

I clucked my tongue against the roof of my mouth. "Good to see you're handling your grief well. Thought you'd be all torn up over Charm's death."

His expression slammed shut like a steel door. He took a menacing step toward me. "Watch your mouth. Charm was a fucking hero in this coven." Damned if he didn't sound like he believed it.

I stepped up to him, getting right in his face. "So you decided to honor his memory by sending a crew out to jump those Sang boys last night?"

"We were trying to honor his memory with this private party until you and your partner disrupted it, Detective," the blonde behind Puck said.

I couldn't read her. She certainly didn't talk like the arm candy of a potion dealer.

"Yeah," Puck said. "We don't need you coming in here throwing out allegations and shit. We're trying to mourn the man."

"You're forgetting that I knew him, too," I shot back. "Charm wouldn't want you starting shit that would put the coven in danger."

"I'd never do anything like that." Puck flashed me an eat-shit smile. "Finding Charm's killer is BPD's job, Detective."

I laughed. "Right. You're a big believer in the justice system, are you?"

"Look, unless you got a warrant, you need to leave and let us mourn in peace," Puck said.

"We're not here to harass you," Morales said. "We just thought you might have information that could help us find Charm's killer seeing how you're such upstanding citizens and all."

The blonde stepped up. "You want to find who did this, all you have to do is talk to the fucking albino."

My brow rose. "Harry Bane?" Harry wasn't technically an albino, but like a lot of blood magic wizards he had the pale coloring of someone who spent most of his life trolling through dark tunnels. "What makes you think he's behind it?"

"Please," Puck said, "ever since he took over his daddy's coven he's been struggling to stay on top. Killing the head of the Votaries would earn him cred with the Sangs." He spit on the floor to indicate what he thought of the rival coven. Several of his flunkies grunted their approval.

I crossed my arms and leaned back against the bar. "Maybe," I said, "but there's been upheaval in your camp ever since Abe went to Crowley. How do we know one of your own guys didn't off Charm for the same reason?"

Puck looked me in the eye. "You might have found it easy to betray this coven, bitch, but some of us know the importance of loyalty. No one would dare, because they'd have to answer to me."

I let the insult slide off my back. It was an old song that had lost its meaning for me. "Anyway," I said, "didn't you hear? Someone jumped Harry Bane yesterday."

Puck didn't bother covering his smile. "Serves him right."

Morales smiled tightly in response. "I guess that's a matter of opinion seeing how we believe Harry was framed for Charm's murder."

The words hung in the air like the dying notes of a song. Puck's left eye twitched. Morales and I just watched him.

Finally, he crossed his arms. "You got proof?" His tone was uncharacteristically serious.

The corner of my mouth lifted. "We're working on that right now." My gaze flicked toward his arms. "Nice tattoos by the way."

His eyes narrowed in confusion, but he recovered quickly. He shot a look at my left arm, where my Ouroboros tattoo was peeking out from beneath my cuff.

"You, too."

"I've been meaning to have it removed. That's the thing about tattoos, people make assumptions about you."

"In your case, they assume you're a traitor."

The tension in the air crackled against my skin. I probably could have taken Puck in right then for questioning, but arresting the apparent new leader of the coven in front of his crew was an invitation for homicide. Plus, something in my gut told me that even if Puck was really involved in Charm's death, he wasn't the kingpin. If we wanted Pantera Souza, we needed Puck to lead us to him.

Finally, I removed a card from my pocket and handed it to him. "If you think of anything that might help us, call me."

Puck slowly tore the card into pieces. Several of his cronies chuckled. "We don't help traitors."

"Suit yourself," I said. "But let me make one thing clear." I looked out over the assembled crowd to make sure I had their attention. "Your cousin," I said, referring to Volos, "has the entire BPD on alert for a coven war. They'll come down hard on anyone caught even looking at a rival coven the wrong way." I looked at Puck again. "If I hear about any of your guys making any more moves against Harry Bane or his crew, we will be back with warrants and lots of guys with big guns."

Puck laughed. "You do that."

"I mean it, Puck. No war."

He leaned forward and snapped his teeth at my face.

"Easy," Morales growled.

Ignoring my partner, Puck whispered, "That's the tricky thing about a war, Detective." He held up a finger like a gun and pulled the invisible trigger. "Lots of stray bullets and collateral damage. Never know who will get caught in the crossfire."

I grabbed his finger and twisted it until he fell to his knees on the ground. The crowd moved forward, but Morales drew his gun to halt their advance. The blonde stood to the side, glaring bullets at me.

I leaned down and looked into the pained eyes of the cocky asshole who'd just threatened me. "Your mouth is declaring wars your ass can't win." His finger cracked under the pressure. He didn't yell out in pain, but his jaw tightened and his eyes watered. "I might not be a member of this coven anymore, but I learned everything I know from a ruthless son of a bitch named Abraxas Prospero. If you come after me, I will end you."

With that, I released his broken finger. "Let's go," I said to Morales and marched away without another glance.

It wasn't until we were both outside and the door slammed behind us that Morales finally spoke. "So that went well."

Adrenaline buzzed through my veins like lightning. "Shut the fuck up, Morales."

He grabbed my arm, forcing me to stop. "Hey! I'm on your side, remember?"

I jerked my arm away but fought to put a muzzle on my emotions. "I—fuck." I ran a hand through my hair. "I lost my cool in there. Sorry."

"Relax," he said. "I get it. Just next time you decide to go She-Hulk you might give me a warning or something."

I pressed my lips together. "She-Hulk?"

He shot me a cocky grin. "Honestly, it was kind of hot."

"You're an idiot." I couldn't suppress my smile, though.

"Yeah, well, I'm a hungry idiot." He put an arm around my shoulders and steered me toward the car. "Let's go get that burger you owe me before we regroup at the gym."

Chapter Sixteen

Spinelli's was an institution in Babylon's Little Italy. Situated in the Mundane part of town, it harked back to the city's old days when, instead of potion covens, Mundane mob families ran the city's dark underbelly. I'd picked the spot because its location meant I wouldn't risk running into any cops I knew—especially the one who had told me going on this date was a bad idea.

I'd arrived early—just as I would for any other high-stakes op. I'd chosen my uniform carefully. Instead of the little black dresses a lot of women wore by default for a date, I'd gone with skinny jeans with dark-brown boots. On top I wore a silky blouse and blazer. It was the kind of outfit that said I'd made some effort but not too much. Plus the blazer hid my gun rig. Maybe most women didn't show up for a date packing heat, but most women also didn't have roving gangs of wizards out for their blood.

And if things went well, maybe I'd let Mr. Hart take a peek at my piece.

The bartender set the glass of wine on the bar in front of me. I wrapped a hand around the stem like it was a lifeline. I briefly considered calling Pen for a quick pep talk, but I refused to give in to the nervousness. I was a cop who faced down potion junkies. I could handle a high school science teacher.

As I swallowed some liquid courage, I let my mind wander back over the rest of my day.

After Morales and I had our little chat with Puck, we'd returned to the gym. The good news was Mez was able to connect the potion used to kill Charm to a rare rain-forest frog that secreted a neurotoxin capable of paralyzing a human. That news certainly went a long way to connect Pantera Souza to the crime. Unfortunately, we couldn't find the shaman. We'd spent the rest of our day calling my informants and Morales's MEA contacts to see if anyone had a lead on his whereabouts only to come up with a big fat goose egg.

I sighed and raised my hand to ask the bartender for something stronger, but right then the door to the restaurant opened and Mr. Hart breezed in. It was a chilly night and the wind had had its way with his hair. The mussed look made him seem younger. He handed his overcoat to the hostess, which gave me a view of his typical uniform of faded jeans, T-shirt, and tweed blazer.

I took a big gulp of my wine and kept my gaze glued on the TV over the bar. Making him come to me was a power play that would have made Pen shake her head, but old habits I'd learned as a kid about the importance of establishing a pecking order had never really gone away.

"Kate?"

I turned and smiled confidently, but the wineglass felt

slippery in my palm. I set it down carefully before rising to give him a hug. He smelled of cold air and a tad too much cologne. But our quick embrace revealed long, lean muscles underneath his hipster academic facade.

"Did you find the place okay?" I knew he'd only been in Babylon about a year.

He nodded and motioned to the bartender. "I live near here, actually."

I acted surprised, but I knew exactly where he lived. While I hadn't gone so far as to use police resources to check his record, I had done an Internet search. He lived in what locals called Snob Hill. The neighborhood used to be called NOLI—North of Little Italy—but the name changed after some enterprising real estate types started buying houses and flipping them for enormous profits. A lot of seniors had had to surrender their paid-off homes after the tax rates for the neighborhood sky-rocketed. Which made it super easy for young professionals to swoop in and get the old bungalows for a song.

Of course, I didn't comment on any of that. Just because Hart lived there didn't mean he'd screwed some old woman out of her family home. However, I was curious how he managed the high rents of the area on a private school teacher's salary. The Internet search hadn't netted me much more than an address and a link to the Meadowlake site, which had a brief, polite bio. I also hadn't been able to find him on any of the typical social media sites.

While I reviewed the meager mental dossier I'd built, he chatted with the bartender about the restaurant's selection of import beer. He finally settled on a Belgian white ale. I tried not to judge him for it. Most of the men I knew wouldn't be caught dead drinking a beer with a monk on the label.

"So," he said finally.

"So." A forced smile. Oh God. This was torture. "Where did you live before you moved to Babylon?"

"I grew up in New York," he said. "Brooklyn."

"Were you a teacher there, too?"

He shook his head. "Went to university in Boston. Majored in biochemistry."

My eyes widened. "Wow."

"It sounds a lot more impressive than it was. I spent most of my time in labs watching mold grow." He shrugged. "I worked for a lab after school but quit after a couple of years and got my teaching degree."

My cop instincts told me there was more to the story than he was telling me. But instead of deciding Morales was right about Hart having a shady past, I brushed it off. People didn't share their entire life stories on a first date, after all.

"I taught at a private school in Boston for a bit, but then I went back home for some family obligations."

I took a sip of my wine and processed that. "Any brothers or sisters?"

"Nope," he said with an easy smile. "Just me. Anyway, I got tired of New York and looked for teaching jobs in other cities. I got lucky when the position opened at Meadowlake. It's got a great reputation."

"Cool," I said. "So you're liking it?"

"Totally, the kids are great." He smiled, flashing a dimple. "Parents, too."

"And what drew you to starting DUDE?"

He paused and held up his hands, laughing. "Are you interrogating me, Detective?"

I cringed. "Sorry, force of habit."

He took a sip of his beer, watching me over the rim. "How about a little role reversal?"

"Bring it on," I said with a bravado I didn't feel. There were a lot of parts of my past I'd have to gloss over, too. I took a gulp of wine and signaled to the bartender for another.

He laid a hand on my arm. "I'm just giving you a hard time."

I blew out a breath. "Sorry, I—uh—I guess I'm kind of nervous."

The corner of his mouth lifted. "Join the club. Do you have any idea how intimidating you are?"

I barked out a surprise laugh. "Please."

"I'm serious," he said. "You're streetwise and tough, not to mention gorgeous. I was shocked as hell when you agreed to go out with me."

"Really? Why?"

"Because you lead this exciting life and I'm just this normal, boring teacher. Figured you'd go for a tough guy like that partner of yours."

I cleared my throat and ignored his mention of Morales. "First of all, being a cop isn't exactly as exciting as the movies make it. And second, did it occur to you that after dealing with junkies and criminals all day, I'd crave interacting with a normal human being?" I looked him up and down over the rim of my glass. "Especially a cute one?"

He sat up straighter and groaned. "Cute? Like a puppy?"

I laughed. "I happen to like puppies." They were so much easier to master than the alpha dogs I usually hung around.

He took a drink of his beer, as if considering whether he should be offended or let it slide. I placed my left hand on his arm. He glanced down to where the sleeve of my jacket had slid back to reveal my tattoo.

"What's that?"

Well, shit, I thought. I'd wanted him distracted, but not if it meant talking about my past. "A teenage indiscretion." It wasn't a total lie. Getting myself marked as a *made* member of the Votary Coven hadn't been one of my smartest ideas, although at the time I'd been damned proud—and so had Uncle Abe. *We're gonna rule the world, Kate Girl.*

I shook off the memory and started to pull the sleeve back down over the tattoo coiled around my wrist.

"Hold on." His voice was as soft as his uncallused hand as he took my wrist and pushed the sleeve back. His fingers traced the delicate skin of my inner wrist where the crowned snake swallowed its own tail. "What's this symbol?"

I swallowed the lump of anxiety in my throat. "It's called the Ouroboros. It symbolizes infinity and the cycle of creation that always follows destruction." I'd certainly felt immortal back then, hadn't I? So full of confidence in my budding cooking skills. So sure my place in the coven was secured. So stupid to believe nothing would ever change.

"That's a heavy symbol for a teenage girl," he murmured.

My smile was self-effacing. "I wasn't much into faeries or rainbows back then." Just potions and profit.

He leaned in over my wrist, which he clasped between his fingers in a grip that was firm but not threatening. "I have a tattoo, too."

"Get it anywhere interesting?"

"This little tattoo shop in Hoboken." He winked to tell me he'd purposefully misinterpreted my question. "On my biceps."

"So? What is it?" I took another sip of wine, enjoying myself now that we weren't discussing my past anymore.

He leaned in as if preparing to share a secret. "A phoenix rising from flames." He touched his right arm.

"Why a phoenix?" It wasn't an idle question. Phoenixes had a long symbolic history—especially in alchemy. Brad Hart was a Righty, but you never knew with some people. Especially since he had a background in biochemistry.

"I got it right after I was released from rehab." He let that sentence hang in the air between us like a dare.

"What sort of rehab?" I asked it in a casual tone, but it wasn't a casual question.

"Potions. That's why I quit the lab. Too much easy access."

I blinked, putting things together. "*That's* why you started DUDE."

A flicker of relief passed over his face, as if he'd been expecting me to walk out of the bar and never speak to him again. "I've seen the effects of addiction on young people firsthand. I was lucky enough to turn my life around, but several of my friends from those days weren't so lucky."

I wasn't sure what to say so I just nodded. I had a ton of questions, but they weren't the kind a woman asked her date. Instead, they were the kind a cop asked a perp.

He pulled back and dropped my hand with an uncomfortable laugh. "I didn't mean to dump that on you tonight."

"No," I said, "it's cool. I guess—I mean, who am I to judge?"

He nodded. "Right—you grew up in a coven." When I cringed, he forged ahead. "I mean you turned your life around, too. We have that in common."

I paused and thought it over. "I guess that's true."

"I have so much admiration for people like you who put themselves on the line to get potions off the streets. I'd love to hear more about your work."

The awkwardness was still there. I couldn't put my finger on it, exactly. He was right. We both helped in the effort to prevent people from getting addicted to potions. But the fact he was a former freaker and I was a woman capable of cooking the magic he used to crave was complicated. Still, he looked so open and genuinely curious to learn more about me that I let it slide for now. We were just having a drink, not discussing marriage for Christ's sake. "What do you want to know?"

"Well, for starters, how did you decide to become a cop? That couldn't have been easy given your background."

I played with the stem of my glass. How much was I ready to divulge to him? I glanced over, and he made an encouraging gesture with his hand. "Oddly enough, it started because I joined Arcane Anonymous."

His eyebrows rose. "You belong to AA?"

"I used to." About five months earlier I'd walked away, but I definitely didn't want to get into the whys with him. "I was never addicted to using potions, but my best friend thought joining would help me keep my vow never to cook again." I took another sip of wine as an excuse to collect my thoughts. "After I joined I met all these people who'd been damaged by addiction, and I was just overcome with guilt because I knew my family had contributed to the problem. Anyway, I was talking to the leader of the group one night about it and he suggested that giving back would help alleviate the guilt."

Hart nodded. I guess if anyone could understand that it was him.

"He probably meant I should volunteer at a mission or something when he suggested it. But about a week later, I saw an article in the paper about how the police were under fire due to the magic-related violence in the Cauldron and how they were having trouble recruiting new officers as a result." I laughed at my younger self. "And I thought, well, hell, with what I know about the Cauldron's covens, I could help. The next day I signed up to take some criminal justice classes at night school. It took me three years to get my degree, and another six months at the academy and probationary patrol before I finally got sworn in."

"Wow, that's some dedication."

I shook my head and laughed bitterly. "Yeah, well, what I didn't account for was that the BPD wasn't real keen on letting an Adept work the Arcane beat—especially one that was also a rookie."

"But now you're on the MEA task force, so you must have done something right."

Now my laugh was more genuine. "Not exactly. I had to kill an MEA informant to land that job."

His eyes widened. "You killed someone? You told the class you hadn't."

My cheeks heated. It had been so long since I socialized with someone who didn't carry a gun that I forgot casually mentioning shooting someone was shocking to a normal person. "If I'd told the class they would have wanted details, which I didn't think was appropriate." After he tipped his head to acknowledge that point, I continued. "He was freaking on a nasty potion and had me cornered." I hated the edge of defensiveness that crept into my voice. "It was him or me."

His cheeks heated and his eyes sparkled with excitement. "That's—"

I adjusted my ass in my seat, cursing myself for not holding my tongue. "I'm sorry—"

"No." He leaned in, and tension zinged from him like small bolts of lightning. "I meant—that's kind of hot." His hand landed on my knee, and his eyes darkened with invitation.

I moved my knee out of his reach. "Brad, no," I said, "it's not hot. Not at all. The guy I killed, he got pulled into this nasty situation. I don't take any pride in killing him."

His face cleared, as if my subtle rejection hadn't fazed him. "I just meant it's extremely attractive when a woman can take care of herself."

Harsh words sprang to my lips at the implied insult in his comment. Every woman I knew took care of herself just fine. But I swallowed the comment because I was determined to get the date back on track. "Thanks," I said instead. Probably he hadn't meant to be insulting. "Anyway, I don't want to talk about work. What do you like to do for fun?"

His face fell, as if he'd had a million other questions about my job. "Oh, I'm pretty boring. When I'm not teaching I like to read."

"I love to read," I said.

As if I hadn't spoken, he said, "Have you killed a lot of people?"

I pressed my lips together and tried to keep a lid on my patience. "I know TV makes all that stuff seem really exciting, but mostly it's boring paperwork."

"Right," he said, drawing out the word. "That's not how it sounded when you were talking to the kids."

I finished off my wine. "It has its moments, but I was hoping to get away from it for a while tonight."

His posture stiffened. "Sorry."

Great. "Let's just talk about something else. What's the last book you read?"

He motioned to the bartender for another drink. "I don't remember."

I frowned. "Have you seen any good movies lately?"

He took his drink from the guy and swallowed half of it. "Huh?"

"I asked if you've seen any good movies."

"I went an indie movie festival a couple of weeks ago," he said absently.

"Is something wrong?" I asked.

"You're just... different than I thought."

I pulled back. "What?"

He shrugged and took another sip. "No offense, but I thought you'd be a little more exciting."

My mouth fell open. "Excuse me?"

"Sorry," he said, sounding petulant, "but if I wanted to talk about books I would have asked out one of the teachers from school. Just figured you'd be a nice change of pace, is all."

My eyes narrowed. "A change of pace?"

He sighed. "I normally date educated women. I thought you'd be more fun."

I turned fully in my seat to stare at him. "Did you just say you asked me out because I'm uneducated?"

He shook his head. "No, I meant—well, you're not, right? Educated."

"I graduated from college." I added a silent *asshole* at the end.

He raised a brow. "Where'd you go?"

"Babylon Community College," I said. "I graduated with honors in criminal justice."

His mouth twitched. "An associate's degree."

Anger rose in my throat. "I worked my way through night school while holding down a job and raising my little brother. Sorry I wasn't in the right sorority or whatever."

He placed a hand on my arm. His palm was damp, and that look was back in his eyes like maybe he thought he still had a chance at some blue-collar ass. "Relax," he said. "There's no shame in that. It's just different from what I'm used to. I'm sure you're smart in your own way."

My left hand itched and the only way to scratch it would be punching this dick in the face. But I pushed down the urge because I was determined to walk out of there with some dignity.

"You know what? I'm suddenly really tired." I stood then,

motioning the bartender as I rose. "Drinks are on me." I tossed two twenties on the bar.

"You don't—" he said, starting to rise.

"Oh, I insist."

"Don't be so sensitive. I wasn't trying to offend you." His eyes strayed toward my chest. "Have another drink with me." He smiled what he probably thought was a charming smile.

I suddenly felt very tired. "I think I'll pass."

The smile disappeared. "You're a tease."

"A tease?" My tone was flat.

"You've been flirting with me for months. Practically begging for it."

I laughed out loud. "Unbelievable. See you around, Mr. Hart."

As I walked away, he muttered, "Bitch."

I walked forward with my head held high. But inside, I was on full burn. Part of my anger had to do with Hart's insulting attitude, but another part was mad that it turned out Morales had been right, after all. Going out with Hart had been a mistake. Not because of his jaded past, but because he was a major dick in the present. So much for giving nice guys a try. Alpha males were pains in the ass, but at least they didn't pretend to be something they weren't.

Chapter Seventeen

B y the time I got home, my anger had mellowed but my mood was still pretty shitty. I just wanted to go to bed and pretend the night had never happened. Unfortunately, there was a BMW I didn't recognize sitting at the curb in front of the house. A bumper sticker on the fender advertised Channel Seven Action News.

Grace Fucking Cho. Awesome.

I trudged up the steps and approached the door. Inside the kitchen, the lights were on and the sounds of two female voices reached me. Remembering what Baba had said about Cho trying to get dirt on me, I rushed inside.

Baba and Cho sat across from each other. Two mugs steamed in front of them, like I'd interrupted a cozy coffee klatch. When I walked in, they both looked up.

"Kate!" Baba said. "Look who stopped by." The overly friendly tone hinted that Baba was uncomfortable.

Grace Cho smiled a catty smile and waved me over with her claws. An open notepad lay on the table in front of her. Considering my shitty mood, I should have just flipped her the finger and walked back out the door. But I knew she'd keep coming at me if I didn't nip her ambitions in the bud.

"What's going on?" I asked, looking from one woman to the other.

Baba started to speak, but Cho jumped in. "How was your date?"

I flicked an annoyed look at Baba. She just shrugged, as if she'd been caught off guard by the reporter's intrusion. "No comment."

Cho chuckled. "You're home too early for it to have been a love connection."

I tossed my keys on the counter. "Baba, can you give us a minute?"

The old woman hesitated, but finally rose. "See ya," she said to Cho.

The reporter nodded with a small smile on her face. "It was nice chatting with you." She sounded totally comfortable, as if she hadn't invaded the sanctity of my home.

I waited until I heard the sound of Baba's bedroom door closing. Crossing my arms, I leaned back against the counter. "How long have you been here?"

Her long black hair was perfect and her makeup was tasteful, instead of the heavy on-camera face she wore for the show. She flicked her hair over her shoulder before answering. "Not long." She raised her coffee mug and blew the steam from the top before taking a delicate sip. "Who was your date with?"

"None of your business."

She nodded amiably. "In case you're worried, Baba didn't tell me anything."

"I wasn't worried. Why are you here?"

"You know why." She set down her mug and turned more fully toward me.

I crossed my arms and blew out a breath. Pen's warning about not antagonizing the reporter rang through my head. "What's it going to take to get you to leave me alone?" She opened her mouth, but I raised a hand. "Besides an on-camera interview. I've already said that's out of the question—as did my boss."

Her eyes took on a speculative gleam. "Would you be willing to answer a few questions off camera?"

I shook my head. "Not if you're going to use it to do an exposé or something."

She hesitated, as if thinking it over. "All right, off the record, then." Off my skeptical look, she rushed forward. "Promise. Whatever you say tonight won't make it into a report."

I laughed but there wasn't much humor in it. "What's the point then?"

"I'm curious about you. It takes a special kind of person to walk away from a crime family and join the other side."

"Flattery won't get you far with me."

"It's just a conversation." She blinked her heavily lashed eyes in a way that indicated she was attempting to look innocent. I turned my back to her and filled a glass with water from the tap. "All right," she admitted, "my producer really wants me to land this interview to complement the series on Mayor Volos. I'm hoping that maybe you'll change your mind once we've talked for a bit."

That seemed about as likely as me punching myself in the

face, but if a simple conversation would get her off my back I'd do it. I nodded curtly and dropped into the seat Baba had vacated. "You've got ten minutes," I said. "I suggest you use them wisely."

"All right." She nodded. "Let's get to it, then. I've been researching your history. Ten years ago, you left the coven almost immediately following the death of your mother. How did she die?"

I took a slow sip while I gathered my thoughts. Finally, I set the glass down with deliberately careful movements. "The death certificate is part of the public record."

"You know as well as I do that death certificates don't tell the whole story."

I rose from my seat. "If you wanted to butter me up for an interview, leading with my mother's death was a really shitty strategy. Conversation's over."

"Who shot her?" The question was asked quietly but I heard it just fine.

I turned. "Excuse me?"

"On the death certificate—it said cause of death was a gunshot wound."

I frowned and lurched back toward the table. "That's bullshit," I whispered. "The coroner declared her death an accidental overdose of an Arcane substance."

Cho's eyes grew wide. "That's impossible." She leaned down and pulled a file from her bag and opened it on the table. "Here it is," she said, holding up a photocopy. For a moment I was too distracted by the thickness of the file. She really had been digging into my life. "See?" She held out a sheet of paper.

I grabbed it. The document listed the deceased's name as *Margaret Ann Prospero, age 34*. I swallowed hard and forced myself to scan the rest of the form's boxes until I found one labeled Cause of Death. Sure enough, the reason listed was *gunshot wound*. My breath escaped my lungs. I dropped into the chair. "What the fuck?" I whispered.

"How did you think she died?"

Distracted, I shook my head. My gut was churning and my mind spun as I tried to make sense of what I was seeing. Part of me wanted to latch on to the death certificate as proof I hadn't really been responsible for my mother's death. But the other part—the rational part—told me I couldn't trust anything Grace Cho put in front of me. She could have forged the documents or doctored them to get a rise out of me. I just couldn't figure out what her angle was.

I pushed away the conflicting thoughts and focused on getting control of the conversation. "I'll talk about my job, but I am not interested in opening old wounds."

Smooth as silk, she took the photocopy and stashed it away. "Then let's talk about why you became a cop."

I licked my lips and leaned back. The words on the paper flashed behind my eyes like a neon sign. "I became a cop because I wanted to help people." *And because I thought it would help balance the scales on my past sins.* Questions about the death certificate rose again—was it possible my mom hadn't really died from that potion I'd cooked?

"I'm not buying that," Cho said. "You belonged to the most powerful coven in Babylon. A coven that was run by your own uncle. You really expect me to believe you suddenly did a one eighty and decided to become a cop?"

I shook my head. "It wasn't exactly that easy. It took five years. I left the coven, got a job as a waitress, put myself through school, and then I signed up for the academy."

"Still, you understand why someone would question your motives. Is it true you don't do magic anymore?"

I narrowed my eyes. She really had done her homework. "Who told you that?"

She smiled. "I can't reveal my sources. So it's true?"

I nodded. "Mostly. I used to stay away from it altogether, but I've relaxed those standards a little."

"Why?"

I shrugged and toyed with my water. "Not all magic is bad."

"Dirty magic is," she said.

"Usually."

"So this relaxed attitude toward magic, did it happen before or after you joined the task force?"

I could feel her prodding at me, trying to find a way to trip me up. "I didn't have much use for it on patrol. But the more dangerous and complex cases I've had on the MEA required the use of magic to get the job done."

"Like with the Babylon Bomber case," she said. "Is it true you summoned the Lake Erie Lizard to help stop him?"

I shook my head. "That's ridiculous," I said. "The Lake Erie Lizard is an urban legend. We stopped him using good old-fashioned police work."

Her eyes narrowed. "Last I checked defusing bombs wasn't standard training for a cop."

The corner of my mouth lifted. "No, but no one stays on the force long if they don't learn how to think on their feet and improvise."

Judging from the expression on her face, she wasn't buying my lie. "I'm confused. You claimed you've had to use magic to solve cases for the MEA, but you just said you used Mundane police work to solve the biggest case you'd had since you joined the team. Are you saying you've used magic to gather evidence, then?"

I clenched my jaw. "Evidence gathered using Arcane means is inadmissible in court, as you well know, Miss Cho."

"Precisely. So how about you give me a specific incident where you used magic in a legal way?"

I sighed. "I don't know what you're fishing for here, but I assure you that when magic is used it's well within the boundaries of the law. You're aware we have a wizard on the team who is in charge of creating protective amulets and other potions that we use to help solve cases."

"So Kichiri Ren is the only wizard on the team who's cooking?"

And there it was. The real reason she wanted to investigate me. She thought that I was a dirty cop using dirty magic to solve Arcane crimes. I leaned forward with my hands on the table. "I am a detective. My job is to arrest bad guys. Mr. Ren handles the cooking."

She pursed her lips and spun the stem of her glass for a moment. "Why did you quit Arcane Anonymous?"

I stood so fast that my chair fell over behind me, causing a racket. Cho didn't flinch, and she had the nerve to smile when I threw open the door. "Time's up."

She rose slowly and gathered her purse before walking toward me. "If you don't tell me the truth, I may be forced to connect the dots creatively. I have enough material to build a story about how a detective on a federal task force might be using dirty magic to solve cases and she's the mayor's former lover to boot. How long until questions arise about the mayor's relationship to dirty magic?"

"You're playing a dangerous game. I might have left the covens a long time ago, but I didn't abandon my backbone. Pushing me is a mistake." I didn't even mention how idiotic it was for her to think she could go after Volos directly.

"Are you threatening me, Detective Prospero?"

I lowered my voice. "Take it however you want—just stay the fuck out of my life."

Head held high, she walked through the door but stopped to issue a parting shot. I slammed the door in her face and turned off the porch light.

Chapter Eighteen

When I got to work the next morning, I found Morales and Shadi loitering near Gardner's closed office door. I slowed my stride at the top step. "What's up?"

"Shh." Shadi didn't even turn to look at me when she made the noise. She was too busy straining her ear toward the door.

I threw my stuff on my desk and went to join Morales at his. He was leaning back in his chair with his boots up on his desktop, but his eyes were aimed at the door like a couple of lasers. "Who's in there?" I whispered, leaning a hip next to his boots.

"Your favorite person."

I frowned, scanning my list of least favorite people for likely candidates. It took me a few moments to narrow it down to a handful of likely suspects. "Captain Eldritch?" I guessed.

Morales shook his head. "Volos."

My eyes flared wide. John Volos hadn't been on the list I'd come up with. Not because he wasn't someone I disliked, but because I hadn't expected the mayor to let himself be seen slumming it at the MEA offices. "Why is he here?" I shot a worried glance toward the door.

"Got here about fifteen minutes ago," said Shadi. "Gardner didn't look surprised when he showed up, either."

"Hmm," I said. They both turned to look at me when I didn't say anything else. "What?"

"Do you know what's going on?" Shadi asked. Morales just looked at me with his best detective stare.

"Why would I know?" I asked.

Shadi shrugged. "You and Volos—you know."

I crossed my arms. "No, I don't know."

With a sigh, Morales pulled his boots from the desk and let them hit the floor with a thud. "Well, if Volos is involved, it's bound to bite us in the ass."

I couldn't argue with that so I didn't say anything. "Where's Mez?"

"Coming in late." Shadi said this without looking at me. "He was up late working on that shaman's potion."

Since sitting there wasn't doing anything for my peace of mind, I decided to be productive and go make some coffee. I pushed off Morales's desk and skirted the boxing ring to access Mez's lab. Normally, it would have been bad form to go into another Adept's lab without them there, but Mez and I had an understanding. Plus, protocol wasn't going to stand between me and coffee—especially when it appeared my morning was going to be full of John Volos drama.

The apparatus Mez used to brew coffee looked like something out of Frankenstein's lab. Really it was just a simple vacuum process using a heating element and two glass chambers with a siphon tube in the middle. I poured filtered water into the lower vessel, freshly ground beans in the upper chamber, and flipped on the heating element. The process took a lot longer than most conventional pots, but the results were a lot tastier.

Since I had a few minutes to kill, I went back to the doorway to check on the peanut gallery. Morales and Shadi had their heads together and were speaking in low tones. No doubt they were theorizing what breed of shitstorm was brewing inside Gardner's office. I went back to watch the water boil.

The sound of a door opening and new voices in the main room drew my attention. I went back to the doorway, careful to stay hidden enough not to get drawn into any unfolding drama. That would happen soon enough.

"...I'm counting on you," Volos was saying. I couldn't see him on the other side of the boxing ring, but the sound of his voice hit me right in the gut just like it always did.

"We appreciate your faith, Mr. Mayor," Gardner said. I could barely see the top of her sleek brunette bob through the ropes.

Volos stepped into view. His dark-blond hair was carefully styled and his suit cost more than the GDP of some third-world countries. But it was more than the accessories he wore that made Volos an impressive sight to behold. He was one of those men who exuded power. He had the kind of confidence that couldn't be bought, but would definitely cost you if you were dumb enough to stand up to it.

"Don't worry about the tension with Eldritch. I've made it clear he needs to focus on keeping the streets safe while you track down the party responsible for creating the chaos," Volos said in his most diplomatic tone. "He understands there's too much at stake here to let a territorial pissing match get in the way of getting the job done."

He paused as something caught his eye. I moved forward an inch or two to see what had distracted him. He was staring directly at the large board we'd posted in the boxing ring. On it, pictures from Charm's murder scene and the junkyard surrounded a large image of Pantera Souza's scarred, black face.

Behind me, the coffee apparatus made a loud hissing noise that indicated the water was about to boil over. I ignored it in favor of watching Volos's face morph from the practiced smile of a politician to the mask of a man hiding something. "Is that your suspect?"

Gardner cleared her throat. "Yes, sir, he is an operative for the Brazilian cartel."

"*A Morte*?" Volos's gaze stayed on the board, as if memorizing every detail. "You didn't mention a cartel connection earlier."

"We're still gathering evidence, but we have reasons to believe they're tied to both the murder and the assault on the head of the Sang Coven."

The mayor's gaze snapped toward Gardner. "Interesting." He cleared his throat. "I'll let you get back to it, then." He glanced at his gold watch. "I need to run to a luncheon at the ladies' auxiliary, but before I go I was hoping to speak with Detective Prospero."

All eyes turned toward me.

Behind me the coffee apparatus boiled over, sending hot coffee spraying all over the tabletop. I jumped, muttering a curse. My reaction had more to do with the request than the spill, but I was happy to let them think otherwise. "I'll be there in a sec," I said in the same tone a person might use to say they were ready to face a firing squad. "Need to clean that up."

Volos smiled and looked me in the eye. "I'll wait."

After I quickly switched off the heat element and wiped up

the worst of the mess, I trudged over to meet Volos. While he waited, he'd pulled on a cashmere dress coat and a red woolen scarf that looked disgustingly good on him. He tipped his head toward the stairs leading outside. It seemed whatever he had to say wasn't meant for the team. That or he was worried about what I'd say to him in their presence. I raised a brow. "It'll just take a moment." He held a hand toward the stairs.

With a sigh, I turned and marched down the steps. His presence at my back felt like an oppressive shadow on my shoulders. By the time I burst out the front door onto the sidewalk, I was thankful for the fresh air and the wide-open space to give me some distance for the conversation. Luckily I'd left my puffer vest on when I'd arrived, and that combined with my flannel shirt, jeans, and boots protected me from the worst of the late-winter chill.

"What do you want?"

He smiled at my preemptive attack. "Well, for starters, hello."

I crossed my arms.

He cocked a brow at that but didn't call out my snappish tone. "How's Danny?"

Impatience pressed like hot air behind my ribs, but he'd get to his point in his own time. Rushing him would only make him delay longer to fuck with me. "He's learning magic."

John's eyes widened. I mentally patted myself on the back for the ability to surprise him. "Since when?"

I forced a causal shrug. "November. I figured instead of fighting it any longer, I'd just make sure he learned about it the right way. Totally clean potion work, by the book." I didn't mention I'd sat in on a few of those lessons, so I could learn more about the clean side of things.

"Interesting," he said in a tone I couldn't interpret. "What's your read on this *A Morte* situation?"

159

The change in topic was too abrupt not to be contrived. He wanted me off guard. "Gardner already filled you in."

He crossed his arms and regarded me with a skeptical look. "But now I'm asking you."

I shrugged. "Brazilians are trying to shake things up."

"Any idea why?"

"Normal reasons, I suppose—money, power." I looked up under my lashes. "You know how that is, right, Mr. Mayor?"

He nodded distractedly, seeming to ignore the dig. "I can't afford for this to blow up right now."

For the first time, I noticed the tension lines between his eyebrows. "Huh," I said.

"What?" he snapped.

"Just don't think I've ever seen you nervous. It's kind of refreshing. Makes you seem almost human."

"I never claimed to be anything but."

"It's cold, and because of you I haven't had any coffee. So state your business or I'm going inside."

He stepped closer. "I need you to keep me in the loop."

I frowned at him. "That's Gardner's job."

He shot me a get-real look. "We both know she'll tell me what's politically advantageous for the MEA. You're the only person I can trust to tell me what's really happening."

I held up a hand. "You seem to have forgotten that we are not friends. I hate you, remember?"

"I remember that you're always trying to convince me of that. I also know you're honest to everyone but yourself."

"Fuck you." I started to stalk around him, but he grabbed my arm.

"I know why you don't want to deal with me. If I were you, I wouldn't, either. But I'm asking you to do this anyway."

A laugh scraped out of my throat. The ego on this guy threatened to suck all the oxygen out of the atmosphere.

"Please?" He looked me in the eyes. "It's important."

Something in his tone gave me pause. It wasn't just that John was basically begging me for help. It was also that he sounded worried. "What aren't you telling me?"

The pleading look disappeared and his mask fell neatly back into place. "Nothing you need to worry about. Just keep me informed. I'll make it worth your while."

I sucked in a deep breath and released it. "I've experienced your warped form of gratitude before. I'm not real eager to go through that again. You want information? Find some other pawn. Like Grace Cho."

He looked at me as if I'd spoken a foreign language. "What's she got to do with this?"

"Thanks to you, she's been stalking me for a story."

"I take it you're not interested."

I just shot him a stony look.

"I'll take care of it," he snapped.

I frowned. "How?"

"Don't worry about how," he said. "Just say thank you and agree to let me know if you have any breaks with *A Morte*."

I sighed and looked at the ground. I really wanted Grace Cho off my back, but I didn't love the idea of having to report to him about the case. "Tell you what, I'll help you if you get Cho off my back *and* tell me what you know about how my mom died."

His expression didn't change. "What are you talking about?" His tone was patronizing.

"I have reason to believe Abe lied to me about how she died," I said. "And I think you know what it was." I didn't mention Cho or the death certificate. Too much detail would give him material he could twist into a lie. But the truth was, Cho was only the latest person to imply there was more to the story. Shayla King, who'd been one of Aphrodite's whores, had mocked me months earlier for beating myself up for my mother's death and intimated Uncle Abe had hidden details from me. I shot the bitch before she could finish laughing. Her death had been deserved, but I regretted not demanding the full story before she bled out.

He put a hand on my arm. "I'm sure Charm's death hit you hard. It's no surprise it would stir up some old wounds, too. But I swear I don't know what you're talking about."

My eyes narrowed. "So you believe she really OD'd on that potion I made?"

He nodded. "I know that's not what you want to hear, but you're going to have to come to terms with it and move on. It's time to stop torturing yourself with the past."

I shrugged off his hand. "You're from my past. Does that apply to you as well?"

He stepped closer and his expression softened. "I—"

The sound of someone whistling arrived a split second before Mez rounded the corner at the end of the building. When he saw Volos and me standing so close, his steps slowed and the tune he'd been whistling died.

"Hey, Mez." I took a pointed step away from Volos.

"What's up?" Mez cast a speculative glance at Volos. "Morning, Mr. Mayor."

Volos tipped his chin. "Mr. Ren." He turned to me. "I'll expect your call."

With that, he walked to the car waiting at the sidewalk. Mez stood next to me, hands in pockets, watching him go. "What was that about?"

"Oh, you know," I sighed. "Same shit, different day."

Chapter Nineteen

Back inside the gym, Mez and I joined the others. Morales, Shadi, and Gardner all looked at me expectantly. I raised both of my brows. "What?"

"What did he want?" Gardner asked.

I shrugged. "He wants me to keep him in the loop about the case." No sense hiding it.

"Instead of me or in addition to?" she asked.

"In addition. Said he trusts me to give him the real story."

She shook her head but didn't look surprised. "I appreciate you telling me," she said. "Do as he asked, but be careful. If he thinks we're not busting our asses, he'll call my bosses in Detroit. They're waiting for us to screw up."

"Understood."

"All right," she said, "where are we on this. Shadi?"

"After Prospero and Morales talked to the Votary crew

yesterday, I went to stake out the bar. Lots of Votary people went in and out, but no Souza. After the bar closed down, I followed Puck Simmons and a blond female—"

"That must have been the chick who gave us lip yesterday," I interjected.

"I followed them back to an apartment," Shadi continued. "Their lights went out at four in the morning. I stayed another hour without another peep from them."

"Do you think it's worth bringing Puck in for official questioning?" Gardner asked Morales.

"We could try," I said, "but I doubt he'd turn on Pantera Souza."

"Why not?" Gardner asked.

"Puck might have betrayed Charm, but he's coven through and through. Squealing isn't in his makeup. Especially when it's against someone like Pantera, who would likely go after the guy's nearest and dearest before he tortured Puck to death."

Gardner nodded. "Mez?"

"I retested the potion and confirmed that the toxin is from South America. There's no way of tying it directly to Souza without using dirty magic, though."

Shadi held up a hand. "Explain for us non-Adepts please."

"Each wizard leaves a sort of magical fingerprint on their recipes. There's a technique some Adepts can use to *read* a potion."

I kept my eyes on Mez, but I saw Morales glance at me from the corner of my eye.

"But the courts deemed that sort of evidence gathering illegal," Mez continued. "And even if it weren't inadmissible, it's not a form of magic I'm capable of doing." He said this last part grudgingly. Mez prided himself on being a magical wunderkind.

"Do you know any wizards who can do that?" Gardner asked Mez.

He shook his head. The boss turned to me. "How about you?"

"No," I said more quickly than I'd intended. My eyes cut toward Morales, who refused to look at me now. My shoulders relaxed when my partner didn't call me on my lie.

Gardner tapped her lip. "I wonder if Val does—or Volos, even."

"Sir," I said hesitantly, "what's the point if we can't use it to build a case?"

"The point, Prospero," she snapped, "is that we're dead in the water without a lucky break in this case."

I crossed my arms and looked at the floor. I'd regretted not admitting I was able to *read* potions when it came up, but I knew I'd made the right choice. When I'd joined the task force Gardner had lectured me about the importance of using old-fashioned police work to solve cases instead of taking magical shortcuts. But now that the case had personal stakes, she was ready to throw all that out the window.

The room had fallen silent. Morales had watched the exchange with a hard look on his face, but now he stepped forward to break the tension. "There's an angle we haven't pursued."

Gardner threw up her hands. "About damned time someone started thinking outside the box. We're all ears, Morales."

"Abraxas Prospero."

My stomach flip-flopped. But before I could utter the curse that immediately sprang to my lips, Gardner leaped on the suggestion. "Make it happen."

"Sir, I really don't think—"

She cut me off. "We don't have time for you to throw a fit,

Prospero. Morales is right. Abe has a dog in this fight since it was his captain who got killed. Besides, a man with his influence and connections is sure to have had run-ins with the cartel."

She was right, but I didn't like it.

"The problem is, I'm not sure we'll be able to get in to see him." Morales shot me an apologetic glance. I responded with a shitty glare.

"That's right," Gardner said, looking at me. "Since you're the reason he won't speak to us, you better figure out how to fix this."

I sucked in a deep breath to hold on to my temper. I wasn't sure why Gardner had suddenly declared it shit-on-Prospero day, but it was wearing on my nerves.

"I have an idea of how to make it happen," Morales said.

Gardner raised her brows. "Well?"

"Duffy."

"Damn it, Morales," I said.

Gardner ignored my outburst. "Volos did say he's read Eldritch the riot act about cooperating." She nodded decisively. "Make it happen."

My head fell back and I looked up at the ceiling, wishing a bolt of lightning would strike the building. The last thing I thought I'd be doing that day was dragging my ass to the precinct to beg Pat Duffy for help.

"You got a problem with that, Prospero?" Gardner's voice was cold.

I lowered my chin and shook my head. I knew when it was time to eat shit with a smile. "No, sir."

She tipped her chin. "Good." She turned to Shadi and Mez. "You two pair up and see if you can track down Puck. He'll go see Pantera Souza eventually, and I expect one of you to be there when it happens." She put her hands on her hips, issuing each of us a don't-fuck-it-up glare. "Let's make this happen, people."

◆ ◆ ◆

Walking into the precinct a while later, I still wasn't speaking to Morales. He paused with his hand on the door and blocked my entrance. "You know I didn't have a choice."

I looked up with narrowed eyes. "Sure you did. Where I come from you don't throw your partner under the bus." I started to brush past him, but he blocked me.

"First of all, I was being a good partner by not calling you on your lie. Would you have preferred for me to inform Gardner that your magical specialty is *reading* potions."

Some of the hot air escaped from my indignant posture.

"Second of all, if I hadn't suggested Abe, she would have pursued the plan to find a wizard who could *read*. How long do you think it would have been until she approached one of your old cohorts who would have asked why you didn't just do it?"

Shit. I really hated it when he was right. "But Abe?" I said, not quite ready to give up the fight.

"You know this is the right move. Your ego just isn't ready to let it go."

"Screw you, Morales." I shouldered him out of the way. He muttered a curse and followed me in.

I nodded to a desk sergeant I recognized, but didn't bother stopping to chat. This precinct had been my home for five years before I'd joined the task force, but it was hardly a welcoming environment for me. Most of my time in the BPD had been a struggle against the brass and my fellow officers, who refused to trust an Adept cop—especially one with my background.

167

The door leading back to the squad room buzzed open. I held it open and held out a hand for Morales to precede me. As he passed, he tossed me a mocking salute. Ass.

The squad room hadn't changed much. Rows of old metal desks provided work space for filling out reports, and along the walls were offices for the brass and lead detectives. A kitchen area had rows of vending machines offering Mundane sodas, energy potion drinks, and carb-and-sugar-laden snacks.

I'd expected to find Duffy sitting in one of the desks in the bullpen, but an officer there directed us to an office directly across the room from the one Eldritch used. A quick glance in that room revealed that the captain wasn't there, which was a relief. I knew Gardner had phoned him because I'd heard the tense call, but he must have cleared out to avoid dealing with us.

I turned left between rows of desks and headed toward Duffy's office. Morales fell into step beside me.

"Looks like Eldritch rolled out the red carpet for his cracker-jack new detective."

"No shit," I muttered. I let the tension from earlier dissolve. We needed to present a united front in the meeting with Duffy. Besides, I was more annoyed at the unfairness of him having an office than I'd been at Morales for being right.

When I'd worked the Cauldron as a beat cop, I'd campaigned for a detective's rank only to be told in a million spoken and unspoken ways that Eldritch didn't trust an Adept at that rank. It had taken me joining the task force and almost getting killed to get promoted, and then only after some political maneuvering on Gardner's part. But Adept Duffy had not only gotten his own office, he'd also been placed at the head of the murder squad. I knew better than to believe Eldritch had suddenly changed his prejudices against Adept officers. More likely, the move was prompted by some ambition Eldritch believed Duffy could help him attain.

The shade was pulled down over the door's window, but when I knocked Duffy's gruff voice invited us to come in. When I opened the door, he was sitting behind a desk stacked high with case reports. "Oh," he said, with as much enthusiasm as if he were greeting the devil, "it's you."

I raised a brow but didn't take the bait. "Eldritch said he'd tell you to expect us."

He tossed a pen on top of the mountain of folders and leaned back. "I expected you, but I don't have to be happy about it."

Morales crossed his arms. "You were happy to see us when you called us to consult on your crime scene."

The detective pressed his lips together. "Consult. Not take over the case."

I raised my hands in what I hoped looked like a diplomatic gesture. "We had nothing to do with that decision."

"Sure." He grunted. "You're here about the violence last night, I assume." He picked up a newspaper from one of the stacks on his desk and held it up. The headline screamed, "Coven Violence Rocks the Cauldron." "Fucking journalists," Duffy said. "A drive-by hexing hardly constitutes a coven war."

I exchanged a look with Morales. "Eldritch didn't tell you why we were coming?" I asked.

Duffy frowned. "He just said you had some questions."

I cursed silently. Gardner had told Eldritch exactly why we were coming, but the bastard clearly hadn't told Duffy. So now we'd have to suffer through asking him ourselves.

Morales took a step forward. "We're not here about the drive-by."

Duffy sighed the sigh of the martyred and pointed at the chairs on the other side of his desk. While Morales and I each took seats, he fished a notebook out of the mess on the desktop. "Val in CSI said she already turned all the files over. Not sure what else I could help you with."

Since this had been Morales's idea, I leaned back and stayed quiet. He picked up on my cue immediately and shot me a glare.

"Well?" Duffy prompted.

Morales cleared his throat. "We need to ask a favor."

Duffy's brows shot up to his receding salt-and-pepper hairline. He leaned back in his squeaky chair and placed his hands over his stomach. "I'm all ears."

"We need you to interview someone who might be able to help us locate our suspect," Morales said.

"Why can't you interview 'em?"

I shifted uncomfortably, but it had nothing to do with the hardness of the chair.

"It's complicated," Morales said.

"Who is it?" Duffy asked.

Morales sighed. "Abraxas Prospero."

Duffy froze for a moment, and then his shoulder began to shake. "You're shitting me."

I rolled my gaze toward the ceiling, but that damned lightning let me down again.

"I assure you we're totally serious," Morales said.

The amusement drained from Duffy's face as he looked at me. "Is there a particular reason you can't interview your own uncle?"

I looked away, my cheeks heating.

"Abe took out a restraining order on Detective Prospero," Morales said in an amused tone.

Duffy's eyes swiveled in my direction. "Why in the hell would a prisoner in a penitentiary for Arcane criminals have to take out a restraining order on his own niece?"

I raised my chin and looked him in the eyes. "Because the last time I visited him in Crowley Penitentiary, I stunned his ass with a Taser."

Chapter Twenty

It had been five months since our last visit to Crowley State Penitentiary for Arcane Criminals. The prison loomed over Lake Erie from a cliff on an island called Crook's Point, several miles off the mainland. Morales, Duffy, and I stood on the deck of the ferry. My legs were braced against both the choppy ride and the knowledge that our meeting would not be a pleasant one.

"Are you sure he'll agree to see me?" Duffy asked. He looked totally comfortable on the deck of the ship, as if he'd spent lots of time on the water.

I shrugged. "I put our chances at sixty–forty in favor of a no."

"Better odds than I was thinking considering what you did to him last time," the detective said.

"The trick is not letting him know Prospero and I are there,"

Morales said. "Man like Abe will have plenty of spies in the general population."

"Not to mention the guards," I added. "I still think this is a waste of time."

Morales shot me an annoyed look. "Your optimism continues to impress, Cupcake."

"If this pans out, you two are gonna owe me," Duffy said. "If it doesn't, you'll owe me big-time."

The ferry bumped into the dock on the island. While the captain moored the lines, we started walking toward the gangway.

"It'll work," Morales said with total confidence. "I bet Abe's been expecting a visit from the moment he found out about Charm. He'll wonder what took so long."

"Maybe." I took the first step down the ramp. "But first we have to convince him to talk to Duffy at all."

◆ ◆ ◆

Thirty minutes later we'd checked in with prison security. The guard behind the desk was a big guy with a shaved head that indicated he was either former military or wanted people to believe he was. Judging from the precision of his movements and his economical budgeting of words, I guessed the former.

While we waited for word about whether Abe would see Duffy, the guard sat on his stool with his arms crossed. He watched us like we were criminals, but I wasn't offended. When you spent your day with the dregs of humanity, it colored your opinion of every person you met, even if they worked on the same side of the prison bars as you.

Morales didn't fidget while we waited. He was former military, too. His hair was longer than the guard's, but I'd seen his more militant side come out plenty of times. Enough to be happy he considered me an ally, anyway.

As for Duffy, he sat quietly several feet from where Morales and I stood. I didn't bother chatting because I figured he was gathering his thoughts for the interview. We'd given him a run-down on the information we were looking for. I'd never seen Duffy interrogate someone, but he had a good enough reputation in the BPD for me to trust him with this, even though I hated needing his help.

The phone on the desk screamed into the silent waiting room. My heart leaped in my chest, but I managed to keep my expression neutral as the guard answered and spoke quietly into the mouthpiece. Every few seconds he'd flick a glance toward us. I couldn't get a read on whether this was a positive sign or not.

Finally the guy hung up. "Mr. Prospero will see Detective Duffy."

"He wasn't informed we are here, correct?" Morales asked.

"You'll be able to watch from the observation room. As long as Detective Prospero isn't in the same room it won't violate the restraining order."

"That will be fine," I gritted out. That fucking restraining order had been the ultimate fuck-you from my uncle. He was about as afraid of me as a viper is a mouse.

Duffy rose to join us. "I don't like this."

"You don't have to," I said. "You just need to get the answers."

He looked me in the eyes for a moment, as if debating whether to continue the argument. I raised a brow to let him know it was a waste of breath. "All right," he said. "I'm ready."

The guard was waiting for us at the first of a series of gates we'd have to go through to get to the interview rooms. A few moments and several turned locks later, he deposited Duffy in a room and led us to the next door down.

The observation room was unremarkable, except for the fact it barely was large enough for both Morales and me. The front wall was made up of a two-way mirror, allowing me to see Duffy standing inside the all-white interview room. A couple of shabby office chairs upholstered in coffee-stained fabric were wedged together in front of the window. I ignored them, preferring to stand at the glass with my arms crossed.

"Relax." Morales dropped into one of the chairs.

"Easy for you to say."

Duffy nodded toward the mirror on his side a split second before the door opened. Two guards led Uncle Abe into the room. His feet shuffled against the concrete floor thanks to the shackles binding his ankles. A chain connected those to the iron cuffs on his wrists, which were held in front of him. The prison-issued jumpsuit was as yellow as a canary's ass. Abe's head was down, which made his bald pate look like a scrying mirror under the harsh fluorescent lights.

The guards deposited Abe at the table and shackled him to the brackets there. The way the table was situated, both Duffy and Abe had their sides to the two-way mirror. I wished I'd been able to see Abe's face head-on instead of in silhouette, but it was better than having to stare at the back of his head.

Duffy mouthed his thanks to the exiting guards before he moved toward the table. I realized then that I hadn't turned on the speakers and flipped the switch in time to hear Abe's opening salvo crackle through the line. "I'm relieved to see the BPD is on the case, Detective. I was concerned the MEA might claim dominion."

Duffy smiled tightly and took the chair across from Abe. "The MEA doesn't investigate murders, Mr. Prospero."

"In my experience, the members of the task force are loose cannons with little respect for the rule of law."

I snorted and crossed my arms.

Duffy's eyes stayed on Abe, but he cleared his throat, as if reminding me to stay cool. "My condolences on the death of Charles Parsons, Mr. Prospero. I understand you two were close."

Abe's head cocked to the left. "That's awfully thoughtful of you, Detective—Duffy, was it?"

He received a quick nod in response.

"You seem familiar," Abe said. "Have we met before?"

"I've been a cop for twenty-five years. I'm fairly certain given your criminal background we've had the opportunity to cross paths."

"Yes, well, I'm afraid I'm still quite overwhelmed by news of my friend's death. He was a good man. Naturally, I'll help any way I'm able."

Duffy flipped open his notebook. "When was the last time you spoke with Mr. Parsons?"

"You'd have to confirm with the prison records, but I believe his last visit was three weeks ago."

Duffy looked up. "What did you speak about?"

"We were just catching up."

"Did he mention if he was having problems with anyone in particular?"

Abe executed a noncommittal shake of the head. His clasped hands lay perfectly still on the tabletop. The man hadn't fidgeted or shifted his weight once since he'd sat. "Not that I recall. This was right after the mayoral election. We mostly talked about that."

I laughed bitterly. "Oh, I bet you did." Volos had once been Abe's protégé—after I'd left the coven, that is—but had turned traitor and testified against my uncle in exchange for immunity. The fact his enemy was now mayor of the city Abe still considered his own had to stick in the old man's craw.

"Did you speak to Mr. Parsons after that day, say, by phone?" Duffy asked.

Abe cocked his head as if trying to recall. "Now that you mention it, he called a week ago."

"He's a real piece of work," Morales muttered. Neither of us believed for a moment that the phone call had simply slipped Abe's mind. More likely, he'd been hoping Duffy hadn't been smart enough to ask and wouldn't check his phone records.

"What did you speak about on that occasion?" Duffy prompted.

"Do you have a cigarette?"

"Don't smoke. The call?"

Abe's hands flexed in the cuffs. I smiled. A megalomaniac like Abe expected people to scramble to meet his every whim. Apparently Duffy hadn't gotten the memo—or he didn't care, which made me like him more.

"Charm was calling to tell me he was having some problems."

"Of what sort?"

"May I be frank?"

Duffy nodded.

"Charm wasn't a saint. Who among us is?" Abe chuckled.

I made a gagging motion with my finger. Luckily Duffy didn't seem to be buying Abe's act.

"Your point?" Duffy said.

"My point, Detective Duffy, is that we both know Charm was involved in certain business dealings that the government frowns upon. A person doesn't last long in that kind of business without gaining some enemies." Abe tapped a finger on the tabletop. "However, Charm's people? They loved him. He was a good leader. Tough but fair."

"Okay," Duffy said. "What does this have to do with the phone call?"

"I mention it because I'm sure it's tempting to look inside the coven for the guilty party. But I assure you, Charm's problem came from outside."

I stiffened and looked at Morales. "Holy shit. Is he actually going to cooperate?" My partner rose and joined me at the window.

"Go ahead," Duffy said.

"I assume, even though you're a homicide detective, that you've a passing familiarity with the cartels."

"Of course."

Abe nodded. "For years, the covens of Babylon have relied on specific suppliers for certain regulated substances."

"Which suppliers would those be?" Duffy asked.

"That really has no bearing on this discussion," Abe said. "The point is, a new supplier has been trying to horn in on the action. Aggressively."

"One of the cartels?" Duffy was playing dumb. We'd already filled him in on what we knew.

"A specific one—*A Morte.*" Abe said the name with dramatic flair, as if he expected Duffy to come down with a case of the vapors upon hearing it. Instead, the detective just watched Abe with a blank expression.

When Duffy didn't react, Abe shifted forward in his chair. "Charm called to tell me a cartel operative had contacted him."

"And he was worried?"

"To put it mildly."

Duffy shifted in his seat, crossing his leg over his knee. "See, this is where you've lost me. If you knew Charm felt threatened by the cartel, why didn't you come forward with this information the moment you learned he'd died?"

Abe held up his bound hands. "I'm in prison, Detective."

"Surrounded by law enforcement agents who easily could have taken your statement."

Abe's shoulders pulled back. "What are you implying?"

Duffy's mouth turned down as he shook his head. "I'm simply curious about why you wouldn't try harder to help solve your friend's murder."

"As you're aware, my niece is on the MEA task force. I had reason to worry she might use Charm's death to implicate me."

"Asshole," I muttered.

"I can't imagine how," Duffy responded drily. "As you said, you're in prison."

"That wouldn't stop Kate," Abe said, his tone spiteful. "Last time she was here she physically assaulted me."

Duffy cleared his throat. "Back to Charm. Why would *A Morte* be making a move on Babylon now?"

Abe shrugged. "I wouldn't pretend to try to understand the motives of those savages."

Duffy tapped his pen on his lip. "Do you honestly expect me to believe that a man of your extensive connections never had dealings with the Brazilian cartel?"

"Absolutely not. I was well aware of their reputation and refused to work with them. I can only assume that's why they waited until I was incarcerated to make their move on Babylon."

"You've been here for five years. Why wait so long?"

"All I know is that Charm had been approached by the cartel operative—"

"Did he give you a name?"

Abe nodded. "Hector Souza."

"Bingo," Morales said.

"Did he mention where this meeting took place?" Duffy asked.

Abe shook his head. "We didn't get into that."

"What did the operative want?"

Abe adjusted in his chair. Not for the first time, I wished I could watch his face directly as he talked to get a read on him. "That's the odd part. Souza said he wanted Charm to make a move against the Sang Coven."

Duffy frowned. "Hold on. I thought you said *A Morte* wanted a cut of the potion trade. Why ask Charm to attack the other coven?"

"All I know is Souza gave him seventy-two hours to comply."

"What did you tell him to do?"

"I told him it was out of the question." My uncle shrugged. "The Sangs and the Votaries have a long history as allies. Even though Harry Bane is leading that coven into the ground, it's no reason to start a war. I told him to circle the wagons and get ready to defend his territory." Abe shook his head. "He seemed like he was going to do it, too. I don't understand how Souza got to him anyway."

"We have reason to believe a member of the Votary Coven betrayed Charm," Duffy said.

Abe's head jerked up. "Who?" His voice burned like a match tossed into grain alcohol.

"We have some theories, but no arrests have been made." We'd told Duffy not to mention Puck's name in the hopes Abe might finger possible cohorts.

"Give me some names," Abe demanded.

"I don't think so."

Abe snorted. "Surely you don't believe I'd tip off someone who killed my best friend."

Duffy's gaze hardened. "I'm willing to believe you capable of almost anything."

Abe's head pulled back in surprise. "Believe what you'd like about me, but don't let that blind you to how dire this situation is."

"I assure you we're all well aware of what's at stake."

"We?" Abe's posture straightened.

"The BPD," Duffy said.

"Hmm. So you weren't referring to my reckless niece and her meathead partner?" Abe swiveled toward the window and waved.

"I'll be damned," Morales said. He crossed his arms and had the gall to smirk.

I glared at my uncle's smug face. "I really wish I'd had something stronger than a Taser last time."

Morales wrapped an arm around my shoulder. "Relax, Cupcake. We got what we needed."

I tilted my head. "Did we? I didn't hear anything we didn't already know."

In the interview room, Abe had turned back toward Duffy. The detective didn't look impressed by the little drama. "Mr. Prospero, if you're done showing off, I have one additional question."

"What's that?" The smile he'd flashed at me laced his tone.

"Do you know of anyone in the Cauldron besides the covens who might have had business dealings with *A Morte*?" I frowned. That hadn't been on the list of questions we'd given Duffy, but now that he had asked it, I really wanted to hear Abe's answer.

Abe froze. "What do you mean? Who would have—I'll be damned."

I frowned and shot Morales a glance to see if he knew what was happening. He just shrugged and turned back to the window.

Abe was practically vibrating in his chair. "I heard a rumor several months ago that there had been a business deal gone sour with the cartel, but I hadn't believed it at the time."

"With whom?"

"Time's up, Detective," the guard said.

Duffy held up an impatient hand. "In a second. Abe?"

Abe motioned to the guard to come unshackle him. The guard moved forward and unlocked the brackets that kept my uncle chained to the table. The metal scraped against the concrete floor. The sound crawled into my ears and scratched down my spine.

Abe whispered something to the guard.

"Mr. Prospero? Who was involved in the business deal?"

The guard led Abe toward the panel of glass separating us. He walked right up to it, directly in front of me.

I had to force myself not to back away. After all, he was looking at a mirror—he couldn't really see me. Regardless, he smiled as if he could. The expression wasn't the amused grin when he'd revealed that he'd known I was there. Instead, this one was mean, like a snake's just before it strikes its prey.

Morales put a steadying hand on my arm. I kept my gaze on my uncle's face because even though he couldn't see me, I'd be damned before I looked away.

"You want to know why *A Morte*'s in Babylon, Katie Girl?" he said quietly. "Ask yourself who has the most to lose if there's a coven war."

I blinked. "What?" But my question didn't reach him because of the glass separating us. "What does that mean?" I asked louder.

Abe was already turning away, and the guard who'd stayed at the door during the interview was already coming forward to take him back to his cell. I hit a hand against the glass to get his attention. If he heard it, he didn't show any sign.

I ran to the door of the observation room and threw it open. I spilled out into the hallway. Just beyond the door to the interview room, the guard and Abe were walking away.

"Abe!" I called.

My uncle paused and turned slowly. The smile on his face was pure evil.

I rushed forward. Behind me, I heard Morales calling after me. The guard held up a hand. "Stop, Detective. You're not allowed within twenty feet of the prisoner."

My boots skidded on the floor. I held up my hands. I sucked in a breath to still my heartbeat and looked my uncle in his eyes. "Who?"

His blue eyes twinkled. "You're the detective. Figure it out."

With that, he turned his back on me and walked away.

Chapter Twenty-One

After the confrontation with Uncle Abe, the day didn't get any less frustrating. BPD patrols all over the city were on the lookout for Pantera, but so far no one had run across the shaman. What they had found plenty of were drive-by hexings, street brawls, and lots of defacement of public property by coven Heralds wanting to issue threats to their enemies. No doubt about it, the atmosphere in the Cauldron was heating up.

After dropping Duffy at the precinct, Morales and I had called it a day. He'd asked me if I wanted to grab a bite, but I begged off. I used needing to spend time with Danny as an excuse, but I really just needed space to think about the things Abe had said.

By the time I made it home, it was already pushing five thirty. I'd stopped at Danny's favorite pizza place to grab a pie for supper. When I pushed my way through the door into the kitchen, I'd expected to find the kid sitting at the table doing homework. Instead, I found Baba cutting coupons from the paper.

She looked up. "You shoulda told me you were getting pizza—I got a coupon." She fished a slip of paper from the stack. "BOGO, too. Damn."

I shrugged. "BOGO?"

"Buy one, get one free," she explained. "One for us and one for the human vacuum."

I joined her at the table and willed the day's frustrations to slide off my back. "Where is he, anyway?"

She shrugged. "Said he was gonna stay after to work in the library. He promised to be home by supper."

"Does he have a paper due or something?"

She shook her head. "Not that I know of."

My brows rose. "And you didn't think it was strange that he'd voluntarily stay at school to study?"

She frowned. "Why would I?"

"Because he's a teenager, Baba. They lie."

She shrugged. "He's a good kid, Katie."

I rose to grab my phone and call the school to see if he was there. I knew that Pen would have already left for the day and was on her way to her weekly AA meeting, or else I would have called her. But before I could dial the number, the back door opened.

Danny didn't walk through the door, he slammed through.

"Hey." I put down the phone. "Where ya been?"

He kept his head down and acted like he planned to walk straight through the kitchen without answering.

"Yo," I called, "I'm talking to you."

He paused at the threshold. "What?" His head was angled

away from us, and the hand gripping the handle of his back-pack had a couple of bloodied knuckles.

I was across the room before I had a conscious thought to move. "Were you in a fight?"

He swung around. The corner of his mouth was streaked red and swelling. "How did you know?"

I rolled my eyes. "Never mind that." I grabbed his chin to get a better look at the bruise forming on his cheek. "Who punched you?"

He hissed and pulled away from my probing fingers. "I ran into a wall."

"Oh, please. Don't bullshit me."

He sighed and leaned back against the wall with his arms crossed. "Look, I've got it—all right?"

I snorted. "Right—"

"I'm sixteen, Kate—not six. I can take care of myself."

I didn't like the stony determination in his gaze, but he had a point. "Just"—I sighed, trying to calm my instinctive need to protect him—"where were you?"

"I told Baba," he said. "I stayed after to work on a project."

"This happened at the library?" I asked, an eyebrow raised.

He rolled his eyes. "No, Kate, it happened on my way out. Just chill, all right? Mr. Hart broke it up before it got out of hand."

My brows shot to my hairline. "Is he planning on calling me to discuss it?"

He shrugged. "I told you, it wasn't a big deal."

I hadn't told Danny about my date with Hart, and now wasn't time to get into it. However, I found it odd that he wouldn't call me about this.

"Don't call him, Kate." Danny's tone was on the border between pleading and demanding. "It's nothing to worry about."

"Forgive me, but I'm allowed to worry when you walk in looking like someone used you for target practice."

He snorted. "You're one to talk. You get beat up all the time."

"I'm a cop, Danny. And it's not all the time." Behind me, a significant throat clearing sounded. I glanced over my shoulder to see Baba making a let-it-go gesture. I blew out a breath. "All right, fine. I'll trust you to take care of this on your own, but promise me you'll ask for help if this escalates." I was lying. I fully intended to at least call Pen so she could keep an eye on things.

He nodded. "I will." When I looked unconvinced, he sighed. "I promise, okay?"

I nodded and watched him make his escape. "There's pizza," I called belatedly.

"Not hungry." A second later the sound of his door slamming in the basement filtered through the house.

"How much you want to bet there's a girl in the middle of this?" Baba asked. When I turned around she'd returned to clipping coupons, but her eyebrows were raised.

"Has he been telling you about Luna?"

"Nah." Baba waved the scissors. "Isn't it always about a girl with a teenage boy?"

Part of me was relieved that Danny hadn't gone to Baba instead of me for girl advice. Not that he'd really told me much, either. It's just one day he suddenly started looking for excuses to bring up Luna's name in conversation and I'd put two and two together.

I looked toward the door again. "I don't like it. He's never had a fight before."

Baba shrugged. "That you know of. All boys fight at some point. Just takes some longer to get pushed to the edge."

I chewed on my lip and wondered what in the hell could

have pushed Danny to that edge. Instead of marching down to his room and demanding answers he wouldn't give anyway, I picked up my phone and tried Pen. As I'd expected it switched to voice mail. I didn't leave a message, though. I'd see her in the next day or so and ask her then. Maybe by then this whole thing would have blown over.

I grabbed a slice of pizza for Baba and handed it to her before taking some for myself. Then I grabbed a beer from the fridge and went into the den. It had been weeks since I spent a night vegging on the couch. I sank into the cushions with a sigh and fished around in them until I came up with the remote.

Taking a sip of beer, I clicked the button and settled back. Unfortunately, the six o'clock news was on, which meant the face grinning at me from the screen was Grace Cho's. I made a disgusted sound, but before I could change the channel I caught what she was saying. "...my exclusive interview with Babylon's new mayor, John Volos, about the recent coven violence."

The screen jumped to an image of Volos sitting behind the desk in the mayor's office. Cho sat across the desk from him, looking poised but determined.

"What steps are you taking to keep the people of this city safe?" Cho asked in her practiced evening-news voice.

"Chief Adams and I are in constant contact. He's upped patrols of the affected areas. I'm also overseeing the efforts of the MEA task force as they work to find the parties driving the violence." He cleared his throat. "In addition, I'm working closely with the city council to increase budgets for the strained precincts, including possible pay increases for officers."

I made a rude noise. "Bullshit."

"What?" Baba called from the kitchen.

"Nothing."

The exchange meant I missed whatever Volos had been saying next. But I definitely caught the last part.

"Mr. Mayor, do you have any messages for the criminals who are behind the recent spate of violence?"

I lifted my pizza, but before I took a bite I muttered, "This'll be good."

The camera panned dramatically toward Volos's face. With the seal of Babylon hanging behind his head, he looked like a civilized warlord. "Babylon will not cower from you," he said. "We will stand up and protect ourselves from anyone who threatens what is ours. And when we find you, our justice will be swift, hard, and absolute."

I took a long swallow of beer to wash down the pizza. I found his strongly worded warning curious. To my ears, it almost sounded like he'd been talking not on behalf of the city, but for himself. Sure, it made sense for a mayor to be pissed that someone was trying to consolidate the criminal powers in the city. Maybe another viewer of the same interview might have had a different impression, but I'd known John Volos for two decades. His words hadn't just been an idle threat. Instead it sounded almost as if John was taking the cartel's interest in Babylon personally.

Uncle Abe's words surfaced in the front of my brain like a flashing neon sign. *Ask yourself who has the most to lose if there's a coven war.*

"Son of a bitch," I breathed.

On screen, Cho was moving on to a new story about a zoning dispute. I picked up the remote and clicked until a dumb reality show popped up. I picked up my phone and hit the button programmed to call Morales.

The call clicked straight to voice mail. I cursed silently while Morales's greeting played in my ear. "Drew, it's me. Call me ASAP."

I tossed my phone on the table and grabbed my beer. Now that the seed of Volos's involvement had been planted, it sprouted into a poison vine that wound through my brain collecting more evidence I'd missed. His reaction at the gym when he'd seen the board filled with evidence linking *A Morte* to the crimes. The way he'd asked me to personally keep him in the loop about any developments. The fact that every freaking crime the MEA had investigated in Babylon had John Volos's fingerprints all over it. As the city's first Adept mayor, he certainly had a lot to lose if he couldn't prevent a coven war.

I took another bite of pizza, but the taste just nauseated me now. I made a disgusted sound. Before I'd joined the task force, I'd managed to avoid John Volos for a decade. But the minute Gardner brought me on to the team, the bastard had kept popping up in my life—and my cases. First, he'd been framed by Uncle Abe for putting a dangerous potion on the streets, then he was robbed by the Babylon Bomber. And now he was all mixed up with *A Morte*'s motivations for trying to start a coven war. In each case, Volos looked like a victim, but I knew better. He wasn't some hapless guy who always found himself in the wrong place at the wrong time. Volos wasn't a survivor—he was a player, a manipulator.

"An asshole," I said out loud.

"What?" Baba called again.

"Nothing," I muttered.

Chapter Twenty-Two

On my way in the next morning, there was a traffic jam leading to the Bessemer Bridge. I was running late as it was, after waking up on the couch with a crick in my neck and creases on my cheek from the cushion's nubby fabric. "Come on," I groaned and tapped the brakes.

As the main artery into the Cauldron, the bridge often got clogged during rush hour. But that morning, traffic wasn't just crawling, it was dead—totally at a standstill. I looked toward the lights of emergency vehicles flashing in the middle of the span crossing over the Steel River.

Normally I would have just written it off as an accident, but a couple of BPD boats bobbed under the bridge, as well. I grabbed my phone and punched in the number of my old patrol buddy Santini.

"Hey, it's Prospero. What's the holdup on the Bessemer?"

"You didn't hear?" he said. "We got a call about a body."

"A jumper?" It wasn't uncommon for someone to decide life was worse than leaping to their death in the frigid waters of the Steel River.

"Don't think so," he said. "Dispatch sent out Duffy."

My stomach dropped. If they'd sent Duffy they thought there was a murder involved. "Thanks, Santini." I hung up and called Duffy's phone number. He answered on the third ring.

"Where the hell are you?" he answered.

I frowned. "Stuck in traffic. Why?"

"Didn't you get my message? You need to get your ass to the Bessemer."

"I'm stuck in the bridge traffic," I said. "Half a mile away."

"Park your car and walk it. You need to see this."

My stomach pitched south. "What the hell's going on, Duffy?"

"I gotta go. See you in a few."

"Shit," I said into the dead line. I hit End on the phone and tossed it on top of my backpack. Then I flipped on my blinker and started the painful process of edging my Jeep out of traffic and toward the ditch on the side of the road. The guy behind me honked to let me know he disapproved of the move. I turned off the car, grabbed my bag, and exited.

As I was locking the door, the guy who'd honked rolled down his window. "Hey! You can't leave your car there!"

I waved with my middle finger and took off jogging. Ten cars up, my cell buzzed in my hand. That's when I realized why I hadn't gotten Duffy's call earlier—the phone was set to silent. "Morales?" I answered.

"You heard from Duffy?"

"Yeah, I'm on my way to him right now."

"I'm stuck in traffic on the way out of the Cauldron."

"I was on my way in and ran into the same thing. I'm hoofing it there now."

"Good idea," he said. "I'll meet you in the middle."

After he hung up, I stashed the phone again and continued to jog past cars. Every now and then, someone would toot their horn. I ignored them and put a little more speed into my run. There was no reason I could think of for the homicide detective to be calling me to the scene of a murder. Well, no good reason. Had Pantera Souza hit another coven leader? Aphrodite had left town and as far as I knew Harry was still safe at the hospital under twenty-four-hour police surveillance. But he could have hit one of the lieutenants from one of the covens.

By the time I reached the start of the bridge, I was winded. Police lined the entrance, but they nodded as I approached and let me through. The waters of the Steel River were churning that morning, and the cloudy sky made the water roughly the color of tarnished silver. I glanced over the edge of the railing to see the police boats bobbing in the water.

Up ahead ambulances had created a perimeter around the action. Most likely this was to block bystanders and the media from seeing what was happening on the other side. It appeared that the action was centered around the railing on the left side of the bridge. I jogged in that direction to try to find Duffy.

I came around the bumper of the closest ambulance. Across the way, I spotted Morales, who appeared to have just beaten me. He was walking toward Duffy, who had his back to both of us as he knelt in front of something at the base of the railing. Morales jogged over.

"Any idea what's up?" he asked.

I shook my head. "Only one way to find out."

Duffy was standing up and turning around as we approached.

He saw us and paused. I tilted my head and opened my mouth to ask him what was going on. But he simply stepped to the side.

My legs locked up, and the coffee I had for breakfast turned into a brick in my stomach.

A rope extended from the metal bracers high up on the bridge's structure. The end of the rope was tied into a noose around the victim's neck. The head tilted down toward the left, and a tongue hung from between blue lips. The victim's expensive suit was mottled with blood and God only knew what else. Her feet were bare except for run-through pantyhose, and her toes reached toward the ground a foot below.

A single white sheet of paper hung around her neck like a bib. Before I could ask what it said, shock descended like a steel door.

"Mother of God," Morales whispered beside me.

My face felt cold. It had nothing to do with the wind whipping up off the river, and everything to do with blood draining from beneath my skin. I didn't speak because I couldn't.

The detective's eyes were on me, but he didn't say anything.

"What do you know?" Morales asked.

Duffy sucked in a breath. "That this is going to be a media shitstorm."

I glanced toward him. "You call Gardner and Eldritch yet?"

He nodded. "They're on their way."

I placed a hand over my eyes and squeezed. "Fuck."

"Kate."

I pulled my hand away to look at Duffy.

"Her phone was on her." He said the words like a verdict.

I just looked at him. Somewhere deep in my gut, I knew what he was about to say was going to make this shit show turn into a real fuck fest.

"The last call was to your cell."

Remembering how my ringer had been off, I tilted my head and ignored the ping of dread in my center. "Of course it was." I pulled out the phone again and saw I'd missed three calls. The most recent was from Duffy with no corresponding voice mail. At midnight, long after I'd crashed on the couch, Morales had called and left a message. But in between those, Grace Cho had called at two in the morning. I held the phone up for Duffy to see she hadn't left a message.

"Any reason she'd be calling you?"

I nodded. "She's been trying to get me to do an interview. I told her I wasn't interested, but she's been pretty persistent."

Duffy wrote that down in a little notebook. "Where were you last night?"

"Fuck off, Duffy," Morales said. He stepped closer to me. "You don't have to answer that."

"Give me a break, Morales," Duffy snapped. "You know I have to ask."

I held up a hand. "It's okay," I said to Morales. "I was at home. Fell asleep just after the ten o'clock news. That's why I missed the call. My ringer was on silent and the vibrate function wasn't loud enough to wake me."

"Can anyone corroborate your story?" Duffy asked.

"Baba—my roommate."

His brows lowered at the mention I had a roommate, but I didn't elaborate and he didn't ask me to. "Why was Cho investigating you?"

"She said doing a piece on an Adept cop would be a nice complement to her piece on the city's first Adept mayor." I ran a hand through my hair and sighed. "Christ, what a mess." The body drew my attention. To avoid the bloated face and blood, I focused on the white square over her chest. "What's the note say?"

Duffy scratched his head. "I can't make sense of it. All it says is *Swift, Hard, and Absolute*."

Gravity seemed to double in force, pulling all the blood from beneath my skin to pool in my gut.

"I take it that means something to you?" Duffy said.

"Fuck." I looked at Morales, who appeared as lost as Duffy. "Fuck," I whispered. "I knew it."

Before they could question me, a new set of sirens ripped through the air. A moment later Gardner ran with Eldritch on her tail around an ambulance. When they saw the hanged woman they both froze. Then they swiveled toward each other and had a low-toned conversation I couldn't hear.

Gardner and Eldritch completed their confab and beelined for us. "Do not go anywhere," she said as she passed by. Then she and Eldritch pulled Duffy away to get a report.

Morales grabbed my arm. "Let's talk." He dragged me toward the opposite railing. "What was that reaction?"

I sighed. "Remember how I called you last night?" He nodded and waited for an explanation. "I'd just watched an interview between Cho and Volos about the coven violence." I pointed toward the body. "He said those exact words."

Morales watched me for a moment with an unreadable expression. "Abe was talking about Volos."

I nodded. "Last night, the connection was just a theory. Volos's words seemed too much like a personal threat." I nodded in the direction of the body. "But with that note—"

"Pantera Souza was sending a message back to the mayor by killing Cho," Morales said. "Shit, Prospero. What the fuck has Volos gotten himself into now?"

"Prospero, Morales," Gardner called, "a word, please."

The wind made her hair flap around her face like crow wings. She wore sensible gray slacks and a black twinset that day. Her lips were free of lipstick and tightened into a tense line. The skin under her eyes had the bluish tint of sleep deprivation.

When she reached us, she angled her body so that we were turned away from Eldritch and Duffy.

"What do you know?" Her eyes angled toward the body.

We filled her in on my theory about Volos's connection to the case. When I was done, she cursed. "Get out of here and find him. I don't care what it takes, find out what he knows. Once Duffy and the media connect the message on the note to the interview, we won't be able to get near him."

"Got it," Morales said. I nodded because I was busy steeling my resolve for the coming confrontation with Volos.

"While you're doing that," Gardner said, "I'm going to have Shadi bring Puck in for a conversation. Call me when you're done. And, guys? I expect usable intel from your meeting. I want Pantera in lockup by sundown."

Chapter Twenty-Three

We arrived at Volos's apartment thirty minutes later. I'd called his office as we ran back to Morales's car. Luckily his assistant recognized my name and easily gave up the information that he was working from home that morning. I didn't question why Volos's assistant felt I was trustworthy enough to share that information with, because it hinted that the mayor considered me a part of his inner circle. Definitely not where I wanted to be. After I told her I'd call him there myself, I'd hung up and told Morales where to go.

We didn't bother calling ahead. All things considered, the element of surprise would work better than giving him a chance to concoct a story.

Morales was quiet on the ride up the elevator. I turned to look at him. Stress lines bracketed his mouth. "What are you thinking?"

He glanced over at me. "Why would Souza kill Cho?"

I frowned. "What do you mean?"

"If he's after Volos, why hasn't Pantera gone at him directly? He certainly doesn't lack the stomach for murder."

I hadn't thought of it that way. "Maybe he doesn't want to kill Volos."

Morales nodded. "Blackmail, maybe. Or extortion."

"Question is, what does Volos have on *A Morte*?"

A few seconds later we knocked on Volos's door. The woman who answered wore a short black robe; her red hair was piled on top of her head in just-fucked waves. Her gaze narrowed on me. "What are you doing here?"

"Hello, Jade." I shouldn't have been surprised to see Volos's lawyer standing in front of me in boudoir attire, but I was. The last time I'd seen her was the previous fall when Volos had been a suspect in my first case for the MEA.

"What do you want?" she asked.

"We need to speak to your *boss*." I couldn't help putting extra emphasis on the last word.

Her eyes narrowed. "John's in the shower." She smiled a catty smile that seemed to say she enjoyed sharing that little tidbit with me.

I barely managed not to roll my eyes.

"Go get him," Morales said, "and while you're at it, you might want to put on something more lawyerly—this is an official call."

She watched us for a moment, as if trying to figure out if we were serious. I raised my brow to assure her we were. "You got a warrant?"

I shook my head. "Not that kind of official. We have reason to believe he's in danger." On the way over, Morales and I had decided to lead with that angle instead of going after him about his connection to *A Morte* head-on. If he thought we were looking out for him, he might be more likely to open up about his involvement. Or most people would be, but John Volos wasn't exactly most people.

Her expression lost some of its bitchiness, and a little bit of concern crept in. "Come in," she said. "There's mimosas on the breakfast bar in the living room."

I smiled. "We know the way."

"We'll be out in a moment." Her hips swaying, she sashayed away toward the hall leading to the bedrooms.

Morales and I closed the door and walked into the apartment. A couple of steps led into a sunken living room with a massive sectional leather couch. The sun had burned off that morning's clouds and glinted off the lake like sparks. The view from the large windows on the far wall was spectacular. Morales walked toward them and stood with his back to me. The light spilling through the glass outlined his wide shoulders. The back of his neck was tense, and his posture advertised that he clearly didn't want to be there. I couldn't blame him. I didn't like being in Volos's home myself. Yet I tended to find myself there with frustrating regularity.

While Morales took in the view, I wandered over to the breakfast bar. A crystal pitcher of mimosas sat next to sparkling glasses. The table in the kitchen still had the dishes laid out from an intimate breakfast for two. Except one of the settings was overturned, as if someone had pushed it out of the way in a fit of passion. A sudden image filled my brain of Volos rising above Jade's body as he took her on the table. I shook myself, realizing I had no interest in the image or the unwanted, hard spike of jealousy it summoned from the shadows.

"Kate?" John's voice carried from the hall.

"In here." I turned in time to see him come around the corner. He wore faded jeans and a T-shirt bearing wet spots that told me he'd dressed quickly after being called from the shower by Jade.

"What's wrong?" He didn't look at Morales, though it would have been hard to miss the big guy looming like a thunderhead by the windows. Instead, Volos looked concerned, as if he expected my reason for being there was to ask for help.

"You might want to wait for your attorney to join us before she answers that," Morales said.

John finally glanced toward my partner. "Oh," he said, "so this isn't a social call?"

I shook my head. "Of course not."

He crossed his arms and leaned against the bar. "Go ahead and tell me. We can fill in Jade once she joins us." He indicated the couch in the sunken living room. "Shall we?"

I shook my head. "I'd prefer to stand."

"As you wish."

Morales pulled away from the windows and came to join us. "Have you seen the news this morning?"

John looked from Morales to me and slowly shook his head. "I've been...preoccupied."

"Police were called to a murder scene on the Bessemer Bridge. There was a traffic jam for two miles in either direction."

John raised his brows. "Another coven killing?"

I shook my head. "Not exactly, but we believe it's connected to that case."

"So who was it?"

I looked him in the eyes so I couldn't miss a reaction. "Grace Cho."

His jaw hardened.

"That's not all," Morales said.

"Of course not." Volos stood straighter, like a man facing a firing squad. "Go ahead."

"There was evidence found on the scene that indicated her death was a message to you. Any idea why?"

"Who died?" Jade said, coming around the corner. She now wore a pair of dress slacks and a cashmere sweater. The bare feet were now encased in expensive shoes with ice-pick heels. Gone was the seductress who'd answered the door—in her place was a no-nonsense lawyer.

"Grace Cho," Volos said.

Jade's steps faltered and she gasped. She looked at John and he held out an arm. She went to him and leaned against his chest. Over the top of her head, he said, "Jade and Grace were friends. That's why I agreed to her request to do a feature on my first week as mayor."

"I'm sorry for your loss," I said to Jade. Cho had been a pain in my ass, but no one deserved to die so brutally.

She sniffed and visibly pulled herself together. She nodded to accept my condolences. "How did she die?"

I hesitated and shot a look at Volos. He squeezed her shoulders. "Maybe you shouldn't be here for this."

She shook her head and stood straighter. "No," she said, "I can handle it. It's just—I was shocked. I just talked to Grace yesterday."

"You did?" Morales asked. "What time?"

Jade pulled away a little bit from Volos, but not far enough that they weren't touching. She sniffed again. "About noon. We were planning on having dinner together last night, but she called to cancel. Said she was working on breaking a huge story and wouldn't be able to make it after all."

"Did she tell you what the story was about?" I asked. My

reason wasn't selfless. I wanted to know if I was the huge story Cho had been so hot to pursue. Her death would be huge news, and it wasn't a stretch to imagine any stories she'd been working on might also be part of the reporting.

Jade shook her head. "We didn't talk long. She said she'd be in touch soon." Her voice cracked at the end of the sentence, as she realized she'd never hear from her friend again. "What happened to her?"

I glanced at Volos, a silent question about whether I should tell her. He tipped his chin. "She was murdered." I didn't repeat the gruesome details about how we found her. "We have reason to believe the man who killed her is also responsible for the death of one coven wizard and the beating of another."

Volos tilted his head but didn't speak.

"We also found evidence at the scene that indicated Volos might be a target," Morales said.

The tension in the room was almost unbearable. Us standing there watching Volos for any sign he knew more than he was telling us, and him watching us, trying to figure out how much we already knew and what he could still hide.

It was Jade who broke the bubble. "What kind of evidence?"

"A note that contained the quote *Swift, Hard, and Absolute*."

Jade frowned. "What does that mean?"

"It's from the interview with Grace that ran last night," he said. "I was referring to how we'd deal with the culprit behind the coven violence. Obviously someone took exception to my strong words."

I snorted and stared at him. "Someone, right."

"What are you implying, Detective?"

"That you know exactly who killed Cho."

Volos stared back at me with a placid expression.

"That's preposterous," Jade said, all indignation.

"Is it?" Morales asked Volos.

"I assure you if I had evidence pertaining to a murder I would have come to you."

I arched a brow. "You may not be able to prove who killed her, but that doesn't mean you don't *know*."

"You obviously have a point to make." Volos crossed his arms. "So make it."

"We believe that the murderer wasn't responding to the interview last night so much as upping his game," I said. "Killing Charm and attacking Harry Bane didn't get the results he wanted so he decided to kick the hornet's nest."

"Who?" Jade said, sounding exasperated.

"Hector Souza." I watched Volos as I said the name. Again, he betrayed nothing.

"Who the hell is that?" Jade demanded.

"He works for the Brazilian cartel. Goes by the street name Pantera," Morales said. "We've linked him to at least two murders—three if our hunch about Grace Cho proves correct."

"What does this have to do with John?" She shot him a sideways glance, but he was too busy looking unaffected to acknowledge her.

"That was our question," I said. "Why would a cartel hit man want to send a message to Babylon's mayor?"

"I can't wait to hear your theories, Detective," Volos said, his tone full of patronizing humor.

I sighed and crossed my arms. "We thought *A Morte* was simply trying to get a cut of the action by destabilizing the covens."

"By starting a war," Morales added.

I nodded. "But that never really materialized except for a couple of breakouts of violence. Then I was talking to someone who knows a thing or two about criminal strategies—"

"Who?" Volos interrupted.

"Abe."

He laughed. "Great sources you got there, Kate."

I ignored him. "And he asked me a question I couldn't answer—at least not at the time."

"Which was?" he asked.

"Who in Babylon had the most to lose if the covens went to war?"

A muscle in his jaw jerked. I forged ahead. "Even if we believed Pantera's aim was to start a coven war, we couldn't figure out why he'd chosen now to make his move. Abe's been in jail for years, and Ramses Bane died almost six months ago. So why now?"

Volos didn't take the bait. He just stared me down, daring with his gaze to make my move. I took the opportunity with relish.

"Did you know Charm was killed the night of your inauguration ball?"

Jade snorted. "Please, Detective. Unless you have more to go on than wild speculation, you're wasting our time."

"Did you also know we suspect your own cousin is helping Pantera Souza?"

Volos's face tightened with anger. "Puck?"

I nodded. "I figured he was just being ambitious, trying to carve out a leadership role that Charm had denied him."

He raised a brow. "But?"

"When we questioned him, Puck had a lot of choice words about how you were a traitor to the coven. Not hard to believe that someone who hates you so much would go along with a cartel plot to bring you down."

Jade sputtered. "This is preposterous. You have yet to do anything besides spout theories and conjecture, Detective."

I held up a hand. "John is the city's first Adept mayor, and he ran on an anticrime platform. Seems he'd have the most to lose if a major outbreak of Arcane violence rocked the city."

"The only question we can't answer," Morales said, "is why *A Morte* would go to such lengths to discredit Volos as mayor?"

Volos remained as locked down as Fort Knox. I chewed my lip for a moment. "How long until he comes at you directly?" I asked. His eyes hardened. "Cho's death will be all over the news, along with the juicy note referencing your interview. That's bad enough. But it's not long until Pantera gets tired of playing games and decides to get real."

"I'd say it's already pretty fucking real," Morales said.

I nodded. "You're going to be so busy managing the media hurricane Souza whipped up that you won't have time to find him on your own." I crossed my arms. "But the MEA is already focused on this case. We just need a break that will help us shut him down."

He started to talk, but hesitated when Jade cleared her throat.

"Let us help you." The words tasted bitter on my tongue. If he was as deep in the Souza case as I believed, he deserved to spend his days in a prison jumpsuit. But we could stop Pantera without knowing the full story, so I was prepared to play the empathy card if it got us what we needed. "We can make this go away for you."

"That's enough," Jade said. "As Mayor Volos's attorney I'm not going to stand here and let you accuse—"

"If I tell you what I know," Volos cut in, "I'll need assurances."

Jade's mouth fell open. I raised my brow. "What kind of assurances?"

"That you won't use what I'm about to tell you to bring me up on charges."

For the first time that day, Morales smiled. "Why, Mr. Mayor, why on earth would you need amnesty?"

Volos shot Morales a look that would have made lesser men quake. But Drew Morales had faced down scarier characters than John Volos. Men who'd cut out your tongue for such an offense.

"Pardon us a moment." Jade grabbed John's sleeve and pulled him away. They walked around the corner. Her higher-pitched voice spoke rapidly. Occasionally his deeper voice would issue a calm response.

Morales raised his brow at me. "What do you think?"

I shrugged. "If he won't tell us now, we'll come back with a warrant."

He shook his head. "No, I mean do you think he knows why *A Morte*'s after him?"

"Of course he does." My confidence wasn't born of any sort of sixth sense. Men like John Volos didn't gain power without knowing their enemies better than they knew their allies. Whatever he and Jade were arguing about would provide the answers to *A Morte*'s motivations. I knew that as surely as I knew Volos would stop at nothing to win Pantera's deadly game.

Before Morales could respond to my comment, Volos came back around the corner with Jade trailing him. She'd lost some of the confidence in her step. His shoulders were back and his chin high.

"Well?" Morales prompted.

Volos nodded toward Jade. She hesitated and then walked out of the room. I didn't see where she went, but a few seconds after she disappeared I heard a door open and close down the hall.

"Before I tell you what I need to tell you, the three of us need to come to an agreement."

"This isn't a negotiation," I said. "If you have information that can aid us in making a case against a murderer, then you're legally obligated to share it."

"Not if I plead the Fifth, Detective," he said, putting mocking emphasis on my title.

"I got five for you, asshole," Morales said, clenching his fist. I shot him a warning glare.

"Why would you need Fifth Amendment protection, Mr. Mayor?" I said sweetly. "I thought you were legit now."

"Therein lies the rub, Detective. In order to tell you that, I'm going to need assurances that you won't turn around and use what I'm about to tell you to build an obstruction case against me."

"You're putting us in an impossible position," I said. "How can we agree not to use it against you before we know what it is? What if you're about to admit you killed Cho?"

Volos shot me a pitying look. "Don't insult me, Katherine."

I narrowed my eyes. "Watch your tone."

At that moment, Jade came back in carrying a file folder. She handed it to Morales. I glanced questioningly at Volos. He shrugged. "Like I said: assurances."

Morales opened the folder. As he read the contents, his expression didn't change, but a muscle in his jaw pulsed.

Volos crossed his arms, and when he looked at me his expression was stony. "Do we understand each other?"

I wasn't sure what was in that folder, but I knew enough about some of the skeletons in my partner's closet to fear what would happen if Volos shared the contents with the MEA—or God forbid, the media.

"Thank you," Morales said. Volos shot my partner a questioning look. "You've just confirmed my complete lack of faith in politicians."

Volos's expression tightened. "Do we have a deal?"

Morales slammed his folder shut and tossed it to me. My fingers fumbled in my haste to open it. Inside, I found a dossier on Morales. But it was the second page that made me curse out loud. It was a sworn statement by a wizard named Gan Ji, a member of the Fangshi Coven in Los Angeles. According to his sworn statement, he'd witnessed Morales helping leaders of the Fangshi cover up the death of a cop.

I looked up from the damning document to glare at Volos. "You son of a bitch."

"Do we have an understanding?" he asked.

Morales executed a curt nod. "This better be good." He crossed his arms, as if he didn't trust himself not to punch the mayor.

"Kate?" Volos prompted.

I folded the file between my arms. "Oh, I understand perfectly." There was no anger in my tone—just resignation. Knowing Volos, he had files on every power player in Babylon as an insurance policy for instances just like this one. He raised a brow to indicate that my retort hadn't been enough of an assurance. "I promise we won't arrest you for *this* crime."

The corner of Volos's mouth quirked as he turned toward the breakfast bar and lifted a glass. He held it up, as if to offer a drink to everyone else. Morales and I just stared at him. He shrugged and poured himself a mimosa. I knew he was stalling, but didn't comment. I wasn't too excited to hear what he was about to say. Any information that required the threat of blackmail wasn't going to be good news.

Morales, however, had had enough. "Time's ticking, Volos."

"Fine," he said. Clearly he knew better than to push us any further. "Do you recall the potion that was stolen from my lab about six months ago?"

I frowned. "You mean the truth serum Dionysus used on us?"

After he'd kidnapped Morales and me, Dionysus had pumped us full of a truth serum that caused severe pain if we lied. The effects of the potion hadn't lasted long, but while it worked it had been excruciating. That was why I wasn't shocked to read the Fangshi wizard's statement. Morales had admitted to covering up that murder under the influence of Volos's potion. That's also how I knew the statement hadn't told the whole truth. According to Morales, who was unable to lie because of the potion, the cop who'd been murdered was dirty.

Anyway, back when it had been stolen, Volos admitted to me that he'd made the potion for a well-paying mystery client.

Volos tipped his chin. "After hearing how it was used on you, I destroyed the formula and refused to deliver a new batch to the people who asked me to develop it."

I closed my eyes and cursed. "Let me guess—the people who hired you were members of *A Morte*?"

He was silent so long, I opened my eyes again. Finally, he said, "I didn't know it was them until it was too late."

"Bullshit," Morales said. "You honestly expect us to believe you didn't vet the request?"

"The man who commissioned the potion was a wizard who worked for the Department of Defense. He had legit credentials. Said he'd been tasked with making the potion to use as an alternative to torture during interrogations on enemy combatants."

"That was what you called an alternative to torture?" I asked, incredulous. When I'd tried to resist the effects of the potion, it had felt like razor blades stabbing at my gut.

"It was still in the testing phase when the formula was stolen," he said.

"So how did we get here?" Morales asked.

"About a week after Halloween the man who'd hired me started calling. I'll admit I avoided his attempts to contact me. But in my defense, I'd just thrown my hat in the ring for mayor and was pretty preoccupied.

"Anyway," he continued, "in January the fed wiz finally showed up on my doorstep. He was pretty agitated and demanded I hand over the formula immediately. Since he put me on the spot, I admitted I'd destroyed it."

"What did he do?" Morales asked.

"He pulled a gun on me."

My brows rose. "I bet that went over well."

The only confirmation was a slight uptilt of his mouth. "Once I showed the gentleman the error of his ways, he admitted that he'd been hired by *A Morte*. He'd promised them he'd deliver the formula by the New Year. When it didn't appear, they started putting on the pressure."

"Wait," I said, "did *A Morte* know he'd hired you?"

"Good question." Volos smiled. "No. They'd hired him and given him a hefty down payment to come up with the formula. He couldn't make it work and came to me."

"Stupid bastard," I said.

Volos nodded. "About two weeks after he confronted me, I saw a report in the paper about the death of a DoD wizard. I called in a few favors to get the full story. The body had been found in his garage. He'd had multiple nail gun wounds, including one to the skull."

Morales crossed his arms. "Let me guess. It was ruled a suicide?"

Volos nodded. "The cartel's reach is vast."

I sucked a deep breath in through my nose and released it. "And it didn't occur to you then to cover your ass by coming to us and telling us what you knew?"

"Once I saw he was dead, I figured I was free and clear," Volos said. "Until I saw the board at MEA headquarters covered in your theories about Pantera Souza being the killer."

"Any idea how they found out he'd hired you?" Morales asked.

"Best guess is he admitted he'd outsourced it to me to try to save his own ass." Volos shook his head. "Regardless, I thought calling them out in the media might make them back down, but I...miscalculated."

"Jesus, Volos." I laughed humorlessly. "Your shitty error got Grace Cho tortured and murdered."

Jade's face fell at the mention of torture. My conscience flared to life, but we were beyond sugarcoating the situation to protect the lawyer's delicate sensibilities.

"Why didn't you come to us earlier?" I demanded. "We could have—"

"What, Kate? What would you have done differently?" he challenged. "How does this change the fact that you haven't been able to catch this guy?"

I threw up my hands. "Don't turn this on us, Volos. If you hadn't been so fucking greedy you wouldn't have *A Morte* on your ass and this town wouldn't be dealing with a coven war."

He tilted his head. "I'm not so sure that's the case. *A Morte* has wanted their fingers in the Cauldron for decades. I simply offered them the excuse they needed to make their move."

"Abe wouldn't deal with them," I said. "Any idea why?"

He held up his hands. "You mean what you've seen so far isn't enough of a reason?"

I shrugged. "Please, Abe would do business with the devil himself if he thought he'd turn a profit."

Volos looked like he was weighing the risks of bullshitting me. But I shot him a look that clearly communicated I'd reached my limit for the day. Finally, he sighed. "It has to do with an old beef between Abe and the leader of the supercoven in New York."

The phone on Volos's hip started ringing. He checked the screen quickly, but muted the ringer. "My office," he said. "We need to wrap this up. If the media and BPD have figured out my connection to Cho's murder, I'm about to be swamped."

I frowned. "You were saying about the Quincunx?"

Unlike Babylon, which had three main covens ruling most of the dirty magic trade in the city, in New York the Quincunx Coven ran everything.

Volos nodded. "The leader of the Fives," he said, using the street name for the New York supercoven, "is an old enemy of Abe's. And since the Fives have ties to the cartel, Abe refused to work with the Brazilians."

"Who's the leader?" Morales asked.

Volos smiled tightly. "I don't know." He was lying, but I had a feeling he'd reached his limit that day, too. I shot Morales a look to let it go; the Quincunx wasn't the focus of our investigation.

I ran a hand through my hair. "So our best guess is that *A Morte*'s pissed at you. They figured they'd knock you out of the mayor's office and take a piece of the potion trade while they're at it." As much as I wanted to pin the blame entirely on Volos's back, it had really only been a matter of time until the power vacuums created a coven war.

Volos's home phone rang this time. At the same time, Jade's cell chirped from her hand. Volos looked at us. "If that's all, I need to plan a press conference to get ahead of this story."

"We're not done with this," Morales snapped.

Volos moved toward the living room and clicked some buttons on a remote. A screen lowered from the ceiling. Another button resulted in three video boxes appearing—each filled with local newscasts. The screen lit up with images of Cho's murder scene, headshots of Volos, and anchors speculating about the mayor's connection to the death.

We all watched the circus in silence for a moment before Jade's phone screamed again. She looked down at the screen and read the incoming text before speaking. "BPD's on their way now to question you."

"Shit," I said. If Duffy found us at Volos's place, he'd go supernova. "All right, we're leaving. I suggest you double your security detail for the time being."

Volos's mouth quirked. "Your concern warms me, Detective."

"Yeah, don't get too excited," I said. "Considering the shit show you've put us in the middle of—again, I might add— you're lucky I haven't killed you myself."

"Lucky, sure." His eyes were on the gruesome video collage and the talking heads. If I weren't so pissed at him, I almost would have felt bad for what he was facing at the press conference he'd mentioned.

But as it was, I was too busy feeling bad for Morales and me. Volos had to face down rabid journalists, but we had to go tell our boss that we were no closer to finding the man who'd killed Charm, Hot Pocket, Grace Cho, and Gardner's old team than we'd been the last time we'd seen her.

Chapter Twenty-Four

After sneaking out the back door to Volos's apartment building, Morales and I got in the SUV and called Gardner. She told us Shadi was on her way in with Puck and wanted us there ASAP.

Morales put the car in Drive and took off. "Well?" he said.

I sighed. "Well what?"

He shot me a sideways glance. "You think he was telling the truth?"

I crossed my arms and slouched down in my seat. "With Volos it's best to assume you're getting at least half bullshit."

He snorted. "At least we have a better idea why Pantera's in town."

"Fat lot of good that does to help us find him."

Morales blew out a breath. "Let's pray we can get something useful out of Puck."

"Don't get your hopes up."

"I gave up on hope a long time ago, Cupcake."

His words hung there for a moment. "You want to talk about that folder?"

He kept his eyes on the road. "Not especially." I nodded, but he wasn't done. "One of these days Volos is going to go too far." His hands tightened on the wheel.

"I hear you."

He looked over at me. "Maybe once this is all done we should take a closer look at him." These words were spoken casually, as if he was testing the waters.

"What? Build a case?"

He tipped his chin.

"Wouldn't be easy," I said.

"The best cases rarely are."

I chewed on my bottom lip as I thought it over. "If we went after him, he'd fight back—hard. I'd bet cash money that folder he showed us today is only the tip of the iceberg. You willing for your skeletons to get paraded out in order to bring him down?"

Morales's jaw hardened. "It would depend on our chances of making the case. If we had enough shit on him to bring him down? Maybe."

I blew out a breath. "Let's leap off that cliff once we get Pantera off the streets." He shot me a surprised look. "What?" I asked.

"I just thought you'd be against it."

"Going after Volos?" I frowned. "Why would I be against that?"

He raised his brows.

I sighed. "What we had was a long time ago. He's not the same guy and I'm not the same lovesick girl. If he's as dirty as we believe, I'd have no problem bringing him down if I thought it would make a difference."

Morales turned onto the street in front of the gym. He parked next to the curb before answering. "Like you said, now's not the time. But eventually, Volos is going to learn he's not above the law."

◆ ◆ ◆

Inside the gym, we found Gardner, Shadi, and Mez standing in the boxing ring. Next to the whiteboard bearing the evidence we'd gathered on Souza, Puck was cuffed to a chair. "I want to call my lawyer," he yelled.

"You're not under arrest," Gardner said. "You're free to leave anytime."

Puck's eyes narrowed. "Then uncuff me."

She crossed her arms and shot him an apologetic look. "Lost the key."

"Bitch," Puck hissed.

"Did we miss anything good?" Morales called. He held the ring's ropes open for me to climb under before following me through.

"Just got started," Gardner said. "Mez, Shadi, why don't you give us a minute." The pair exited the ring like we were fighting a tag-team match.

"Where ya been, Puck?" I asked.

"Pain," he said. "I told you I don't go by Puck anymore."

I crossed my arms. "All right, where ya been, *Pain*?"

He slouched in his seat. "Oh, you know, little of this, little of that."

"By that do you mean conspiring with Pantera Souza to bring down your cousin?" I asked.

At the mention of the *A Morte* hit man, Puck's eyes widened, but he quickly schooled his features. "Who?"

217

"About this tall"—Morales raised his hand to his shoulder—"midnight-black skin. Sometimes becomes a cat."

Puck's eyes narrowed. "I don't know no one like that."

I sighed. "Cut the shit, we know you were at the junkyard with Pantera the day Harry Bane was beaten."

"Bullshit."

I grabbed his uncuffed right hand and raised it, pushing back the cuffs of his shirt as I did. "You stupid son of a bitch, did you really think I wouldn't recognize Votary tats when I saw them?"

"Every fucker in the coven has tats like mine."

"Yet you're the only one who's leading the coven now that Charm's dead."

"What the fuck are you talking about?"

I waved a hand to dismiss that dead end. "Where's Pantera Souza?"

"I told you," Puck drawled, "I don't know anyone named Pantera."

I sucked on my teeth for a moment, watching him. "Gardner, Morales, you want to give me a minute?"

Morales looked like he wanted to argue, but after shooting me a speculative glance, Gardner nodded. "Let's go see if we can find that key."

Puck watched them leave. His expression told me he actually believed he'd walk out of this building without spilling his secrets. I smiled at him because I knew different. "Sorry you had to wait for Morales and me to arrive," I said.

He frowned. "Huh?"

"Earlier," I said. "We were coming from a meeting, so the interview was delayed. Sorry about that."

His expression turned wary. "Whatever."

"It's kind of funny, actually. Your name came up in our meeting."

He looked at the floor, as if dismissing me.

I laughed. "I wish you could have seen the look on your cousin's face when we told him we suspected you were helping Pantera kill Charm."

Puck's head jerked up so fast he almost overturned the chair. "You told Volos I killed Charm? Why?"

I shrugged. "The mayor wanted a status report on the case, so we told him what we knew. Needless to say, he was extremely interested to learn of your involvement."

"Shit, tell me you're kidding."

"I assure you I'm not." I looked him in the eye. Stupid asshole bought it, too, if the sudden paleness of his skin was anything to go by. I didn't bother telling him Volos hadn't even blinked when I'd mentioned Puck's possible involvement. Men like Volos didn't give a shit about kittens like Puck when real predators like Souza were prowling. "Especially now that Souza's pulled Volos into this mess by killing that reporter—"

"What reporter?" Puck's voice pitched an octave higher than normal.

I crossed my arms and pursed my lips while I stared him down. "Lying to me right now would be a very bad fucking idea."

He raised his right hand like a freaking Boy Scout. "I swear. I don't have a fucking clue what you're talking about. As far as I know Harry Bane killed Charm."

"Who told you that?"

He shook his head. "The street told me. My gut told me."

"I don't know. Maybe if I took you to Volos he could get the truth out of you."

"Fuck no. Please, I'm telling you everything. Honest."

I narrowed my eyes. "You scared?"

"Um, yes! Look, put me in jail, read me my rights—whatever. Just don't hand me over to Volos. He'll kill me. No doubt."

"But you're family." I was playing devil's advocate. There was no doubt in my mind, either, that if I handed Puck over, Volos would hurt the kid.

Puck snorted. "Family—right. He don't know the meaning, otherwise he wouldn't have betrayed the coven five years ago."

"Is that why you decided to work with Souza? To make Volos pay for betraying the Votaries?"

He sighed as if exhausted. "I'm not working with anyone."

"If it wasn't you, someone else in your crew killed Charm and beat Harry Bane. Who was it?"

"I'm telling you, no one in my crew would dare do something like this. Charm and I had our moments. I told Charm that if we didn't adapt we'd continue to lose street cred, but he didn't listen. But I didn't take him out and neither did any of my people."

"You sure about that? Maybe you aren't as in charge as you think."

Puck's eyes hardened. "Find that fucking key and call my attorney. I'm done talking to you."

I looked over my shoulder to the doorway to Mez's lab, where Gardner and Morales were watching us. "Call Volos, will you? Tell him we got Puck."

Behind me, laughter crawled up my spine like spider legs. I turned slowly to see Puck's gaze on the small, muted TV on a nearby desk. I guess Gardner had clicked it on to watch the news reports on Cho's death. When I saw what was on the screen, I cursed silently.

"Yeah," Puck said, shooting me a victorious smirk, "call Volos."

On screen, the mayor stood behind a podium fielding questions from reporters. Tension lines bracketed his politician's smile. A scrolling ticker at the bottom of the screen read, "Mayor Volos holds press conference on the death of reporter Grace Cho."

"Looks like my cousin's got problems of his own right now." He shot me a superior look. "And I got a call to make to my lawyer."

◆ ◆ ◆

An hour later the door to the building slammed closed behind Puck and his attorney. We couldn't hold the shit because we didn't have any hard evidence to connect him to the murder or the junkyard beating. We'd tried to convince him to make a statement implicating Pantera Souza in the crimes, but he'd told us to go fuck ourselves. Unable to hold him without a charge, we'd had no choice but to let him walk.

"Fuck," Morales said, his eyes on the empty stairs.

Gardner looked like she wanted to either throw up or punch something. "Please tell me you got something we can use from Volos."

We quickly filled her in on his theories about why *A Morte* might be targeting him. We were careful to avoid mentioning Volos's ill-fated deal over the truth serum. It was still too risky to expose his direct influence, since he could still send that file on Morales to Gardner.

When we were done, she rose slowly from the desk she'd been leaning against. "So basically we've got nothing?" Her tone was too quiet to be trusted. "Is that what you're telling me?"

Morales deflated. "Yes, sir."

Gardner turned and stalked away. Slack-jawed, we watched her enter the office and slam the door. The glass on the window vibrated from the force.

I blew out a long breath. "Shit."

"When you were talking to Puck, she told me her boss called from Detroit."

I dropped into a chair. "Let me guess, if we don't shut Souza down, he's shutting us down?"

Morales shook his head. "No, they'll bring in someone to replace Gardner. They're concerned that her personal history with *A Morte* is compromising her ability to get the job done."

"Jesus. What else can we do?"

"I still think Puck's in contact with the shaman. *A Morte* isn't known for leaving people alive who can testify unless they have plans for them."

I nodded. "We can put Shadi on him again. See if we rattled his chain enough to get him to make contact with Pantera."

"That's what I was thinking, too."

"What about us? Should we see if LM's found out anything new?"

He shook his head. "We're going to spend the rest of the day hitting the pavement. Souza isn't exactly the kind of guy who'd blend into a crowd. Someone's seen him, and I intend to knock on every door in the Cauldron if that's what it takes."

I sighed. I didn't love the idea of spending my day getting doors slammed in my face, but it beat sitting around waiting for the shaman to make his next move. "Should we tell Gardner?"

At that moment, the sound of a raised voice came from the office. We turned to see Gardner yelling into her phone.

"On second thought, maybe we should give her some time," I said.

Morales nodded gravely. "Unfortunately, until Souza makes another play, time is the one thing we got."

Chapter Twenty-Five

S everal hours later I dragged myself up the steps into the gym. After a long, frustrating day knocking on doors and visiting real shitholes looking for someone who'd seen Pantera Souza, we'd turned up nothing. Morales had dropped me back at my car an hour earlier with promises to pick me up the next morning to get back at it. But I hadn't been able to relax enough to go to bed, so I'd decided to grab crime scene reports from the office to go over while the rest of the world slept.

The lights in the gym were all extinguished, except for a dim glow coming from Mez's lab. Instead of heading for my desk, I went to say hi to Mez and see what was keeping him working so late. But when I came around the corner and entered the lab, it wasn't Mez I found there—it was Gardner.

Her back was to me and her head was bent over the worktable.

She was so intent on her project that she hadn't heard me. I cleared my throat, so as not to spook her. "Sir?"

Her head snapped up and she spun on her stool. "Jesus, Prospero. You scared me."

"Sorry, I thought you heard me come in."

She cleared her throat and shook her head. "What's up?"

I pointed a thumb over my shoulder. "I dropped by to grab some files." I tried to see over her shoulder, but couldn't make out what she'd been doing.

She nodded and yawned. "What time is it?"

"About ten," I said. "What you working on?" I tried to keep my tone casual, but I was curious as hell.

"It's nothing," she evaded. "Just a side project."

In all my time on the team, I'd never seen Gardner working in the lab. She was an Adept, so she knew how to cook, but I'd never actually witnessed her do it. "You're cooking?"

Her gaze skittered to the right. "Not really."

The scent of ozone in the air betrayed the lie. I also detected the bite of sulfur and something spicy-sweet—frankincense, maybe.

"How'd your rounds go today?" She sounded tired.

"Frustrating. We're going back out in the morning."

"Okay." She nodded absently and glanced back at the glass flask filled with bubbling liquid. I watched her, wondering if I should force the issue about her cooking.

"Did you need anything else?" She stared at me without blinking.

It didn't take a detective to read the evasive body language. Whatever she was working on, she clearly didn't want to share the details. "No," I said slowly. "I'll just grab what I came for and get out of your hair."

She nodded. "See you tomorrow." With that she spun back

on her stool. Next to the cooking apparatus, there was a bottle labeled BUCHU. A quick scans of my mental Rolodex of herbs told me an infusion of the herb was often used to enhance psychic powers and induce prophetic dreams. It was especially effective when mixed with frankincense.

"Sir?" I said quietly.

"Yes?" She didn't turn again. Instead, she picked up the bottle and added a little to the potion. The mixture hissed as the new ingredient caused a reaction.

"You're not doing anything stupid, are you?"

She sat straighter and turned very slowly, as if giving me time to run. But I held my ground. If she was doing what I thought she was doing, someone needed to talk some sense into her. "Prospero?"

"Yes, sir?" I raised my chin.

"Have I ever done anything to give you the impression I'm dumb?"

I shook my head. "Until now? No."

A single brow rose. "Mind your own business, Detective."

"If you're cooking a potion to help you track down Souza, it's very much my business, sir."

A flicker of something crossed her expression, but she quickly replaced it with her poker face. "Don't be ridiculous."

I crossed my arms. "Good. Because you were right—you are too smart to do something like track down a dangerous cartel hit man on your own."

She didn't react.

I sighed. "Look, I know you've got history with this guy. And if I were you, I'd probably be tempted to track him down myself. But I would hope if that were the case that someone would stop me and remind me that it was a really dangerous idea."

She placed her hands between her knees. "Just because an idea is dangerous doesn't make it bad."

I cocked my head and looked my superior officer in the eye. "I'll be sure to repeat that to you next time I get a shitty idea in my head. If you're still around, that is."

Her mouth tilted up into a tight smile that didn't reach her eyes. "Watch yourself, Kate."

"No, *Miranda*, you watch yourself. We're all working our asses off to catch Pantera and make sure he feels the full brunt of the MEA's boot heel to his ass. If you go off half-cocked because your need for vengeance overrides your sense, you could risk the entire operation."

In the dim light, her eyes glinted dangerously. "You. Are. Dismissed."

Our gazes collided and held. Hers dared me to say one more word. Just one word calling her on her bullshit. One more word that would give her justification for suspending me for insubordination. Instead of handing her the ammunition to use against me, I simply nodded and turned away without another word.

I walked on wooden legs toward my desk, picked up the file, and grabbed my purse. The entire time, my heart thudded in my chest. I was almost at the stairs when her voice reached me. "Prospero." She said it quietly, but in the silent gym with its tall ceilings, it sounded as loud as a gunshot.

"Yeah?" I said, my foot hovering over the first step.

"Whatever you think you just saw—keep it to yourself."

I swallowed hard but nodded. "You're the boss."

Her head tilted. "You want that to continue to be the case, keep your mouth shut."

I didn't respond. Just jogged down the steps and slammed out the front door. I grabbed my phone as I stiff-legged it toward Sybil. I didn't dial until I was in the car and speeding away from the office. He answered on the third ring.

"What's up?"

"I'm coming over."

A significant pause followed, followed by a cleared throat. "I'm not alone."

I paused, trying to sort through the mixture of emotions that comment caused. "Really?"

"Nah, I'm just fucking with you. Bring a sixer."

I smiled. "Will do. Be sure you put on some pants before I get there."

"You're no fun, Cupcake."

I hung up and turned the Jeep in the direction of Morales's apartment. I may have agreed not to tell anyone about her late-night cook session, but I hadn't promised not to find Hector before she could use that potion.

Chapter Twenty-Six

I'd never been to Morales's apartment before. I wasn't sure what I'd expected, but it wasn't a space filled with books. Two entire walls of his living room were taken up by mismatched bookcases filled to the gills with paperbacks.

I wandered over to one of the cases and started reading titles. There didn't seem to be a method of organization. Mysteries were stacked with Westerns, and science fiction pressed against political thrillers and fantasy novels.

The hiss of a cap top twisting from a beer bottle announced Morales's return. I turned to take it from him. "I'm impressed."

"What? I'm not a total Neanderthal, Cupcake."

I lifted a book from one of the shelves. "Vampire romance?"

He almost spit out his beer. "An ex-girlfriend left that one."

I raised my brows in challenge, but he wouldn't look at me. I smiled and put back the book instead of teasing him more.

Not that I'd admit this out loud, but the idea of him reading a romance novel was kind of endearing.

He cleared his throat and took another sip of beer.

An awkward moment of silence passed between us. Odd. We'd worked together for months and spent countless hours in the car in silence without the merest hint of discomfort. So why now?

"Anyway," Morales said, "shall I assume from the stack of files in your hands this isn't a social call?" Disappointment shadowed his words.

"Hitting all those doors today didn't turn up shit. Figured it wouldn't be a bad idea to go back over the crime scene reports. Maybe we missed something."

He nodded and took another sip of his beer. "Actually, I called a buddy in Miami this evening. Works lots of *A Morte* cases. He sent me a couple of reports on cases where Souza's name has cropped up."

My brows rose. "That's great."

"I was just printing them off to go over when you called. I'll go grab them." He disappeared down the hall. I peeked around the corner. At the end of the hall, an open door revealed a made bed with a simple beige comforter. Morales disappeared into a different room that he must have used as an office.

While I waited for him to return, I plopped onto the over-stuffed sofa and set my beer on one of the coasters obviously left there by a man who expected them to be used. A few magazines were on the table. Couple of gun rags, as I expected, but also a high-minded news journal and a magazine about cigars and spirits. They were displayed in a perfectly square stack in one corner of the table. The three remotes on the table were likewise lined up. I couldn't reconcile the man who preferred such order in his home with the rough-and-ready partner with the scuffed boots and carefree smirk.

He emerged from the hallway with a couple of file folders in his hands. "Found them."

I scooted over to make room for him. When he sat the leather cushions inflated under me, pushing me toward him. I bumped into his side with my hand open on his biceps. "Sorry," I said. He shot me a look but didn't say anything.

"What?" I asked.

"Nothing."

I frowned at him as I moved out of bumping range. "I went by the gym before I came over," I said, trying to keep my tone casual.

He was busy putting the printouts in order. "Yeah?"

"Gardner was there."

He looked up. "And?"

I forced a casual shrug. "I'm worried about her. I think the case is taking its toll."

A dismissive flick of his brow indicated he thought maybe the case was affecting me, as well. "It'll be fine. She's a pro."

I bit my lip to hold in the words that rushed forward. It would have been so easy to tell him what I saw, but something told me he'd brush it off. Morales respected Gardner too much to believe she was on the edge. So instead of bringing it up, I sighed. "Maybe you're right."

There was that cocky smirk. "'Course I am, Cupcake."

He held my gaze for a moment too long. As much as I complained about his cocksure attitude, it also kind of pushed my buttons. There really was nothing like a man who could handle anything. I'm sure deep down, Morales had doubts like the rest of us mortals, but you'd never know it by dealing with him.

I cleared my throat and looked down at the files in my lap. "I brought Val's forensics report from the Charm scene, as well as Mez's from Harry's."

"Okay, you read over those and I'll handle the ones my colleague sent."

I nodded and settled back to start reading Val's exhaustive notes. About thirty seconds passed before Morales spoke.

"Kate?"

"Yeah?" My eyes were on the top picture from Val's report—an image of Charm's head cradled in the saint's arms.

"Never mind."

I frowned at his weird mood, but brushed it off. This case was making all of us edgy. I started reading again. "Listen to this," I said. "Val's report says there were traces of hematite found on Charm's limbs."

He frowned.

I continued reading. "She noted here that it's possible it's from wherever they killed and dismembered the body."

"Where would one find hematite?"

"Lots of places around Babylon." Off his questioning look, I waved a hand. "I forget you didn't grow up in a steel town. Hematite is one of the main iron ores. All of the old steel refineries, the train yards, and the ports would have traces of it."

Morales's eyes narrowed. "Considering most of those places are now abandoned, any of them would make a great place to commit a murder."

I nodded. "Oh, wait," I said, reading. "Val made a handwritten note here. Apparently, she did some research and the world's largest supplier of hematite ores is a mining company in Brazil."

Morales's eyes widened. "Interesting."

I shrugged. "Maybe. Could be a coincidence."

"Or not."

"What did you find?"

He sighed and closed the folder. "A list of seriously fucked-up

231

crimes linked to Hector 'Pantera' Souza, but nothing that will tell us where he is now."

"Grab your computer and let's look up this company in Brazil and see if there's any links to *A Morte*."

He paused. "What's working in that head of yours, Cupcake?"

"Even though none of the steel factories is still producing, tons of ore come through the city's ports for manufacturing companies across the country. That's where the largest concentrations of hematite would be at present."

"How does that connect to Souza?"

"Okay," I said, "stick with me here, but if the shaman was trying to enter the country, Miami would be the worst place because the MEA would be watching all the ports as well as the airports. But a Brazilian freighter wouldn't be as closely monitored in Babylon."

Morales frowned. "You're right. The MEA in Miami would have people watching all the normal entry points down south for him."

"There's lots of warehouses and slips and boats down there that would make excellent spots to kill someone."

Morales grabbed his laptop from the floor next to the table. "I'll access the MEA database and see if I can find any references to the Brazilian cartel using ships to smuggle people or potion-making supplies into the country."

Now that we had something concrete to research, excitement surged through me. I scooted closer, but in my enthusiasm overshot and ended up pressing my thigh against Morales's. He looked up from his typing. "Sorry," I said, and shifted back a bit.

"No worries." He looked back at the screen and cleared his throat. "Okay, according to a report from a couple of years ago, a shipment of ayahuasca was confiscated in the Port of Miami from a ship out of the Port of Tubarão in Brazil. One of the MEA agents got a statement from a worker on the ship that it was from *A Morte*, but before they guy could testify his body was found hanging from a crane at the port."

"Jesus. Way to send a message."

Morales nodded. "So your theory isn't as wild as you thought."

He leaned back into the cushions and took a celebratory swig of beer. "Looks like we'll be headed to the docks in the morning."

"I'll call one of my friends in the port authority and ask them to help out."

"Good thinking, Cupcake."

The corner of my mouth lifted. "You know when you end a compliment with that nickname it becomes backhanded, right?"

"Only if you choose to believe I call you Cupcake as an insult."

I tilted my head. "It's not?"

He shrugged and shot me a slow smile. "Maybe it was in the beginning. When you showed up on your first day in that short skirt and those fucking pearls."

I slapped his arm. "Shut up! I didn't know."

He laughed, and it totally transformed his face. With his stubble and overtly masculine angles, he usually looked like he was searching for an ass to kick. But when he laughed, he looked...approachable? No, that was too tame. *Doable*, a voice in the back of my head whispered.

Whatever he saw on my face made his laughter drift away. "Hey, Prospero?"

"Yeah?"

"You ever have that date?"

The question was so unexpected it slapped me out of my trance. "What—with Hart?"

"Yeah."

I swallowed some beer. "Uh-huh."

He nodded, but his face showed no sign of that smile anymore. "Oh."

The silent question hung between us like smoke. *Are you going to see him again?*

I looked away. "It, uh—didn't go so well."

"No?" His tone was casual, but I thought I heard a note of hope buried in that one syllable as well.

I shook my head. "Turns out he only asked me out because he thought it would be fun to slum it."

The air shifted in the room. The careful casualness of his posture and tone disappeared, and he practically crackled with anger. "What the fuck?"

I looked at him. "It's no big deal."

"He actually said that shit to you? That he was slumming?" He gripped his beer bottle so hard his knuckles turned white.

"Not in so many words, but he did say he usually dates polite, educated women. Thought dating a cop would be exciting."

"Jesus, Kate, is he still walking?"

A shocked laugh escaped me. "What?"

"I'm just saying, I wouldn't put it past you to show him a little excitement in the form of a couple broken bones."

I chuckled again. "Believe it or not, I don't always manhandle my dates."

He cocked a brow. "That's too bad."

Heat rose up my neck at the innuendo. "Not the ones who can't defend themselves anyway. I doubt Brad Hart's ever gotten into a fistfight."

He leaned closer a fraction. "Is that what you like—" His deep voice pitched lower. "—a man who can fight?"

The heat in my neck rushed further south. I licked my lips to buy some time to recover, but those two brown eyes that missed nothing watched the movement with keen interest. "Uh."

The corner of his mouth turned up. "I think you do. Maybe you convinced yourself you wanted a brainy guy, but once you had one you realized you like someone a little more . . . physical."

Lord Jesus. I squirmed on the cushion. "Morales—"

The kiss came out of nowhere. I'm not even sure who moved first. But one second we were arm's length away, and the next my back was back up against the cushions and Morales was pressed to my front.

His scent surrounded me—the clean smell of soap, the hot tang of lust. My mouth tasted the flavor of beer and arousal his lips. Calluses on his hands scratched the delicate skin of my inner arms. The heat of his skin burned my fingers as they dug into the nape of his neck.

The first thrust of his tongue forced a blood flow into regions that had been starved of sensation for too long. His hands possessed every inch of skin they touched, like he was branding me.

After months of antagonistic flirting and denial and dancing around each other, this first kiss was wild, unrestrained. Not polite. Exactly what I'd hoped it would be. Morales was a force of nature. He wasn't too rough, but he wasn't gentle, either. He didn't hesitate like he was worried I might change my mind. He was a man with his mind on conquest and I was the enthusiastic prize.

He pulled away, dragging his lips across my cheek to speak in my ear. "Come on." His voice was filled with gravel and heat. He took my hand and pulled me, dazed, from the couch.

After being surrounded by his hot skin, the shock of cold air shook me from my aroused haze. "Wait." I pulled on the hand tugging me toward his bed.

He raised a brow. The color was high on his cheeks, and his lips were wet and swollen from kissing me. He was sin incarnate and I suddenly felt like Eve being offered a very juicy apple.

My body wanted him. But my mind had reservations.

"Don't think, Cupcake." He pulled again, but I resisted.

My gut twisted with indecision. It had been close to two years since I'd slept with anyone. Add to that spending the last six months stuck in close quarters with the extremely hot man currently urging me toward his bed, and I felt ready to combust. But that twist in the gut? It was fear—the only emotion more powerful than lust.

"This is a bad idea," I said. "A really, really bad idea."

He stepped closer. "Being bad is really good. And I promise you, it will be good. Very good."

And that was the problem. Men like Morales? They didn't play to win, they played to conquer. If I allowed those hot hands on me again, he'd make me forget all my good intentions.

I stepped back and held up my hands to ward off his advance. "I'm not the slut." The words rushed out before I knew they were coming.

He froze. Confusion passed over his flushed face. A beat passed and that confusion morphed into anger. "Jesus, Kate, I've been waiting for this for months. I know you're not easy."

"No," I said in an exasperated tone. "Look, it's something one of my sergeants said in the academy."

He narrowed his eyes and crossed his arms, as if he was barely restraining himself from grabbing me again and shutting me up with his mouth. "The academy."

I swallowed. "She said if you want to make it in law enforcement as a woman, you have to be a lesbian"—although she'd used more colorful terminology—"a slut, or a bitch."

He frowned and ran a hand through his hair. "Are you telling me you like girls?" he asked in an incredulous tone. "Because I gotta call bullshit on that after the way you just kissed me, Cupcake."

I shook my head, knowing I was fucking this up. "No, it's just—I never sleep around with other cops. It's too easy to get labeled the precinct slut and then no one takes you seriously unless you're willing to drop to your knees."

"Christ," he muttered, "I think I'm insulted that you're lumping me in with the kind of assholes who see female colleagues that way. I've worked with you for months, Kate. Have I ever once acted like I thought you weren't capable?"

I shook my head. "No, but—"

He held up a hand. "Have I ever acted like I felt handicapped by being partnered with a female cop?"

"No, but that's not the point."

"It is the fucking point." His voice rose. "You know what your problem is?"

I pressed my lips together. "I'm sure you'll tell me."

"You got a chip on your shoulder that makes the Rock of Gibraltar look like a pebble. I asked you on a date months ago. You remember that?"

I nodded jerkily.

"I waited patiently for you to make your move, but you're so tied up in that head of yours that you won't let yourself have anything good."

My back stiffened. "Don't psychoanalyze me. Is it so hard to believe that I wouldn't want to complicate our working relationship by fucking you?"

He sucked in a long, frustrated breath and released it before answering. When he did, he sounded tired. "Is it so hard for you to believe that I'm interested in more than just fucking you?"

"Yes!" I yelled before I realized what I was saying. His eyes instantly softened and he stepped forward. Shame washed through me and I backed away from his touch. He'd hit the nail on the head. I'd known for a long time that Morales was interested in more than being my fuck buddy. That's what really scared me about him. Because a man like Morales didn't screw around—he possessed. And what frightened me the most was that part of me wanted him to.

"Kate—"

I shook my head and drew a cleansing breath into my tight lungs. "It doesn't matter. I told you—I don't sleep with my partners. I'm sorry if you can't deal with that, but that's not my problem."

The tenderness on his face disappeared just like I'd hoped it would. That razor-sharp brow arched. "Well, you certainly got the bitchy cop role down to a T, sweetheart."

His words stung like a slap. Emotion gathered like a low pressure system in my chest. I had to get the fuck out of there before the storm broke. I turned and gathered my files in a haphazard mess.

"Kate," he said.

I shook my head and hurried toward the door.

"Hold on a minute." The sound of him storming across the room reached me as my hand grabbed the knob. "Stop!"

I made the mistake of looking back over my shoulder. He looked confused and sorry and determined all in one. But I felt too shitty and scared and sad to let him convince me to stay. "I'm sorry."

With that, I made my escape, running from the door like a woman with demons on her tail. It wasn't until I was safely inside Sybil that I realized he didn't try to follow me. And that made me feel shittiest of all.

Chapter Twenty-Seven

The next morning I ran from my car toward the front doors of the school. Banks of snow lined either side of the sidewalk. Snow clouds overhead dampened sound; the only noise was my breathing, the clank of the flag's hook against the pole, and the squawk of a crow in a nearby tree. The bird's beady eyes tracked my progress toward the school.

I punched the buzzer at the front door. A voice crackled over the speaker, "Can I help you?" Memory rose of another voice coming through a different speaker the day Harry Bane had been beaten. I had a bad feeling this time I'd be the one walking away feeling like I had my ass kicked.

"It's Kate Prospero," I said.

"Oh," the voice said. "Come in."

A loud click accompanied the door's lock opening. I pulled open the massive door and rushed into the two-story foyer.

The scent of old wood, young pheromones, and industrial floor cleaner hit me. Classes were in session and the sound of teachers' voices filtered into the large space like the voices of overeducated ghosts. I walked into the office, where a woman wearing a red twinset and glasses sat behind a massive desk.

"Miss Prospero," she said. The tone reminded me of the one my old teachers in school would employ when I got out of line. I stood straighter, reminding myself I wasn't the one in trouble here. "They're waiting for you in Principal Anderson's office." She pointed down the hall.

"Thanks." I scooted around the desk and started down the long wooden hallway. With each step the wood announced my advance. Too late to turn around. Too late to stop to collect myself.

The call had come in when I was driving to meet Morales at the docks. I'd had to execute an illegal U-turn and figure out how to let my partner know I'd be late without having to actually talk to him. In the end, I'd called Shadi and told her what was going on at the school. She offered to go meet Morales at the docks. I felt bad asking her to fill in, but she'd sounded relieved to have something to do besides watch Puck's apartment. I knew I'd have to talk to Morales eventually, but I needed some time for the embarrassment to wear off and also to figure out how to play the fallout from our argument the night before.

The door to the principal's office was open. Inside, my little brother slouched in a chair. Brad Hart sat next to him. When I walked in, he looked up with a hard look on his face. I tilted my head in question, but he looked away as if he couldn't stand the sight of me.

"Detective Prospero." Principal Anderson stood and came around to shake my hand. "Thank you for coming. I hope we didn't pull you off an important case." He motioned to the third seat, which sat empty. I noted a slight mocking tone to his comment.

"All my cases are important, but not as important as Danny." I looked at my brother. "You all right?"

He looked up. His left eye was swollen shut. I clenched my jaw and shot an accusing look at the principal. "What happened to him?"

Anderson raised his hands for patience. "If you'll sit we can discuss it in a calm manner." He'd clearly already labeled me a hothead he needed to manage.

"Where is Pen?" I asked. As the school's counselor, she was normally called in when kids got in trouble serious enough to require a visit to the principal.

"We felt she would be unable to be impartial, all things considered," Hart said. "That's why I'm here instead."

I bit my tongue instead of asking him if he'd be able to be impartial. I hadn't spoken to him since our ill-fated date, but I was pretty sure the assholish smirk on his face meant he was still pissed. But since I hadn't told Danny about the date, and I was pretty sure admitting it in front of Anderson wouldn't do anything to endear me to the man, I kept my mouth shut about Hart's presence.

I sat slowly and scooted my chair closer to Danny. "Go on."

"It seems Danny and another student got into a bit of an argument this morning before the bell rang."

"It certainly appears so." I shot a significant look at the wounds on the kid's face. "Where are the other boy's parents?"

"At the hospital with their son," Hart said.

My head swiveled to look at him. "What?"

"Danny, why don't you tell your sister what you did to your friend?"

"He's not my friend," my brother growled. "He's an asshole."

241

"Watch your mouth, son," Anderson snapped.

Danny crossed his arms. "Fine, but he's still a bully."

The principal raised a challenging brow. "If that's true why is he the one in the hospital?"

I held up a hand. "Who is the other boy?"

"I'm not at liberty to share the other party's name."

"Forgive me, but how am I supposed to understand what happened if I don't know who all was involved?"

"It was Pierce Rebis," Danny said before the principal could brush me off again.

I closed my eyes and cursed silently to myself. When I opened them again, I caught a look pass between Hart and Anderson.

"Can someone please tell me what the hell—" The principal shot me a sharp frown. "Excuse me, can someone tell me what the heck happened?"

"I'll tell you," Hart said. "Pierce picked on Danny, and your brother retaliated by ambushing Pierce with a dirty magic potion."

My stomach plummeted, as if someone had pushed it off the Bessemer Bridge. "Danny?" I whispered because I didn't trust myself not to scream.

He wouldn't look at me. "Wasn't dirty," he said. "It was clean." He looked up then, his eyes like those of a wounded animal. "I swear, Katie."

I spoke low and slow so as not to yell. "What kind of potion?"

Danny's gaze dropped again. I looked at Hart and then the principal, hoping someone would tell me. Finally, Hart said, "It made all of the boy's hair fall out."

I bit my lip.

"I fail to understand what is so amusing, Detective."

"Forgive me, you're right." I cleared my throat. "Danny

shouldn't have retaliated like that, but I don't really understand why it was allowed to escalate like this."

Anderson frowned. "What do you mean?"

"A couple of days ago Danny came home with a bruise on his face. When I questioned him, he said he'd intervened when Pierce was harassing another student. He said Mr. Hart witnessed Pierce punching him and broke it up." I turned to look at Hart. "So I'll ask my question again, why wasn't this matter dealt with before it escalated?"

Hart's expression stayed the same but two spots of red appeared on his cheekbones. "At the time, I thought it was just two boys getting hot under the collar. No real harm done."

A mocking laugh escaped my lips. "Clearly." I pointed to Danny's black eye.

"Detective Prospero, if you had concerns at the time, you should have come to me," Anderson said.

"Why is it on me—or Danny for that matter—to demand that Pierce Rebis be held to the same rules as everyone else?"

"You're assuming your little brother told you the full story about what happened that day," Hart said. "When I walked out and saw the pair, Danny pushed Pierce first. He's hardly the innocent you're painting him to be."

I waved a hand. "Regardless, you knew there was an issue yet I received no call and the boys weren't dealt with then. And now you're putting all the responsibility at Danny's feet when clearly this was not a one-sided thing."

The principal adjusted himself in the chair. "As for today's events, we don't have any witnesses willing to corroborate Danny's story that Pierce hit him first, but several went on record to say they saw Danny attack Rebis with the potion."

My eyes narrowed. With deliberate calm, I said, "I just bet."

"Excuse me?"

"I just find it interesting that everyone's backing the wealthy Mundane kid and no one's taking the side of the middle-class Adept."

"Detective, I understand that in your line of work the lines between Mundane and Adept are stark, but we do not tolerate that kind of prejudice at Meadowlake."

I snorted and crossed my arms.

"Luna was there," Danny said. "She saw Rebis punch me."

I looked at the principal for reaction. He shuffled some papers on his desk. "That's true. Luna did stand up for you. But you two are dating, correct? She's hardly an impartial witness."

"All right," I said, "this isn't productive. What's going to happen next?"

Hart leaned forward to look at me. "Well, he's out of DUDE, that's for sure."

I tilted my head and stared at him with a look that made him pull back.

The principal cleared his throat. "I've talked to Mr. Rebis and he said they wouldn't press charges—"

"Generous of him, but I'm not so sure we won't be pressing some of our own."

Danny looked at me, as if shocked to hear me taking his side. I shot him a look to remind him we'd be having our own reckoning once we got home.

"—as long as Daniel is never allowed to step foot on school property again," Anderson finished.

My mouth dropped. "You're expelling him?"

"My hands are tied, Detective. We can't have students hexing each other with potions every time they have a disagreement."

"But it's fine to have them punch each other?" Danny asked.

"Danny," I snapped.

"Sorry," he grumbled.

I rose, grabbing my coat from the chair. "I could fight this," I said. "But I have no interest in subjecting Danny to an environment that is so hostile to Adepts and so permissive to whomever has the biggest bank account."

"Detective, forgive me, but given your history and profession," Hart began, "it's hardly a surprise that your little brother is acting out."

"Excuse me?"

"Even if this incident hadn't happened, I was planning on calling you to have a discussion about your decision to allow Danny to take magic lessons from a wizard."

"First of all, the wizard you're talking about graduated from the most prestigious Arcane university in the country, and works for the government to create legal, clean potions in an effort to stop major crimes. He's hardly a street-level criminal as your tone implied." I leaned forward. "And as for Danny following in my footsteps? There are worse paths, Mr. Hart. I might have come from a rough past, but I've worked like hell to provide a better life for this kid. And I won't sit here and be insulted by a couple of pretentious assholes who've never known a hard day's work in their goddamned lives."

"Careful, Detective," Hart said, "your persecution complex is showing."

"Like you're some saint," I said. His eyes narrowed at my shot about his past with addiction.

"I'm not the one who taught him how to use magic like a weapon."

I snapped my mouth shut because I didn't have a defense against that—not that they'd listen to one even if I had it. "You will keep this off his record or you will hear from my lawyer. I won't have this miscarriage ruin his chances for getting an education elsewhere."

"Fine. We just want him gone."

"Let's go, Danny." I grabbed his arm and jerked him out of his chair. "Do you have all your stuff?"

"I got some stuff in my locker."

"We'll send it on with Miss Griffin," Principal Anderson said. Obviously they couldn't stand to have us taint their precious school any longer than necessary.

Before we walked out the door, Hart called my name. I pushed Danny through the door ahead of me before I turned to look at the man who a couple of days earlier had tried to get in my pants. "Do the kid a favor and get him in counseling."

I looked him in the eye. "Go fuck yourself, you self-righteous prick."

Chapter Twenty-Eight

M ez was waiting in his car when we pulled up to the house. Pen had caught us on our way out of the school and followed us home. All four of us were silent as we filed into the house.

Danny's shoulders drooped like he was being led to his execution. Pen's face was tense, which wasn't a surprise given the weird position the situation had put her in. But it was Mez who had me worried. In the all the months I'd belonged to the task force, I'd never seen the wizard angry. Annoyed, sure. Frustrated and grumpy, yes. But the twin spots of red on his cheeks, the muscle working in his jaw, and the way his hands clenched made him resemble a winter storm roaring in off Lake Erie.

As for me, well, I guess I was in shock. The indignation I'd felt in the principal's office had dissolved into a sort of detached disbelief. The situation had deteriorated so rapidly, I'd felt like I'd been blindsided—especially by Hart's refusal to stand up for Danny.

Even though our date had been a disaster, I'd thought the guy genuinely liked my kid brother. But I guess when it came down to it, Hart was as vulnerable to the pressures of the class system as anyone.

I leaned back against the sink and crossed my arms. Pen sat next to Danny at the table. Her hand rubbed his back in sympathy. But Mez paced back and forth between the fridge and the door.

The only blessing was that Baba was volunteering at the community center that morning, so I didn't have to juggle her chaotic energy, too. No doubt she'd have plenty to say once she got home, though.

I opened my mouth to ask if anyone needed anything, but Mez jumped the gun. "I can't believe you," he said. "How many times did I tell you that magic should not be used in anger? How many times did I tell you that if you're going to learn the craft, you have to respect it?"

"Mez," I warned.

"What? You're going to defend him? You of all people should be livid. You didn't even want him to learn magic. Why aren't you screaming?"

I squeezed the bridge of my nose. "Because I know Danny would never have done this without a good reason." I sighed and looked at the kid. "What really happened this morning?"

He shot a glance at Pen. Resentment that he'd look to her for encouragement instead of me rose briefly in my chest. But I squashed it because it wasn't productive or healthy to think like that. Pen herself had taught me that. And right then, she nodded encouragingly to my brother.

"Pierce has been picking on one of my friends for a while—"

"Is that what happened the other day?"

He nodded. "Yeah, after school I walked up on Pierce harassing my friend and I confronted him. We didn't fight exactly, but he punched me and told me if I didn't stay out of it he'd make it even worse on my friend."

Pen and I exchanged a significant glance. We both knew he was talking about Luna, but confronting him about that now would only distract him from telling us the whole story.

"Anyway, she called me last night. She was crying, Kate," he said, his tone angry. "Pierce has been calling and harassing her. Saying he was going to do horrible shit to her."

I glanced at the curse jar I kept on the counter, but didn't say anything. After the day he'd had, the kid deserved to blow off some verbal steam.

"What kind of shit?"

Danny shook his head. "I don't want to repeat it. But it was bad enough that I decided it was time to teach that asshole a lesson."

"Why didn't you come to me?" Pen asked.

Danny raised his chin. "Some things a man has to do for himself."

Mez cleared his throat. "I should have known this was over a girl."

Danny frowned. "Why?"

"Because nothing makes a boy want to become a man faster than a pretty girl."

"It's Luna?" Pen asked quietly.

Danny shook his head too quickly, and the blooms of red on his checks betrayed him further.

"You can tell us the truth," I said. "We're not going to get her in trouble."

He nodded reluctantly. "She wouldn't ever tell me exactly what happened, but I think he did something to her. Something really bad."

My stomach clenched. How was Danny old enough to be in the middle of this kind of bullshit? As much as I'd tried to shield him from the darker sides of life, it looked like life was determined to bring the darkness to him. But underneath that cramp of denial was a warm orb of pride. "I don't approve of using magic for revenge at all," I said in a stern voice that had Danny's shoulders drooping in shame. "But I am proud of you for standing up for your friend." His head came up in surprise. "I mean it. You talked about being a man? Real men stand up for people who can't stand up for themselves even if it means they'll suffer consequences."

"She's right." Mez's earlier anger had mellowed, but his tone was still tight. "You were trying to do the right thing. But you should have come to one of us."

"Why, so Anderson can tell you no one trusts the Adept kid?" Danny's tone was defeated. Couldn't blame him. Some of life's lessons were particularly hard to swallow.

"No," Mez said with a grin, "so I could have helped you make a potion that no one can trace."

A shocked laugh escaped Danny's mouth. Even Pen had to cover her mouth with her hand to hide her amusement.

"I wouldn't go that far," I said. I would, of course, but I had to maintain the illusion of being a good parental influence. "And all things considered, the magic lessons end now."

Danny opened his mouth to argue, but Mez spoke over him. "Agreed." His hard tone shut down the kid's protests. The wizard turned to me. "Kate, I'm so sorry this happened. I know you had reservations about him taking lessons—"

I waved a hand. "This isn't on you. It was Danny's decision to misuse magic. You didn't teach him that."

Danny's head lowered. "I know I screwed up," he said. "I was just so angry!"

"Which is why the first thing I taught you was not to use magic when your emotions are unpredictable," Mez said.

The kid nodded. "You're right."

Pen leaned back with a sigh. "Jesus, Mary, and Jerome—what a mess."

"Is there anything you can do, Pen?" Danny pleaded.

Pen shook her head. "It's out of my hands."

My phone rang into the silence following Pen's statement. I jumped in shock and pulled it from my pocket. It was Morales. I considered not answering, but I knew he'd keep trying until he got me. "Be right back, guys."

I answered on the third ring. "Hey."

"Where are you?" No hello. He was pissed.

"At home."

"Shadi said you were going to the school."

I sighed. "Danny got expelled. We just got here."

"Shit," he muttered. "What happened?"

"It's too long to get into now," I said. Normally I would have filled him in, but given the weird limbo following our argument I wasn't sure I was ready to confide in him about anything. "Are you at the docks?"

A beat of silence followed my question. "Yeah. Nothing yet, but there's a lot of territory to cover."

"Sorry I'm not there to help."

"Don't worry about it." His tone was aloof, distant. "Anyway, I was calling to see if you heard from Gardner this morning."

I frowned. "No, why?"

"She wasn't at the gym this morning when I checked in and she hasn't returned my calls."

"Hold on, I'll ask Mez."

"Mez is at your house?"

"Yeah." I didn't explain because it would take too long. Besides, I didn't owe Morales an explanation for everything. I walked to the doorway and covered the phone. "Hey, Mez?"

He looked up from where he and Pen were talking quietly. Danny had reverted to sullen silence with his arms crossed and his chin tucked. "What's up?" the wizard asked.

"You heard from the boss today?"

He shook his head. "Why? Is something the matter?"

I shook my head. "Not sure yet. She hasn't checked in with Morales." I lifted the phone to my ear and told Morales what Mez had said.

"Shit. All right. Let me know if you hear from her, okay?"

"Yep."

"Should I assume you're in family-crisis mode for the rest of the day?"

"Pretty much, yeah."

"Is everything okay?" His tone had changed from distant to concerned.

I paused, unsure whether he was asking about Danny or about us. "It will be," I said, because it covered both circumstances.

"All right," he said. "Tell Mez to come pitch in once he's done at your place."

With that he clicked off without saying good-bye. I pulled the phone from my ear and watched it for a moment. A low curse escaped my lips. How had everything gotten so fucked up?

"Kate?" Mez said, coming to the door. When I looked up, he continued. "Everything okay with Morales?"

I briefly told him about the conversation. "I'm worried about

Gardner," I said. "Last night I found her in your lab cooking something."

He frowned. "Really? When I got in this morning, nothing looked out of place."

"She asked me not to tell anyone, but considering she's not returning any calls, I'm worried she's done something stupid."

"Maybe she just needs some time alone. This case has brought up a lot of shit she thought was behind her, you know?" He looked so confident that I grabbed on to it and borrowed some of it for myself.

"I guess you're right," I said. "Still, I'd feel better if she checked in."

"I'm about to head out. I'll swing by the gym. She might have her ringer off or something and didn't see the calls. After that, I'll go meet the others at the docks and pitch in on the search."

I nodded and blew out a breath. "Thanks, Mez."

I glanced over toward the table where my crestfallen brother and my best friend sat side by side. I had a feeling while Mez, Morales, and Shadi were tracking down the bad guy, I'd have my hands full trying to figure out where to send Danny to school now.

"Let us worry about Souza and Gardner." Mez put a hand on my shoulder. "You just worry about keeping things tight here. We'll call if anything changes."

Chapter Twenty-Nine

Late the next morning Morales and I were on our way to Gardner's place. After not hearing from her all night, the entire team had gone into emergency mode. Shadi and Mez were manning the phones at the gym, but thus far none of Gardner's contacts had seen her. Morales had stopped by Gardner's apartment the night before, but no one had answered. We were headed back there in the hopes any evidence or signs of struggle would be easier to find in the daylight.

"So did you ground him?" Morales asked.

I sighed and shook my head. "No. I mean, don't get me wrong, I wasn't happy about him using magic for revenge like that, but in the end he was trying to defend the girl."

"Have you talked to her?"

I shook my head. I'd filled him in on the Luna situation because I knew he'd keep it quiet. "Pen thought that pressure from me might ruin any chance of Luna coming forward to implicate Pierce."

"Do you know her parents?"

"It's just the mom. I've seen her at a couple of school events. According to Danny she's a Mundane and doesn't allow Luna any contact with magic."

"Sounds familiar," Morales said.

I raised a brow. "Yeah, and look at what coming around on that topic has led to."

He reached across the center console and squeezed my hand. "For what it's worth, I still think you made the right call there."

I looked down at the connection. He withdrew his hand quickly, as if belatedly realizing his mistake. "Thanks, but he won't be cooking again for the foreseeable future."

His support meant a lot to me even though it was unexpected. Ever since he'd called that morning to tell me to come to the gym for a meeting before we headed out to look for Gardner, I'd been bracing myself for The Talk. But so far, he'd been acting totally natural, as if the drama a couple of nights earlier never happened. And for that, I was more grateful than I'd been for his support of my parenting decisions.

He shot me a look at my sudden silence and cleared his throat. "Anyway, what's next?"

I shook my head. "I'll have to find him a different school. Probably public."

The previous afternoon I'd spent a couple of hours on the phone trying to figure out how to transfer him to our neighborhood public high school.

"Aren't there other private schools?"

I nodded. "But I was receiving a hefty discount at Meadowlake because of Pen. Not sure I could afford any of the other schools. Plus, I'm pretty sure we'll run into this sort of thing at most of the private schools in town since most are Mundane-dominant."

He nodded and we both fell silent, watching the buildings of the Cauldron give way to the Bessemer Bridge. The spot where Grace Cho's body had been found now had a bunch of flowers and candles set out in memorial. "I have to tell you something," I said.

"What's up?"

"The other night I walked in on Gardner cooking."

He glanced over. "Which night?"

"Two nights ago." My eyes lowered at the unintentional reminder of the night of the kiss. Regardless, he made the connection and shot me a look questioning how that was possible when I'd been at his place. "Before I went to your place."

"Why didn't you tell me this then?"

"I told you she was acting off, but you said she was just upset. I figured I was overreacting."

A muscle in his jaw worked. "What kind of potion was it?"

I shook my head. "I couldn't tell exactly."

He raised a brow. "But you have a theory, right?"

I pressed my lips together, cursing him silently for knowing me that well. "Like I said, there was no way to be certain, but there were a few herbs that are common in a potion to enhance psychic powers or induce prophetic dreams." I looked up. "The kind that might help a person locate an enemy."

His hands gripped the wheel tighter. I couldn't help but worry he was wishing it had been my neck. "Let me see if I understand. You saw Gardner cooking a potion to locate an enemy, and you didn't think to tell me about it until after she's been missing for hours?" His tone was low and mean. When Morales got angry he didn't shout—he seethed. "What the fuck, Kate?"

"I told Mez." Judging from the anger flaming behind his

eyes, it had been the wrong thing to say. I rushed forward. "But either way, I didn't think she'd be dumb enough to actually go through with it."

He made a disgusted sound, but some of his anger drained from his posture. "You're right. She's not that reckless." He sounded as if he was trying to convince himself more than me.

"But as much as I hate to say it, after she lost her last team to the bastard I'm pretty sure she'd do anything she could to save us from meeting the same fate."

He didn't respond, but a muscle in his jaw started clenching like a fist. The SUV turned in to a modest apartment building, which was little more than a large gray rectangle with no adornments of any kind. No balconies, no shutters, no hedges or flower boxes.

Morales pulled his car into a space near the far end of the building.

"Which unit is it?" I asked.

He got out of the car before answering. I joined him in front of the building. He took so long to answer I worried he'd decided to just stop talking to me. "Morales?"

"Top floor, corner." He pointed toward the unit on the top right-hand corner of the building. "When I came by last night the place was totally dark."

He started toward a set of metal stairs leading to the second floor. I followed him more slowly, and took the opportunity to scan the building and area for signs of anything suspicious. I was so focused on my task, I didn't see him paused on the third step until I slammed into his back. "Damn, sorry," I said, catching myself before I fell.

Without a word, he turned to the side and backed against the wall to the right of the steps. I looked up at him, confused, but then he pointed to the fifth step.

The smear wasn't large but it was definitely blood. "Shit," I gasped.

My gaze climbed the rest of the steps and saw several more drops of blood leading up to the landing.

"They're dry," he said. "Missed them last night because it was dark because the damned exterior lights were out." Regret made his tone gritty.

I sucked in a breath to try to tamp down the spurt of panic that climbed from my stomach into my throat. "It may not be hers. Gardner is a fighter. If someone came after her, they wouldn't walk away without an injury."

He didn't answer me. Instead, he took the rest of the steps two at a time, careful not to touch any of the bloodstains as he went. At the top of the staircase, he pulled something out of his jacket.

By the time I reached him, he had his shoulder bent over the doorknob. "What are you doing?" I whispered.

"Letting myself in. Cover me."

I stepped in front of him, which gave me a view of his face. His expression was determined and grim, almost as if he expected to walk in and find Gardner's body inside. But something in my gut told me we wouldn't find her there. Whatever was going on, it wouldn't be as easy as Pantera killing Gardner and leaving her body for us to find. Fast, easy deaths weren't his style, for one thing. For another, no matter how I tried to look at it, I couldn't figure out what he would gain from her death.

Before I could voice any of these theories to my partner, he popped the lock and the door opened. Yet another reason I didn't think Gardner was inside. Why would Souza lock the door on his way out?

Morales stood on the threshold. He held his breath and

stared into the dark room beyond. I could practically hear the argument in his head. Instead of telling him to relax, I pushed past him into the room. "Wait—"

Ignoring him, I continued inside. As I went, I pulled my weapon from my waistband. The room smelled like spent ozone and dirty copper. Light streamed through the windows and highlighted the bloodstains on the cream carpet.

This time Morales slammed into my back. His hands came up automatically to steady my shoulders. When I didn't react, his eyes must have followed my gaze. "Fuck."

I turned quickly. His face had morphed into a mask of rage. "Drew, listen to me," I said, grabbing his shoulder with my right hand. "She's not here. We have to see that as a positive."

His eyes looked over my shoulder toward the bloodstain. I grabbed his chin and forced him to look at me. "She is still alive. As long as we keep it together she has a chance."

He swallowed hard, as if trying to get control of his temper. Finally, he nodded. "Clear the rest of the residence."

Hearing him switch back into mission mode helped ease some of my own tension. I gripped my gun with both hands again and began to clear the place room by room. As I moved through the motions of checking closets and bathrooms for unfriendlies, I took stock of Gardner's home. I'd never been to her place before, and exploring it felt like an invasion. The living room had a simple but elegant sofa and a single armchair with a reading lamp. There was no TV. The room had plain white walls with no artwork. No plants added life to the spot. On the table in front of the couch lay journals focused on the academic sides of police work. At some point during my time on the team, Morales had mentioned that Gardner had started working toward her PhD in criminal justice. Looked like she spent her free time studying.

The kitchen counters were empty, as was the sink. Not a dirty fork or coffee-stained cup to be found. In fact, the only room in the place that had any personality was her bedroom. Unlike the monastic furnishings of the other rooms, the bed had a wrought-iron canopy and a deep-purple-velvet bedspread. The walls were covered in pen-and-ink sketches of entwined nude bodies—lovers. I cringed inwardly knowing I'd entered her private sanctuary; it felt like having an uninvited peek beneath the no-nonsense facade she wore like armor.

I moved beyond the bed and looked into the walk-in closet. All of Gardner's suits were lined up like soldiers on the rods. Even though everything was in neutral hues, she'd sorted them by color and her shoes beneath were arranged by heel height. There were shelves at the front that were filled with neatly folded shirts, but I didn't see one T-shirt or pair of jeans anywhere.

"Prospero?" Morales called.

I left the closet and went to join in him in the second bedroom. "All clear," I said from the doorway. He was standing behind a simple wooden desk. The top was covered in stacks of files and books. It looked a lot like her desk at the gym. Still, Morales stared down at it like he'd found a smoking gun on the surface. "What's up?"

"C'mere."

I went to join him. In the center of the desk, a file folder was open. Lying across it was a picture of Gardner's old team, and next to that was a half-empty bottle of Scotch. "Looks like someone was walking down Memory Lane."

I frowned. "I don't get any of this. She was planning on finding Souza. So why the blood?"

"Maybe he found her first."

A loud vibrating sound came from the desk. The noise made

me flinch, but Morales just leaned over and fished a cell phone from under the open file folder.

"Is that Gardner's?" I asked.

He nodded and held up the screen for me to read. The call was coming from an unknown number. He punched the button to answer the call on speaker. Neither of us spoke, and for a moment the line just crackled.

"Morales." Hearing my partner's name said with a Brazilian accent made a chill crawl up my spine.

"Who wants to know?"

"Don't play games. Trust that Gardner doesn't have time for them."

"Get to talking, then, since you called me."

The phone beeped to indicate an incoming text. "I just sent you a present."

Morales looked up at me, and I nodded. My stomach twisted with nausea. I didn't want to see any picture an *A Morte* hit man would send, but at that point he was calling the shots. Morales licked his lips and hit the button to display the image.

I put hand over my mouth to hold in my gasp. Morales's knuckles turned white on the phone. I used my left hand to grab his right. He squeezed it back but wouldn't look at me.

Inside a darkened room, a spotlight glared at Gardner's face. Both eyes were open, but the left was a mere slit tucked into a bruise. Her sight was clear and shooting bullets at the person taking the picture. A dark bruise marred the right side of her mouth, and a trickle of bright-red blood dripped from the corner to her chin. Someone had set a newspaper in her lap to show that morning's date. The image on the front page was John Volos at the press conference two days earlier; the headline read, "Mayor Vows End to Violence."

Morales growled. "I'm going to make you bleed, motherfucker."

Souza's low chuckle oozed out of the speaker. "You'd have to find me first, and that won't happen until I am ready."

"What do you want from us?" I asked. No man sent a picture like that without following it up with a demand.

"Not what, Detective—who."

Morales and I looked at each other. A bitter cocktail of emotions mixed in my gut—frustration, anger, fear. Finally, I said, "Volos."

"Very good, Detective. From what I understand, the mayor has a special affinity for you."

"You can't honestly expect us to hand over the mayor for you to murder," Morales said.

"I expect you to do whatever I say or I will kill Gardner and then come after you. I understand Detective Prospero has a little brother, yes?"

"You son of a bitch."

He clucked his tongue. "You're wasting all of our time. Bring Volos to me and Gardner lives."

"Why are you doing this?" I asked, trying to buy some time.

"You forced my hand after you interrupted me at the junkyard."

"Why did you kill Cho?" Morales snapped.

"I'd hoped her murder would keep you running in circles so I could get to my real target. But once again you proved inconveniently clever. So I decided to do the only thing that would ensure you would bring Volos to me."

"How can we trust that she'll be alive when we get there?" Morales asked. I flashed him a look—was he really considering capitulating? He avoided my gaze.

"Despite her vocal hatred of me because of the actions of my cartel, I have no beef with your boss. But I will not hesitate to kill her if you try to screw me. You have until six o'clock. When I call again, I expect you to have him in custody and ready to hand over. Or Gardner dies."

The call went dead.

Morales dropped the phone onto the carpet. Instead of speaking, he pivoted and punched a fist through the wall. I didn't bother trying to calm him down. I wasn't feeling so tranquil myself. While Morales took his anger out on the wall, my heart was trying to pound its way through my ribs. I ran a hand through my hair and tried to push down the surge of adrenaline. We didn't have much time and I needed cold clarity to guide us, not hot tempers.

"Morales," I said.

He pulled his knuckles from the ruined drywall and shook off the dust. "What?"

"We have two choices."

He paused and looked at me. "You heard Souza—we don't have any choice at all. If we want to save Gardner, we have to hand him Volos."

I shook my head. "What if we find him first?"

"Kate, we spent most of the day yesterday combing the docks with no sign of Pantera. Face it, he's got every advantage here."

"So, what? We're supposed to just hand the fucking mayor over to Souza to murder?"

"Yes." There was no doubt in Morales's expression. "Yes, we fucking hand over the mayor. He's the reason Pantera Souza is here to begin with, remember? We hand him over and in the process rid this city of two menaces."

I crossed my arms. "Assuming I'd willingly do that, which isn't too fucking likely, Ace, there's no way you could get close to Volos right now. Ever since Cho's death his team has circled the wagons. He's got a posse around him twenty-four seven."

"You're right. I can't get near him." He looked me in the eye. "But you could."

I snorted. "That's bullshit."

He popped a brow. "Really? Has he ever denied you anything, Kate?"

"He's refused every demand I've made that he leave me the fuck alone," I said, exasperation adding an edge to my tone.

"Exactly. He won't leave you alone because he can't. Don't you get it? He's still in love with you, Cupcake."

The words bounced off my brain. They were just sounds, really. Ones that made no sense to me. "What the hell are you talking about? Volos doesn't love me. He's done nothing but blackmail me, manipulate me, and be a general pain in my ass for the last six months."

Morales crossed his arms. "Don't kid yourself, sweetheart. The man's got it bad for you."

I blinked and shook my head. "Look, you're wrong. The only person John Volos loves is John Volos."

He shrugged. "You want to be in denial? Fine by me. But the fact remains that you're the only person who can get close to him right now. We just have to figure out how to use it."

Even as my brain tried to reject the words, an idea formed. Unfortunately, if we acted on it, it would make me no better than Volos. It was deceitful, dangerous, and damned if it wasn't the perfect solution to our problems.

I'd gone very still as I grappled with my own conscience.

"What's going on in that head?"

I looked up and cringed. "I think I know what to do. It's

illegal as hell but it might be the only way to ensure both Gardner and Volos walk away from this alive."

Both brows rose. "I'm all ears."

I glanced at my watch. It was already after eleven. "I'll tell you in the car, but first I need to make a call. Let's go."

Chapter Thirty

The SUV idled half a block from our destination. "I really wish we had time to recon this," Morales said. "If things go pear-shaped, we're toast."

I put down my binoculars, which had basically been useless since the midday glare of the windows prevented seeing inside the restaurant. "If wishes were horses, poor men would ride."

"Huh?"

I shook my head. "It's just something my mom used to say." I cleared my throat. "Anyway, I don't love doing this, either, but neither of us has been able to come up with an alternative that doesn't end with someone dying."

A deep sigh heaved from his chest. "All right, let's get you wired."

A call to the mayor's office revealed that Volos was having a lunch meeting at this bistro, which was a couple of blocks from City Hall. I hadn't met any of the members of his security detail directly, but I knew that a few of them were old BPD officers, as well as a few security guys from his company, Volos Real Estate Development. But I wasn't worried about them. Whether or not Morales was right about Volos's feelings for me, the fact remained that the man always seemed to have time for me.

My second call after locating Volos had been to Mez. Luckily he'd been at the gym so we could swing by, pick up what we needed, and give him and Shadi instructions. Morales grabbed the ampoule we'd gotten from Mez and exited the car to go open the rear door. I followed him and hopped onto the bumper.

We were parked at the mouth of an alley, and behind us were nothing but trash cans and hungry pigeons. The privacy was a blessing, since Morales was strapping a wire to my chest. If any of the mayor's security detail looked out the window, seeing that going down would have sunk us before we had a chance to get started. I had to lift my shirt to give him access, but I didn't bother being self-conscious. Ever since that morning, we'd both done a decent job of pretending the kiss and the fight that followed had never happened. I guess that was the one good thing about Gardner's disappearance—it gave us the perfect excuse for denial. And even if I had the energy or interest to act like a chick about showing Morales my bra, he didn't seem to notice. He'd been as focused as a heat-seeking missile ever since the call with the murderous shaman.

Once the wire was in place, Morales handed me the ampoule. Mez hadn't balked or acted shocked when we told him our plan. He just warned us not too use too much of the potion or it might stop Volos's heart.

"Don't tempt me" was all Morales had said.

267

When we'd gotten in the car after leaving Gardner's, Morales had vented for a good five minutes about how the entire mess was Volos's fault. While I wasn't exactly an apologist for our new mayor, I wasn't ready to sacrifice his life, either. Not to say my motives in this operation were pure. A small, dark part of me relished the idea of turning the tables on the man who'd repeatedly tricked and blackmailed me. I'd do everything I could to ensure he survived this operation, but by the time it was over he was going to think twice about trying to screw me over again.

"You ready?" Morales asked.

I took a deep breath, held it for a moment, and released it in a rush. "Yeah."

As if he couldn't help himself, he touched my cheek. "Be careful." I felt the bass of his voice somewhere below my breastbone. He held my gaze, daring me to pull away. Instead, I met his stare directly.

"Piece of cake," I said carelessly. Then I pulled away as gently as possible so as to lessen the rejection and checked the ampoule in my pocket.

He was silent for a moment, but I could feel the heat of his gaze. Finally, he sighed. "Remember, it only takes a couple of drops. We don't want him out for long."

Something hard formed in my gut. I looked into Morales's eyes. "I got it." I couldn't keep the snap out of my words.

He held up his hands. "All right," he said slowly. "Let's get this over with. You want to explain to me why you're mad at me?"

I jerked my hair back over my shoulder. "I'm not mad."

He sat back and crossed his arms, daring me to lie to him again.

I sighed. "I'm not mad," I repeated. With another sigh, I continued. "I'm embarrassed."

He frowned. "Why?"

I looked at him. "Um, because I freaked the fuck out the other night."

He blew out a breath. "Look, you shouldn't feel embarrassed. I get it."

"What?"

He smirked. "I scare the shit out of you."

My mouth dropped open. "No, you don't. I just need some time."

"Kate," he said, "please."

"Egotistical ass," I muttered. "Only you would read a rejection as me being intimidated by your awesomeness."

"Look, Cupcake, like it or not, there's business between us. You're not ready to deal with it?" He shrugged. "Fine. But understand that I won't be forcing the issue again. When you're ready you can come to me, and then I can decide whether or not I should bother."

"Whether or not you should *bother*?" I asked, my voice rising. "You're a real piece of work, Macho."

"Pot. Kettle. Black, babe."

I huffed out a frustrated breath. "Whatever. I'm going in."

I jumped off the bumper before he could speak and jogged across the street. The movement helped work off some of the residual frustration.

He'll decide if he should bother, my ass.

I rolled my shoulders and tried to focus. Morales's dickishness notwithstanding, I had a job to do. According to Souza, we had only three hours to secure Volos before he called again with instructions. That meant I didn't have time to waste on my infuriating partner. I needed to keep my eyes on the mission.

As I jogged across the street and up a block toward the bistro,

I felt better. Having a goal made my brain focus with laser-like precision. There was no room for worry about interpersonal drama.

As I approached the door, I looked into the large windows out front and spied Volos sitting at a table with a couple of men in suits and his lawyer, Jade. I hadn't anticipated her being there, but I wasn't worried. The story Morales and I had come up with ensured Volos would send everyone away.

Instead of a maître d', there was a security guard in a slick navy suit standing at the front door. Unfazed, I approached the podium.

"May I help you, ma'am?"

"I'm meeting Mayor Volos," I said. I removed my badge from my waistband and flashed it.

He tilted his head and regarded me with suspicion. "The mayor is already in a meeting, Detective."

I smiled and flashed my badge. "Pretty sure he'll see me."

"One moment." He walked toward Volos's table. I leaned an elbow on the podium and watched the drama unfold.

The guard was all apologies as he interrupted something Jade was saying. Volos nodded at something the man said and then listened as the security guy whispered something in his ear. A moment later those intense eyes searched the front of the restaurant. I smiled and waved.

Volos frowned, as if taken off guard, and said something to the muscle, who motioned me over. I took my time walking toward the table. As I approached, I watched Volos say something to his companions. The suits rose immediately and shook his hand in farewell. That done, Volos turned toward Jade. The lawyer didn't look nearly as accommodating. In fact, she leaned in and her body language was argumentative.

To his credit, Volos didn't raise his voice. If anything, he seemed to lower the pitch. Whatever he said to her, it seemed to do the trick, because while I was still two tables away, she rose from her chair and grabbed her designer purse from the floor with twitchy movements. Without a parting word to Volos, she stomped away on her impossibly high heels.

She was almost on me when she saw me. She froze and looked me up and down. Judging from the scowl on her pretty features, she didn't like what she saw. "Jade," I said with a nod.

She took a step forward, bringing her within striking distance. I held my ground. "I don't know what game you're playing, but I will advise you to tread carefully, Detective."

I shrugged. "Relax, counselor. I'm not here on official business." I paused to make sure she could hear me and smirked. "It's personal."

Her eyes narrowed. "Whatever." As she stalked away, I heard her mutter, "Bitch."

"Drive Miss Turner back to the office," Volos said to the security guard.

"Sir, I—"

Volos flashed him a tight smile. "I'll be perfectly safe with Detective Prospero. I'll call you to pick me up when I'm ready to leave."

The guard executed a clipped nod, flashed me a warning look, and then walked away to catch up with the pissed-off attorney.

Volos came forward. "Has there been a break on the case?" He sounded hopeful.

He leaned forward as if to hug me, but I held out a hand to shake instead. "I'm afraid not. I'm here on a personal matter, Mr. Mayor." He paused and smiled, as if amused by the formality of my greeting. When his hand wrapped around mine, the contact was warm and familiar. Before I could withdraw, he'd quickly bent over my knuckles and grazed them with his lips.

I jerked my hand from his grasp and wiped it on my jeans. I'd be damned before I let him take charge of this meeting. Also I was really glad that the wire taped to my chest was only a one-way communication device. Otherwise, I'd have had to deal with Morales's profanity in my ear.

"May I?" I asked, motioning to the empty chair next to his.

"Of course." He stepped behind the seat and pulled it out like a gentleman. He only took his seat once I was settled. "Are you hungry? I'm afraid I've already eaten."

I shook my head. I hadn't eaten since coffee and a handful of cookies that morning, but my stomach curdled at the idea of food. Not least because I was about to potion the man who'd just offered me lunch.

A waiter ran up. "May I bring you something, miss?"

I smiled at the waiter. "Hmm, yes." I drew out the moment, relishing the intense scrutiny of my tablemate. It wasn't often I was able to catch Volos unawares. "I'll have a beer." The carbonation would settle my stomach, and the alcohol would give me courage—the perfect elixir.

"Of course, ma'am. What brand do you prefer?"

I waved a hand. "Doesn't matter. Just no IPAs or stouts."

He nodded. "Foreign, domestic?"

I shrugged. "Cold."

His mouth twitched. "Right away." The waiter turned to Volos. "Anything else for you, Mr. Mayor?"

He shook his head and flicked a hand to dismiss the young man. Once he was gone, Volos leaned forward with his elbows on the table. "Now, why don't you tell me what is so urgent you had to interrupt a meeting with two of my most generous donors."

My brows rose. "You didn't have to cancel the meeting for me."

He laughed. "Bullshit. You wouldn't willingly seek me out without a very good reason. So spill it, Katie."

I tensed at his casual use of the old nickname. "It's about Danny."

His expression darkened. "Is he okay?" No doubt he was remembering the last time I'd asked for his help regarding my little brother. Back then, Volos helped me save Danny's life—just before he blackmailed me.

I held up a hand. "He's not in danger, if that's what you mean. Well, not direct danger, anyway."

The waiter brought my beer in a frosty pint glass. Before he ran off, Volos grabbed his arm. "On second thought, bring me a bourbon, neat."

The waiter nodded eagerly and took off to the bar. Inside, I did a little victory dance.

"Tell me," Volos said to me.

"There's been trouble at school." I proceeded to fill him in on the basics of Danny's issues. In the middle of my explanation, the waiter returned with his bourbon. As I talked, he sipped on the drink.

"Wait," he said, "Pierce Rebis? You're sure?"

I nodded. "Anton Rebis's son."

"And Danny hexed him?" He couldn't hide the smile on his face, which made him look younger. And more dangerous to my equilibrium. Morales's words drifted like a poison cloud through my head. *He's still in love with you, Cupcake.*

My chest felt tight, but I blew the words away and focused on my mission. If I let my guard down, Volos would for sure turn the tables on me.

"Don't look so amused. I still haven't decided on how to punish him for misusing magic."

"Oh please, Kate. Back in your day you would have done a lot worse to anyone who dared mess with one of your friends." He shot me a look daring me to argue, but I couldn't. He was right. I'd gotten in my share of brawls with girls and boys in school who dared even look at people in my coven the wrong way.

"I think we can both agree that our goal is for Danny *not* to follow in either of our footsteps."

He took a sip of his bourbon and watched me over his glass. "Oh, I don't know. Considering the gutters we came from, we cleaned up pretty good."

He was the mayor and I was a detective on a federal task force, so I had a hard time arguing with the point. "Despite our résumés, we've both done things we wouldn't want Danny to get messed up in," I said pointedly.

"Touché, Detective."

I nodded. "Anyway, I need to figure out how to get Pierce to admit what he did."

"To what end? Danny still attacked the kid using magic. The Rebis family is well within their rights to press charges."

"Not if they're interested in keeping Junior's little rape hobby out of the papers." Off his frown, I quickly filled him in on that twist to the story without naming Luna as the victim.

Volos's face changed. Instead of looking amused by Danny's exploits, he looked proud of me. "You should go into politics. You've got a killer instinct for blackmail."

"I know you meant that as a compliment, but I'm not taking it that way."

He shrugged and toyed with the crystal tumbler. "Where do I come in?"

"I was hoping you could talk to Rebis. See if you can get him to drop charges... or whatever."

The corner of Volos's mouth tilted up. "It's the 'or whatever' that interests me. Are you really asking me to use my office as mayor to put pressure on a political opponent?"

"I'm asking you to do whatever you're comfortable with to help Danny."

He took another drink of the bourbon and rose.

"Where are you going?" I asked, panic seeping into my voice.

He pulled his phone from his pocket. "I'm going to call Rebis and see if he's free for a chat."

I sat back in my chair. Despite the fact I'd manufactured the reason to approach him, I was shocked at how easily he'd agreed to help me.

"What's wrong?" he asked.

"I just—I'm just surprised."

"That I would help you?"

I nodded. "Something like that."

He touched my chin with the fingertips of his left hand. "You haven't figured it out yet."

I jerked my chin away from his touch. "Figured what out?"

He watched me for a moment. Panic surged like an electric shock under my skin. I absolutely could not handle Volos declaring his feelings for me right then. But something in my expression must have made him change his mind. He pulled back a fraction and held up the phone. "Be right back."

To make the call, he disappeared down the hallway leading to the restroom. I watched him go for a moment. As much as I liked to cast him in the role of archvillain, the truth was he clearly had a generous side. Unfortunately he usually used that generosity to manipulate and deceive. Or that's what I told myself—what I had to tell myself—to do what I had to do to save Gardner.

A waiter dropped a glass somewhere near the bar. The sound of shattered glass surprised me out of my thoughts. I shook myself and reached into my pocket for the ampoule. None of the tables nearby was occupied, and all of the nearby staff had pitched in to help clean up the spill.

Now was my chance. My left hand closed around the small glass vial. My conscience flared. Less than a year ago, I wouldn't have let a potion ampoule within ten feet of my person. And now here I was about to use one to incapacitate a man who'd just offered to help me. What was worse, I planned to hand him over to an enemy who'd proven himself a fan of torture.

I blew out a determined breath. I assuaged my conscience by promising to do everything in my power to make sure we walked out of the confrontation with Souza with both Gardner and Volos alive.

That decided, I quickly popped the top off the ampoule and poured the yellow potion into the glass of bourbon. Only half an inch of liquid remained, but it was enough. It had to be.

I'd just stashed what was left of the potion in my pocket when Volos emerged from the hall. His expression was blank, and for a moment I had a spurt of fear that maybe he'd figured out my plot. Had he seen me?

"Our friend answered," he said. I managed to nod. "But he said if I wanted to speak to him I'd have to go to the hospital."

I feigned disappointment. "Damn."

Volos frowned at me. "Well?"

"Well what?" Having him stare at me was making my palms itchy and damp.

"Are you ready to go?"

"Where?"

"To the hospital," he said slowly. "Are you feeling okay?"

I licked my dry lips and tried to look like I was overwhelmed with worry. "I'm just worried about Danny."

"Don't worry, Kate. We'll figure it out." He patted my shoulder. The patronizing tone set my teeth on edge. "I just need to call my driver."

Shit. I'd forgotten about his goon/driver. "Finish your drink and then we'll go."

His eyes narrowed, but instead of calling me on my strange suggestion, he lifted the drink and drained it. I watched to the last drop, and only when he swallowed it all did I relax.

"Happy?" he said, sounding exasperated.

I forced a smile. "You know what? My car's outside. I'll drive."

He hesitated. "You still driving that shitty Jeep?"

I nodded. "What's the matter? Is your ass too important now to touch anything but Corinthian leather?"

He laughed, pulling out his phone. "Let me just text my driver and let him know he's off for the rest of the afternoon." While he did that, I let out the breath I'd been holding. Once he was done, he shoved the phone in his pocket. "All right, Detective, I'm in your hands."

My smile wobbled a little. "Great."

◆ ◆ ◆

An hour later I was sitting in an expensive leather armchair in Volos's penthouse. Morales paced back and forth in front of the granite breakfast bar. "How much did you give him?" he demanded.

"I told you, I was in a hurry. I think it was only a few drops."

He pointed at the man on the couch. His arms were sprawled toward the floor, and a line of drool dripped from his slack lips. "That doesn't look like a few, Cupcake."

I threw up my hands. "I don't know what you want me to say."

277

Morales ran a hand through his hair, making it all spiky. He would have looked handsome if he weren't so busy being an ass. "How in the hell are we supposed to put him on the phone with Souza when he calls?"

I leaned back against the chair's back, which cupped me like a large hand. "We still have an hour. Maybe he'll wake up by then."

He seemed to ignore me. "I'm going to check in with Mez and see if there's an antipotion we could give him."

I pressed my lips together to keep in my retort. I knew Morales wasn't really mad at me. He worshipped Gardner, and the stress of being responsible for her safe return was getting to him. "Do whatever you want."

He didn't respond. Just grabbed his phone and left the room. His footsteps retreated down the hall and then a door slammed.

Shaking my head, I rose from the cocoon of leather and went to the bar. If I had to wait for Mr. Mayor to wake from his beauty sleep, I decided to help myself to his very good bourbon. I poured two fingers of Pappy Van Winkle and went to look out the bank of windows overlooking Lake Erie. It was late afternoon and the sun had begun its descent on the far side of the horizon, bathing it in bloody hues.

I closed my eyes against the sunset and stretched my neck muscles. It had already been a long fucking day, and I expected it to be an even longer night. Last night worries about Danny's future had chased away sleep, which meant I wasn't firing on all cylinders to begin with. "Christ," I whispered. I almost envied Volos his unconsciousness.

The door down the hall clicked. "Mez says the potion should wear off soon," Morales said. "I'm going to run down to do a sweep of the lobby just in case Pantera decides to make a surprise appearance. Call me if he wakes up."

"Got it."

After he was gone, I took a mouthful of bourbon and let it burn against my gums and tongue before swallowing the smooth fire. In front of me, the luxurious apartment reflected in the wide expanse of glass like a mirage.

The whole thing was surreal. Ten years earlier—no, more than that, twelve?—John and I had been working for Uncle Abe. While the Grand Wizard of the coven had plenty of money, he kept everyone working under him lean and hungry. Desperation made people more pliable, he'd said. As his niece, I was better taken care of than most—especially since my mother's jobs brought in money in addition to what I earned doing basic potion work and running errands for Abe.

But we'd never known luxury. Especially John, who'd been abandoned by his potion freak parents to a grandmother who'd let him run wild. Back then his hair was shaggy, his cheekbones were sharp blades on his too-thin face, and his eyes held hungry shadows. The streets had chiseled away his soft edges early. However, his innate talents for strategy and cooking served him well, and it wasn't long before he found his way into Abe's fold. Once he'd joined the coven, he'd learned quickly how to fit in and, even quicker, how to stand out in the right ways. I never questioned his ambition or his ability to turn his dreams into realities—by force, if necessary.

But I never imagined he'd eventually live the way he did now. When we were teens, this frivolous display of wealth was something we saw only in the movies when we managed to scrape enough dollars together to pay for a show—or we snuck in, which was more common. We'd both had ambitions, sure. I was supposed to take over for Abe, and John would have been either my co-leader or my right hand. Sometimes we'd sit around and talk about what our house would look like once we ruled the coven. As kids, we'd imagined ridiculous luxuries like golden toilets and a bowling alley in the basement.

Once I'd left the coven, I'd pretty much given up those dreams. And frankly, seeing John's place now made me glad I had. His need to surround himself with the best of everything seemed like an attempt to absorb some of the class from those objects into himself. But under the designer duds and expensive haircut, he was still that lanky kid who had to wear the same black T-shirt every day because his grandmother was on the dole and spent most of her money on lotto tickets and luck potions.

I drained the liquor from the heavy crystal tumbler. Despite his fancy apartment and designer clothes and his hard-won power, John Volos was as hollow as that glass. He could keep pouring expensive things into it, but a hole is a hole, even if it's surrounded by crystal.

A small voice in the back of my mind warned me to be careful. Romanticizing John Volos as some lost little boy role-playing as a mogul was dangerous. Whatever motivated him was less important than his actions. Over and over he'd proven himself a ruthless survivor. If I let my guard down, he'd have an opening to make me pay for my betrayal in spades.

The sound started as a hushed whisper of fabric against leather. Subtle. In fact, it didn't even register in my conscious mind until the groan sounded. My eyes flew open and I spun. My hand automatically went to my salt flare. It was my go-to draw when there was magic involved. It wasn't lethal, but in a pinch the ability to strip skin from bone was a potent demotivator.

I looked toward the couch. Volos no longer lay prone on the leather. Instead, he sat up with his head in his hands.

"John?" I stepped forward, my flare still hot in my hands.

"What did you give me?"

A lump of fear in my throat. I knew better than to trust his quiet tone. "Knockout potion."

He nodded into his hands. "The bourbon."

I nodded even though he couldn't see me.

"Why?"

I sighed. I really should call Morales back, but I hesitated. Adding my partner to the situation would be like adding a match to a bucket of gasoline. For the moment, Volos was calm, so I held off. "Souza has Gardner."

A bitter laugh escaped his mouth. He turned his head in his hands. His face was pale, almost gray, and shadows darkened his eyes. "A trade, then?"

I nodded, not trusting myself to speak. Shame washed through me. Up until that moment, the entire plan had been like a game. Figuring out how to outsmart Volos and get him to drink the bourbon had been like a match of chess. But now, with those haunted eyes watching me, I realized how very real the situation was and how very wrong I'd been to think I had the stomach to trade his life for Gardner's. "I—it's not—"

"Not what?" he demanded. "You're not about to tell me you have a plan where no one has to die, are you?" He made a disgusted sound. I pulled myself up to my full height, but before I could respond, he continued. "You're a lot of things, Katie, but you're not naive."

He let his weight fall against the back of the couch. "What I don't get is why you felt the need to hex me." He turned his head to look me in the eye. "You just had to ask me."

I snorted. "Sure."

"When have I ever denied you anything? Hell, I'd just offered to blackmail a political rival just so Danny could get back in that school."

Guilt bloomed cold in my gut. "You said it yourself: I'm not naive. Helping Danny get back in school isn't the same as asking you to risk your life to save Gardner."

"Did you make up the story about Danny?"

Something about his tone told me the answer to this question was important. I considered lying, but I couldn't force it out of my mouth. "No, it was true."

He nodded, taking that in. "I guess it's a moot issue now, isn't it? We're here now. The question is, how do we go forward?"

"You don't get it. You're the reason we're all in this situation. You don't get to call the shots anymore."

"Can I ask if you plan on me being alive at the end of all this?" His tone was dry.

"If you cooperate."

"Christ." The heels of his hands pressed against his eyes. "What the hell was in that potion?"

"It was clean."

He laughed and continued to squeeze his head. "Clean— sure. I feel like I was hit by a horse tranquilizer."

"Said it was clean—not weak."

He absorbed that with a nod. "May I have some water?"

With the gun still in my left hand, I sidestepped toward the wet bar. I filled a tumbler with water from the faucet and brought it to him. He accepted it with a nod and drained it. I retreated to the far side of the coffee table. When he finished, he nodded resolutely as if he'd decided something. "I suppose if I'm going to die, I might as well tell you."

"Tell me what?" I asked.

He looked up. The shadows in his eyes had retreated. Lines bracketed his mouth and his shoulders slumped, as if he'd surrendered. "You're not going to like it."

My left hand clenched the gun I'd lowered to my side. "Tell me anyway."

"Come on." He nodded toward the hall. Morales was still downstairs. I knew I should call and tell him to come back. But I hesitated. Something told me if I did, the secret Volos was about to tell would remain unshared. And something in my gut told me I'd regret that more than not calling Morales. Besides, I had my salt flare if Volos tried anything.

"Morales is coming back any minute." I wasn't sure if I was warning him or reassuring myself.

"It's in my office." He waved me on, and disappeared down the hall. I followed him slowly, gripping the brass flare in my damp left hand.

The hallway contained four doors. It was the third one on the right that he turned into. I was surprised he hadn't put his office in a room overlooking the lake view. In fact, the only windows here were set up high into the wall. They let in light, but no one could see in or out.

He went about turning lights on in the office. "Come on in." Something about the tension in his tone put me on edge. Even if I'd been considering holstering my weapon, that alone would have convinced me to rethink the choice. I stopped at the threshold. He shot me a disappointed look. "Kate, I'm not going to hurt you."

Something told me he was promising not to physically harm me, but knowing him, my emotions were fair game.

A glass-and-steel desk sat in the center of the room with a black lacquered credenza behind it. Over that hung a massive painting of a black crow sitting on a golden egg against a blood-red background. A shiver passed over me. The living room had been warm with all its wood and leather, but this room was cold. The phrase *war room* came to mind. This was, after all, where John Volos planned all his campaigns, both political and criminal.

He went to the credenza and pulled out a file. It reminded me of the folder he'd shown Morales.

My stomach spasmed. "You're going to blackmail me *again*?" I didn't bother disguising the incredulity in my tone. Although, where Volos was concerned, I shouldn't have been surprised by any form of manipulation he threw at me.

His expression soured. "To what end? You already know if I go down you'll go down, too, especially after tonight."

My stomach twisted at the reminder. By kidnapping and hexing Volos, Morales and I had tricked the devil.

"So what is it?" I prompted.

He paused, as if choosing his words carefully. "You asked me before what happened to your mom." He wouldn't have surprised me more if he'd punched me. I could only stare at him.

He waved a folder. "I have the answers you wanted."

I lurched forward to grab it, but he pulled it back. "Hold on." He put his free hand up to hold me back. "You might not be ready for what's in here."

"I've spent the last decade blaming myself for her death, John. I'm ready to know what really happened."

He released a long breath. "All right."

I snatched the offered folder from his hands. My eyes narrowed at the top page inside. It was a death certificate. The same version Cho had showed me. I blinked. "You lied to me." I looked up. "You looked me in the eye and told me I really was responsible for her death."

He jaw tightened. "It wasn't the right time to tell you."

My hand curled around the document. "The right time to

tell me was ten years ago, you bastard." I paused. "Besides, I already saw this."

His eyes widened. "When?"

"Grace Cho shoved it in my face the other night."

"Cho showed it to you?" He'd come around the desk and leaned back against it with his arms crossed, watching me. The mood in the room had shifted the instant he'd mentioned my mother. But the tension wasn't just from me. It radiated off him, too, almost as if he were bracing himself.

"I told her it had to be a mistake."

He shook his head. "It's not."

I took a slow, bracing breath. "Why did Abe lie to me? Why would he let me believe she'd died from taking my potion?"

His gaze drew away from mine. "He was protecting you."

"By blaming me for her death?" I would have laughed at the ridiculous notion if I hadn't spent the last decade flailing myself with guilt.

He sighed. "Kate, there's something—there's more to it."

I waited expectantly. On some level, I was aware that I should be screaming. But shock weighed down my limbs and protected me from imploding—yet.

"Abe got word that someone in the coven was selling information to one of his rivals."

"Which rival?"

"The Quincunx."

"The supercoven in New York?" I frowned. "You mentioned them the other day, too. Something about Abe having an old beef with the leader."

He nodded. "The Philosopher."

I ran a hand through my hair, as if it could somehow help me sort through his confusing switches in topics. "What does this have to do with my mom?"

"Like I said, Abe got word someone in the coven was selling secrets to the Quincunx. He started by watching his inner circle, but no one showed any signs of having been turned."

"What? How is it possible I never heard anything about this?"

He just watched me for a moment, letting me draw my own conclusions. A burning sensation began in the pit of my stomach.

"He asked me to watch and see if anyone made unusual purchases, which might indicate a sudden infusion of cash." He hesitated but held my gaze steady. "She had just bought Danny a new bike."

"No. Fuck you." I shook my head. "She worked two jobs to earn that money."

"I know, but she also paid a lot of money to a man who specialized in forging documents, like birth certificates and driver's licenses. The kind someone would need to start a new life."

The burning grew until it was a red flame in my chest. "You're lying."

"I wish I was," he said. "Trust me, telling him that was the third-hardest thing I've ever done."

My head jerked up. "The third?"

"The first was letting you walk away from the coven," he said.

I bit my cheek to keep from screaming. "And the second?"

I'll give him this—the bastard gave me the respect of looking me in the eye. "Not telling you the truth to make you stay."

"You fucking knew," I whispered. "You knew I was eating myself from the inside for her death."

He swallowed and nodded. "Abe told me if I told you what really happened he'd kill you and the kid."

"But—" I cleared my throat because it felt like it was filled with buckshot. "Why? Why did he want me to think I was responsible?"

"He said he needed to see how you reacted. I guess he thought maybe you were in on it with your mom. He let you go because he wanted to see if you went to The Philosopher. When you didn't, he figured it was only a matter of time until you'd come back."

I put my right hand to my mouth as my mind processed everything he was saying. But my fingers were trembling, so I lowered into a chair and dug my fingertips into the wood. My left hand was busy pointing the salt flare at Volos. "Did you pull the trigger?"

His eyes closed. "I know you think I'm a monster, Kate, but even I am not evil enough to kill the mother of the woman I love."

I didn't miss that he'd used that four-letter word in the present tense. I was beyond caring about his fucking feelings. "That didn't stop you from investigating her and ratting her out to Abe!"

His eyes popped back open, and the intensity in his gaze made me back up a step. "I was trying to prove her innocence, goddamn it!" He blew out a breath and physically struggled to get hold of his temper before he continued. "And I had to stop her, Kate," he continued in a quieter tone. "She was selling information to earn money to get all of you out of Babylon. I couldn't lose you."

Now it was my turn to close my eyes. I felt breathless and empty, as if I were that empty glass now. "Why?" I whispered.

He laughed bitterly. "Good question. You left anyway, didn't you?"

I shook my head. "No, why was she trying to get us out?"

"Same reason you left, I'd imagine. She saw what working

287

for Abe was doing to you, and wanted to save Danny from the life."

A rebellious tear seeped out from under my lid. I swiped it away and opened my eyes. "If it wasn't you, who pulled the trigger?"

"Charm."

A humorless laugh escaped my lips. "Of course."

I dropped my head in my hands. A warm hand landed on my shoulder. It reminded me of the time Charm had performed the same movement to comfort me over the death of my mother. I shrugged him off. Volos didn't say a word—he just gave me my space.

I'd been a fool to mourn Charm at the crime scene. The hand he'd put on my shoulder to comfort me had been the same one he used to pull the trigger on the gun that killed my mother. Souza should have kept the bastard alive while he dismembered him. He deserved that and worse pain for killing my mother.

Burn in hell, asshole.

A vortex of memories opened around me. The past and the present swirling together until I couldn't tell them apart. When I'd left the coven I thought I'd taken control of my own life for a change. And for a few years I had. But here I was right back where I began—being manipulated by power-hungry men.

Just like my mother.

I didn't kill her, I didn't kill her, I didn't kill her.

The words marching through my brain should have made me feel relief. They should have released the pressure valve on my guilt, but instead all I felt was rage at the fucking futility of it all.

I thought about the decade I'd spent abusing myself and trying to make amends for a sin I hadn't fucking committed.

Meanwhile, the assholes responsible for her death had gone about their merry way without consequences. Worst of all, I'd never let myself properly mourn Maggie Prospero's soul because I'd been so busy trying to save my own.

"Kate." John's voice shattered over me—or maybe it was me who was shattering.

The little fissures of pain cracked open my chest. Any illusions I'd protected in the center of myself took flight like startled birds. The hollow space left behind flooded with a rush of cold, dark clarity.

"You're a monster." I didn't raise my voice or let any emotion color the words. They were simply spoken as a statement of fact. "You held on to the truth like money in a savings account." A bitter laugh rose like a frigid wind in my throat. "And now you're trying to cash it in to save your life."

His expression didn't change. "Wrong," he said. "I told you—"

The phone in my back pocket rang.

"Don't answer it." His voice was seductive as the devil's. Those eyes that had looked at me for so many years pleaded with me to spare his life. "Please, Katie."

If what he'd said was true, my mother had been trying to make a better life for all of us by doing the one thing she'd always done well—selling herself for money. For the O Coven, she'd sold her body, but to escape Abe she'd sold her soul to The Philosopher—and it had cost her life.

The phone rang again.

No, I thought—this was worse. At least my mother had been paid for selling parts of herself to the highest bidder.

John Volos wanted me to hand my soul over for free.

The sound of the front door opening echoed through the penthouse. "Kate?" Morales called.

"In here."

On the third ring, Volos's shoulders relaxed, as if he already smelled victory.

Tears fell freely now. Small, wet circles bloomed hot on my legs, like a baptism.

I pulled the phone from my pocket. John's eyes widened. "Don't—" He lunged toward me. I raised the salt flare. He stumbled to a halt with his hands raised.

"Kate?" Morales said from the doorway.

I thumbed the answer button. "Mr. Souza?"

"Katie, no." Volos's voice cracked.

I smiled at the flash of fear in his eyes. If he hadn't tried to manipulate me by absolving me of my mother's murder to gain my sympathy, I would have filled him in on the plan. But right then I wasn't too eager to alleviate his worries. He deserved to suffer a little. Lord knew he hadn't done anything to alleviate my suffering over the last decade.

"Yeah," I said into the phone, "we've got him."

Chapter Thirty-One

The tanker loomed over the dock. Its hull was rusty and covered in thick barnacles, like scabs. In this part of the docks, all of the lights either had burned out or were broken by punks or criminals looking to conduct illegal business under the cover of shadows.

The vessel's name was painted in white at the prow. "*Eris,*" I read.

"Goddess of discord," Volos said absently. I refused to look at him or acknowledge his words.

"It's sailing under a Dutch flag," Morales said. "Not Brazilian, as we'd assumed. That explains why we kept striking out yesterday."

The air smelled of algae, rotting wood, and decaying fish. Beside me, Morales kept his gun on Volos. I studiously avoided looking directly at our prisoner despite his attempts to engage me. It's not that I was afraid he'd make me change my mind about turning him over to Souza. I just didn't trust myself not to let my temper take over and punch him in the face.

After I'd taken the shaman's call, I'd handcuffed Volos to his desk and pulled Morales into the hallway. Getting some space between Volos and me had been crucial. The way I'd been feeling, I'd have been completely capable of killing him myself.

Naturally Morales had demanded to know why he walked in on my crying and Volos looking like he'd lost his best friend. I'd quickly explained how the mayor had tried to buy his life by telling me the truth about my mother. I shared this in a robotic tone that made Morales frown with worry and pull me in for a hug. I resisted the contact at first, but soon found myself sinking into the comfort he offered. But I didn't allow myself to cry anymore. I was done shedding tears.

After that, we'd put phase two of the plan in motion and called the rest of the team to put it into action. To his credit, Volos never demanded to know what we were planning. He'd gone very quiet, but I could see the gears moving behind his eyes. When the time was right, Morales could tell him how we were going to pull this off, but I refused to be the one to ease his mind. I knew I was being petty. Hell, I'd hexed the man and kidnapped him. I was far from an angel. Still, I reminded myself that Volos was the reason several people were dead and Gardner had been kidnapped.

The area in front of the ship was quiet and still. The three of us were ducked behind a large shipping crate closer to the row of warehouses near the docks themselves.

"What do you think?" Morales said in a low tone.

I sucked in a breath through my nose. My eyes scanned the ship's deck for signs of life. The only movement I saw was the flags on the mast whipping around in the cold winds coming off Lake Erie. "I'll go in first."

Both men spoke at once and they both said the same word: "Bullshit."

After that I tuned them both out as they competed to be the one who talked me out of my plan. Morales's protests bugged me more than John's. As my partner, he knew I could hold my own, but I was worried that the personal stuff would make him see me as someone to protect instead of as an equal.

"Enough!" I hissed. "Jesus, you two. I swear it's like neither of you knows me." They shut up then. Morales looked more contrite than Volos did. "If we walk in with Volos we have zero leverage. I'll go first, get the lay of the land, and then give you and Mez the signal when the time is right."

"But—" Volos began, then drifted off in the face of my glare. He might be mayor, but he'd seen that expression on my face and heard that tone in my voice enough to know he wouldn't win this one.

Once he was quiet, I looked at each man in turn and nodded when they didn't argue. "Mez?" I said into my intercom.

"Yo."

"You all set?"

"If by set you mean armed to the teeth with potions, yes."

"Good man. Remember to wait for the signal."

"Understood."

We'd called Mez with the plan on our way to the docks. He'd met us there with the supplies we'd requested and then retreated to provide backup. Shadi, meanwhile, was stationed on a roof somewhere nearby with the all-seeing eye of her sniper rifle. I quickly did a check-in with her, too.

"I'm going to radio silence," I said before signing off with her, "but Morales will be connected for the time being. You see anything off, you let him know."

"Ten-four."

I pulled the earpiece out of my ear and held it toward Morales. His expression had testosterone all over it, but my own told him I was immune to macho tactics. Finally he sighed and took it from me. But when I repeated the procedure with my gun, he couldn't keep quiet anymore.

"I'm not sending you in there unarmed."

"Thank God," Volos breathed. "A voice of reason."

"How long do you think Souza will let me keep a weapon? Besides, I have one of Mez's magic-dispersing amulets under my Kevlar-and-salt vest."

"A vest won't stop a bullet to the head, Kate." Volos's tone was quiet but the point hit home.

"He won't shoot me until he has you," I said. "Then all bets are off."

I rose from my crouch and peered around the corner of the shipping crate. Morales scooted over to join me. He didn't touch me, but I could feel the tension burning off his skin.

"I don't like this."

I turned to look at him. Just beyond his shoulder, Volos was doing an unconvincing job of trying to look like he wasn't eavesdropping. To Morales, I said, "You don't have to like it. You just have to let me do my job."

"But who's going to watch your ass? That's my job."

"No, your job is to trust me."

"I do." He placed a hand on my arm. It was a simple gesture, but combined with the sudden gravity in his gaze it took on new meaning. He moved closer and I could smell the sweat on his skin. The scent memory reminded me of the taste of him. A warm feeling bloomed in my chest. "Be careful," he whispered.

Behind Morales's back, Volos cleared his throat. My gaze strayed toward him. He wasn't bothering to pretend he wasn't watching us anymore. His eyes were narrow and his jaw hard. He hadn't missed the intimacy of the touch and the tone, either.

I looked back at Morales and stepped away. A stung look passed over his features. I pointed at Volos, whom I wasn't convinced wouldn't run and screw us all. "Watch him or he'll try to escape." With that, I turned and ran before he could say anything else. I heard him say my name, trying to call me back, but ignored it. The confusion tugging me in two directions was dulled by the thrill of adrenaline in my veins. I savored the jolt and picked up my speed to outrun the pair of magnetic forces willing me not to go.

The shadows along the pier provided ample cover. Closer to the boat, the scent of rotting fish grew stronger and the air grew colder. About twenty feet from where I crouched, a set of steps led up to the deck. I was surprised not to see any armed guards watching the entrance. I'd figured Pantera would have a thug there to pat me down before I boarded. Instead, the ramp lay empty, like a silent invitation to come aboard. Something about the silence felt ominous, but I didn't have the luxury of being cautious. I knew the shaman had tricks to play, but the only way to get him to show his hand was to play along for now.

Taking a deep breath, I stepped onto the ramp. As I did, a wave of energy passed over my skin. Like a sizzle of static electricity. My hair stood on end and my nerve endings tightened. I was wearing Mez's protective amulet, so whatever magic the shaman had just thrown at me passed by useless. Most likely, though, it had been an Arcane sensor—meant to detect whether I was packing any magical weapons. I prayed he'd warded only the stairs and not the entire ship.

I reached the top of the ramp without further incident and stepped onto the metal deck. Wind whipped up from the water, buffeting my clothes and making my hair lash at my face.

The main part of the cargo ship's deck was made up of a series of tall hatches that opened to allow filling from loaders above. There was also a several-stories-tall pilothouse to my left, but it was totally dark. I stopped and closed my eyes, listening. In the distance the sound of boat horns echoed mournfully in the dark. Water slapped against the ship's metal hull. The muted sound of traffic thumping across the seams on the Bessemer Bridge created a steady rhythm. But underneath all that, the high-pitched sound of metal beating against metal echoed from somewhere deep in the ship's bowels. I opened my eyes and started forward, toward the hatches. Most were closed, but about halfway up the row, one massive lid lay open. Above it, a large loader—which looked like a crane but with a spout instead of a hook at the end—hung over the opening.

I approached the open hatch slowly. The banging sound got louder the closer I got to the opening. Moving carefully, I edged up until I could look over the lip that rose a couple of feet off the deck. The hole was dark, but I had a sense of vastness and depth below. I blew out a quiet breath. The tapping sound was coming from inside that cavern, which meant I was going to have to go investigate.

Pain exploded across the back of my skull. I jerked and started to turn, but a low, mean voice said, "Stand up. Slowly."

"Shit." I put my hands into the air and did as instructed.

A light way down inside the hole flashed on. I blinked at the scene below. "Gardner."

Far below, a man with a machine gun jerked back my boss's head. Her face was barely recognizable from all the swelling. Her brown hair was matted with blood. But she was still wearing the pantsuit she'd been wearing two days before—albeit now bloodstained and torn. Her hands were bound behind her, and wire bound her ankles to the legs of the chair. She was unconscious.

"Where is Volos?" the man behind me said in an accented voice. I glanced out of the corner of my eyes and saw Pantera's midnight-black skin.

"He's close. I want to see Gardner first."

He pointed his gun toward the hole. "You can see her."

I shook my head. "I need to make sure she's okay."

He sighed. "I don't like games."

"Good," I said, "because I'm not playing any. Once I see she's okay, I'll call my partner to bring Volos to you."

"Fine." He nudged my shoulder. "Use the ladder."

I moved toward the opening, where a metal ladder descended into the bowels of the cargo area. My boots clanged against the rungs as I made my way slowly down. Pantera stood above, watching my descent. I paused. "Aren't you coming?"

He smiled wide, his teeth impossibly white against the pitch black of his skin. The expression made his green eyes sparkle like poison under glass. "I'll be here."

I sucked in a breath through my nose. If he stayed up there, Gardner and I would be like two fish in a very empty barrel. He could shoot us both and clear out before Morales and Volos even heard the bullets ricochet off the steel walls.

The shaman raised a single brow at me. "Well?"

I resumed my descent. I wasn't about to leave her down there alone. Souza smiled down at me. Probably, he'd known I wouldn't show up with Volos. He'd have concocted his plan around it, and I was playing right into it.

By the time I reached the bottom, I also realized just how freaking deep the cargo area was. I looked up, up, up at Pantera.

The height made him look small at the mouth of the hold, but no less menacing.

Her head hung low and to the left side, as if her neck had simply lost the ability to hold up her head. Her hair covered her face. Before I got close enough to move it out of the way, the asshole with a homemade TEC-9 stepped in front of her.

He didn't look familiar, and his Hispanic features indicated he might be a henchman the shaman brought with him from home. Because no shaman worth his weight in ayahuasca would dare travel without an armed gunman. The gun, too, hinted at his origins. A while back I'd read a report in the MEA files about a trend within *A Morte* for members to make homemade submachine guns. Agents had even found gun workshops within larger potion labs in São Paulo.

The henchman met my eyes, his lips curled in an anticipatory smile, as if he'd love nothing more than to put a bullet between my eyes. "Souza?" I called up.

"Yes?"

"Tell your friend to stand down or you won't see Volos."

His laughter echoed down to me. "You talk a big game, *menina*. But if your partner doesn't bring me Volos, I'll kill both of you."

I turned and put my hands on my hips. "Do it, then."

He paused and tilted his head as if trying to see my bluff shimmering in the air like a hologram. He said something in Portuguese. I wasn't anywhere near fluent in his mother tongue, but I was certainly well versed in the tone of a superior telling his flunky to stand the fuck down.

The asshole didn't look up at his boss because he was too busy trying to intimidate the little woman with his big gun. I raised a brow and flicked my thumb to indicate he should move aside. He took his sweet time before turning and sauntering away to go stand nearby.

Finally free, I skidded to my knees in front of my boss. "Gardner?" I pushed the hair back and tilted her battered face toward the light. Up close I could see the true extent of the damage. The lacerations and bruises on her face I'd expected, but she also had them on her arms and legs—her neck. They hadn't just beaten her. They'd tortured her.

The senselessness of it hit me like a fist to the gut. Souza didn't do things on a whim. He'd planned to use Gardner as leverage to get Volos. Torturing her for information was unnecessary, but the sick fuck had probably just done it to get his rocks off.

I ran my hands over her arms to check for breaks. Two fingers on her left hand were bent at odd angles. I touched them gingerly. It took me a moment to realize that her tiger-eye ring was gone. The only time I'd ever seen her without that thing on was the night I walked in on her cooking in the lab. For some reason, knowing that they'd taken that from her—something she considered sacred—was the final straw.

Rage roared behind my sternum. My hands itched to overpower the asshole, steal his machine gun, and perforate the hull of the ship.

"Detective Prospero," the shaman called.

"What?" I yelled louder than I'd intended. I closed my eyes and tried to get my temper under control. It would only be a weapon for the homicidal shaman to use against me.

"Now that you've seen Gardner is alive, it is time to summon Mayor Volos to the party, yes?"

I cleared my throat and prepared to stand. But just before I engaged my thigh muscles to rise, Gardner's hand squeezed mine. I was standing between her and the asshole, so he couldn't see her right eye open a mere slit. It was enough. Enough to show me she was alive and lucid enough to know who I was and that I was there to help her. But also, I thought, the squeeze was a warning to be careful. I nodded and licked my suddenly dry lips. "Be ready," I said under my breath. The only response was the closing of that single lid and the release of my hand.

"Hey," I said to the asshole.

He tilted his head down. "What?"

"You got any wire cutters?"

"Fuck you."

"Yo, Panther Boy?" I called up.

"Yes, Detective?" His voice was weighted with exaggerated patience.

"I need something to cut these wires."

I rose slowly and turned to look up at the shaman. His body was a dark silhouette against the lights above.

"That was not the deal, *vadia*." Something in his tone made the hair on the back of my neck stand on end. I turned slowly. The asshole had his knockoff TEC-9 pointed at me again. My gaze shifted up and I took in the image Pantera portrayed. He had a booted foot propped on the edge of the hatch, like a fucking pirate.

I ignored the rapid flutter of my pulse. "If you think I'm going to hand you Volos with her here so you can kill all of us, you seriously underestimated my intelligence."

He made a dismissive noise. "Why do all cops think they're smarter than everyone else?"

I crossed my arms and squinted up at him. "Same could be said for most criminals, dickbag."

He sighed. "You test my patience."

Yeah, I thought, that's the fucking point.

"At least let me get her unbound," I said. "Obviously it's going to be hard to get her out of the hold until Morales gets here to help me."

He raised something into the air and waved it. "The number first?"

I pursed my lips, weighing my options. If I continued to stall one of two things would happen. Either Souza would lose his patience—or Morales would. If I wanted to maintain some control, I needed to get things moving. I read off a series of numbers.

A few moments later the muted sound of the shaman speaking into the phone filtered down to me. I clenched my fists until my nails dug into my palms, trying to remain still and continue to look unworried. But inside, adrenaline coiled like a viper in my gut, ready to strike. Adding Morales and Volos to this scene would be like throwing a match into a barrel of gunpowder.

Something in his posture shifted toward anger. "No, you listen to me. The two bitches stay here until you produce Volos."

I closed my eyes and cursed under my breath. Morales wasn't doing anything I wouldn't have done. But seeing how I was the one with a machine gun pointed at me, I found myself praying that my partner would listen to reason.

"You bring Volos here or I will kill one of them. I think I'll start with the young one. She's pretty but not as valuable, I think, as the special agent." Souza punched the End button on the phone and inhaled a long breath. "It's time," he said, almost to himself.

Time to get Gardner ready to go. I moved back toward her and knelt. The wires around her ankles and wrists had cut through the skin, and blood coated her palms and bare feet.

"Think about this, Mr. Souza," I called. "If my partner hears a gunshot, he'll take Volos and get the fuck out of here."

301

The shaman's laughter boomed through the empty cargo hold. "Or he'll rush in to save you. That's the fatal flaw of all cops—the instinct to run toward danger."

While the asshole kept his gun pointed at me, Pantera Souza raised a pistol into the air and pulled the trigger.

I closed my eyes and tried to center myself and get my pulse under control. Souza's move had just fucked shit up, but at least he hadn't actually killed me as he'd promised Morales. I needed to get Gardner free before he arrived and bullets started flying for real.

Using my fingers, I started untwisting the ends of the wires. They were slick with Gardner's blood so my grip kept slipping. Finally I gave up on that tactic and pulled at the wires. They stretched a little, giving me enough room to work them farther down Gardner's hands. She was passed out now, so her hands were slack and the blood acted like a lubricant for the wire to slip over her skin.

The sound of boots against metal made me look up. Souza was climbing down the ladder. I frowned. Why not stay on the deck where he could hide and shoot at Volos and Morales?

Above, the sound of multiple feet running across the deck pounded throughout the ship's metal walls. I moved around to Gardner's front. "Wake up," I whispered, my voice sounding panicked to my own ears. When she didn't respond, I slapped her cheeks. "Wake up!" I commanded. "Miranda, wake up!"

Her head swiveled and a groan escaped her bloody lips. "Good," I said. "I'm going to move you."

As carefully as I could manage, I tipped her chair to the side and lowered it carefully to the ground. She cried out, as if the movement had put pressure on a particularly nasty injury. I gritted my teeth together from the strain of not dropping her to the floor. Finally, the edges of the chair reached the metal floor and her torso collapsed on its side. Using my booted foot, I brought it down hard on one of the chair's legs. It cracked on the second kick, but the movement forced another cry from my boss's mouth. I didn't have the luxury of trying to remove the wires from her ankles, but I could at least get her free. The other chair leg was flush with the floor, so I could only push the wire down the wood until it came off. The whole thing probably took less than a minute, but it felt like a lifetime.

By the time I got Gardner free and got her body upright and braced against my side, the shaman had reached the bottom of the ladder. There were a few crates pushed against the far wall of the hold, which he knelt behind. The guy with the TEC-9 had taken cover behind some barrels on the opposite wall. That left Gardner and me out in the open. Not that I thought Morales would shoot at us, but bullets had a nasty habit of ricocheting off metal.

I dragged Gardner over toward the corner of the cargo hold. There, a pallet of boxes was shrink-wrapped and pushed into the corner. I helped Gardner to the floor and leaned her against the boxes. Then I turned and stood in front of her. My body wasn't a great shield, but it was better than leaving a defenseless, injured person out in the open.

"Shit's about to hit the fan," I whispered. "Stay behind me."

She swallowed and nodded. "Be careful." An immediate wince followed the words.

I planted my feet and crossed my arms to brace for the fireworks. But the ambush I expected didn't appear. What the hell was keeping Morales? The footsteps on the deck had quieted, and now the only sounds were my harsh breath and the creaking of the ship in the water.

I glanced over toward Souza. As if he sensed my gaze, his head turned to look toward me. Something lit his eyes.

Anticipation? Realization that my backup wasn't coming? Either way, that look caused a corresponding ping of fear in the center of my chest.

The shaman rose from his crouch. Under his loose-fitting pants and roomy shirt, his muscles began to twitch. His limbs shifted in odd angles. Holding my gaze, he lowered his head with a feline smile on his face.

The ears shifted up, the face grew forward, and his eyes spread toward the sides of his head. His black skin sprouted fur, which gleamed in the harsh lights. His hands and feet grew and morphed into claws.

A loud growl echoed through the hold.

My heart kicked up speed. Bullets I could handle, but a magical panther? Hell no. I was suddenly regretting giving Morales my gun. "Anytime now, Morales," I whispered, backing up.

When the backs of my legs hit Gardner's shoulder, I stopped. My eyes scanned the cargo area for anything I could use to defend us. The boxes behind me were covered in plastic and appeared to contain electronics from China. The barrels across the way were yellow and had warning symbols on the outside indicating that whatever was inside was poisonous. Hard to make use of in an enclosed space. The crates behind the panther might have held something useful, but would require me to get around the pissed-off animal. Not an option.

The cat growled again and began to slowly stalk forward. Its glossy black shoulder muscles rose and fell with each step.

"Hector," I said quietly, appealing to the name his mother gave him, instead of what he was called on the streets, "don't do anything stupid. Morales will be here." Inside my head I thought, *Please, Morales, get here.*

The panther paused, lowered the front of its body, and licked its chops.

"Shit," I said.

The next few moments happened in slow motion. The panther sprang forward. I braced my muscles for impact. But before it came, the air sizzled with magic. It filled with the overpowering stench of ozone. Then—*poof*—three dark figures materialized between the panther and me. Everything froze for the span of a single heartbeat.

Then, chaos in motion.

One man tackled the cat and rolled away, struggling with the animal. The second man swiveled and aimed a Glock at the asshole with the poor man's TEC-9. The bullet's trajectory was relentless, hitting the guy square between the eyes. His brain exploded back out of the skull and spattered all over the wall.

I barely had time to digest what I was seeing before the third man slammed me to the ground. Pain exploded in my back and spread through my hips. My head bounced off the hard metal of the ship's floor. Before I could cry out in pain, the heart-stopping scream of an angry jungle cat ripped through the air. The large body on top of mine shifted to the side. I sucked air into my lungs and looked into his face. "John?"

His hands were still clasped protectively around my waist, and his eyes were busy looking over very inch of my body. "Where are you hit?"

I tried to wiggle out of his grasp, but he held me down. Fed up with fighting him, I grabbed his chin and made him look at me. "He didn't shoot me." I pointed to where Morales was wrestling the panther while Mez assisted with magical weapons. "I need to help them. Let me go."

Relief flashed across Volos's face, but a frown quickly replaced it. "He's fine." He grabbed me in a hard hug. "Jesus, I thought we were too late."

Magic sizzled through the air. A loud yelp responded. A low

male curse. Then the sound of gunfire exploded. I looked up in time to see the panther fall at Morales's feet.

I scrambled out of Volos's hold and leaped toward Mez. He was panting and lying on his back. A visible wound bled freely from his right shoulder. Sweat coated his forehead. Large scratch marks created red canyons on his cheek and neck. A nasty bite on his left arm forced the limb to lay useless by his side. His shirt was torn to ribbons, exposing red gashes all over his torso. I pushed his hair back from his forehead and looked into his eyes. "Talk to me."

The corner of his mouth lifted in a lame attempt at a smile. His tongue darted out to wet his lips. "Remind me to stay in the van next time."

I snorted a laugh, not because I was amused, but because I was relieved he was alive. Mez wasn't a fighter. He was a badass wizard, but he normally left the violence to the rest of us.

Morales knelt next to us. "How you doing, man?"

Mez swallowed hard. "Next time, don't worry about my ego and just shoot the killer panther."

"I thought you were just toying with it." A smirk spread across my partner's face.

A wheezing chuckle came from the wizard's mouth. I patted his shoulder and looked at Morales. "What took you so long?"

"Once we filled him in on the plan, it took some convincing to get *Mr. Mayor* to take the potion." His tone was mocking.

"I'm just glad it worked so well."

"Hey," Mez said, protesting my doubts about his potion.

I smiled at him. "No offense, but you have to admit it was a long shot."

After we'd told Mez about how Souza had disappeared from Harry Bane's trailer, he'd been working on his own version of the potion. He'd even called in some favors from wizards who specialized in potions created by South American shamans to figure it out. We'd taken a major gamble relying on the untested product to get Volos and Morales into that ship, but it had worked a treat.

"I'm pleased," Mez said. "Especially since we got to use that asshole's own magic against him."

Speaking of the shaman shifter, the panther growled and attempted to shift its heavy weight. But its sides heaved from pain and the effort, and it fell still again. I patted Mez's shoulder, ready to relax. He and Gardner both needed medical attention, but at least we were all alive.

A sound came from the opening above us. Morales and I had guns pointed up before we realized it was just Shadi coming to join the party. She shot us a give-me-a-break glare before descending the ladder into the hold. When she reached the bottom, she jogged over.

"You missed all the fun," Morales said.

"Some of us don't cheat," she said, hefting her assault rifle up onto her hip. Despite her petite frame, she looked like a total badass. "While you were beaming up here like some *Star Trek* motherfuckers, I had to rappel down a building, climb up a ramp, and climb down a deep-ass ladder."

Morales bumped her shoulder. "Pussy."

She pursed her lips and dismissed him. "Where's the boss?"

"Here."

We looked over to see Volos helping her stand. For a man who thought we'd planned on trading his life for our boss's, he was being suspiciously helpful.

But before I could stand and wrap my mind around his cooperation, the panther on the ground began to shift. The fur disappeared and the paws morphed back into hands and feet. The process moved more slowly than it had the first time—a result of the blood loss and pain. Morales, Shadi, and I formed a shield around Mez. We had lots of guns trained on the man-imal, but we didn't want to take any chances.

When Souza completed his shift back into his human form, he was naked and the right side of his body was covered in blood. He staggered to stand and pulled himself up to his full height. His eyes were glossy from pain, but his expression was nothing short of enraged. "How did you work this magic?" he asked. I assumed he was referring to the way Volos and Morales had materialized in the ship.

I raised a brow and tipped my chin toward Mez. "The cartels aren't the only ones with powerful wizards."

His chin lifted and he made a dismissive sound. "You have accomplished nothing. My lawyers will have me out in less than a day." He smiled. "Next time, *A Morte* will send an army."

"Your first mistake is in assuming you'll walk out of here." I spun around. The threat had come from Gardner, who limped forward with Volos's help.

She stopped next to Morales, who rose from his crouch. She held out her left hand without speaking. Morales paused, but lay his gun across her palm.

"Sir?" My stomach dropped.

She eyed me. Her pupils glowed with a violent fervor that had me shifting my weight to the balls of my feet. "What, Prospero?"

I held up a hand. "Think about what you're doing."

Her left brow, which was split apart, lifted ironically. "It's all I've been thinking about since this bastard landed the first punch."

"If you kill him, more will come," I said. "It'll be like kicking an anthill."

She smiled. "Not if we hide the body and no one knows he's dead."

I looked around to the rest of the team. Shadi had fallen back with her eyes down. Mez was inspecting a particularly nasty wound on his arm. Morales met my gaze, but shook his head to tell me I was fighting a losing battle.

I ignored my partner. "Arrest him," I urged. "Make him face justice. Maybe he'll turn on his superiors."

Behind me, Souza snorted. I knew the suggestion had been insane. Cartels demanded ultimate loyalty from all their people. As an insurance policy, the leaders collected lists of family members' names from everyone who was accepted into the cartel. Snitching on your bosses lost a lot of appeal when you knew the cartel knew your mom's maiden name and address. I'd heard stories about family members being boiled in acid in retaliation for disloyalties as minor as even mentioning the name of the cartel you belonged to.

"Okay, fine. Maybe we can't flip him, but we're not murderers, sir." I'd done a lot of shitty things on this case, but that was a line I was not willing to cross.

Now it was Volos's turn to snort. I shot him a glare, but he smiled at me with an ironic tilt to his lips.

I'd grown up on the same streets he had. We'd played Wiz versus The Fuzz with all the other Adept kids. No one ever wanted to be the cops because to a bunch of kids raised in the Cauldron, the police were definitely not the good guys. But I needed us to be. I needed to know that I wasn't like Uncle Abe or Harry Bane. I needed to believe that where I'd come from wasn't my destiny. And if I stood by and let Gardner do this, then I was no better than the coven leader I'd been groomed to become.

I glared at Morales, urging him to help me. He looked from me to Gardner, indecision clear in his expression. In the end, his shoulders dropped and he looked away.

"Shadi?" I said, my voice raising with panic.

She shook her head. "Sometimes the only choice is to put down a rabid animal."

"She's right," Volos said in a quiet tone.

I looked at him. Of course he agreed. He was the kind of man who disposed of anyone who stood in his way regardless of the law or morality. But that wasn't who I was. Not anymore. I'd become a cop because I truly believed I could do good. Sometimes we had to do bad things to reach the good result, but the line had to be drawn somewhere. If we murdered an unarmed—not to mention naked—man, no matter how evil he was, then we'd never be able to get back over that line.

"Sir," I said, "killing him won't bring them back."

She froze. The gun in her hand twitched. Her gaze slowly pulled away from the shaman to zero in on me like a laser. "What did you say?"

I cleared my throat and stood straighter. "This won't balance the scales. Your old team is gone. Resorting to cartel tactics won't make you the winner in this. It'll just mean you're no better than him."

Her eyes jerked toward the Brazilian again. He ignored her and smirked at me. His teeth were threateningly white against his onyx skin. "The MEA ain't the good guys, girl. Who do you think armed the cartels to begin with?"

I looked at him. "What?"

"We helped your president unseat some dictators in South America. In exchange they gave us weapons and raped our lands. The only way we could recover was to get into the supply side of the potion trade to ensure our people had enough to eat."

I raised a brow. "Now who's moralizing?"

"Enough," Gardner said. "I hear what you're saying, Prospero. But he's right. He'll be out by noon tomorrow. Then he'll disappear back into the jungle and the cartel will send a crew of assassins after all of us."

"Not if you give me Volos."

All the air in the hold disappeared. Gardner and Morales exchanged a look. I glanced at Volos, who, for the first time, looked worried.

"He's who they want," Souza said, referring to his bosses. "You let me walk out of here with him and you won't have to worry about either of us again." Hector shot a challenging look at Gardner. "Your life would be easier without him around, right?"

I felt sick to my stomach because Souza was right. Volos had caused one complication after another since I'd joined the task force. He might have convinced the people of Babylon he deserved to be mayor, but he was as dirty as any cartel hit man or coven wizard.

The question was: Did Gardner agree? It seemed likely. If not for Volos, *A Morte* would have left Babylon alone and Gardner never would have been tortured. On the other hand, if she agreed to Pantera's deal, she'd be allying herself with the cartel that had killed her team.

Chewing on my bottom lip, I glanced at Volos. He raised his chin, but said nothing to save himself.

Something shifted inside me. A realization that if we let Pantera take Volos, he'd die without ever publicly facing consequences for his actions. He'd die, sure, and probably painfully. But what I finally understood was that I didn't want Volos dead—I wanted him exposed.

"Sir," I said, my voice hard. "I demand that you read this man his rights."

Gardner's hand twitched. Her eyes had gone unfocused, as if she was so busy fighting an internal battle she'd had to withdraw from the scene.

"Morales," I said, "talk to her." The edge of desperation had seeped into my voice, but I didn't care. I knew if Gardner killed Souza it wouldn't just be the end of his life—it would also be the end of my time in the MEA.

"I understand your hesitation," Souza said. "But be reasonable. I have no beef with you at the moment."

I raised a brow. This guy was a real fucking piece of work.

"Give me Volos and you won't see me again."

Gardner's gaze sharpened as she plugged back into the moment. "Your promises hold as much water as a desert, Shaman." She lowered the gun. "You have the right to remain silent..."

I blew out a breath and allowed the adrenaline to drain out of my limbs. While Gardner continued to read the shaman his rights, Morales moved forward with his cuffs. Souza's expression went from cajoling to deadly. If he'd been able, he probably would have turned back into the panther and attacked.

I ran a hand through my hair and met Gardner's eyes as she continued to Mirandize Pantera Souza. She nodded and held my gaze. I knew it was probably as close to a thank-you as I'd get from her, but it was enough.

Morales completed clicking the iron cuffs onto Hector's hands and stepped to the side. The shaman lifted his chin, a sneer on his face. "You will regret this, bi—"

His words exploded into a shrapnel cloud of bone, skin, and blood.

Chapter Thirty-Two

The blast from the gun ricocheted against my eardrum. In slow motion, I crouched and turned toward the noise. Volos stood still with the gun in his hands. The shaman's body slammed to the ground in a pool of blood.

I blinked once, twice. My brain sped forward, putting together what Volos had done.

"No!" Before I knew what I was doing, I launched myself at the bastard.

Shock registered on his face a split second before I slammed into him. The impact of my body into his forced the weapon from his hands.

"Son of a bitch!" My fist connected with his jaw. Pain exploded in my hand and radiated up my arm. Red bloomed from his lips, but instead of warning me to stop, it spurred me on. Bone crunched into soft cartilage with a satisfying crunch.

I raised my throbbing fist back to punch him again, but two strong arms wrapped around me from behind.

I screamed and fought against the backward momentum. Unable to connect with his face, I kicked my legs.

"Damn it, Kate!" Morales grunted in my ear. "Stop!"

"Let me go," I screamed.

Morales jerked me away and all but threw me. I landed on my side a few feet away. The impact stunned me, but I quickly got my feet under me.

Volos wiped the back of his hand across his mouth. The smile on his bloody lips made me lunge again.

This time Morales was ready for me and caught me around the middle. His arms were steel bands and the impact knocked the air out of me. "No," I panted. "No!"

"Enough!" Gardner's voice cut through the air. "Stand down, Prospero."

Morales's muscles tensed around me, as if he expected me to start kicking again. But all my strength escaped me as the full weight of what had just happened settled on my chest. I sagged against Morales's chest. His grip changed from restraining to comforting.

"He just fucked us," I whispered.

"Wrong." Volos's eye was rapidly swelling, his nose was bleeding freely, and the cut on his mouth was already swelling. "I saved you."

I could only shake my head and try to breathe through the tightness in my chest.

"Explain yourself." Gardner hadn't moved through the entire altercation. Her arms were crossed. Behind her, the man Volos killed had been reduced to a rapidly cooling, bloody mess on the ground.

"Sir—" I started to tell her not to listen to him. But a hard squeeze on my arm and a shut-the-fuck-up glare from my boss closed me down.

Volos pushed himself slowly off the floor. He was listing to his right, as if in pain, but managed to look confident anyway. "Kate was right. You couldn't kill him. It would have bitten you in the ass down the road." He straightened his collar. "And I couldn't have him put in jail because Mr. Souza was also right. Once his lawyers cut him loose, we'd have had a real war on our hands."

Gardner sucked at her teeth. "So your solution was to commit murder in front of federal agents, Mr. Mayor?"

Volos smiled tightly, but the move caused him to cringe. "You got a tip that a cartel shaman was receiving a shipment of illicit supplies. You assembled your team and set up a raid. Only when you arrived, Souza and his cohort were both dead. From appearances it looked as if one of Mr. Souza's local accomplices betrayed him for trying to take over Babylon's dirty magic trade."

Fear sizzled up my spine. How in the hell had he formulated that plan in such a short time?

"That's bullshit," Morales said. "No one would walk into this scene and believe that story."

"They would if we disposed of the murder weapon and the injured members of our party leave before the BPD arrives."

"There is a slight wrinkle to your plan," Gardner said.

Volos shot her an incredulous look, as if he couldn't fathom any angle he hadn't covered. "What's that?"

"Your flaw is assuming anyone in this room would be willing to cover this up for you."

"You hexed me and kidnapped me with the intention of handing me over to a known murderer. No jury would find me guilty for killing a man to save my own life."

My stomach dipped. The bastard had our balls in a vise and he knew it.

When no one argued with him, he continued to press his case. "You think he's the last wizard who's going to try to take over Babylon, Special Agent? Trust me, Souza was a choirboy compared with some of the sick fucks who have their eyes on this town. If you let me go down, who will protect this city from them?"

"We will, asshole," Shadi said.

"Right," Morales said. A vein worked in his neck. "You're the reason that fucking shaman came here to begin with, remember?"

"I'm also the one who got the job done." Volos stared down Morales. "Face it, the only way to protect this city is for all of us to team up. The MEA is limited by laws that can't touch me."

"Jesus," I breathed, "you're not above the law."

"Which is exactly why we should already have this murderer in cuffs, sir," Morales said to Gardner.

"Let he who is without sin cast the first stone, Agent Morales." Volos's tone was quiet but damning.

Gardner glanced quickly at Morales. My partner's expression went as blank as any professional gambler's. My throat felt tight, as if a noose had closed around my neck. I'd tried so hard to do the right thing by encouraging Gardner not to kill Souza, but as usual Volos had twisted the situation into a complicated moral knot. His threat was clear: If we arrested him, he'd bring all of us down.

"Enough," Gardner said. "He's right."

Morales's expression went cocky. "Damn straight."

"Not you," Gardner said. Morales looked at her like she'd just crotch-kicked him. "Volos is right. If we arrest him, every wizard with a product to sell will swarm into Babylon. We don't have the resources to stem that tide. But if we all work together..."

Morales's expression turned into a mask of frustrated anger. "You motherf—"

"Special Agent Morales," Gardner snapped. "A word?"

He looked like he wanted to argue, but the expression on her face hinted that would be a really fucking bad idea. Gardner limped toward the other side of the hold with Morales following like the dutiful soldier he was.

Shadi made a disgusted sound and shook her head, as if she was done with everyone in the ship. She turned her back on me and went to kneel next to Mez. It wasn't until then that I realized the wizard had passed out from pain and missed the entire confrontation.

"Kate?" Volos called softly.

I refused to look at him. My fists clenched at my sides. I felt fractured, like I'd never be able to pull all my pieces together again. I'd walked into this case believing I knew the difference between right and wrong, but now nothing seemed right. There were no good guys left in this scenario. Just scavengers scrambling to save their own asses.

"Katie."

My chest felt full. Like dirty water had rushed in through all my cracks and I was drowning. Like I'd never know the miracle of breathing clean air again.

"Please look at me." There was an emotion I couldn't place in his voice.

Something dark swirled in the dirty water. A beast born of grief and fed by my anger. It consumed what little hope remained for a good life, a decent one. One where every decision wasn't tainted by magic and death.

I could see John's shoes from the corner of my eyes. Drops of blood marred the expensive leather. I knew this wouldn't be the last time I'd see blood on John Volos. And considering the deal Gardner was about to make, it wouldn't be the last time I'd be forced to help him clean it up.

He didn't speak again. The only sound in the cargo bay was the whispered argument between Morales and Gardner. I already knew she'd talk him into doing what she wanted— what Volos wanted. Morales was a lot of things, but he wasn't a snitch or a rebel. He'd toe the line because that's what good soldiers did.

I glanced toward the arguing pair. Morales looked up then, and our gazes collided. It was instantly obvious they were talking about whether I could be trusted to go along with the plan.

Was I a good soldier?

I used to be. I used to take orders and carry them out. Only back then, I'd had a different commander. Uncle Abe might have been a criminal, but there was no doubting that the street rats, cooks, and corner boys under his control were his private army.

An army I'd deserted.

I glanced at the Ouroboros tattoo on my left wrist. There were specks of blood on the snake. Just like there was metaphorical blood on my badge.

"Look at me, damn it!" This time it wasn't a whispered plea, but an order.

I looked up. Volos's face was solemn, not angry. From the sound of the conversation across the room, Gardner and Morales were about to rejoin us. Not much time, then. "I want you out of my life."

He looked like I'd slapped him. I wished I had. Wished I could feel the sweet sting of his pain on my skin again. "You're not a child, Kate. Wishing me away won't make me disappear."

But before I could respond, Gardner and Morales returned.

"You okay?" Gardner asked, shooting me a worried look.

I swallowed hard and nodded.

She tipped her bruised chin to acknowledge she'd heard me. "Here's the deal." She paused and lifted a hand to her side, as if to ease pain. "We don't have much time if we're going to make this believable, so we need to get the story straight."

Volos closed his eyes briefly in relief. Morales looked like he'd been forced to swallow poison. I knew how he felt. Bile climbed the back of my throat, but I swallowed the bitter fluid. There'd be time enough later for being sick over my actions; right then we couldn't afford to contaminate the crime scene we had to create.

Gardner had been speaking while I struggled to get a grip on myself. "...Morales and Shadi will stay and call it in. Kate?"

All eyes turned on me. I cleared my throat. "Huh?"

Morales tilted his head. "You sure you're okay?"

"Fine," I lied.

"Good," Gardner said. "Mez and I both need medical attention."

"Hospital's out," Shadi said.

I nodded. "We can go to my place. Baba will keep things under wraps."

Gardner nodded toward the gun on the ground. I realized that Volos had used the gun Souza had discarded before he'd shifted into the panther instead of the one Gardner had held on the shaman. "Take that and dispose of it in the lake."

I paused, eyeing the murder weapon. Volos stepped forward and held it out. Setting my jaw, I stepped forward and took it in my left hand, which was wrapped in the cuff of my shirt so my prints wouldn't land on it. But he refused to let it go and held my eyes. I narrowed my eyes and focused the full weight of my hatred into my glare.

"Mr. Volos," Gardner prompted. "Kate promises to properly dispose of the weapon. Don't you, Prospero?"

My left eye twitched. His eyes burned into mine, but I refused to look away. "Of course," I said. "I'm an expert at taking out the trash."

The corner of his mouth quirked. He finally released the gun into my hand. Stepping away slowly, I wrapped the weapon more carefully in the cloth.

"Good," Gardner said. "Now, Volos will say he was kidnapped by Souza."

"Wait, he's staying?" I asked. "Why?"

"It's my ship." The look in his eye dared me to get pissed again, but I was beyond that now. I just wanted to leave.

"Of course it's your ship," Morales said, his tone heavy with irony. He turned to Gardner. "How in the hell are we going to explain him looking like he went three rounds in the ring?"

Volos licked at the wound in the corner of his mouth. "Souza brought me here to kill me. He roughed me up, but before he could finish the job a Votary Coven member showed up and killed both the shaman and his friend."

I frowned. "Votary—" I stopped as the realization hit me. "You're going to frame Puck for this?"

He raised a brow and began to speak. I held up a hand to interrupt him. "You know what? Fuck it. I don't care anymore. I'm going to go get the car." To Morales and Shadi, I said, "Bring them when you're ready."

With that, I turned my back and did something I should have done months ago. I walked away.

Chapter Thirty-Three

Two hours later I covered Mez with one of Baba's quilts. He was passed out from the sleepy tea Baba had forced on him after she'd treated his wounds. I sighed and turned off the lamp before going to the kitchen.

When I'd arrived with two injured cops, Baba had transformed into Florence Nightingale. She brewed teas and issued orders for clean sheets and blankets for the patients. Because I didn't want to think anymore, I followed her instructions. I'd put fresh sheets on my bed for Gardner and set up a pallet on the couch for Mez. I'd boiled water and gathered bandages. I'd gone down to check on Danny, who thankfully was sound asleep.

Once all that was done, I closed myself in my bathroom, turned on the shower, and let the water scald my skin. I'd expected tears, but they never came. I was simply beyond the place where self-pity could touch me. Maybe I was in shock. Or maybe I was simply too afraid to let myself feel anything because the emotions would consume me.

By the time I'd done a final check on Mez and joined Baba in the kitchen, I needed a drink more than I needed oxygen. My roommate was sitting at the table sipping something from a mug. She looked up when I walked in and shook her head. "You look like shit."

I smiled. "Feel like it, too. That tea in your cup?"

"Bourbon." She pulled a flask out of the pocket of her blue housecoat.

"Thank Christ," I breathed. She rose and grabbed me a mug while I plopped into the chair. Bless the old witch, she filled it to the rim.

I took the mug and took a greedy sip. Unlike the expensive brand I'd had at Volos's earlier, this brand was cheap, hot, and spiced with aluminum from the flask. But I swallowed it eagerly, enjoying the liquid fire searing a path down to my gut.

"You want to talk about it?" she asked quietly.

I stared down into the mug and shook my head.

She reached across the table and touched the abrasions on my knuckles. "Let me get some ointment for those."

"It's fine." I raised my left hand and clenched it into an experimental fist. The skin pulled taut, sending a sharp sting through the knuckles. Memory of that fist connecting with Volos's face made me grimace. Not because I regretted hitting him, but because I wished I'd done more damage.

"Kate—"

"Am I interrupting?" I looked up quickly and found Gardner standing in the doorway of my bedroom. She had on one of my old T-shirts and a pair of flannel pajama bottoms. Her face still looked like hell.

Baba clucked her tongue. "You should be in bed, missy."

"Couldn't sleep." She took an experimental step into the kitchen. "You got anything to drink?"

Baba rose. "I can make you some tea that will help you sleep."

My boss shook her head. "I was hoping for something with more of a punch than tea."

I lifted my mug. "Bourbon?"

"God yes." She limped to the chair across from mine. I rose and got her a glass. Baba's flask was empty, so I poured half my mug into hers and handed it over.

Baba yawned so wide her jaw cracked. "I think I'm done." She turned to Gardner. "The liniment I put on the wounds will prevent infection, but your body needs rest."

Gardner raised her glass. "I'll hit the sack once I finish this. Thank you for everything, Baba."

The old woman flushed, but waved a hand. "It was nothing. Just take it easy on yourself." She turned to me. "Same goes for you."

Since I wasn't wounded, she'd meant I should take it easy on myself emotionally. I hadn't told her exactly what had happened, but she was well acquainted with the emotional hangover that always followed a particularly fucked-up case. "Yes, ma'am."

Once Baba left, the kitchen fell into silence. I sipped my drink and studied the wounds on my knuckles. I didn't believe for a moment that Gardner had come out because she couldn't sleep. She had something to say, but I wasn't sure I was ready to hear it.

She cleared her throat and shifted on her seat. The movement forced a hiss of pain out of her mouth. I finally looked up. "You need anything?"

She shook her head and tried to adjust to a more comfortable position. Once she found it, she took a long, bracing gulp of her bourbon. "Jesus, that's horrible."

I chuckled. "Baba likes her hooch cheap. Says she can afford to drink more of it that way."

She met my eyes. "I knew I liked her."

I nodded. "Me, too."

She sighed and leaned forearms on the table. "I think we need to talk."

My stomach flipped over. "No, we don't."

Despite the swelling around her eyes, I could see the moment the steel entered her gaze. "Fine, I'll talk. You can just listen."

I sighed and leaned back in my chair. My palms cradled the mug against my chest. "Go ahead."

She nodded and licked her cracked lips, as if gathering her thoughts. "You were right."

I wasn't sure what I expected her to say, but it sure as hell wasn't that. "About what, exactly?"

"A lot of things." She ran a finger along the lip of her mug. "When you caught me cooking the potion, when you talked me out of killing Souza, when you beat the shit out of Volos." Her lips twitched. "You've got a mean left hook, by the way."

Her attempt at levity fell flat. I just watched her, waiting for her to continue.

She cleared her throat. "But the thing is, being right isn't always enough."

I frowned. "How do you figure?"

"Did you know I didn't finish the potion you saw me cooking? I realized you were right and tossed it." She paused to let that sink in. "I did the right thing, and for my effort I was ambushed outside my own front door by Souza. If I'd used the potion I would have been able to meet him on my own terms. But since I didn't, I was kidnapped and tortured." She shrugged off the irony, but her fingers were trembling.

"Sir, I can't imagine how horrible that was for you. But you did the right thing."

She laughed bitterly and took a bracing sip of her bourbon. "The truth is, Kate, sometimes you gotta get your hands dirty before things come clean. Until you come to terms with that, you'll always be at odds with the job."

I gaped at her. "You sound like Volos."

She shrugged, letting the insult slide off. "Maybe. I've been in this job a long time. Seen shit that would make most people lose all faith in humanity. It takes a toll. Changes you. Makes lines blur."

"Do you remember my first day on the team? When you read me the riot act about how things were done in the MEA?" I shook my head at how nervous I'd been that day. "You warned me that if I wanted to stay on the team I'd have to do things by the book."

Her lips thinned into a narrow line.

"But tonight," I said, "you didn't just ignore the book—you set it on fire."

Her eyes narrowed. "What should I have done, Kate? Arrest Volos and let him take all of us down with him?"

"I'm not talking about that part," I said. "No one understands what it's like to be trapped in Volos's snare more than I do." I looked up. "You were going to kill an unarmed man."

"One who'd tortured me and killed my team." Her voice shook. "Did you know I was engaged to one of the men he killed, Kate? Or that his funeral was on the day we were supposed to be in Vegas getting married?"

I closed my eyes and muttered a curse. My stomach cramped imagining how horrible that must have been for her. Especially when, hot on the heels of that loss, the MEA had treated her like it was her fault. "I'm sorry." I opened my eyes. "I knew you were involved with one of the agents, but not the rest."

She nodded curtly to accept my apology. "The point is that if the tables were turned, you would have considered killing him, too. Hell, before Morales stopped you, you were trying your best to end Volos."

I looked at my hands and swallowed to ease the ache in my throat. "Point made." I looked up, my eyes stinging. "I'm tired. I'm so fucking tired of the game. When I became a cop I thought I'd make a difference, you know? Make things better. But after tonight?"

"Yeah?"

"I'm not sure we aren't part of the problem."

"You don't like the way the game's played? Change it."

"Every time I try, I get the shit kicked out of me."

"I didn't say it'd be easy." She smiled sadly. "Your problem is you're too rigid. It's like you've created all these criteria for what it means to be good, to be righteous. But those rules don't leave any room for being human."

I frowned. "What is that supposed to mean?"

"You deny yourself what you want because you're convinced everything you want is wrong. Then you beat yourself up for not being able to follow your impossible rules."

I looked at her for a moment. "No offense, sir, but I don't need this bullshit. You're my boss, not my shrink. And I'm not going to sit here and be told that wanting to do the right thing is a weakness."

She leaned back and crossed her arms. "Fair enough. But let me ask you this: Do you know what you want?"

"Of course I do."

She raised a brow. "Name it."

"I want to bring down the covens."

"How much?"

"With every cell in by body."

"Enough to kill for it? Enough to lie? Steal? Cheat the system?" She leaned forward. "Because that's what it's going to take to make it happen. The game is rigged, Kate. The covens aren't bound by rules. They don't have to deal with budget shortfalls and political bullshit. They aren't hamstrung by conscience."

I held my ground. "Which is why they're criminals. Those rules keep us honest."

"You want honesty? How's this: The rest of us on the team are only tourists in this world, Prospero. It's your home. You want to make it a better place? You're gonna have to get over yourself and start fighting the war in the real world, not some fictional battle where the lines between the good guys and the bad guys are clear-cut. In a perfect world our moral choices would be simple, but our world is far from perfect."

The room fell silent as her words soaked in. A moment later, my phone buzzed on the table. "It's Morales," I said. She leaned forward and nodded for me to answer. "Hey."

"It's done."

"Where are you?"

"On my way home." He sounded tired. "Duffy's working the scene. Jade came to go with Volos to the station to make his statement. They've already picked up Puck."

"Any problems?"

"Went just as the bastard said it would."

I sighed. "You want to talk to Gardner?"

"In a sec. How are you?"

"Good."

"Liar. If you need me, I'm here." There was weight to his words that implied he was speaking about more than being a shoulder for me to lean on. But I was very aware of Gardner's eyes on me, and didn't care to get into that particular discussion with her looking on.

I smiled because it was surprisingly nice to be worried about, to be wanted. "'Night, Macho."

Gardner took the phone and turned in her seat to speak with him. She mostly listened, but occasionally clipped off a question. I sipped my bourbon and tuned out the conversation. As much as I didn't want to think about anything, Gardner's words echoed in my head.

You're going to have to get over yourself and start fighting the war.

Fight for what, though? A long time ago, Captain Eldritch told me he didn't believe it was possible to bring down the covens. He said even if it was possible, he was more afraid of what might take their place.

I realized then that I hadn't been totally honest with Gardner. My goal wasn't really to bring down all the covens. My goal was to balance the scales. Maybe it wasn't possible to rid the world of evil, but it damned sure was possible to make it harder for evil to win. To protect the pockets of good and help them expand a little.

But balancing the scales also meant I needed to make those who'd wronged me feel the boot heel of justice. The top of that list was Uncle Abe. Just under him, but rapidly working his way up to a tie for first, was John Volos. The man who would have been third on my list, Charm Parsons, had died before I even knew he belonged there. But Abe and Charm hadn't been the only ones responsible for my mother's death. Thanks to Volos's revelations, I now had a fourth name to add: leader of the Quincunx supercoven. Because of The Philosopher's attempts to screw over Abe, my mom was dead. For the last ten years, the scale had been weighted in favor of the guilty. It was time to fix that.

If I left the MEA, I'd give up access to resources that would allow me to settle those overdue accounts.

Which brought me to the other part of Gardner's assessment. The part about me denying what I really wanted in an effort to be righteous. The truth was that ever since I'd left the covens, I'd overcorrected to compensate for my past.

As a cop, I'd tried my best to prove to everyone I wasn't that same girl who killed her mom and had once wanted to follow in my uncle Abe's footsteps. However, to do that, I'd had to deny and push down a lot of things I wanted because I believed myself to be inherently tainted by my upbringing.

But I was exhausted from constantly beating myself up for *wanting*. Maybe it was time to start taking.

Gardner clicked off the call with a sigh. "Christ. Volos has us by the balls."

I polished off my bourbon. "You were right."

She pulled her head up. "Yeah?"

"If we don't like the game, we have to change the rules. Eventually he's going to fuck up, and when he does we'll take him down."

Her brows rose. "Why does that sound like you have a plan?"

I shrugged. "I don't really. Not yet."

"Right." She stood and took the last sip of her drink. "When you figure it out, let me know. In the meantime, I'm going to go pass out."

I rose, too, but not because I was headed to sleep. "Good night, sir."

She paused and looked at me. "We good?"

I thought about it for a moment. About fighting the fight and taking what I wanted instead of denying myself all the time. I nodded slowly. "Yeah, we're good." She smiled and turned to go. "But, sir?"

She looked back with her brows raised.

"I can't promise I won't stop being a pain in your ass."

She laughed. "I'd be disappointed if you did, Prospero."

"Good night, sir."

Once she shuffled off to bed, I rose from the table. I took the mugs and put them in the sink. Dried my hands on a dish towel and carefully hung it from the handle of the oven.

Under the sink, I found a pair of the rubber gloves Baba always wore when she washed dishes. I stuck them in my back pocket along with a zip-top bag. The backpack I'd dropped when I'd helped Mez into the house was still there.

The hallway outside my bedroom was dark. No light came from under the door, which indicated Gardner had indeed kept her promise to go to sleep. I carefully opened the linen closet door. Kneeling down, I pulled out the old comforter that usually sat in the floor of the closet. I removed the pin light from the carabiner on the outside of my backpack. I fumbled a couple of times for the latch, but once my fingers found it the trapdoor opened easily. Inside the hole, I shone the light on the keypad for the safe and entered my code. The door popped open.

I pulled on the rubber gloves before I opened the lid the rest of the way. Inside, there was a small wad of bills, Danny's and my birth certificates, and a couple of items that had belonged to my mother—things I didn't want found if our house ever got robbed.

I hesitated before removing a small velvet box. I hadn't looked at its content in years. But after the night's revelations, I couldn't resist. The lid cracked open to reveal a necklace that had belonged to my mother. The pendant was shaped like a star and set with rubies. According to my mom, a favorite client had given it to her. She'd worn that necklace every day I knew her. I should have buried her wearing it, but I couldn't. She left so little of herself behind when she died, I'd refused to bury the necklace, too.

I let out a shuddering breath and closed the box. I started to put it back in the safe, but something stopped me. Maybe it was that I'd hidden it away for so many years because it was a reminder of my guilt. But now that I knew I was not responsible for her death, I found myself wanting to keep it near me as a reminder—a totem of my new purpose. I had spent too many years avoiding reminders of her because they were too painful, but now I wanted to keep her close to my heart, where she belonged.

I tucked the box into my right hand. Using my left, I reached into the backpack and removed what was about to become the most precious item in my safe.

Before I'd left the ship, I'd told Gardner I'd dispose of the gun that killed Hector Souza. At the time, I'd intended to throw it in Lake Erie before leaving the docks. But when I left the boat, I'd been so pissed off it had slipped my mind.

I pointed the light at the black metal. If Volos ever found out I still had this gun, my life expectancy would diminish rapidly.

You don't like the game, change the rules.

I looked down at my hands. In my right, I held a symbol of my past, and in my left, the key to my future. There was an odd sort of equilibrium to the moment, as if the scales were already beginning to balance.

I slid the gun into the plastic bag and zipped it up tight. Then I buried it under the documents and cash to wait for the day John Volos learned the hard way that no one fucked over a Prospero.

Chapter Thirty-Four

Three days later Danny and I exited Sybil and began the walk up to the doors of Meadowlake Prep. The temperature still required a jacket, but winter's harsh bite had softened into spring's warm kiss. I looked up at the blue sky and inhaled the dewy air. Along the base of the school's flagpole, a handful of yellow crocuses were struggling to raise their faces to the sun.

We were almost at the door when my phone rang. Duffy's number. I held up a finger to Danny to give me a sec and answered it. "What's up, Detective?"

"Prospero." His tone wasn't friendly. Uh-oh. "You got a minute?"

Danny crossed his arms and shot me an impatient look, but I ignored it. Something in Duffy's tone had started a warning signal flashing behind my eyes. "Yeah. What's wrong?"

His sigh carried over the line. "I've been closing up the paperwork on the Pantera Souza murders."

"Okay," I said slowly.

"Why was Grace Cho investigating you?"

My stomach dropped. "I told you, she wanted to interview me because I'm an Adept cop."

The sound of his chair squeaking carried through the phone. "The cops who searched her house for evidence linking Souza to Cho found her notes on you. Are you aware she was working on a theory that you've illegally used dirty magic to solve cases for the MEA?"

"No."

"Maybe it's nothing."

"Of course it's nothing. She was desperate for any sort of angle to use on me."

"I just find it peculiar, is all. But that's not the only thing that has me scratching my head. Did you know that Puck Simmons has an alibi for the night Pantera Souza was murdered?"

I started to curse, but remembered Danny's presence. "Are you telling me you're releasing him?"

"He said he was at his girlfriend's house, but she denied it."

I frowned. "Really? That's odd."

"Not really. One of our undercovers is reporting that Puck's girlfriend is now running the Votary Coven."

"You're joking."

"It's peculiar, don't you think? Makes me wonder if maybe we got the wrong guy for that murder."

"It's your case, Duffy. Why don't you investigate it?"

He continued as if I hadn't spoken. "Once Puck's in the can, the cartel will have him eating a shiv within a day. If I was a conspiracy nut, I might think that Puck's a sacrificial lamb."

"Listen, I—"

"And thinking about that got me remembering how you assaulted your uncle in prison."

I paused, trying to keep up with his mercurial switches in topics. "What's your point, Duffy?"

"No particular point, I suppose. Just been pondering things." He paused. "Tell me, why weren't you, Gardner, or Kichiri Ren with the rest of your team the night Pantera Souza died?"

Danny sighed and pointed at his watch. I thrust a finger in the air.

"I'm in the middle of something, Duffy. Family stuff. Maybe you should take this up with Gardner."

"I assure you she's the next call I'm making. I just wanted to give you a chance to explain yourself."

"I don't need to explain myself to you."

"You're mighty defensive."

I huffed out a breath. "And you're mighty presumptuous calling me with accusations."

"Didn't accuse you of a thing. Just letting you know I've noticed some troubling patterns. And that I'll be watching."

"Thanks for the heads-up," I said through gritted teeth. "I've got to go now." I punched the End button and stared at the phone for a moment.

"Who was that?" Danny's eyes were wide with concern. I cleared my throat and pushed the anxiety down before dragging my gaze from the cell to look at him.

"Just a guy."

"Are you in trouble, Kate?"

I looked over at my brother. "I don't think so." Duffy didn't have shit. He wouldn't have called me if he had evidence that I'd broken the law. He just wanted to fish a little and see if he could get me to bite on one of his theories. Still, I shot a quick text to Gardner telling her Duffy might be calling with questions about the Souza murder and promised I'd call her later to discuss what he said.

That done, I blew out a long, slow breath. It eased some of the tightness in my chest, but not all of it. I wondered if it ever would totally go away.

"Kate?" Danny's tone was impatient. "Come on."

I couldn't blame him his eagerness to get inside. When Principal Anderson's secretary had called, she'd refused to tell me what the meeting was about. I had a feeling I knew, but I didn't mention it to Danny because I didn't want him to get his hopes up. "Listen, play it cool in there, okay? Let me do the talking."

He tilted his head and shot me a look full of teenage scorn. "I'm not a toddler, Katie."

Despite his petulant tone, he was right. The kid stood taller than me now, and his body had somehow morphed from that of a gawky teen into that of a young man seemingly overnight. But it wasn't the broadening and lengthening of his body that concerned me. Instead, it was his eyes. The events of the last couple of weeks had removed some of the light from those baby blues.

I hated that. I had hoped to protect him as long as possible from some of the harsher realities of the world. That's why I'd fought against him learning magic. Even though it would have been tempting to say I'd been right after he used a potion against Pierce Rebis, I didn't feel smug. Something told me that even if Danny hadn't had access to magic, he would have found some other way to punish Pierce for hurting Luna.

"No, you're not a toddler." I wanted to go to him and smooth down the lock of hair dancing in the spring breeze, but I knew he'd reject it. "But you're also not an adult. So let me do the talking. Okay?"

He nodded reluctantly. "Let's *go.*"

A few moments later we walked into Principal Anderson's office. To my relief, Brad Hart wasn't in the room, but Pen was. She smiled tightly when we entered. When I raised my brows to ask for some hint of what was coming, she shook her head.

My stomach dipped, but I turned to greet Anderson with a smile.

He didn't shake my proffered hand. He simply nodded toward the two empty chairs. "Please sit."

Once we were settled, I shot a reassuring look to Danny. I knew he was hoping he'd be reinstated at the school, but I didn't want him getting his hopes up.

"Thank you for coming today," Anderson said. "I know some harsh words were said the other day, but I'm hoping we can put that behind us and move forward."

"I'm not sure I understand how it's possible to move forward when Danny has already been expelled."

A pained expression passed over Anderson's face. "You have to understand, Detective, my hands were tied. If I didn't expel Danny, Anton Rebis would have pressed charges against him."

I raised a brow. "And he would have withdrawn his generous donations, right?"

"Worse." Anderson shook his head. "He would have sued us. Even if we'd been able to win the suit, our reputation would have been destroyed."

"Nice to know your reputation is more important than the kids you teach. You threw Danny under the bus instead of standing up to a bully."

Anderson's face paled and he cleared his throat. "As I said, mistakes were made. I'd like a chance to rectify that, if you'll agree."

I crossed my arms. "Agree to what, exactly?"

Anderson shot a quick look toward Pen before returning his gaze to me. "Rebis has changed his mind. If we reinstate Danny, he won't sue us or press charges against any of the parties involved."

"Yes!" Danny pumped a fist.

"Hold on," I said to the kid. To Anderson, I said, "What changed?" But I knew. I *knew* what—or rather, who—had orchestrated Rebis's change of heart.

Anderson shifted uncomfortably in his seat. "It would seem you have friends in higher places than Anton Rebis, Detective."

He glanced down at the newspaper on the desk. I leaned forward and saw John Volos's face smoldering at me from the front page. The headline read "Babylon Celebrates Heroic Mayor." A story to the side of the main one showed a picture of Puck being led into the precinct in cuffs.

My lip curled. "John Volos is not my friend."

The principal's mouth curled down in confusion. "Regardless, he considers you one. He called me this morning and assured me that he'd consider it a personal favor if we allowed Danny to rejoin the Meadowlake family."

My gaze swerved toward Pen. Her expression was grim. She didn't know what had gone down in the ship, but she knew my feelings about Volos wedging himself into my life.

Oblivious to Pen's expression or the tension coiling my body for a fight, Danny smiled widely at the principal. "That's awesome!"

Danny had always idolized Volos. When we'd dated, the kid had always treated John like the dad he'd never had, and, later, after Volos steamrolled back into our life, he'd saved Danny's life and encouraged him to learn magic. And now this.

I shook my head. "I don't know."

"Aw, c'mon, Kate," Danny said. "John just fixed everything. Now I don't have to go to a new school." I was pretty sure his enthusiasm had more to do with being able to stay near Luna than excitement over Meadowlake's excellent academics.

I gripped my fists in my lap. Volos hadn't just managed to fix everything for Danny, he'd also put me in an impossible bind—again. If I refused to let the kid back into that school, I'd take the fall as the bad guy. But if I accepted the favor, I'd be in Volos's debt.

"Danny, it's not that simple." I glanced at Anderson. "I'm not sure this is the sort of environment I want influencing you anymore. Besides, how long will it be until Pierce Rebis decides he wants revenge?"

Anderson met my gaze steadily. "According to Mayor Volos, Pierce is being sent to a military boarding school out of state."

My brows rose. It seemed Volos had thought of everything. Military school wasn't as bad as prison, but since rape was incredibly hard to prove this far after the fact, the chances of Pierce getting time even if Luna had pressed charges were slim. At least this way, he was getting some sort of punishment rather than being able to resume his old life.

"The fact remains that your treatment of Danny was unfair and prejudicial. I'm not comfortable allowing him to spend more time here."

Two red spots appeared on his cheeks. "Now, wait just a—"

I held up a hand. "No, you wait. You've said your piece. It's now time for me to say mine." I took a breath. "I know where Danny and I come from seems like it's beneath you. I know that because you are not an Adept you find it hard to under-stand the challenges we face. But as an educator your job is to help all students—not just the privileged few—achieve their potential. Yet time and again all I have seen here is an interest in maintaining the status quo between the haves and the have-nots. You let a few disadvantaged kids in for appearance's sake, and then you leave them to navigate social strata designed to punish the unprivileged."

"That's preposterous!" he sputtered.

"I bet if a rich girl had been raped you would have done something." The words came from Danny's mouth and were spoken with damning calm. I gaped at him. This was the first time he'd indicated he knew exactly what had happened to Luna.

"What the hell are you talking about?" Anderson blustered.

Pen crossed her arms. "You know exactly what he's talking about."

Anderson's face was red, and a trickle of sweat rolled down his temple. "When you told me there *might* be an issue you didn't tell me who the victim was, so don't try to paint me as some sort of evil bigot here."

Pen's expression tightened into a disgusted slant. "With all due respect, sir, you can shove that up your ass. I told you who was accused and you told me to keep it quiet unless the girl decided to press charges." She rose from her chair and faced her boss. "It's up to Kate and Danny what they decide to do, but I am tendering my resignation."

Anderson looked like a pressure cooker about to blow. "Get the hell out of my office."

"Gladly," Pen said. She went to Danny, who looked shell-shocked. "Let's go have a chat while they finish."

He rose blindly, but before she could lead him out the door, he stopped and turned back. "Principal Anderson?"

The older man stopped and looked at Danny. "What is it?"

"My answer is no. I wouldn't come back to this school if you paid me." He looked at Pen. "Let's go."

As I watched my kid brother walk out with his head held high, pride blossomed in my chest. I'd thought I'd have a fight on my hands to convince the kid, but he'd gone and made the right decision for himself.

"But what am I going to tell the mayor?" Anderson sputtered.

I rose from my chair to follow Pen and Danny out, but before I did, I looked the principal in his eyes. "That's not my problem."

The principal's mouth curled. "It's for the best. We don't need your sort of trash in this school."

I laughed bitterly. "We may be trash, but at least we aren't whores. I hope you have fun being under Volos's thumb. I promise you won't enjoy it when he fucks you over."

♦ ♦ ♦

None of us spoke until we were outside. The wind had picked up, and the American flag's hooks rattled against the pole with a spastic *dingdingding*.

"Are you okay?" I asked Danny.

Before he could answer, the door to the school burst open and Luna ran out. "Danny!"

He turned and the frown on his face morphed into a radiant smile. "Luna?"

I grabbed Pen's arm and pulled her away. "Let's give them a minute."

We walked toward the end of the walkway, leaving the teens near the flagpole. I glanced over Pen's shoulder in time to see Luna throw herself into Danny's arms. He wrapped his arms around her and tucked her head beneath his chin.

Emotion made my chest feel overly full. Pride, for sure, but also sadness. Like it or not, Danny wasn't the little boy who needed his boo-boos kissed anymore. Now he was becoming a man who would be someone else's soft place to land.

"They're cute together," Pen said.

I nodded. "I just hope he doesn't get hurt. She's got a lot of heavy shit going on."

Pen exhaled a loud rush of breath. "Don't we all?"

I turned to my best friend. "How are you doing?"

The corner of her mouth lifted in a wry smile. "Surprisingly okay considering I'm unemployed."

"You did the right thing."

Pen turned and looked back at the dignified stone walls. "Even if I wasn't, it's too late now." She laughed, and I was surprised it sounded genuine. She shoved her hands in her pockets and peeked at me from under her lashes. "Truth is, it's been a long time coming."

"What will you do now?"

She shook her head. "Damned if I know. Baba said something about the community center looking for people. Maybe I'll start there."

I bit my lip to stop from commenting on the idea of my best friend and my roommate both working for Volos's pet project. Truth was, no matter what I thought about the man himself, the center was doing good things for the Cauldron's kids. "That actually sounds like a great fit."

She shot me a wary look. "But?"

I shrugged. "But what? I meant it."

"Don't tell me you're not pissed at Volos for interfering."

A tight smile pulled back my lips. "I'm never not pissed at Volos."

"He won't be happy you turned down his help."

I looked up to watch a crow spreading its black wings to circle overhead. "It's about time he's the one who's unhappy."

She shot me a speculative look, but didn't comment. Instead, she said, "Who knows? This may end up being a positive change for all of us."

"I hope so." My gaze strayed back to Danny and Luna. They were holding hands now and speaking in low tones. Judging from the body language, the fact they wouldn't be in school together anymore wouldn't keep them apart. I sighed.

"She started her period," Pen said quietly. "She told me this morning."

"Thank God," I breathed.

"She still needs counseling, though, and I'm still trying to convince her to share what happened with her mother. She's got a long road ahead of her to recover."

I blew out a long breath. As grateful as I was that Luna wouldn't have to deal with an unwanted pregnancy, Pen was right: The kid's problems were far from over. "Of course he goes for the troubled Adept girl."

"Of course." Pen shot me a knowing smile. "His other favorite woman in the world is one."

We laughed and shared a quick hug before she said her good-byes. The couple by the flagpole were still deep in discussion, but the door to the school opened and Brad Hart came out. "Luna! You're supposed to be in class."

She jerked away guiltily from Danny. "Coming," she called.

While she and Danny said their good-byes, Hart crossed his arms and met my gaze. I waggled my fingers and smiled at the jerk. His eyes narrowed. "Luna—now!"

The girl jogged away from Danny and disappeared inside the open door. Before Hart closed it, he called out to Danny, "Take care of yourself, kid."

My little brother nodded and turned with his hands in his pockets. As he walked toward me, I noticed the flush on his cheeks. "You ready, Romeo?"

His shoulders came up to his ears. "Jeez, Kate."

I reached up and wrapped an arm around his shoulders. "I'm proud of you, kid."

He swallowed before answering. "I hated this place, anyway," he said dismissively.

"Then let's get out of here."

Together we walked toward the Jeep, which stood out like a turd in a parking lot full of sparkling luxury cars. "Hey, Kate?"

"Yep?" I climbed into the car.

"I'm glad your date with Mr. Hart sucked."

I froze. "You knew about that?"

"Baba told me."

I closed my eyes and cursed.

"Don't be mad at her."

I opened my eyes. "I'm not. I'm mad at myself for not telling you."

He shrugged. "Whatever. I'm just glad you didn't fall for him and stuff."

"Why's that? I thought you liked him?"

"You mean before he took Anderson's side on expelling me?"

"Right," I snorted, "before that."

Danny clicked his seat belt in place. "I dunno. I guess I kind of hoped you'd start hanging out with Morales."

I paused with my key halfway to the ignition. "What?" I choked on a shocked laugh.

"He's cool, Kate. And he's totally into you."

I took my time responding. "It's not always that simple. Morales and I work together."

"So? I think if you like someone you should try to make it work."

I glanced over at my little brother, who suddenly sounded a lot like a very wise adult. "You think so, huh?"

"Plus, he makes you smile. That's important." He sighed, and I knew immediately he was thinking about Luna.

"When did you get so smart, kid?"

"Born this way, I guess," he said with sly smile.

I laughed out loud and put the car in drive. "All right, smarty-pants. Let's get you home, and then I need to run out to take care of something."

He looked up. "What?"

I shook my head and focused on the road. "A long-overdue message that needs to be delivered."

Chapter Thirty-Five

Two hours after we left the school, I exited the apartment building's elevator. My palms were sweaty so I wiped them on my dark jeans. The hallway leading to my destination felt impossibly long, but before I knew it I was standing in front of it.

Instead of knocking immediately, I adjusted my shirt and lifted my chin. When I raised my left hand, my eyes went to the snake tattoo around my wrist. That symbol used to be a source of shame for me, a reminder of a past I didn't want to claim. But now I saw it differently. In alchemy, the Ouroboros is a symbol of the infinite cycle of life and death.

It seemed like lately I'd been grasping too tightly to parts of myself that I needed to let die. Guilt over my mother's death, for one. The hope that deep down under all his expensive clothes and machinations John Volos was the same boy I'd once loved so fiercely. But also the shadow of shame that hovered over all of my decisions. It was time to make a fresh start. To leave behind the parts of myself that didn't work anymore.

My knuckles struck the door before I had time to second-guess my decision. A male voice called out for me to hold on. My heart tripped over itself and then raced like a nervous rabbit in my chest. I wiped my sweaty palms on my jeans one more time and braced myself for the confrontation that would begin the instant the door opened.

I took a deep breath. It was time to change the game.

A moment later, the door opened. The man across the threshold froze when he saw it was me. He was wearing faded jeans and a black T-shirt. When he recovered from his momentary shock at my unexpected visit, he leaned against the jamb and crossed his arms. The move pulled the fabric taut across his broad shoulders. His eyes traveled down my body, taking in my nicest jeans, a low-cut red blouse, and the high-heeled boots. A smile turned his lips up into the smirk that always got me right in the gut. "What's up, Cupcake?"

I licked my lower lip. The flavor of my lip gloss reminded me of my mission. And like all good missions, I couldn't let myself get distracted, even if the diversion happened to look incredible in jeans. "Hey."

"Hey, yourself." He raised his brows expectantly.

"I, um—" I paused and shifted uneasily on the heels I'd worn on a whim. With him standing there watching me with that unreadable expression, all my nerve escaped me. "I'm sorry. I should have called first."

He shook his head. "No worries. What's on your mind?" I noticed he hadn't invited me in. Not a good sign.

The phone in my right hand vibrated. My immediate thought was it might be Gardner. I'd called her after the school meeting to fill her in on the Duffy situation. She'd reaffirmed my original theory that the detective didn't have any hard evidence, but she'd said she'd call me back if he contacted her. I held up a finger to Morales. "One sec."

But when I looked down at the screen, I realized it wasn't my boss, but John Volos. No doubt he'd heard from Anderson and was calling to read me the riot act. I smiled and took great pleasure in punching End. I shoved the phone into my back pocket and turned my full attention back to the man who deserved it.

He tilted his head and frowned. "Everything okay?"

"Yeah. It's all good." I blew out a breath. "You know how the other day, you said that you weren't sure if you should"—I cleared my throat—"bother?"

His eyes narrowed. "Yeah."

I shifted my weight. "Well, the thing is, I'm kind of an idiot."

A shocked smile broke across his lips. "Oh yeah?"

I nodded. "See, the thing is, I suck at this stuff."

He moved forward a little bit. "What stuff is that?" His voice had lowered to a pitch that hit me right in the diaphragm.

I looked down at the floor. "Man–woman stuff."

"I knew it—you are a lesbian!"

My head jerked up in shock, but when I saw the laughter on his face, I put my hands on my hips. "I'm trying to be serious here."

He schooled his features. "Sorry. You were saying you're hopeless with men?"

I narrowed my eyes at him. The good news was my annoyance made a lot of my nerves melt away. "Jesus, you're not going to make this easy, are you?"

He rocked back on his heels. "No way." He looked so smug and utterly masculine. As much as I wanted to be annoyed by it, it kind of turned me on instead.

I stepped forward. His eyes flared. Good, I wasn't the only one affected. "The thing is, I've decided something." I leaned in and lowered my voice to a whisper. "I want you to bother."

"You do, huh?" His expression was unreadable, but he moved forward another fraction. He was playing it cool, but a muscle in his jaw twitched. "How exactly do you want me to bother you?"

I blinked. "Wh—what do you mean?" I thought I'd been pretty clear.

"Do you want me to bother you nice and slow?" He reached out and lifted my chin. "Or do you want me to bother you hard and fast?"

I gulped. Before I could second-guess myself, I launched myself at him and kissed him. He tensed in surprise for a moment, but then gave back as good as I was giving. We kissed until we were both breathless. "You taste like strawberries."

I used my thumb to wipe away the red smear of gloss on his lips. "I think this color looks better on you."

"Christ, Cupcake." He blew out a breath. "You're going to be the death of me."

I smiled slowly. "At least you'll go out with a grin, Macho."

He smirked at me. "Does this mean you're ready to play slutty cop after all?" He lifted a finger to touch my mother's ruby star necklace, which lay right over my heart, where it belonged.

My mother had spent too much of her life playing the role of slut to men who used her and controlled her and, finally, killed her. I didn't intend to follow in her footsteps, but I'd use the lessons I learned from her mistakes to take control of my own life. Starting now.

"Nope." I shook my head. "I decided to give you a label, instead."

He pulled me fully inside and shut the door. He bent his head down toward my lips, but stopped just shy of kissing me. His hand teased up along my ribs. That's when I realized that coming over had been the best idea I'd ever had. "Oh yeah?" he asked.

I put a hand against his chest and slid it down toward his waistband. "*My* bitch."

"Lord have mercy," he whispered.

And with that, I took his hand and led him toward his bedroom so he could bother the shit out of me.

Acknowledgments

As always, thanks to Devi Pillai for her stalwart editing and support of my writing. Lauren Panepinto continues to amaze with her beautiful covers. I also owe a huge debt of gratitude to the rest of the Orbit team who oversee production, publicity, and sales efforts.

Rebecca Strauss, my agent, is a patient woman, and I owe her many drinks for her advice and support over the years.

A special shout-out to Laís Roque Gonçalves, my biggest fan in Brazil, for her help with the Portuguese phrases.

Thank you to the Secret Sassenach Bitches for the laughter and loyalty in a business that often feels lacking on both fronts.

Thanks to Team Awesome, my amazing street team, for the camaraderie and for spreading the Wells Gospel across the land.

Thanks to Suzanne McLeod, Tricia Skinner, Jamie Henry, and Shelley Bates for the insightful critiques.

The writing life is a strange one, and I am incredibly lucky that Mr. Jaye and Spawn weather the ride with good humor and patience. ILYNTB.

But most of all, thank you, dear reader, for spending your time and money on the crazy tales I weave for you.

extras

orbit

meet the author

Emily Tirado

Raised in Texas, *USA Today* bestseller Jaye Wells grew up reading everything she could get her hands on. Her penchant for daydreaming was often noted by frustrated teachers. She embarked on a series of random career paths, including stints working for a motivational speaker and at an art museum. Jaye eventually realized that while she loved writing, she found facts boring. So she left all that behind to indulge her overactive imagination and make stuff up for a living. Besides writing, she enjoys travel, art, history, and researching weird and arcane subjects. She lives in Texas with her saintly husband and devilish son. Find out more about Jaye Wells at www.jayewells.com.

introducing

If you enjoyed
DEADLY SPELLS
look out for

RED-HEADED STEPCHILD

Sabina Kane: Book 1

by Jaye Wells

*Sabina Kane is half mage, half vampire, and all attitude.
Despite her red-headed stepchild status in the vampire
community, she remains loyal to the vampire leaders
who raised her to be an assassin.*

*When a routine mission uncovers startling secrets that could
destroy the uneasy truce between vampires and mages, Sabina
must find a way to prevent an all-out war. Helping Sabina
navigate this treacherous world are a high-maintenance hairless
cat demon, a prognosticating nymph who used to work in
faery porn, and a mysterious mage with an agenda....*

1

Digging graves is hell on a manicure, but I was taught good vampires clean up after every meal. So I ignored the chipped onyx polish. I ignored the dirt caked under my nails. I ignored my palms, rubbed raw and blistering. And when a snapping twig announced David's arrival, I ignored him too.

He said nothing, just stood off behind a thicket of trees waiting for me to acknowledge him. Despite his silence, I could feel hot waves of disapproval flying in my direction.

At last, the final scoop of earth fell onto the grave. Stalling, I leaned on the shovel handle and restored order to my hair. Next I brushed flecks of dirt from my cashmere sweater. Not the first choice of digging attire for some, but I always believed manual labor was no excuse for sloppiness. Besides, the sweater was black, so it went well with the haphazard funerary rites.

The Harvest Moon, a glowing orange sphere, still loomed in the sky. Plenty of time before sunrise. In the distance, traffic hummed like white noise in the City of Angels. I took a moment to appreciate the calm.

Memory of the phone call from my grandmother intruded. When she told me the target of my latest assignment, an icy chill spread through my veins. I'd almost hung up, unable to believe what she was asking me to do. But when she told me David was working with Clovis Trakiya, white-hot anger replaced the chill. I called up that anger now to spur my resolve. I clenched my teeth and ignored the cold stone sitting in my stomach. My own feelings about David were irrelevant now. The minute he decided to work with one of the Dominae's enemies—a glorified cult leader who wanted to overthrow their power—he'd signed his death warrant.

Unable to put it off any longer, I turned to him. "What's up?"

David stalked out of his hiding place, a frown marring the perfect planes of his face. "Do you want to tell me why you're burying a body?"

"Who, me?" I asked, tossing the shovel to the ground. My palms were already healing. I wish I could say the same for my guilty conscience. If David thought I should apologize for feeding from a human, I didn't want to know what he was going to say in about five minutes.

"Cut the shit, Sabina. You've been hunting again." His eyes glowed with accusation. "What happened to the synthetic blood I gave you?"

"That stuff tastes like shit," I said. "It's like nonalcoholic beer. What's the point?"

"Regardless, it's wrong to feed from humans."

It's also wrong to betray your race, I thought. If there was one thing about David that always got my back up, it was his holier-than-thou attitude. Where were his morals when he made the decision to sell out?

359

Keep it together, Sabina. It will all be over in a few minutes.

"Oh, come on. It was just a stupid drug dealer," I said, forcing myself to keep up the banter. "If it makes you feel any better, he was selling to kids."

David crossed his arms and said nothing.

"Though I have to say nothing beats Type O mixed with a little cannabis."

A muscle worked in David's jaw. "You're stoned?"

"Not really," I said. "Though I do have a strange craving for pizza. Extra garlic."

He took a deep breath. "What am I going to do with you?" His lips quirked despite his harsh tone.

"First of all, no more lectures. We're vampires, David. Mortal codes of good and evil don't apply to us."

He arched a brow. "Don't they?"

"Whatever," I said. "Can we just skip the philosophical debates for once?"

He shook his head. "Okay then, why don't you tell me why we're meeting way out here?"

Heaving a deep sigh, I pulled my weapon. David's eyes widened as I aimed the custom-made pistol between them.

His eyes pivoted from the gun to me. I hoped he didn't notice the slight tremor in my hands.

"I should have known when you called me," he said. "You never do that."

"Aren't you going to ask me why?" His calm unsettled me.

"I know why." He crossed his arms and regarded me closely. "The question is, do you?"

My eye twitched. "I know enough. How could you betray the Dominae?"

He didn't flinch. "One of these days your blind obedience to the Dominae is going to be your downfall."

I rolled my eyes. "Don't waste your final words on another lecture."

He lunged before the last word left my lips. He plowed into me, knocking the breath out of my chest and the gun from my hand. We landed in a tangle of limbs on the fresh grave. Dirt and fists flew as we each struggled to gain advantage. He grabbed my hair and whacked my head into the dirt. Soil tunneled up my nose and rage blurred my vision.

My hands curled into claws and dug into his eyes. Distracted by pain, he covered them with his palms. Gaining the advantage fueled my adrenaline as I flipped him onto his back. My knees straddled his hips, and I belted him in the nose with the base of my hand. Blood spurted from his nostrils, streaking his lips and chin.

"Bitch!" Like an animal, he sank his fangs into the fleshy part of my palm. I shrieked, backhanding him across the cheek with my uninjured hand. He growled and shoved me. I flew back several feet, landing on my ass with a thud.

Before I could catch my breath, his weight pinned me down again. Only this time, my gun stared back at me with its unblinking eye.

"How does it feel, Sabina?" His face was close to mine as he whispered. His breath stunk of blood and fury. "How does it feel to be on the other end of the gun?"

"It sucks, actually." Despite my tough talk, my heart hammered against my ribs. I glanced to the right and saw the shovel I'd used earlier lying about five feet away. "Listen—"

"Shut up." His eyes were wild. "You know what the worst part is? I came here tonight to come clean with you. Was going to warn you about the Dominae and Clovis—"

"Warn me?"

David jammed the cold steel into my skull—tattooing me with his rage. "That's the irony isn't it? Do you even know what's at stake here?" He cocked the hammer. Obviously, the question had been rhetorical.

One second, two, ticked by before the sound of flapping wings and a loud hoot filled the clearing. David glanced away, distracted. I punched him in the throat. He fell back, gasping and sputtering. I hauled ass to the shovel.

Time slowed. Spinning, I slashed the shovel in a wide arc. A bullet ricocheted off the metal, causing a spark. David pulled himself up to shoot again, but I lunged forward, swinging like Babe Ruth. The metal hit David's skull with a sickening thud. He collapsed in a heap.

He wouldn't stay down long. I grabbed the gun from his limp hand and aimed it at his chest.

I was about to pull the trigger when his eyes crept open. "Sabina."

He lay on the ground, covered in blood and dirt. The goose egg on his forehead was already losing its mass. Knowledge of the inevitable filled his gaze. I paused, watching him.

At one time, I'd looked up to this male, counted him as a friend. And now he'd betrayed everything I held sacred by selling out to the enemy. I hated him for his treachery. I hated the Dominae for choosing me as executioner. But most of all, I hated myself for what I was about to do.

He raised a hand toward me—imploring me to listen. My insides felt coated in acid as I watched him struggle to sit up.

"Don't trust—"

His final words were lost in the gun's blast. David's body exploded into flames, caused by the metaphysical friction of his soul leaving his flesh.

My whole body spasmed. The heat from the fire couldn't stop the shaking in my limbs. Collapsing to the dirt, I wiped a quivering hand down my face.

extras

The gun felt like a branding iron in my hand. I dropped it, but my hand still throbbed. A moment later, I changed my mind and picked it up again. Pulling out the clip, I removed one of the bullets. Holding one up for inspection, I wondered what David felt when the casing exploded and a dose of the toxic juice robbed him of his immortality.

I glanced over at the smoldering pile that was once my friend. Had he suffered? Or did death bring instant relief from the burdens of immortality? Or had I just damned his soul to a worse fate? I shook myself. His work here was done. Mine wasn't.

My shirt was caked with smears of soot, dirt, and drying blood—David's blood mixed with mine. I sucked in a lungful of air, hoping to ease the tightness in my chest.

The fire had died, leaving a charred, smoking mass of ash and bone. *Great,* I thought, *now I have to dig another grave.*

I used the shovel to pull myself up. A blur of white flew through the clearing. The owl called out again before flying over the trees. I stilled, wondering if I was hearing things. It called again and this time I was sure it screeched, "Sabina."

Maybe the smoke and fatigue were playing tricks on me. Maybe it had really said my name. I wasn't sure, but I didn't have time to worry about that. I had a body to bury.

As I dug in, my eyes started to sting. I tried to convince myself it was merely a reaction to the smoke, but a voice in my head whispered "guilt." With ruthless determination, I shoved my conscience down, compressing it into a tiny knot and shoving it into a dark corner of myself. Maybe later I'd pull it out and examine it. Or maybe not.

Good assassins dispose of problems without remorse. Even if the problem was a friend.

introducing

GOD SAVE THE QUEEN

Book 1 of the Immortal Empire

by Kate Locke

Queen Victoria rules with an immortal fist.

The undead matriarch of a Britain where the aristocracy is made up of werewolves and vampires, where goblins live underground and mothers know better than to let their children out after dark. A world where being nobility means being infected with the plague (side effects include undeath), hysteria is the popular affliction of the day, and leeches are considered a delicacy. And a world where technology lives side by side with magic. The year is 2012.

Xandra Vardan is a member of the elite Royal Guard, and it is her duty to protect the aristocracy. But when her sister goes missing, Xandra will set out on a path that undermines everything she believed in and uncover a conspiracy that threatens to topple the empire. And she is the key—the prize in a very dangerous struggle.

CHAPTER I

POMEGRANATES FULL AND FINE

London, 175 years into the reign of Her Ensanguined Majesty Queen Victoria

I *hate* goblins.

And when I say hate, I mean they bloody terrify me. I'd rather French-kiss a human with a mouth full of silver fillings than pick my way through the debris and rubble that used to be Down Street station, searching for the entrance to the plague den.

It was eerily quiet underground. The bustle of cobbleside was little more than a distant clatter down here. The roll of carriages, the clack of horse hooves from the Mayfair traffic was faint, occasionally completely drowned out by the roar of ancient locomotives raging through the subterranean tunnels carrying a barrage of smells in their bone-jangling wake.

Dirt. Decay. Stone. Blood.

I picked my way around a discarded shopping trolley, and tried to avoid looking at a large paw print in the dust. One of them had been here recently—the drops of blood surrounding the print were still fresh enough for me to smell the coppery tang. Human.

As I descended the stairs to platform level, my palms skimmed over the remaining chipped and pitted cream and maroon tiles that covered the walls—a grim reminder that this... *mausoleum* was once a thriving hub of urban transportation.

The light of my torch caught an entire set of paw prints, and the jagged pits at the end where claws had dug into the steps. I swallowed, throat dry.

Of course they ventured up this far—the busted sconces were proof. They couldn't always sit around and wait for some stupid human to come to them—they had to hunt. Still, the sight of those prints and the lingering scent of human blood made my chest tight.

I wasn't a coward. My being here was proof of that—and perhaps proof positive of my lack of intelligence. Everyone— aristocrat, half-blood and human—was afraid of goblins. You'd be mental not to be. They were fast and ferocious and didn't seem to have any sense of morality holding them back. If aristos were fully plagued, then goblins were overly so, though such a thing wasn't really possible. Technically they were aristocrats, but no one would ever dare call them such. To do so was as much an insult to them as to aristos. They were mutations, and terribly proud of it.

Images flashed in my head, memories that played out like disjointed snippets from a film: fur, gnashing fangs, yellow eyes—and blood. That was all I remembered of the day I was attacked by a gob right here in this very station. My history class from the Academy had come here on a field trip. The gobs stayed away from us because of the treaty. At least they were *supposed* to stay away, but one didn't listen, and it picked me.

If it hadn't been for Church, I would have died that day. That was when I realised goblins weren't stories told to children to make us behave. It was also the day I realised that if I didn't do everything in my ability to prove them wrong, people would think I was defective somehow—weak—because a goblin tried to take me.

I hadn't set foot in Down Street station since then. If it weren't for my sister Dede's disappearance I wouldn't have gone down there at all.

Avery and Val thought I was overreacting. Dede had taken off on us before, so it was hardly shocking that she wasn't answering her rotary or that the message box on said gadget was full. But in the past she had called me to let me know she was safe. She always called *me*.

I had exhausted every other avenue. It was as though Dede had fallen off the face of the earth. I was desperate, and there was only one option left—goblins. Gobs knew everything that happened in London, despite rarely venturing above ground. Somehow they had found a way to spy on the entire city, and no one seemed to know just what that was. I reckon anyone who had the bollocks to ask didn't live long enough to share it with the rest of us.

It was dark, not because the city didn't run electric lines down here any more—they did—but because the lights had been smashed. The beam from my small hand-held torch caught the grimy glitter of the remains of at least half a dozen bulbs on the ground amongst the refuse.

The bones of a human hand lay surrounded by the shards, cupping the jagged edges in a dull, dry palm.

I reached for the .50 British Bulldog normally holstered snugly against my ribs, but it wasn't there. I'd left it at home. Walking into the plague den with a firearm was considered an act of aggression unless one was there on the official—which I wasn't. Aggression was the last thing—next to fear—you wanted to show in front of one goblin, let alone an entire plague. It was like wearing a sign reading DINNER around your neck.

It didn't matter that I had plagued blood as well. I was only a half-blood, the result of a vampire aristocrat—the term that had come to be synonymous with someone of noble descent who was also plagued—and a human courtesan doing the hot and sweaty. Science considered goblins the ultimate birth defect, but in reality they were the result of gene snobbery. The Prometheus Protein in vamps—caused by centuries of Black Plague exposure—didn't play well with the mutation that caused others to become weres. If the proteins from both species mixed the outcome was a goblin, though some had been born to parents with the same strain. Hell, there were even two documented cases of goblins being born to human parents both of whom carried dormant plagued genes, but that was very rare, as goblins sometimes tried to eat their way out of the womb. No human could survive that.

In fact, no one had much of a chance of surviving a goblin attack. And that was why I had my lonsdaelite dagger tucked into a secret sheath inside my corset. Harder than diamond and easily concealed, it was my "go to" weapon of choice. It was sharp, light and didn't set off machines designed to detect metal or catch the attention of beings with a keen enough sense of smell to sniff out things like blades and pistols.

The dagger was also one of the few things my mother had left me when she . . . went away.

I wound my way down the staircase to the abandoned platform. It was warm, the air heavy with humidity and neglect, stinking of machine and decay. As easy as it was to access the tunnels, I wasn't surprised to note that mine were the only humanoid prints to be seen in the layers of dust. Back in 1932, a bunch of humans had used this very station to invade and burn Mayfair—*the* aristo neighbourhood—during the Great Insurrection. Their intent had been to destroy the aristocracy, or at least cripple it, and take control of the Kingdom. The history books say that fewer than half of those humans who went into Down Street station made it out alive.

Maybe goblins were useful after all.

I hopped off the platform on to the track, watching my step so I didn't trip over anything—like a body. They hadn't ripped up the line because there weren't any crews mental enough to brave becoming goblin chow, no matter how good the pay. The light of my torch caught a rough hole in the wall just up ahead. I crouched down, back to the wall as I eased closer. The scent of old blood clung to the dust and brick. This had to be the door to the plague den.

Turn around. Don't do this.

Gritting my teeth against the trembling in my veins, I slipped my left leg, followed by my torso and finally my right half, through the hole. When I straightened, I found myself standing on a narrow landing at the top of a long, steep set of rough-hewn stairs that led deeper into the dark. Water dripped from a rusty pipe near my head, dampening the stone.

As I descended the stairs—my heart hammering, sweat beading around my hairline—I caught a whiff of that particular perfume that could only be described as goblinesque: fur, smoke and earth. It could have been vaguely comforting if it hadn't scared the shit out of me.

370

I reached the bottom. In the beam from my torch I could see bits of broken pottery scattered across the scarred and pitted stone floor. Similar pieces were embedded in the wall. Probably Roman, but my knowledge of history was sadly lacking. The goblins had been doing a bit of housekeeping—there were fresh bricks mortared into parts of the wall, and someone had created a fresco near the ancient archway. I could be wrong, but it looked as though it had been painted in blood.

Cobbleside the sun was long set, but there were street lights, moonlight. Down here it was almost pitch black except for the dim torches flickering on the rough walls. My night vision was perfect, but I didn't want to think about what might happen if some devilish goblin decided to play hide and seek in the dark.

I tried not to imagine what that one would have done to me.

I took a breath and ducked through the archway into the main vestibule of the plague's lair. There were more sconces in here, so I tucked my hand torch into the leather bag slung across my torso. My surroundings were deceptively cosy and welcoming, as though any moment someone might press a pint into my hand or ask me to dance.

I'll say this about the nasty little bastards—they knew how to throw a party. Music flowed through the catacombs from some unknown source—a lively fiddle accompanied by a piano. Conversation and raucous laughter—both of which sounded a lot like barking—filled the fusty air. Probably a hundred goblins were gathered in this open area, dancing, talking and drinking. They were doing other things as well, but I tried to ignore them. It wouldn't do for me to start screaming.

A few of them looked at me with curiosity in their piercing yellow eyes, turning their heads as they caught my scent. I tensed, waiting for an attack, but it didn't come. It wouldn't either, not when I was so close to an exit, and they were curious to find out what could have brought a halvie this far into their territory.

Goblins looked a lot like werewolves, only shorter and smaller—wiry. They were bipedal, but could run on all fours if the occasion called for additional speed. Their faces were a disconcerting mix of canine and humanoid, but their teeth were all predator—exactly what you might expect from a walking nightmare.

I'd made it maybe another four strides into this bustling netherworld when one of the creatures stuck a tray of produce in my face, trying to entice me to eat. Grapes the size of walnuts, bruise-purple and glistening in the torchlight, were thrust beneath my nose. Pomegranates the colour of blood, bleeding sweet-tart juice, filled the platter as well, and apples—pale flesh glistening with a delicate blush. There were more, but those were the ones that tempted me the most. I could almost taste them, feel the syrup running down my chin. Berry-stained fingers clutched and pinched at me, smearing sticky delight on my skin and clothes as I pressed forward.

"Eat, pretty," rasped the vaguely soft cruel voice. "Just a taste. A wee little nibble for our sweet lady."

Our? Not bloody fucking likely. I couldn't tell if my tormentor was male or female. The body hair didn't help either. It was effective camouflage unless you happened upon a male goblin in an amorous state. Generally they tried to affect some kind of identity for themselves—a little vanity so non-goblins could tell them apart. This one had both of its ears pierced several times, delicate chains weaving in and out of the holes like golden stitches.

I shook my head, but didn't open my mouth to vocalise my refusal. An open mouth was an invitation to a goblin to stick something in it. If you were lucky, it was only food, but once you tasted their poison you were lost. Goblins were known for their drugs—mostly their opium. They enticed weak humans with a cheap and euphoric high, and the promise of more. Goblins didn't want human money as payment. They wanted information. They wanted flesh. There were already several customers providing entertainment for tonight's bash. I pushed away whatever pity I felt for them—everyone knew what happened when you trafficked with goblins.

I pushed through the crowd, moving deeper into the lair despite every instinct I possessed telling me to run. I was looking for one goblin in particular and I was not going to leave without seeing him. Besides, running would get me chased. Chased would get me eaten.

As I walked, I tried not to pay too much attention to what was going on in the shadows around me. I'd seen a lot of horrible things in my two and twenty years, but the sight of hueys—humans—gorging themselves on fruit, seeds and pulp in their hair and smeared over their dirty, naked skin, shook me. Maybe it was the fact that pomegranate flesh looked just like that—flesh—between stained teeth. Or maybe it was the wild delirium in their eyes as goblins ran greedy hands over their sticky bodies.

It was like a scene out of Christina Rossetti's poem, but nothing so lyrical. Mothers knew to keep their children at home after dark, lest they go missing, fated to end up as goblin food—or worse, a goblin's slave.

A sweet, earthy smoke hung heavy in the air, reminding me of decaying flowers. It brushed pleasantly against my mind, but was burned away by my metabolism before it could have any real effect. I brushed a platter of cherries, held by strong paw-like hands, aside despite the watering of my mouth. I knew they'd split between my teeth with a firm, juicy pop, spilling tart, delicious juice down my dry throat. Accepting hospitality might mean I'd be expected to pay for it later, and I wasn't about to end up in the plague's debt. Thankfully I quickly spotted the goblin I was looking for. He sat on a dais near the back of the hall, on a throne made entirely from human bones. If I had to guess, I'd say this is what happened to several of the humans who braved this place during the Great Insurrection. Skulls served as finials high on either side of his head. Another set formed armrests over which each of his furry hands curved.

But this goblin would have stood out without the throne, and the obvious deference with which the other freaks treated him. He was tall for a gob—probably my height when standing—and his shoulders were broad, his canine teeth large and sharp. The firelight made his fur look like warm caramel spotted with chocolate. One of his dog-like ears was torn and chewed-looking, the edges scarred. He was missing an eye as well, the thin line of the closed lid almost indistinguishable in the fur of his face. Hard to believe there was anything aristocratic about him, yet he could be the son of a duke, or even the Prince of Wales. His mother would have to be of rank as well. Did they ever wonder what had become of their monstrous child?

While thousands of humans died with every incarnation of the plague—which loves this country like a mother loves her child—aristocrats survived. Not only survived, they evolved. In England the plague-born Prometheus Protein led to vampirism, in Scotland it caused lycanthropy.

It also occasionally affected someone who wasn't considered upper class. Historically, members of the aristocracy had never been very good at keeping it in their pants. Indiscretions with human carriers resulted in the first halvie births, and launched the careers of generations of breeding courtesans. Occasionally some seemingly normal human woman gave birth to a half or fully plagued infant. These children were often murdered by their parents, or shipped off to orphanages where they were shunned and mistreated. That was prior to 1932's rebellion. Now, such cruelties were prevented by the Pax—Pax Yersinia, which dictated that each human donated a sample of DNA at birth. This could help prevent human carriers from intermarrying. It also provided families and special housing for unwanted plagued children.

By the time Victoria, our first fully plagued monarch—King George III had shown vampiric traits—ascended the throne, other aristocrats across Britain and Europe had revealed their true natures as well. Vampires thrived in the more temperate climes like France and Spain, weres in Russia and other eastern countries. Some places had a mix of the two, as did Asia and Australia. Those who remained in Canada and the Americas had gone on to become socialites and film stars.

But they were never safe, no matter where they were. Humans accounted for ninety-two per cent of aristocratic and halvie deaths. Haemophilia, suicide and accidents made up for the remaining eight.

There were no recorded goblin deaths at human hands—not even during the Insurrection.

I approached the battle-scarred goblin with caution. The flickering torches made it hard to tell, but I think recognition flashed in his one yellow eye. He sniffed the air as I approached. I curtsied, playing to his vanity.

"A Vardan get," he said, in a voice that was surprisingly low and articulate for a goblin. "Here on the official?"

Half-bloods took the title of their sire as their surname. The Duke of Vardan was my father. "Nothing official, my lord. I'm here because the goblin prince knows everything that happens in London."

"True," he replied with a slow nod. Despite my flattery he was still looking at me like he expected me to do or say something. "But there is a price. What do you offer your prince, pretty get?"

The only prince I claimed was Albert, God rest his soul, and perhaps Bertie, the Prince of Wales. This mangy monster was not *my* prince. Was I stupid enough to tell him that? Hell, no.

I reached into the leather satchel I'd brought with me, pulled out the clear plastic bag with a lump of blood-soaked butcher's paper inside and offered it to the goblin. He snatched it from me with eager hands that were just a titch too long and dexterous to be paws, tossed the plastic on the floor and tore open the paper. A whine of delight slipped from his throat when he saw what I'd brought. Around us other goblins raised their muzzles and made similar noises, but no one dared approach.

I looked away as the prince brought the gory mass to his muzzle and took an enthusiastic bite. I made my mind blank, refusing to think of what the meat was, what it had been. My only solace was that it had already been dead when I bought it. The blood might smell good, but I couldn't imagine eating anything that... awful... terrible... *raw*.

The goblin gave a little shudder of delight as he chewed and rewrapped his treat for later. A long pink tongue slipped out to lick his muzzle clean. "Proper tribute. Honours her prince. I will tell the lady what I know. Ask, pretty, ask."

The rest of the goblins drifted away from us, save for one little gob who came and sat at the prince's furry feet and stared at me with open curiosity. I was very much aware that every goblin who wasn't preoccupied with human playthings watched me closely. I was relatively safe now, having paid my tribute to their prince. So long as I behaved myself and didn't offend anyone, I'd make it out of here alive. Probably.

"I want to know the whereabouts of Drusilla Vardan," I said quietly, even though I knew most of the goblins had keen enough hearing to eavesdrop without trying. Their sensitivity to sound, as well as light, kept them deep underside.

The prince raised his canine gaze to mine. It was unnerving looking into that one bright eye, seeing intelligence there while he had yet to clean all the blood from his muzzle. "The youngest?"

I nodded. My father had gone through something of a mid-immortality crisis about two and a half decades ago and done his damnedest to impregnate every breeding courtesan he could find. The first attempt had resulted in my brother Val, the second in me and the third and fourth in Avery and Dede. Four live births out of nine pregnancies over a five-year period—pretty potent for a vampire.

"She's missing." He didn't need to know the particulars—like how she had last been seen at her favourite pub. "I want to know what happened to her."

"Nay, you do not," the prince replied cheerfully. "Pretty wants to know where her sibling is. The prince knows." He petted the little goblin on the head as he bared his teeth at me—a smile.

Sweet baby Jesus. Even my spleen trembled at that awful sight.

Trying to hide my fear was futile, as he could surely smell it. Still, I had to give it a go. "Would you be so kind as to share my sister's whereabouts, my lord? Please? I am concerned about her."

If there was one thing goblins understood it was blood—both as sustenance and connection. Offspring happened rarely because of their degree of mutation, and were treasured. No decent goblin—and I use "decent" as loosely as it can possibly be construed—would turn down a request that involved family.

"New Bethlehem," he replied in a grave growl.

I pressed a hand against the boned front of my corset, and closed my fingers into a fist. I would not show weakness here, no matter how much the prince might sympathise with my plight—he was still a goddam goblin. "Bedlam?" I rasped.

The prince nodded. "She was taken in two nights ago, in shackles."

Albert's fangs. I blasphemed the Queen's late consort to myself alone. My mind could scarcely grasp the reality of it. "You're wrong," I whispered. "You have to be wrong." But goblins were never wrong. If he hadn't known, he wouldn't have said. That was their way—so I'd been taught. "Honourable monsters", Church had called them.

"Alexandra."

I jerked. I shouldn't be surprised that he knew my name. Of course he knew it. It was the posh way he said it—his voice sounded almost like my father's.

He stood before me—I was right, he was my height. The little one remained glued to his side. I had the sudden and inexplicable urge to reach out and pat her on the head, just as I had wanted to do to a tiger cub I once saw in a travelling exhibit. The comparison kept my hand fisted, and at my side. I wanted to keep it.

"Your prince regrets telling the pretty lady this news."

I turned my attention back to him. The pity in his eye almost brought me to tears. Why should a monster pity me?

"There was an incident at Ainsley's. The Vardan get tried to stab the earl, she did."

That I believed, and therefore I had to believe my sister really could be in Bedlam—where all the special barking mad went to die. Dede and Ainsley had history—a painful one.

The goblin held out his furry hand, and etiquette demanded

I take it. The prince was offering me friendship, and my getting out of there alive just might depend on my taking it, treaty or no.

I nodded, my throat tight as his "fingers" closed around mine. He was warm. For a moment—and only one terribly mad one—I could have hugged him. "Thank you."

He shook his head. "No thanks, lady. Never thank for bad news."

I nodded again and he released my hand. The goblins watched me as I turned to leave, but no one spoke. They didn't even try to tempt me to stay; they simply let me go. I think I despised them most at that moment, especially that little one who waved goodbye.

My sister was essentially in hell and goblins felt sorry for me. As far as I was concerned, things couldn't get much worse.

◆ ◆ ◆

I stumbled cobbleside on shaky, numb legs. The heavy door closed with a thud behind me as I braced a palm against the closest chipped and pitted brick wall. Scorch marks and faded maroon paint marred part of the once impressive frontage. The two buildings flanking the old station had been empty since the fires of '32, their derelict state a blemish on the formerly opulent neighbourhood. This end of Down Street looked like it belonged near the docks rather than within the walls of Mayfair. It was still the most exclusive neighbourhood in London, but for the past eighty years it had existed behind high walls of stone and wire, guarded against the possibility of another human uprising. Broken lamps kept this part of the street, unaffectionately nicknamed "Gob Lane", in the dark. Further up, just past Brick Street, the lamps retained their bulbs, casting a golden glow over the worn cobblestones. Here, grass and weeds poked up from between the cobbles, and someone had propped a broken carriage wheel against the side of the building to my right. Mayfair had its share of ruins, but this was the only one with ABANDON ALL HOPE above the door in flaking white paint, and the only one that still had bloodstains on the threshold.

My ride was waiting for me where I'd left it—no worries about theft on Gob Lane. I swung my leg over the Butler 1863 motorrad and started the engine. The machine roared to life, and I tore off down the street on three hundred kilos of rubber and steel, my frock coat whipping out behind. I stopped at the gates because I had to, but I couldn't remember anything John or Mick, the Royal Guards on duty, said to me. I must have given the correct answers because they let me go.

It wasn't until I neared Wellington district, and my part of it—the area formerly known as Belgravia—that the numbness eased and I began to feel like myself again. I'd entered the plague den and survived, and now I knew where Dede was. It did nothing to make me feel better, but at least I knew.

Bedlam. Fang me.

Why couldn't she have run off with one of the wolves who were down from Scotland for the season? That was what other Peerage Protectorate girls—and boys—did. Shagged the hairy brutes and protected them at the same time—not that weres needed an abundance of protecting. The Scots were looked down upon by some aristos for being a little too physical, but they were impressive in their strength.

I pulled the Butler to the kerb outside the house my sister Avery and I shared on the upper west side of Belgrave Square. The closer to Buckingham Palace and Mayfair you got, the older the neighbourhood appeared. In the East End they'd repaved some of the streets, and even had tall buildings, but here almost everything looked as it had two centuries ago. Even the parts that were new had been made to look old.

It was the same in most cities across Europe with a strong concentration of aristo citizens. The plague had spread across trade routes, taking the Prometheus Protein with it. There were vampires and werewolves all across the continent—halvies too, though the first of my kind had been born right here in London. Or at least, the first halvie in historical record had been. Aldous James was born in 1900. His father was Devonshire, but this was before we took titles as our surnames.

My house had been built in the 1820s. It was a large town house that used to be part of a huge mansion. My father had bought it for his children, but only Avery and I lived there now. Val had his own flat, and Dede had moved out six months ago, claiming she wanted her own space as well.

I unlocked the door, slipped inside the darkened foyer and punched the code into the alarm. That was as fancy as we got. When you were half-vampire, and trained to survive and protect at any cost, you didn't really need much outside security.

I ran straight up the winding staircase to my bedroom. So far my night off had been a nightmare, but it wasn't over yet. There was one person who would try to help me if what the goblin prince said was true. I had to get changed and haul my arse to a party in Curzon Street before sunrise in order to find him.

I had several decent gowns in the walk-in off my bedroom. I had to—Queen V didn't like what most of us considered fashion, so at fancy aristo functions the Royal Guard and the Peerage Protectorate had to dress to code, females in gowns and men in black tails. Sometimes it was a bit of fun, but other times—like now—it was an exercise in frustration. It wasn't that the aristocracy fought progress; just that time moved so slowly for them, it took change longer to take hold. They clung to that which was familiar.

I grabbed the easiest to get into—a pewter-coloured silk with tiny sleeves and long concealed slits on either side of the skirt in case I needed to move quickly or fight.

My shower took exactly four minutes, including waiting for the water to get hot. I didn't have time to wash my bright red hair, so I dusted it with shampoo powder, gave it a bit of a back-comb and twisted it up on to the top of my head.

The hair thing was often copied by humans looking to emulate halvies, but wigs and dye couldn't quite get the same shine. Aristocrats had gorgeous hair—thick and rich, with extraordinary highlights due to the plague's mutation of the pigmentations that determined hair colour. The only way I can describe it is to say that the plague seemed to make everything "more". With halvies, this pigmentation was often sent into overdrive by our unique maternal genetics. It didn't happen in all halvies, but the brighter colours were something of a status symbol amongst our kind. My colour, the same red as Christmas barley candy, was highly unusual.

Clean undies and a fresh corset that hooked up the front went on as quickly as I could manage, followed by stockings, boots and then the gown. I was still fiddling with the zip on the side as I raced back downstairs. I had to get to Curzon Street. I had to find Church.

It was quarter past three in the morning. Most aristo functions ended around four to give everyone time to get home and into their dark chambers before the sun rose, so that gave me forty-five minutes. Luckily, my destination was less than a mile away.

I thought of Dede—not of her locked up in Bedlam, but as she had been when we were younger. She'd always been tiny, sprite-like. Shiny and sweet and full of life. Our family, especially me, had been so protective of her, but even we couldn't save her from herself. She'd fallen for Ainsley's charm as though her bones were made of lead. I'd held her after she lost the baby, crying myself as she sobbed as if the world was ending. I suppose for her it had. I thought she was done with the bastard.

I turned on to Grosvenor Place. Checking the traffic, I saw something in the park to my right that made me put my foot down to stabilise the Butler and look again.

"Fang me," I muttered. Why now, of all times? I had somewhere to be. I did not have time for betty-bashing.

I lifted my foot and whipped the machine between two cars—the space from the boot of one to the bonnet of the other was just large enough for my ride. I kicked the stand and jumped off. Skirt hitched, I raced along the pavement, wishing I'd worn my arse-kicking boots instead of the pointy-toed, hourglass-heeled ones that matched my gown. Still, I was fast and quickly caught up with the people I was chasing.

There had to be at least a dozen of them. From their swagger and their cricket bats I pegged them as bubonic betties— humans who injected themselves with aristo hormones. Eight male and four female, dragging what appeared to be two unconscious people along the dimly lit path. Despite the dark I could see the two of them very well, see the blood on their faces and the jacked-up state of their captors. And I could see their hair—the girl had blue and the bloke's was purple. They were halvies, and they were in trouble.

"Oy!" I shouted as I approached. I didn't even have a weapon in my hand. My ID I'd shoved inside my corset as soon as I jumped off the motorrad.

The men didn't listen to me, of course. I hadn't expected them to. The females at least glanced in my direction. I yelled again and picked up the pace, running past them to cut them off. "Let them go," I said as I stood before them. I had no delusions of getting out of this unscathed, but defeat wasn't an option.

"Sod off," retorted one in a deep, low-brow voice.

They were all in the vicinity of six feet tall and wore black clothing. In the sparse light I could see the sores on their faces, the blackened tips of their fingers. Aristo hormones gave them heightened senses and strength, but the price was an early and painful death. Sometimes they cut the drug with silver nitrate to lessen the harmful side effects, but it weakened the potency and increased skin-blackening.

That was what the plague did to those not of royal blood.

"Let them go," I repeated through clenched teeth. I had somewhere else to be, damn it, and these fuckwits were taking up minutes on my ticking clock. Still, wouldn't have been right of me not to intervene.

One of the males from behind came forward. The breeze that carried his scent to me brought the smell of unwashed flesh, stale sweat, blood and the early whiff of decay. "It's another one," he said in a cockney accent so thick I could have spread it on toast. "Another dirty half-blood."

Well, at least I now knew that these Samaritans weren't simply helping two sick halvies home—as if the thought had even crossed my mind. Fucking humans. They hated us, tried to kill us, but poisoned themselves so they could be more like us. "Hand them over to me and there won't be any trouble," I said.

The betties laughed. They always did—like the laughter track on those American sitcoms broadcast on the pirate box stations. With my bright hair and my expensive gown I obviously didn't look like much of a threat.

The chuckles stopped pretty abruptly when I slammed my shin into Stinky's wedding tackle. The breath rushed out of him in an animalistic moan. As he sank to his knees, I jobbed him between the eyes—twice—and laid him out cold.

"You beauties going to let them go now?" I asked sweetly as the betty crumpled at my feet. "Or do I have to humiliate each and every one of you?"

Of course they didn't oblige me. I'd just relieved their mate of his manhood and my taunting only made them further obligated to exact a little revenge. Two of them came at me—one straight on and the other sneaking around behind.

Albert's fangs. I was still shaky from the goblins, hungry, tired and I'd forgotten to take my supplements—again. All I wanted was for them to leave the halvies alone so I could get to the bloody party on Curzon Street and talk to Church. They were standing in the way of me getting help for Dede and I did *not* have time for this shit. Those limp halvies had better hurry up and metabolise whatever the betties had given them, because I was on a schedule.

The betty up front came at me swinging. I ducked, but not enough. He caught me on the right jaw with a solid blow that knocked my head back and pissed me off. I came back with two quick punches to his gut, and when he bent double, the wind knocked out of him, I brought my knee up and broke his nose. Then I pivoted, whipped that same leg up—thank God for my split skirt—and brought the back of my heel down on his skull. He hadn't hit the ground when I whirled around to take on the next betty. She wasn't expecting me, so she went down a little faster than her friends.

Somebody really ought to tell them that bubonic-derived steroids might make you faster and stronger, but that wasn't much help up against someone even faster and stronger and better trained. It would be like me taking on Church—no contest.

Three down. Only nine more to go. *C'mon, halvies, wake the hell up.*

Two more came at me. These two actually had weapons. No matter how strong you are, a crowbar to the temple *hurts.* I tried to shake it off, but while I was recovering from that, another betty punched me hard in the stomach, and I wasn't wearing a reinforced corset. When he attempted to break my nose as I had his friend, I kicked him hard in the side of his opposite knee. He screamed, but he didn't go down immediately. That required a tap or two on the noggin with his own crowbar, which I then used to render his companion incapacitated. She went down a bit easier than he had.

Seven more. My head hurt—enough that I couldn't quite ignore it. I would probably bruise.

One of the women came at me. Her lips were grey, and the skin on one side of her neck was patchy and black—swollen. She wouldn't live much longer than a fortnight. I could be merciful and kill her here and now, but I wasn't feeling overly merciful at the moment. She'd taken the plague willingly; let her ride it right to its ever-suffering end.

My knuckles split those cadaverous lips. Infected blood splattered across the backs of my fingers, soaking through the thin silk of my gloves. I had the sudden urge to suck the coppery warmth out of the fabric, but I ignored the craving as the bleeding betty recovered and came back swinging. I grabbed her raised arm with one hand and twisted hard.

It's an odd sensation, feeling bone break beneath your fingers. She crumpled with a scream. I backhanded her with my other hand, hard enough to knock her backwards and end all that nonsense.

The other betties didn't seem to know what to do. Out of the six remaining, only two of them had their hands

386

free—the others were supporting the dead weight of the battered halvies.

One of the female halvie's eyes was swollen shut. The fact
that she hadn't woken up yet worried me. And then, as the next
goon stepped up, I saw her foot move. One boot came up, the
sturdy sole planted firmly on the pavement. She was waiting
for me to dig in before she caught her captors unawares. Smart
girl. Lazy, though, letting me do the brunt of the work. How
long had she been awake? The male was coming round as well.
This was going to become knobbed-up very quickly.

I didn't have any more time to wonder about it as another girl
betty came at me, brandishing a cricket bat as though I was the
only thing standing between her and total victory. She swung
and I ducked, the edge of the bat bouncing off my shoulder.

"Fucking hell!" It hurt—but only for a couple of seconds.
Adrenaline is a wonderful thing.

I didn't have much time, as the rest of them had finally
begun to think with that one dim-witted brain they seemed
to share, and had realised that if they ganged up on me they
might stand a better chance. Thankfully, the halvies chose that
moment to jump into the fray and began battling it out with
the betties who had been holding them. The humans never saw
it coming.

Blood screamed through my veins, my heart thumping
wildly. Fang me, but I loved a good punch-up. At the Wellington Academy—where all halvies were educated and trained—
I'd excelled in violence. Church held me up as an example to
other students of how to fight. No goblin was ever going to
take me down without a struggle again.

As if to prove that point, I delivered a walloping kick to the
betty's head with the side of my boot. She was a little tougher
than the last, however, and came staggering back at me, bat

held high above her head as though it was a claymore and she was William fucking Wallace. I rolled my eyes.

"Bored with this," I said, at the same time whipping my arm up to smash the heel of my hand into her nose.

She dropped the bat behind her, and then fell to the ground. She didn't move. For a second I wondered if I had killed her. I'd never killed anyone before.

Any remorse I might have felt was eclipsed by the large bulk blocking out the street light. The other halvies were making sport of their opponents, leaving me just this one last betty.

He was big—the biggest of the lot. And he was much faster than the others—graceful as well. Anticipation hummed inside me. He was a real fighter, an actual challenge. Smacked me a hard one on the jaw before I was ready for it—same side as the crowbar, bastard.

I shook off the stars dancing before my eyes and came back with a few shots of my own. His head flew back, but he didn't fall. He hit me again in the same spot. The pain made me grit my teeth and want to make him eat his own spleen. Enough of this. I caught him with two quick jabs to the stomach and then one between the eyes. He staggered backwards, then came back at me with a solid punch to my mouth. I tasted blood as I pulled my dagger out of its sheath.

That was when what I always referred to as my "aristocratic genes" kicked in, and the vampire half of me really woke up. It was something I kept to myself, because it wasn't a typical halvie reaction to blood, and it didn't matter whether it was my own or someone else's, and it was the equivalent of flicking a switch inside me—like going from low to high. It was why blood-sharing was more of an intimate thing for halvies. It made sex incredibly intense—switching off our humanity and making us all instinct and sensation. Appetite.

I had planned to gut him if necessary, but now...I wanted to eat this betty—and not in a sexy way. Fangs extended from my gums with the sweetest of aches, eager to pierce some flesh regardless of how diseased and disgusting it was.

I smiled, enjoying how his eyes widened.

Then I pounced—straight at his jugular.